A DRUG LORD.
AN EX-NARC.
ONE-ON-ONE . . .

Fields drew a second, searing breath and drove his knee forward a second time, using both hands to steady the bloody mass of Savannah Pink's pumpkin-sized head. Instinctively, Pink leaned into the thrust, grabbed the swinging leg with both arms, and rolled to the side. His massive weight pulled Fields to the carpet, wrenching the knee out of its socket . . .

A high-pitched scream whistled from Fields's grimaced lips as the brutal strength of Savannah Pink flung him across the cabin. With a horror born of pain Fields crabbed backward on his elbows, dragging the mangled leg. Pink, snuffling, filled his lungs with a bushel of frothy air and crawled forward, a bloody grin fixed on his pulped face.

Fields's intellect reeled. He had delivered three killing blows in rapid order and yet the man crawled steadily forward, his demented smile flashing . . .

SAVANNAH SCORE

LEW DYKES
SAVANNAH SCORE

BERKLEY BOOKS, NEW YORK

SAVANNAH SCORE

A Berkley Book / published by arrangement with
the author

PRINTING HISTORY
Berkley edition/November 1987

ISBN: 0-425-10411-7

PRINTED IN THE UNITED STATES OF AMERICA

10 9 8 7 6 5 4 3 2 1

CHAPTER 1

THE sculptor stood in a sand pit the size of a boxing ring. Waves of virgin-white sand filled the pit, and on the sand stood a lobed granite boulder, its natural contours bearing the first tentative strike-offs from his chisel. The sculptor turned, a predatory intensity in his deep-set eyes. He circled the immense bulk of the stone. Moving on silent cat's feet as he glided over the hot sand, his gaze focused on the segmentation of his rock. He danced in the sand, striking, circling, a heavy, short hammer clenched in one hand, a razor-edged masonry chisel in the other. He was stripped to the waist and clad in brief shorts that showed a dark, even tan. He had the build of a gymnast and ginger-specked dark hair.

The beauty locked within the granite absorbed his concentration and walled the artist off from his surroundings. A white sun burned down through palmetto fronds, a sun hot enough to drive the tourists from Hilton Head's beaches and tennis courts into the air-conditioned stores and lounges. The sculptor didn't notice. He took no special notice, either, of the spectator who stood silent in the cooler shadows of the live oaks, for spectators and kibitzers were part of the process of art. Without them there would be no audience, no minds to reflect the intended image, and even worse, no likelihood of a sale. Sometimes they watched and left, sometimes they stayed to talk. In the pit he ignored them all, for he would not let anything interfere with the planning of hammer strokes. No sound could disturb him, no sight catch his eye. However, once he'd backed out of the combat zone, he again became a civil man and could welcome a guest and conversation.

He tapped once, then rapped the heavy hammer down hard and sure onto the forged steel of his chisel. A thin sheet of mica-flecked granite sheared off the vertical face of the rock. With blunt certainty a young woman's hip and thigh asserted their shapes from the stone. He backed a step, nodded, and stepped out of the pit.

"I heard you was supposed to be some kind of sculptor now," rasped an abused voice, "but I didn't believe it. I thought it was just another cover." The speaker was a dark man, paunchy, and bowed at the legs.

The sculptor, Dan Fields, blinked once, placed the face, the voice, the posture, and said, "Party John. I didn't know you were an art lover." Field's voice was dry sand.

"Can't say as I am," chuckled the man, scrabbling forward on unsteady land legs. He held out a hand.

Fields hesitated a beat, then shifted his chisel and took Party John Maltessa's hand. "It's been a long time, John," he said. Then, in a rush, "I'm retired. Everyone in the business knows I don't have anything to do with the Trade anymore. And my art is my business. What makes it yours?"

"Hey!" said Party John, "I've seen narcs 'retire' before. Seen them resign too. Shit! I even seen them get fired and still come back and be testifying on a Ricoh charge a year later in Miami." His face was burned and cracked by a generation lived at sea. Spidered crevices linked the hollows of his eyes to the dense black thicket of his hairline.

"Believe what you want," said Fields. "I could give a damn." He eased into the shadow of a huge gnarled oak. His eyes were like glaciered ice, blue-gray and arctic.

Party John laughed. "It's a damn good cover, though. I'll have to give you that much, Dan. A damn good cover. Christ! Getting yourself written up in an honest-to-God art magazine, having a goddamn one-man show in Savannah, hell! I haven't seen a cover that good since—"

"Since I retired?"

Party John grinned, and his face showed itself to be a thousand-edged mosaic of facial lines.

"Yeah, since then, at least." Party John's smuggler's eyes didn't share in the mirth. He inclined his head toward the immense stone. "Looks like you might know what you're doing."

Dan Fields studied the little man with the basketball paunch. "John, I don't know what you're after." He waited. A man's past belongs in the past, said his eyes.

Party John Maltessa took out a thin, hand-rolled marijuana joint from a stained pocket, lit it, and inhaled noisily. "You owe me, Dan," he said when he exhaled. "I don't ask nobody to give me nothing, ever. You ought to know that. If I go to collect, it's because someone owes me." He sucked on the joint again. "You owe me. If you can look me dead in the face and tell me you don't, well, go ahead, and you won't ever see me again. But goddammit, you owe me."

Fields flexed iron-tendoned fingers around the smoothed handle of his hammer. He remembered the circumstances of his debt.

Dan Fields had been an apple-green undercover agent more than twenty years earlier. After graduation from the BNDD academy—when the agency still had been known as the Bureau of Narcotics and Dangerous Drugs—he'd made a rapid series of drug penetrations and was beginning to make a name for himself when an assignment had dropped him into Party John Maltessa's world. Fields had been following a Mexican heroin network using a deckhand cover. As often happened in the drug trade, illicit shipments overlapped and were combined, and Fields found himself crewing on a trawler loaded with not only the six kilos of brown heroin he'd been tracking but thirteen tons of marijuana as well. Party John had been the pilot of that craft, and in the course of their association Fields and the captain had become friends in the manner of shipmates and outlaws. When, days later, Fields was sold out, fingered as a narc by one of the smuggling cartel's many federal informants, Party John had risked his own death to tip the young agent. Fields had dived over the side that night, slicing into the dark waters without a word. He'd survived but barely, after a confused three-mile swim in darkness through a changing tide. For days afterward, Fields had worn a body-plaster of pain from the lashes of jellyfish and poisonous sea nettles. The shipment eluded the authorities while Fields recovered. Through the years Party John Maltessa had gone on, much as had the young agent, to climb the rungs of his own chosen subculture. The smuggler and the agent. Time had passed, but the indebtedness remained.

"I owe you," said Dan Fields. Sand skittered in a salt-tanged gust and blended with his voice.

They were inside Dan Fields's home, a vaulted cathedral of light. The rooms were large and airy, filled with greenery.

"I need your help," said John. He was plumped on a comfortable sofa, a second joint burning between his fingers, a cold beer in his hand. A recent jolt of uncut cocaine froze his nose and throat. Party John, a man who earned new title to his name each and every day of his life, said, "I hooked up with a new outfit a while back." He began easily, as if their friendship hadn't been interrupted by decades on opposite sides of a career wall. "It's a new group for me, but then, most of them are these days. Everybody we knew is mostly out of the game now, either dead or too rich to worry about dealing."

"Or in jail," suggested Fields. A light glimmered in the iced void of his eyes.

"Yeah, you bastard! Plenty of them in jail." John sucked at the beer, toked on his joint. "Like I said, they're new to me, but they've been around for a while and run a tight operation. Shipments arrive on time and with full weight. The usual protections are there too. You know, bail guarantees, safe payouts, no rip-offs. A gentleman's organization."

Fields listened without reaction. He padded on weightless feet to an alcove of glass where light had been prismed into warm red, blue, and yellow bands of color. Offset from the rainbowed spill, a mighty, stone-cut arm reached up. Fields touched his fingertips to the corded tendons in the huge hand.

"Anyhow, I hooked up with these dudes. I agreed to run three shipments from off of Brownsville, Texas, up to north of where we are now, up past Beaufort into Charleston." John had slumped into the cushions and was balancing an ashtray on his thigh and the beer on his belly. "I was gonna do shrimping runs for them, across the Gulf, then up the coast and into the islands."

Fields grunted acknowledgment. Party John would command a commercial trawler with full working crew, and they would shrimp all day long, convincing the Coast Guard or whoever else might care to observe them that the craft was legitimate. With special cavities carpentered into the hulls and several tons of iced shrimp to move before contraband could be exposed, the ploy guaranteed to a high degree a safe and uneventful delivery.

"The first run was smooth," said Party John. "One of the smoothest I've ever had. I had decent weather all the way—my kind of decent, that is," he explained, then chuckled. John favored traveling in mist and cloud and storm when he was running, as Fields remembered all too well. "Everybody showed on time at every meet all the way in. I couldn't believe it. The off-loading and payout went like a goddamned military operation. Slick. It was all very slick."

Dan Fields walked along the room's perimeter. He touched the base of one of his first pieces, a bust of an old man. Fingers with independent memories of the work traced the slabbed jaw and the strong line of the nose.

"The second run scared me like I ain't never been scared before," the smuggler said intrusively. He lit a menthol cigarette from the ember of his joint and hissed. "You remember Henny Ix?"

Fields, his encyclopedic memory for names and faces snapping in unbidden, nodded. Henny Ix. Henry Ichtenstein, a man nearing his sixties, a fisherman and occasional smuggler with a boat and cabin on Daufuskie Island. He said, "I remember him, John. He's a big man with a bad limp."

Party John stood erect, lurching off his perch, scattering ashes and foam. "He's dead, Dan! Dead, and I watched the whole damn thing through my own binoculars!" His eyes bugged out; the weathered flesh at his neck twitched with a pulse.

"What happened?" Fields stood with a corona of reflected brilliance behind him.

"Pirates!" shouted John, blowing spittle, waving his short arms in outrage. "Goddamned sonofabitchin' pirates! Animals! Acting like it was the motherfucking sixteenth century or something!" He swigged from his beer, then jiggled a pocket and touched a small, dark bottle to his nose, snorting once into each nostril. He found the sofa, lowered himself, ripped the top from a second can of beer. "See, I don't know if you've kept up with these things, but these pirates, a bunch of hard-ass black moth out of Savannah, they been in half-ass business for at and for a while, if they bothered anybody in the trade would dump a couple of bales over the side and the up and that was enough. But this last time they w used to paying grease, but I guess a little free do

Someone over there decided he'd take it all, whole shipments, and never have to pay a dime. Never have to worry about the police, either. I was running a load on *The Atlantic Maiden* and Henny Ix had another load on that nasty little trawler of his, the *Miss Elizabeth*. We're just coming in south of Savannah when these fucking pirates show up in our wake. I mean, we know about them, it's pretty much their territory. So Henny Ix is closest to them and he sees them and dumps a couple of bales over the side. They stop and scoop up the bales like they always do, but then they go after Henny Ix, anyhow. He won't stop for them, so they fire some kind of fucking cannon across his bow! No shit, Dan! It was like something out of a movie. I thought I'd OD'ed! They used a cannon, maybe a bazooka or something like that, roaring and spitting fire. If they hit you with it, I swear they'd blow you right out of the water!" John squirmed, and his words rattled out in a rush. "Anyhow, Henny Ix sees this big ball of flame shoot over his bow, and I know he must've been thinking, 'To hell with this shit!' you know, 'cause nothing's worth getting killed over. So he stops dead in the water, and these black fuckers are laughing and hooting like crazy and climbing on board. I'm watching through the glasses and you can bet your ass I'm putting some kind of distance between us, you can be sure of that. I got my engines wide open. But I see them on deck with Henny Ix, and I'm thinking they're gonna take his shit and then let him go, right?"

Fields nodded.

"Well, that ain't what happens, man! They slit him open right there, Dan! I mean, they gutted that poor old fucker like he was some kind of panfish right on the deck and then tossed his ass over the side! Christ, I couldn't believe it! I still can't believe it." He heaved a great sigh and sniffed and snorted. "I don't have to tell you Mrs. Maltessa's only son got himself the fuck out of there in a hurry. I had that old tub going so fast, you could've skied behind her!

"So I get to the drop point and I do the drop like it's planned, and the guy who sets it up and pays out the bread, he comes to see me and asks if I know what happened to Henny Ix and the *Miss Elizabeth*, 'cause they're late. Well, I tell him they're a lot more than late. I lay it all out for him and he's some kind of pissed. But ___ this, Dan, he ain't so much pissed at what those animals did to ___ Ix, but this dude is freaked, worrying about what's he gonna tell his boss!''

"Who's his boss?'' asked Fields.

"Some military type is the word I get. These guys don't exactly go around broadcasting their pedigrees, right? Well, my contact man, he had to go and make some calls, I guess. Anyhow, he comes back, and now he's all calm and everything, talking about 'inevitable business losses' happening once in a while, and how he doubts it'll happen again, and would I kindly get my ass in gear to get ready for the third run. Shit! I says, 'No way, you silly-assed motherfucker!' and this guy, he's a nasty shit, anyhow, he gets kind of purple and twitchy and says there ain't gonna be no money at all, not for the trip I already made, nothin'! Says he's gonna put the word out on *me* that *I* fucked the whole thing up, that I caused it or planned it, maybe, and that I for sure won't be getting no more work from him or anybody else in the business. Well, that's okay with me, if only they'll pay me off for what I already done, but he says, 'No, you made a deal for three trips, and three is what you gotta do.' And down deep I agree with him. I mean, I been out here for as long as you have and I've never broken my word to anybody, at least not to anybody in the business. So we went at it some more and I got a little loaded and he softened his side of it a little, gave me enough cash to pay my mate, and the end of it is that I still gotta do the last run. But if I do, they'll spring for an extra twenty grand for a shotgun rider, and then they'll pay me off for everything. I wish I hadn't agreed to it, but I did, and that's what I want from you. I want you to ride with me.''

After a moment's thought Fields said, "Can't you just walk away from it?''

"I can," Party John answered, "but only if I walk away broke and with no chance of getting another score. They can ruin a guy if they really want to.''

"How much money are we talking about?''

"Altogether for both trips, it'll come to a hundred and fifty grand," John answered. Then quickly, "Dan, if twenty grand isn't enough, I'd cut you in for part of mine.''

Fields wagged his head in irritation. "How about making a deal with these guys from Savannah?" he asked. "I've never heard of a spot you couldn't talk yourself out of. Can't you go to them and work something out so they let you skate?''

John answered. "They butchered the last man I saw who tried

to talk to them. Don't you understand? They aren't your normal kind of guys.''

''What are you going to do if I say no?'' Fields asked him.

''Christ, Dan,'' John replied, ''it's my get-the-fuck-out money! And I'm getting out too! No matter what. If you can't do it, then I'll just have to get somebody else.''

''And probably get killed?''

''Right,'' John replied, ''and probably get killed. That's why I'm asking you. I figured you're the one guy I know who could handle it.'' He did not need to mention why he held the belief. To anyone in the trade, Dan Fields had been known as a shooter. He'd been in three of the most famous combat exchanges in the Drug Enforcement Agency's history. He'd even captained the first DEA shooting team to beat the FBI pistol instructors on their own course.

''What makes you think they'll pay you after this one?''

''Three things,'' said John. ''First, they've never stiffed anybody before; second, I'm gonna hold back the last shipment until I've been paid in full, and then there's the third thing.''

''What's that?''

''I'll have you with me,'' said Party John. He tried on a coked-out smile.

Dan Fields measured the floor in uneven strides. He said, ''What about my background? My identity?''

''Hey!'' John shouted. ''I didn't give him your biography! I don't do business like that. He knows I want you with me, that's all. He won't ever see your face, man. He don't need to know all that other shit.''

''Twenty thousand?''

''Yep.'' Then, ''I can add to that. I—''

''Twenty,'' said Fields. ''Twenty, and I owe you nothing.''

''Done,'' said Party John.

''Done,'' said Dan Fields.

A noise jarred Party John. ''What's that?'' He turned to the rear of the house, where it sounded as if someone were tearing the door from its hinges.

''The Outlaw.''

''The Outlaw? Who the fuck is the Outlaw?''

''An Airedale.'' Fields shrugged, turning within himself, moving to the door. ''A dog. He's my roommate. We go everywhere together. Almost.''

"I hope you aren't thinking of bringing him on my ship. I don't—''

"Humor me," said Fields over a shoulder. "He keeps me company.''

"Why not?" said Party John. "Why the hell not?"

CHAPTER 2

AS a drug enforcement agent with the Bureau of Narcotics and Dangerous Drugs, and later with the DEA, Dan Fields had from the first been aggressive, fast, thorough, and successful. His energy on the job was not motivated by the morality of any issue but was closer to the reasons why professional athletes choose to play as they do. Fields played, and played hard, because he was in love with the game. He thrived on the cycle of pursuit, infiltration, impossible odds, danger, and then victory and validation. Adrenaline had been his drug, and as an enforcement agent, it had been readily available. All one had to do to "score" was to stand up and say, "I volunteer." And adrenaline, Fields was the first to admit, stood second cousin to violence. In part it was this recognition of the forces within himself that led him to take up the hammer and chisel. For just as violence was kin to his drug of abuse, adrenaline, violent action, even when wrought upon a lifeless stone, served to drain away and neutralize the longing for a "fix."

Again he filtered twenty years of action, tension, peril, disaster, and conquest through his mind. As often happens to hard-charging men nearing their forties, Fields's unexpected career change was triggered by a divorce. Dan Fields, at the age of forty-one and after a full twenty years of service with the DEA, had not given ten minutes' thought to retirement. He had been deep in the game, had been living out his years in a state of predatory fever when his home life exploded. Yes, he'd been a gung-ho team player for decades, and yes, everything else in his life took an immediate second place if a case was in progress, but Fields had his emotional needs. He'd found time to fall in love with a secretary in the U.S. Attorney General's office in D.C. and had married her and bought a home in Rockville. They had one child, a daughter, and as long as they did not conflict with his appointed duties, Fields was happy in his roles of husband and father.

No marriage is without conflict, and certainly Mrs. Fields had on more than a few occasions pleaded with Mr. Fields to be more often at home and less often in the marijuana and poppy plantations. But all in all, these tearful scenes aside, Dan Fields thought himself one of the most fortunate of men. He had been blessed not only with the skills necessary to keep him always close to his all-important game but also was further gifted with a domestic existence that made his forays to the field all the more rewarding. Wife and child made his departures into brave rituals, then made his every return a celebration of family joy. His wife was attractive, pleasant, and sexy. His daughter was a beautiful child, alert and bright. His home, the small family's third and presumably last, carried a mortgage he easily could meet. In the last few years he'd even begun to learn some of his neighbors' names and had actually been to his first PTA meeting. For Fields, life had been perfect.

Until the day he climbed out of a D.C. cab, walked up to his front door, and opened the lock to find the house denuded of its furnishings, Dan Fields had had implicit faith in his performance as husband and father. And then he had none. Empty rooms where once he'd known laughter and fullness assaulted him with accusations. And Dan Fields, alone and barking out choking noises as he cried in a barren room, admitted to all the previous charges.

Only when forced into the daily and absolute isolation of an empty house did the agent at last slow down long enough to confront himself and his life. It happened while he was searching the basement, hunting for anything he might use as a temporary window shade. He'd looked up to the rafters, remembering once when he'd been home in the summer that he'd seen a carpet rolled and stored there. Instead Fields had looked up and found the hooks where a seven-year-old girl had hung her bike in winter. The emptiness he felt had taken him to the cold cellar floor as if struck by a car. The empty house was so final. Vacant rooms told him the matter was beyond negotiation. Fields understood at last. He had failed as a husband and father. Failed. Dan Fields—perfectionist, overachiever—had failed. And the case was closed, beyond appeal. His hand grasped the checkered grip of the service automatic at his side, drew it from the holster. He'd failed, not as an agent but, more deeply, as a human being.

He imagined a life without the woman he loved, the child he loved, a life still in the game but with no one to go home to. It was not enough. The game had lost its magic, as if his obsession had destroyed itself only after it destroyed his family. Fields turned the weapon, touched the barrel to a spot beside his ear. No man could be forced to live with failure, not if he owned his own life. No man could be compelled to—

The force of an idea struck him as he was taking up the pressure on the trigger. Even now he was still playing the game! In the game men solved problems with violence, with bullets and death. Other human beings, those who hadn't spent a lifetime with a weapon in hand, confronted life, faced and survived their failures.

With stunned wonder at his own prolonged blindness, Dan Fields lowered the pistol. He sat, strangely calm, and challenged the validity of the game. He weighed the crimes and punishments, the penalties and rewards he'd seen. He recalled the men who'd died, opponents and comrades, men he'd held at their deaths. And found it all a horrible waste. In that moment of harsh truth he revolted at sending one more man into prison, knowing the sentence carried with it the certainty of sodomy and gang rape. And in that one heretical moment he knew he would never send another human being undercover or into combat, or to jail. And with the knowledge that never again would he commit the life of another to achieve his own success, Dan Fields acknowledged the ultimate value of this new insight. He embraced it with the grip of a drowning man. Life, all of life, was a beauty to be seen, a taste to be savored.

And without doubt or hesitation he decided to proclaim his newfound revelation with art. He turned to his first and longest love, sculpture. As a child, when all of the other children had abandoned playing with clay and moved on to other exciting activities, little Dan Fields stayed behind and made figures out of the accumulated piles of clay. In later years he limited his love for the modeled figure to museums, studying sculpture, kinetic structures, everything available to the public. He studied, not in a classroom but from sculpture he could touch, sculpture he could feel. And as his travels for the DEA took him from one city to another, waiting for this informant or that case agent to be free, he wandered the museums. When they were closed, he sought out sculpture where it lived in the secret places of the cities. He'd touched those pieces, traced their folds and ridges, and always longed to pick up his own hammer and chisel. Dan Fields, given the luxury of being stripped of everything, decided to sculpt. Not to go to school to sculpt, not to write away to learn about sculpting, but to sculpt.

Making a living wouldn't be a critical problem. Twice in the past four years the DEA doctors had suggested he think about taking a medical retirement. Shiny scars and bullet entry and exit wounds marked each of his several hospitalizations. A government pension paying eighty percent of his salary had been available anytime he wished. And he had enough accumulated vacation pay that if the money took a while to catch up with him, he would still be all right.

The drug-enforcement agent had retired and implemented his plan. He divorced himself from the game, from the seduction of combat and adrenaline highs. He taught himself to wield his hammer and chisel to the point where his pieces began to sell once in a while, sometimes before they were complete. His child, now several years older, remained estranged from him, while her mother appeared to blossom in newfound freedom. They acknowledged Fields with polite distance.

And now, a debt owed called to Dan Fields with a promise of one last, sharp thrill.

CHAPTER 3

THIRTY miles from the Georgia coast the Atlantic was gray-green, opaque, and secretive. The breeze from the Gulf Stream was moist and warm, moving soundlessly from the southeast. The humidity poised just short of precipitation, as it had for two days.

Frantic gulls worked the rippling wake from the trawler's nets, wafting spread-winged and white-bellied, watching for the snapping leap of an escaping shrimp. Dipping and diving, splashing down, complaining loudly at their unsuccessful efforts, they fled quickly and quietly when rewarded with a flicking gray morsel. Their plaintive cries gave counterpoint and balance to the muted thrumming of the trawler's diesels while the chop-slosh of the slow-gaited hull provided rhythm to the swirl of life and death.

The trawler, sixty-four feet of pitted metal and petroleum-based science, rode red and salt-scoured-black upon the sea. She was like a Leviathan wading heavy-legged, dipping eight degrees to port, eight degrees to starboard, eight degrees to port.

The crew groped their way through the glare and drone, moving with an economy of motion common to those who exist in grudging compromise with the bounty, famine, peace, and violence of deep-water living.

In the skewed wheelhouse the bandy-legged captain scanned the electronic marvels of his trade. Ship's papers identified him as

John L. Maltessa, licensed master, captain of *The Atlantic Maiden*, trawler, owned and operated by Bronson's Seafood Industries out of Brownsville, Texas. His name was John Maltessa. The rest was fiction.

New England–born and educated, "Party John" Maltessa cursed. He started in English, then rolled into Spanish and Portuguese, switched to gutter French, spat something in Afrikaans, and ended his befouled prayer in a thieves' dialect of Japanese. He was a world traveler, world citizen, and smuggler of the highest caste, and the alarm bells sounding within him had been tuned by more than twenty years of hard-won experience. He repeated his sweep of the instrumentation and the horizons. He tugged a watertight plastic cigarette case from the pocket of his loose-fitting tan cotton slacks, extracted a perfectly rolled marijuana cigarette, placed it between his fleshy lips, and lit it with the flaring flame of a wooden kitchen match. Drawing and hissing as he mixed pungent smoke with salt-seasoned air, he exhaled and willed his fears into oblivion. Instead the influence of the drug increased his unfocused paranoia. His gauges, screens, radio, binoculars, nose, and hearing told him all was well. His internal alarm system told him to run like hell.

Party John edged sideways from the pilothouse and shuffled down the roughened concrete deck. He passed the galley, evading its spiky Gullah scent of peppers and okra by hissing in his own sweet smoke of rarest Jamaican, compelling his lungs to admit the expanding cloud of blue-tinted smoke. Ten paces farther and his inflamed bronchii could endure no more. They rebelled. Party John rounded the cabin bulkhead, fighting a losing battle with his scarred lungs, and arrived on the rear deck in spluttering asphyxiation.

The mate, Ritchie Weaver, had skin the color of rubbed mahogany. Bare-chested, outfitted in loose trousers and high rubber boots, he stood to greet the captain's arrival on the stern. "Sheee-it, *Buckra!*" Weaver's words, full of disgust, were sliced out in a lilting chirp, carrying the sound of the sea islands against the cadence of an African tongue. Gullah was his language and *Buckra* translated as "white man." But when Weaver spoke it, it took on all the hatred and anger one word could hold. This constituted no breach of shipboard protocol, since the captain was not a fisherman and the Gullah mate, Ritchie Weaver, was on board for purposes of camouflage and profit. The shrimp, netted, beheaded, and packed in crushed ice below decks, were his and his alone. During their journey Ritchie had caught and packed away twenty-six hundred-pound boxes of brown shrimp. At two dollars and twenty cents per pound he would unload his catch at the Hilton Head processing plant and cash out with more than fifty-seven hundred dollars for the past four days. And added to that sum was the five-thousand-dollar cash bonus he insisted on at the start of each trip. The trawler, the auxiliary equipment, the fuel, and the ice were all supplied by Party John at no cost. Ritchie Weaver was sullen, self-reliant, racist, uncommunicative, and, above all, a capitalist. There was money, big money, to be made from the nets; none to be made in conversation with the paranoid white man. Ritchie kicked the brake lever on the clangorous winch, and the bright green nets, weighted by chains and large oaken sleds, dropped to the surface of the murky sea with a splash. He played out several hundred feet of wire rope cable, then braked the winch. The oaken sleds dived below the foaming surface and slowed the trawler with their descent. Both nets spread wide, and fishing from either side, *The Atlantic Maiden* resumed her stiff-legged, rolling gait.

Hacking, Party John approached the third crew member. The red-faced captain extended his sinewy arm to the seated man, offering the glowing remnant of his joint. Fields declined it with the barest of nods and continued to scan the western horizon. On board as the third crewman or "striker," his shipboard duties were to separate the salable catch from creatures to be returned to the sea and then to behead the still flicking shrimp. He was derelict in that regard. Clad in khaki shorts and a faded shirt, Fields sat against the gunwale and scanned the open sea, alternating between the glasses and his naked eyes.

"See anything?" the captain inquired between coughs.

"No," Fields replied in a soft voice, nearly a whisper. "Nothing of interest. You getting anything on the scope?"

"Not yet"—Party John hissed and toked—"but I can feel them out there, Dan. I can sure as shit feel them."

Fields's averted face discouraged further attempts at conversation.

Party John smoked and hacked his way back to the pilothouse and its technological assurances. He was twelve hours from his destination and safe delivery of thirty-two bales of marijuana and another, separate package holding ten kilograms of cocaine. Safely delivered, his net fee would be in excess of one hundred and fifty thousand dollars. That figure was comforting, but his internal alarms would not desist.

Party John fingered a small brown bottle from the pocket of his wrinkled trousers. He unscrewed the black cap, dipped lightly into the white, crystalline powder inside with a small, spoonlike appendage to the cap, and brought the spoon and its contents to his right nostril. He inhaled sharply, drawing the powder into his nasal passages. He repeated the process once again to the right nostril and twice more to the left. He had another coughing seizure. His nostrils and sinuses burned painfully and then grew numb. The back of his throat experienced a "freeze," and his pulse rate climbed rapidly. In the midst of those various physical manifestations of distress, Party John began to feel good. He lit a harsh menthol cigarette and opened a can of iced beer, partaking greedily of each. While so engaged, he continued his scan of the instrumentation and the horizon.

His black hair was coarse, curly, and uncombed. It was cut short and shot through with gray and silver. His naturally dark complexion was augmented by a permanent tan. He stood shirtless at the controls, and beneath their covering of dense, ectopic hairs his arms had a tough, sinewy quality garnered from years of oceanic sailing. Those active years, however, were not adequate to conquer the sagging mass of his paunch, nor were they sufficient to overcome the enlargement of his breasts from decades of protracted marijuana usage.

Nothing dispelled his unease. The memories of his last passage through the same waters filled his body with an adrenaline-charged fear no amount of chemical alteration would diminish. He turned his thoughts to the man quietly scanning the horizon at the rear deck. With the reality of danger so close, his mind raced to reexamine the facts that had led him to choose this one man to guard and protect his life, his ship, and his cargo. A man didn't get to live through too many mistakes in his business, and Party John did not make many. True, he often bragged how he'd used up all nine lives of his first and second cats getting out of Cuban prisons and Colombian jails and laughed about how he was well into spending those of his third cat in supposedly safer waters. But not once did he believe it. He made no mistake giving credit to luck. Party John survived because of his ability to read a man's face and hands and body. He knew when they were lying, knew when they were telling the truth. He could sense if a man planned to betray him, just as he knew when a man stood a good enough risk to be trusted. And through the last twenty years he'd had the opportunity to "read" Dan Fields on several occasions. His first judgments stood. Onshore his choice had seemed well founded and wisely made, but riding alone on such a large sea he regretted not bringing an entire navy.

He saw the first radar blip. From the southwest, from the Georgia coastline, it—whatever it was—followed a course to intercept *The Atlantic Maiden*. Party John forced himself to watch the luminescent lines through three more sweeps. The data did not change. A vessel was pursuing his ship and would intercept his wake within minutes. He tumbled from the pilothouse and trained his binoculars on the southwest. He could see nothing on the horizon; the glare was blinding. He checked again. The radar blip sent him trundling down the deck, leaning on the bulkhead for stability. The thundering in his chest shook him with each step, each breath.

Words were not necessary. Fields had focused his binoculars in the exact direction of the radar blip. The Outlaw braced against him, leaning against the defined muscularity of his bunched thigh. The huge Airedale held its head at an improbable angle, maintaining a conscious tension of neck muscles to remain in contact with his master. At John's approach the dog turned, stretched its sprawled legs, and arched its torso. The Outlaw's placid brown eyes and lolling tongue mocked the captain's tension.

"I could feel 'em out there!" shouted John. "I knew they were fucking gonna get me! Goddamn!"

Fields lowered the mottled gray glasses and stroked the black and gold of the Airedale's powerful shoulders. "Ritchie," he called over the thrumming of the diesels. "Get your nets in now. Both of them."

The black didn't acknowledge the command but slid to the winch controls and began the deafening retrieval of the nets.

"Jesus Christ!" yelled Party John. "Why did I agree to do this? I knew this was gonna happen. Damn! Damn! Damn!"

"Shut up, John." He threw back the besplattered tarpaulin at his side. The clownlike Airedale sprang up in anticipation, his huge jowls gaping in a silent grin, his nose working the sharp new scents. Beneath the tarp were two large bales wrapped in dense plastic and bound with thin metal baling strips. Adjacent to the bales lay a long, rectangular wooden box painted a dark green.

The crank and clatter of the incoming chains and weighted sleds competed with the shriek of the cable and the roar of the winch motor while the ever-present gulls issued their complaints at the interruption of their feeding. Ritchie lashed his nets and scrambled down into the hold, down among the iced shrimp to comparative safety. His contractual obligations in no way compelled him to risk his presence above decks.

"John!" Fields called, turning to face the immobilized captain. "Head out to the northeast and put on some more speed." Then he added, "Hold a steady course and avoid the chop." His voice was firm and casual, and a slight smile played at the corners of his lips.

Confident of his impending doom, Party John scrabbled herky-jerky to the pilothouse and tortured himself with the last images of Henny Ix's death. He bumped the diesel rpms to maximum speed and wheeled his course a few points out to sea.

Dan Fields stroked the arched neck of the rough-coated Airedale, and the dog leaned into his touch. "Well, Outlaw," he murmured with the mournful voice of an alcoholic poised over his "first" drink. "So much for going home with a big bag of money just for taking a cruise." The deep-chested, wasp-waisted animal squirmed and wiggled closer. Dan Fields drew in a long, deep breath through his nostrils and exhaled slowly through his parted lips. His eyes, the color of the colder depths of the North Atlantic, focused on the now visible speck approaching the wake of the trawler. He bent and, using the strength he'd acquired as a sculptor of heavy stone, hoisted the forty-kilo bale to his shoulder and tossed it in an arc from the trembling steel of the trawler to the churning froth of the ocean. Without pause he repeated his fluid motion, and a second bale quickly righted itself in the opaque, green water, bobbing to the opposing eddies of the trawler's wake and the incoming tide. Field appraised the drift of the bales and the course of the oncoming craft. His deeply set eyes were framed by dark brows, and across his broad forehead were four parallel furrows accented by the sunlight reflected from the sea. His cheekbones proclaimed his Celtic heritage, and his medium-size nose was made larger by the flared nostrils common to that savage race. The hollows of his cheeks emphasized the angular line of his jaw leading to the centrally cleft chin. His mouth was drawn into a thin, inexpressive line.

Fields raised the field glasses to his eyes. The craft was a cabin cruiser, less than thirty feet in length, piloted from a flying bridge by a black man. Four other blacks were braced on the decking. Two of them casually held rifles at port arms. Their craft displayed neither name nor number, and its hull lifted precariously out of the water as it sped to intercept the two discarded bales.

Fields stroked the broad space between the pricked ears of the Airedale and knelt to the rectangular wooden box. Unhurriedly he flicked open its three pitted brass catches. Inside lay the gleaming blond stock and blue-black metal of a Weatherby Magnum Mark V, a .44. Above the long barrel, a Weatherby Imperial scope was affixed to a Buehler mount. The gleaming cream finish of the handcrafted stock was unmarred by smudge or fingerprint. Taking care to remain below the gunwale and out of sight of the oncoming pirate craft, Fields lifted the weapon from its resting place. The grooved stock and pistol grip accepted the intricacies of his hands and fingers as only the finest of custom carving will allow. He checked the action of the precision-machined bolt and the tension of the strap. He cradled the exotically worked wood and metal in the crook of his left arm and turned again to the smaller craft.

The pursuit vessel had slowed to a near stop at the first of the bales. One of the blacks leaned precariously from the stern of the cruiser and extended a ten-foot gaff. Fighting the lurch of the boat and the swell of the hissing sea, he snagged the bouncing bale and pulled the hook in, hand over hand until the bale was bumping vigorously against the side, threatening to pull hook and holder overboard. A second and third black joined him at the stern, and together they lifted the bobbing parcel out of the water and onto the deck. They pushed the bale to the side without further examination. The pilot of the small craft gunned his engines, and the craft raced to the second bale, bouncing corklike in the swells. It was rapidly hooked and landed.

"Turn around and leave," Fields prayed. "Turn around. Take your tribute and leave and we'll all sleep well tonight."

As if in response to his incantation, the craft again leapt to life and headed on a course parallel to that of the trawler. Fields held his breath. The hull of the cruiser raised higher out of the water, spreading a frothy white wake. On the flying bridge a black garbed in dingy white shorts brought a cumbersome rifle to his right shoulder. The cruiser pulled slightly ahead of the red hull of the trawler. The black on the flying bridge fired his weapon.

On *The Atlantic Maiden* the window of the pilothouse imploded, showering Party John with particles of tinted safety glass. "Oh, Jesus jumpin' Christ!" he screamed, and flattened himself on the deck. "Am I shot?" he screamed to himself. "Am I bleeding?" Wedged and jammed headfirst into a corner of the wheelhouse, he examined his skin and found no injury larger than a scratch. "Great, just great!" he murmured. "They can have more fun when they cut me open and feed me to the fucking fish!"

Fields raised the magnificent Weatherby, grand prize from his last federal marksmanship tournament, fitted it snugly against his shoulder, tightened his fingers uniformly around the pistol grip, snaked his left hand through the strap, and sighted into the cross hairs of the Imperial scope. Passing over the rifleman and the other animated figures, he focused upon the center of the tribute bale, visible in their stern. He inhaled, exhaled half of that breath, and gently, gradually, increased the pressure of his finger pad upon the grooved trigger until the Weatherby detonated with an acute crack.

The stern of the pirate cruiser erupted in a hot, white flash. A rolling red fireball obscured the vessel and those on board. A palpable boom followed as a second, larger explosion racked the cabin cruiser. Debris hurtled skyward, rapidly pursued by the orange-red flames of a towering fireball.

In one abrupt moment the sea was silent and the craft was gone. Swirling black clouds broke free and climbed in silence. The boat sank quickly, definitively, out of sight, out of existence. The straining diesels of *The Atlantic Maiden* broke the silence of the sea.

Fields ejected the spent cartridge, drove a replacement into the chamber, cradled the Weatherby in the crook of his left arm, and sped for the wheelhouse. He peered into the compartment. Crammed into an impossibly small condensation of flesh, Party John lay crouched and quivering on the deck, trying to hold a kitchen match to a broken marijuana cigarette. The Outlaw, unperturbed and unaware of danger either past or present, bounded forward. He slurped his tongue all over John's face and his bedraggled joint.

"Get off me, you dumb son of a bitch!" squawked Party John. A large and enthusiastic pink tongue bathed him. "Dan!" he croaked. "Help me, you bastard! I come within a cunt's hair of having my head blown off and end up being licked to death by this fucking clown!"

The Outlaw was undaunted. He straddled the man, licking, slobbering, then stepped firmly onto John's crotch.

"Oh, goddamn!" screamed Party John. "Dan, get this dummy off me!"

"Let him up, Outlaw," Fields managed to say through his laughter. "He's okay, you can let him up now." The dog backed two paces and sat, his tail stump wagging and his head cocked to one side.

"Damn, his breath is worse than mine!" marveled John.

Fields helped him to his feet. "You were right earlier," Fields said, ending his laughter with a weary grin. "I used a touch too much plastique. They went to the bottom like a rock. Except for a slick and some planking, there's not a trace."

"Sounded like fucking Nagasaki when that thing went off!" Party John exclaimed. He held up his arms and checked the backs of them for injuries. He checked his legs and patted his bottom. "I recognized the boat. That's the same one the bastards used when they got Henny Ix." His hands fumbled with the broken joint. "Let's get the hell out of here before anybody else tries to blow my head off," he said, and sniffed with near violent force. "Dan, I swear I'm getting out of this business. I quit! I can't take this shit!" He brushed fragments of powdered glass from his middle. "They could have killed me! Sure as shit!"

"Take it easy, John," Fields said soothingly. "They didn't get you. You're okay." He smiled an easy smile. "Compared to them"—Fields gestured at the receding debris—"you came out way ahead." He gripped Party John on the shoulder. "Relax, John. Relax and play the game you know best. You're home free now if you keep your head and get your shrimp back to Hilton Head. You're just a little nerved, that's all."

"That's easy for you to say. You didn't have goddamned bullets trying to cut your nose off! Christ! I thought I was dead!" With the flow of words Party John dispelled some of the fear flooding his system. "Look, Dan, you're used to this kind of shit. You think it's normal to blow up a bunch of guys and not get excited. But not to me. I can't be calm!"

"You may be right," Fields replied. "But you need to relax and put the *Maiden* back into her shrimping routine or you'll attract the attention of the Coast Guard, for certain." He looked down at the wild-eyed captain. "I don't know about you, John, but I've already had all the excitement I want today."

John pulled the throttle controls back to shrimping speed, and the bulky trawler resumed her waddle; chugging, deep-water wading, northward and homeward. Fields patted his thigh and left the pilothouse, followed by the Outlaw with his lurch, pause, sniff, leap, and natural joy.

Fields walked to the stern of the trawler and returned the custom-crafted weapon to its casings. As he fastened the latches he gave thanks that he had not needed to use the matched pair of Giles Colts stowed beneath the velvet lining. They were aboard for close and personal contact, each one a finely machined modification of the 1921 automatic pistol. Their clips were loaded with 45-caliber rounds Fields had prepared with soft lead projectiles filed into six-pointed crosses, each shell carrying a heavier than standard powder charge. They were inaccurate at more than forty yards, but at closer distance the filed projectiles spread into tumbling, flattened discs. Striking at more than eight hundred feet per second, they were devastating. The exact precision of the famous Florida gunsmith's design enabled the normally unwieldly pistols to be used with speed and minimal recoil despite the alteration of the ammunition.

Fields stroked the body of the Outlaw, reassuring the sensitive beast. He knelt and hugged the solid dog and let his mind travel to peaceful times and places when love came not only from an adoring pet but from a woman and a little girl.

Shipboard routine resumed. Ritchie Weaver busied himself with separating the catch upon the smeared and stained deck. Party John swept the glassy debris from the pilothouse, corrected his course, and resumed his realistic imitation of a working shrimper heading to port with filled holds, fishing for every last shrimp along the route. He stabilized his unique body chemistry with a mixture of marijuana, cocaine, beer, and chain-smoked cigarettes. While he toked, snorted, gulped, and inhaled from his chemical warehouse, he adjusted the rpms of the diesels upward to compensate for the increased drag generated by the relowered shrimping nets. The pitted hulk of *The Atlantic Maiden* fell into her slow, deep-water waddle, and the gulls returned to waft on the currents above the nets.

CHAPTER 4

THE *Atlantic Maiden* lay anchored off a shallow flat. The predawn humidity cloaked men and machines with a fine mist of sticky droplets as darting river craft rushed out to the trawler, loaded quickly and silently, then sped back to their destinations. Fields stood shrouded in shadow upon the roof of the pilothouse, the twin Giles Colts holstered at his sides. The Outlaw sat perched on the deck below, his broad head uplifted, his eyes alert, his large, black nose tasting the scents.

"It's all there. I counted it myself three times," said the man with the pale skin. His printed shirt was slicked with perspiration, and he mopped his face again with a crumpled handkerchief.

"Right, Weems," Party John mouthed, but he kept counting. The stacks of twenties were neatly bundled and wrapped in piles of five hundred dollars each.

"I'm very pleased with the way your man handled that nasty situation with the pirates," Weems offered. He checked his wristwatch. "I'd like to talk to him when we're finished here."

"What?" asked Party John, annoyed.

"I said I want to talk to your man when we're done."

"I don't think that's such a good idea," John mumbled, dropping another stack of twenties into his duffel. "He don't want to talk to you."

"I think he'll want to talk to me," Weems countered. He pulled the tops of his knee-length support hose a quarter of an inch higher onto pale calves. "If he expects to be paid, he'll talk to me." The man's projected baritone was out of place on the water, and it carried farther than he intended.

"And that's the last one," said John, tossing the final packet of twenties into the duffel. "Now, what's this shit about my man's bread? I promised him twenty grand, and he sure as shit earned it, Weems. I'll tell you one thing. You don't want to cross that man out there."

"Why do you types always have to be so difficult?" Weems asked in irritation. He wiped at his face and pushed a straying comma of dark hair from his unlined forehead. "All that's involved here is for me to thank him for his assistance and to pay him his well-earned money. I don't see where that's too complex for you to understand, Captain." His voice was too large for the tiny compartment. "Get him in here and let's be done with it."

"He ain't gonna like it," said Party John.

"Oh, come on, Captain!" barked Weems. "He'll like it, all right. He'll like it twenty thousand dollars' worth. Get him in here. I haven't got all night to fool around."

"Look, Weems"—Party John slid out from the cramped booth—"he's got no interest in anything you've got to say. He took care of business, that's all you need to know. Something like this, you don't ask too many questions. You just pay up and forget it. Why not do yourself a favor and leave it like that?"

"Because I like to meet the men who work for me," replied Weems. "I like to look into a man's eyes and shake his hand when I pay him. Take his measure, if you know what I mean." He ran the handkerchief around the inside of his shirt collar. "Send him in, Captain."

"He ain't gonna like it," said Party John as he lifted the duffel to his shoulder, "not even a little bit."

Weems arched an eyebrow and drummed his manicured nails on the Formica tabletop.

Party John trudged out of the tiny compartment.

Weems checked his timepiece and saw that it said five minutes after four, then scanned the bulkheads of the compartment for a wall clock and found none. He patted the wrapped parcel on the wooden bench beside him. The moment of sticky panic he'd experienced when Party John had refused to deliver the cocaine had passed as soon as Weems had produced the man's money, but he checked again, just to make sure. Yes, the cocaine was still there. He mopped his clammy skin with the damp square of linen and readjusted the crotch of his knee-length shorts.

"Ah," said Weems as he spied Fields in the passageway, "it's a real pleasure to meet you."

Fields stepped into the cone of light cast by the single bulb overhead but didn't reply. The twin Colts were no longer in sight, and he was dressed in comfortable, faded jeans and a light blue oxford shirt. Weems rose as far as the bolted bench and tabletop would allow him, and offered his hand. Fields refused it with a flicker of cold blue eyes.

Weems lowered his hand. "I hope you don't mind, but I did want to have a word or two with you before I pay you." He smiled a plastic smile.

Fields's continued silence suggested perhaps he did mind.

Weems cleared his throat and leaned down to tug at the tops of his support hose. "You see," he projected, "in a business such as ours, the wise man is always on the lookout for talent, talent to increase the productivity of his business. I'm sure you understand."

Fields's eyes darkened and suggested perhaps he didn't understand.

"First," said Weems as he mopped droplets from his pallid face, "I want to commend you for the manner in which you dispatched that rabble. They've been quite a nuisance to us, and I just wanted to say I'm truly impressed."

Fields released a sigh and lowered his lids.

Party John moved from behind Fields's shadow and stepped into the cramped space of the compartment. "Come on, Weems," urged Party John, the duffel snugged securely over his arm. "Get on with it. I told you he wasn't going to like it."

Weems shifted his wet eyes from John to Fields and back to John. He pulled a thick paper envelope from a briefcase beside him on the galley bench. He peeked inside just to be sure the contents hadn't mysteriously disappeared and offered the envelope to Fields. "Twenty thousand dollars. Worth every penny too. I wish you'd let me talk to you about some very attractive opportunities. I can help you an awful lot," he added. Weems's arm began to tremble. He lowered the envelope to the scarred table.

Party John said, "You better be going, Weems. I don't care

what kind of fix you have in with the feds, I'm getting this ship the hell out of here.''

Weems arched an indignant brow at the captain. "Aren't you going to count it this time?''

Fields's stare answered him.

Weems checked his watch. "I do have to go,'' he offered, as if it were his own idea. "I've other appointments to keep.''

"Right,'' said Party John.

"One thing, though.'' Weems turned to them from the bulkhead. "You know, a dog can be either a pleasure or a pain in the ass,'' he said to Party John, "and that one you've got traveling with you is undoubtedly the latter. Any animal that can't behave properly is a very poor reflection on its owner.''

With a wicked smile Party John said, "The son of a bitch ain't mine.''

Weems was puzzled for a brief second, then the lights went on. He turned to Fields and said, "He's really quite a beautiful animal, but he doesn't have a place in our business. Do you know what I mean?''

Fields's glower told him he didn't know what Weems meant and might never.

"Right,'' said Weems. He pushed his face back into a smile. "I do have other appointments, as I told you, but I hope you'll give some thought to what I've said. I happen to be in an excellent position to be of tremendous help to you.'' Weems hefted the packet of cocaine and made his way out of the compartment. He tried once more to show the qualities of a good manager. He turned to Ritchie Weaver. "Mr. Weaver,'' he called, mindful how blacks felt more important if you addressed them as "mister.'' "I want you to know your performance hasn't gone unnoticed. I'm very pleased with your contributions and hope to do business with you again.'' He held out a hand three shades too white for Weaver to shake.

Ritchie looked Weems full in the face. "Sheee-it, *Buckra*,'' he whispered.

Weems, red-faced in the darkness, clambered over the side.

It was dawn, the gray sky streaked with red. Seabirds cried out in morning hunger, and the slack halyards of moored sailboats slapped and clattered in the freshening east wind. The fat-bottomed lady, *The Atlantic Maiden*, was lashed to the loading docks of a shrimp packinghouse, and Ritchie Weaver was waiting on board for the first packinghouse shift to unload his catch. John, his private craft hidden as usual with no one but himself knowing exactly where, stood in a corner of the marina parking lot. Dan Fields faced him.

"Uh, look, Dan," Party John said. "I—I didn't know that ass was going—"

"We're even, John," said Fields. His eyes were cold and accusing. "I don't owe you now."

John was nodding with vigor. "Right! Damn right!" He spread his arms. "What can I say? I should've checked Weems out a little better, I know that. I fucked up and had us hooked up with a goof, but, Christ, Dan, you—"

"I," said Fields, overriding John with uncustomary force and volume, "I don't want to have to look at you again. I paid the debt, now leave me alone. Do you hear me, John? Am I getting through to you?"

Party John was wounded. "What? What'd I do? What—"

"I'm giving you fair warning. I don't want to see you again. Every time I look at your face, I remember what happened out th—"

"But they were animals!" John was windmilling, his arms wild exclamation points. "Fucking savage animals! You shouldn't—"

"Stop it," hissed Fields. "I'm not inviting you to debate. I'm telling you to leave me alone. I'm out of that life because I chose to be. I should have remembered that. But I don't owe you anymore, and the next time we meet, I'm going to act accordingly." His voice had dropped to a whisper, and his eyes were narrowed to half their size.

"I know!" tried Party John. "It's the money, and I can't blame you—not at all, Dan. I was thinking myself that I hadn't been as fair with you as I sh—"

Fields turned and glided toward a battered pickup truck. The Outlaw sat human-fashion in the front passenger seat, mapping the windshield with the moisture from his nose. Fawn-bellied pelicans were making their dawn journeys seaward in formation. The big dog marked each passage with a smear and a dribble.

"Dan, wait!" Party John was at his elbow, holding him with one hand, digging for his money stash with the other. "Hey! C'mon! I want you to have—"

Fields lashed out with one hand. Party John fell like a dead man. Fields bent, grabbed the smuggler, and hauled him a yard away from the truck. John's mouth was working, blowing like a landed fish, and his eyes were panicked. Fields said, "Leave me alone, John. For the rest of your life I want you to do anything and everything in your power to leave me alone."

Party John Maltessa, fighting for air against the rebellion of his own tissues, his eyes goggling, bobbed his head.

CHAPTER 5

MOST people are born into the environment that shall be called home for all their lives. Some will leave one area to find work in another city or town. Some will relocate for marriage. But only a small minority, those cut off from family and tradition or those exposed to travel at an early age, actually choose and select the very geography of their own homes. Dan Fields was one such man.

The very concept of choice implies a certain familiarity with the options available, and it was true that Fields's professional pursuits had granted him a panorama of "homes" from which to choose. As a child, he'd played and run upon the gentle, rolling green carpets of central Maryland, but as an undercover federal narcotics agent, he had seen the world. Fields had pulled extended tours in Chicago, Detroit, Washington, D.C., and Atlanta. He'd worked flying investigations, operations an agent took "on the road" as he milked a source for drug connections over a spread of states. He'd worked from Key West to New York City and across the path of old Route 66 all the way to the other coast. He'd seen South America, "up-close and personal," from penthoused sunsets in Rio to the packed earthen floors of filthy tin-can huts in Bogota. He'd seen and smelled southeast Asia, too, for BNDD, had gone to 'Nam—oh, yes, and Laos too.

Then, when time had telescoped inward on Fields and he'd

been running agents of his own, broadjumping the continent, hopping planes at midnight, he'd peeked at all of America from above. He knew the snake-spined rivers and patchworked fields, the greens and blues and golds and reds. He'd run on a treadmill then, an infinity loop of adrenaline, taking life at thirty thousand feet and directing undercover lies each time he hit the ground.

Hilton Head Island, near the coastal borders of Georgia and South Carolina, not much smaller than the island of Manhattan, is a subtropical lowland. It is teeming with life from the sands and marshes to the clear skies above. Without air-conditioning and malathion the place would be uninhabitable to most humans. But every home is air-conditioned, and light airplanes fly overhead, spraying the mosquito poison with predictable regularity. Wealth is conspicuous on Hilton Head. Property values are high. Most who play there are tourists, riding onto the island in overloaded station wagons, spending their savings and then fleeing. But tucked away in the lesser known corners, others play on Hilton Head. The northern coast is filthy with successful writers and artists and the most famous of professional athletes. The houses of doctors and attorneys in their youthful retirement dot the landscape. Mercedes and BMWs are common, not worth notice.

Island life tends to insulate one from the passions of the mainland. Everything is informal. To borrow half a million dollars from the bank the client arrives in stained sailing ducks, ripped boat shoes, and a two-hundred-dollar shirt. Everyone is late for everything. Work is canceled for any occasion; parties last for days. Natural beauty is preserved, coaxed, and manicured, but commercial enterprise proliferates. And litigation abounds, maintaining a precarious balance between the greed of investors and the wishes of naturalists. Most of the developed acreage is divided into "plantations," glorified housing developments, each with its mandated portion of commercial and recreational areas. Hilton Head. That was the world, the home of choice for Daniel Fields.

His steep-sloped wood frame house existed beyond the protective confines of a plantation. His surrounding plot of land was not manicured in accordance with itemized covenant but was a tangle of underbrush and poison ivy, pierced by palmetto trees and live oaks. The thick-bodied oaks were draped with light, dry-spun Spanish moss and gave welcome to an ever-changing cast of bird life. The open, vaulted design of the house was an invitation to light. The interior was bright and spacious, granting unobstructed views of the life outside while preserving his possessions within. In the sandy drive sat a rust-consumed and battered pickup truck. Its seats were torn, and gray cotton tufts poked out randomly and littered the thin floorboards.

Adjacent to the house itself, constructed of similar material and design, stood a garage large enough for one vehicle. Inside rested a gleaming, yellow machine, perfect counterbalance to the decaying truck outside. It was an MG roadster, a 1954 TD with rolled fenders and running boards, lovingly and accurately restored to its original condition. Along the walls of the tiny garage, tools were perfectly placed and arrayed, spotless but showing signs of frequent use and meticulous care.

The man and the dog came down the sandy lane. The Outlaw's hind end was jacked up and springloaded, as he bounded with stiff-legged glory. They came from the beach, the cranked Airedale splattering foamy clods of damp sand at each rebound. Within the very private and complex bond of man and beast, Fields and the huge terrier each served the other. The Outlaw filled a space, a dark emptiness within Fields, and in return Fields participated in frantic gallops on wet-slicked beaches. That morning they'd scattered a flock of New Jersey tourists, chased seagulls, and the Outlaw had caught and killed a small blue Frisbee, all without stopping to enter the house. The run was their rule, and if they'd been absent ten minutes or ten days, the Airedale would always insist on it.

Fields worked his key, opened the carved door, and padded in, the Outlaw playing bump and run behind him. The jungle of indoor plants was in glowing, blooming health. Despite his prolonged absence, the temperature was coolly comfortable, and his accumulated correspondence was bundled neatly upon the marble-topped counter separating the small but efficient kitchen area from the bookish spaces of the first floor. After first laying out ample provisions of food and water for the Outlaw, Fields marched in slow time through the first floor, passing the heavy wood and leather of his personally selected furnishings, and climbed the stairs.

On the second-floor loft he drew the drapes that hung upon the expanse of window, nodded silent acknowledgment to the frozen photographs of a blond girl-child and a darkly wild and beautiful woman and fell exhausted upon the gray silk coverlet of the custom-crafted cherry-wood bed. He was instantly asleep, vaguely conscious of the protective presence of the quietly subdued canine.

The animal sniffed lightly at his outstretched hand and padded silently down the carpeted stairway. The large, moist black button of his nose quivering, the Airedale completed his patrol. Only after each fluctuating air current had been tested and accepted as normal and posing no threat to the dog or his master did the beast return to the kitchen and consume his food with wolfish voracity. His meal completed, the Outlaw began a second, more thorough, patrol. He recognized the scents of the neighbors who had given custodial care to the dwelling in their absence. He noted the acrid man-scent of the white-haired naturalist and the intermingling scents of the two young women. Each had entered the house either to bring in the daily mail or to water and care for the rainbow assortment of indoor plant life. No threat perceived, the dog padded cumbersomely up the enclosed stairway and lay to rest at the head of the hall. His vantage point would enable him to hear and smell both his master and anyone or anything else entering his territory. Circling counterclockwise three times, the animal gave out a long, barrel-chested sigh and slept the light, foot-twitching, ear-cocking sleep of chosen duty and happy dog dreams.

CHAPTER 6

THE tavern was littered with the previous evening's debris of ashes, butts, paper wrappers, and dried blood. The bartender busied himself with the bottle count and tried his damnedest to be invisible.

To the rear of the darkened club a bull of a man bellowed, "What the fuck are you telling me, man?" The words reverberated through the empty shadows.

"They're gone, boss," wheezed the smaller black, standing stiffly, his arms tightly at his sides. "They're gone. The boat ain't nothin' but splinters and sticks and a spot of oil on the water." He paused, then the growing silence frightened him even more. "Turtle Eater and his crew went out just like normal," he continued, backing a half step from the huge man. "They were gonna stop that *Atlantic Maiden* shrimper, like you told them to. Last thing I heard, Turtle Eater comes on the CB, tells me he sees the ship and he's gonna go get 'em." The little man blinked three times. "Then I don't hear nothing," he said. "I call 'em and call 'em, and finally I take the fast little boat out to see what's going on, you know, like to see if maybe Turtle Eater is having a bad time or something. Well, I got out there where he's s'posed to be, but all's I see is that ugly old shrimper going like hell. Then I see some sticks and planks on the water and check it out. Where Turtle Eater and the others should be, there's oil on the water and some burned sticks and that's it." The small man shrugged.

The innocent motion triggered the monstrous black. He whipped the pool cue at unbelievable speed, snapping the tapered end with a dry crack over the narrow shoulders of his subordinate. A nine-inch shaft of dry wood clattered behind the bar, but the smaller man remained rigidly still. Suspicion and malevolence shrouded the face of Savannah Pink. He said, "If you're lying to me, you're dead meat. You know that?"

"I know that, boss," the smaller man said quickly. "It's the truth. I went and checked out Turtle Eater's old lady soon as I got back. Checked out that other piece of trash he been stayin' with too,'' he added. "Don't neither one of them know nothin'." The little man paused to measure Pink's anger. "Boss," he said in a whisper, "I don't think he skipped on you. I think Turtle Eater and them others, I think they're dead. And I think that fine boat of theirs and all of those rocket shooters is sittin' on the bottom too."

Savannah Pink laid the splintered cue on the grease-stained pool table. Speaking in a controlled and modulated voice, he looked down. "That trawler's heading for the packinghouse on Skull Creek up behind Hilton Head. That's where she'll dump her shrimp. When she comes in, you find out who is on board. Then you let me know." He wheeled, took two catlike steps forward, and grasped the frightened man by the ears, pulling his head violently down and forward. He rattled the man's head and yanked until the man's nose was pressed flat against Pink's zipper. "You let me know right away, nigger!" he roared, "'cause sure as hell somebody's gonna pay for this, and if it ain't somebody else, it's gonna be your black ass that pays!" The last five words were each punctuated by short, powerful jerks that pulled and pushed the man's head back and forth and from side to side. "And find out what happened to them rockets, dammit! I paid a thousand bucks apiece for those fuckers, and they're all I got. You hear me?" The little tavern had no more room for sound.

His mouth jammed against the fabric of the monster's trousers, he said, "I hear you, Pink. I'll take care of it, I'll find out."

Savannah Pink dropped him at once and stalked to the barman.

Regaining his balance and the ability to control his legs, the frightened man fled as quietly as possible. It could have been worse. Taking that much bad news to Savannah Pink could have been much worse.

Savannah Pink, six feet five inches and three hundred pounds of tarnished bronze brutality, found a new stick and resumed his practice on the scuffed table. The slender cue emphasized the dimensions of his powerful form. Leaning forward to align a straight shot to the far corner pocket, his posture created no less than four folds of rubbery flesh at the rear of his short, thick neck. His torso was massive, and his pendulous abdomen, while grossly large, carried very little fat. His arms hung meaty and unusually long, ending in outsize hands. But despite the man's height, his legs were short and squat and as thick as telephone poles. Pink stroked the uncomplicated shot, sinking the chipped yellow of the nine ball. He moved to the far end of the table with the rolling, wobbled gait of the North American grizzly and searched for his next shot. He squinted close-set, maroon-tinted eyes, not because he couldn't see but to show the extra effort he took to comprehend the spread of the table. He ran a sausage-fingered paw over the short nap of his hair, feeling the shaved line that functioned as his part, following the line of short nubs down past his broad temples and onto the closely trimmed sideburns that extended to his lower jaw and flared into stirruplike points. Pink chose a short, direct stroke on the twelve. The ball clinked into the leather webbing of the pocket, and he smiled in satisfaction. On his upper left incisor a full gold crown with a star-shaped cutout exposed gleaming white enamel beneath.

The bartender completed his nervous-fingered bottle count and placed a fresh pitcher of draft beer on the counter. He busied himself with reorganizing the spotted glassware, fearful that Pink would insist on a game. The monster played nine and eight ball regularly but poorly; since the necessary angles were beyond his geometric comprehension. Pink's gambling losses on the game were frequent and sizable, but it wasn't at all uncommon for him to lose and accuse the winner of cheating. And, once accused, the victor became a victim. Pink had been arrested by the Savannah police on several occasions for murder and on many others for aggravated assault, but he had never gone to trial. Witnesses to his crimes changed their testimony, became unsure of the facts, or disappeared. The bartender, a prudent man in a difficult situation, found more than enough to keep himself busy.

The first delivery truck of the day lurched to a halt at the front of the darkened tavern, and the barman exhaled in relief. Now he could legitimately avoid Pink and his rage. At least that was his hope, for with Savannah Pink one never could be certain. The bartender shuddered as the driver backed in, pulling a loaded hand truck behind him. Today the driver was a white man, and Pink's hatred for whitey was legend. The huge man moved on incongruously tiny feet to the bar and gulped from the pitcher, emptying it as if it were a small glass. His shirt was a broad expanse of pastel pink silk, his trousers a complementary maroon knit, and his shoes a similarly colored alligator. Perched on his basketball of a head was a broad-brimmed pastel pink Panama hat.

The delivery driver blinked at the mountain of pink and said nothing. He looked away quickly, eager to complete his duties and leave. Everyone, including those only tangentially involved with the inner decay of Savannah, knew the man. He was ponderous, slow to start, and lightning when aroused; monstrosity masquerading as a man. As his anger increased, as his rage at being opposed increased, all of those around him would be systematically terrorized and demeaned until his will was done.

Savannah Pink had swarmed out of a red-clay Georgia backwater town at the age of fourteen. Fleeing from prosecution for the murder of his father, Pink had found immediate welcome on the Savannah loading docks. His size, enormous even at that age, protected the youth and found him favor with the gang bosses. He had the strength to do the work of three men and did so each and every day without complaint. One hundred and ten miles away, the local sheriff's department, perhaps influenced by his father's reputation for drunken abuse, failed to pursue the fugitive.

Pink matured. His adolescent form gave way to a fully developed body full of strength and endurance. And violence. A white dock supervisor with a penchant for racist talk made the wrong comment to Pink one morning and spent two months at Savannah General Hospital recuperating from multiple fractures of his ribs and arms and legs. Naturally an arrest followed, but Pink had come to the attention of the union by then. The young giant was bailed out and recruited as an ''organizer'' for local officials. When the trial date arrived, the injured dock supervisor dropped his charges and took delivery on a new car for his trouble.

Pink prospered, learning his lessons with speed, practicing them with zeal. After three intense years with the union he moved on to independent ventures. At times he offered Savannah blacks lottery numbers. At others he dealt them their heroin and cocaine. But at all times Savannah Pink surrounded himself with violence. If a gambler fell behind, Pink himself rendered debt counseling. If a dealer screwed up drug money by sticking his own nose into his stash too often, Pink performed a personal termination. He surrounded himself with followers, men of similar dispositions, but at no time did any of them challenge Pink for leadership.

Pink also possessed a cunning in excess of his peers. Not a man to be overconfident of his own size, Savannah Pink built and established a complex web of intelligence in Savannah. He was feared, but also admired, by many. He peeled off twenties and handed them to hungry children or haggard churchmen. He donated barrels of beer to any wedding he attended, brought trucks of fresh-killed chickens to community picnics, and on many occasions picked up the hospital tabs for injured local black athletes.

Dockworkers held him up as a legend, a man with terrible power but unlimited generosity, a man to be respected. And he rewarded his followers without regard to his own pocket. Pink would do without rather than let a worker go unpaid, just as he would break a man's spine rather than let him survive handing Pink an insult. The years of his reign reinforced his power, strengthened his network. With his newest endeavor, drug piracy in shallow water, Pink had combined all of his assets, violent and organizational, to spin a web of intelligence around the drug trade. Blacks with allegiance to Savannah Pink loaded smuggler trawlers in foreign ports and reported back to him. Other blacks, watermen, dockworkers, and bar brawlers crewed Pink's pursuit craft and brought the "liberated" drugs into port. Pink's own distribution network then took over, cutting or packaging the drugs and moving them out at once. And through it all, directing his people, spreading his rewards, delivering his punishment was the man himself, Savannah Pink.

And he was pissed.

CHAPTER 7

IN Winchester, Virginia, George Washington's office, the one he had rented while still an obscure surveyor, was located down the street and around the corner. It was a shockingly small log-and-plaster building, faithfully and accurately restored, open to the public from ten in the morning to three in the afternoon. The public never went there.

Located scant blocks from that well-tended, but nonetheless neglected, structure, the gray mansion on Cork Street was an immensity that in any other environment would have been an ugly albatross of a house. But in historical Winchester it was a thing of grotesque beauty. The mansion sat well back from the infrequently traveled street, screened from view by a sturdy stone wall eight feet in height and topped with liberally distributed pieces of broken glass. The ornamental black iron of the gates was fashioned in a Gothic arch, the initial *B* emblazoned thereon in a flowery script that defied deciphering. The close green thatch of the lawn stretched nearly eighty yards from the wall to the house, broken only by molded boxwood hedges and three large magnolia trees. The drive from the gate to the house's main door was freshly covered with a uniform coating of black macadam.

The house was a discordant architectural medley. Originally constructed in Colonial times as a two-story log home with several outbuildings, it had been consecutively enlarged in a variety of styles. The resulting concatenation was an immense white stucco edifice that soared, rambled, turned a corner, enclosed a courtyard, and rose three towering stories to a black slate roof of indescribable pitch. In all of its bizarre majesty it was much admired by the local populace, for in that community the standard for admiration was longevity.

Colonel Thomas Vernon Burgess, USMC (ret.), was the master of the house, having extended his family's continuous occupancy of the dwelling for a period of eighty-three years. The original house had been constructed by a successful apple orchardist, but it only began to approach true glory under the Burgesses. The family had amassed power and considerable wealth from their contributions to the nation's military efforts, producing son after son who distinguished themselves mightily in battle and even more so in peacetime administration. The Burgess wealth, it was rumored, sprang from their uncanny ability to award military purchasing contracts to grateful contractors, but others in the community attributed the family fortune to frugal habits and investment savvy.

"Good morning, sir," said Weems. He crossed the Persian carpet to the midpoint of the room and compared his own timepiece with the gold antique on the far wall. He was reassured by the concurrence of the two devices but felt his colon twitch when he saw the lower lip of the Colonel pursed, as if he were trying to dislodge a morsel of food from his teeth. Forcing an insurance salesman's smile, Weems stood at semi-attention before the desk. His instincts told him to tread lightly.

"I have the reports on the Maltessa matter, Colonel," he offered, his glance jumping from the hard man's face to the desk. "I know you're going to be well pleased," he said. "We experienced absolutely no losses this time out. Off-loading was accomplished well within schedule. And, most importantly, we dealt once and for all with the Savannah problem." He took a half step forward and placed a manila folder on the desk.

The hard eyes of Colonel Burgess took in his body movements, then looked at the folder. He said nothing.

"The distribution was perhaps the smoothest, well, if not the smoothest, one of the smoothest operations under my direction. The captain followed the commercial routes you suggested in our conversation of, um, I guess it was the fourteenth. Oh, let's see," he continued under the baleful glare and now steadily pursing lower lip of Burgess. "Okay, yes, the shotgun rider we picked up handled our entire blockade problem in literally a matter of minutes." Weems paused because the Colonel had upturned his palm upon the folder. "Oh, yes, sir," he continued, "the analysis of the cocaine is in; it checked out between ninety and ninety-two percent. There was a minor fluctuation from one packet to another, but there was no sample that showed less than a solid ninety and—"

"Shut up, you ass!"

"I'm sorry, sir?"

"I said, 'Shut up, you ass!' "

Burgess tilted his head, jutting his chiseled jaw and purplish lower lip forward. He savored the moment, relishing each ticking second of Weems's discomfort. He lowered his reptilian eyes to the folder resting upon the desk and slid it contemptuously toward him, snapping it open with a practiced flick of his corded wrist. He scanned the documents, flipping the pages with disdain. The wattles of flesh formed by the constriction of his starched white collar bounced with the intensity of his abrupt movements.

The pages were flawlessly typed and assembled and, as always, stapled in the upper right-hand corner to facilitate his one-handed examination. His left arm was useless. Twisted and withered, he clutched it close to his chest. Its wrist bent sharply down, and the scarred fingers curled tightly into a permanent fist. At their tips the fingers, looking to have been burned, fused and flowed together to form an obscene bud.

A career man, the Colonel had entered the Marine Corps as a junior officer in late 1941 and served with distinction in the Asian theater. He returned to stateside duty until the Korean conflict. He served in Korea in an intelligence capacity until his appointment to a command position at Paris Island, South Carolina. Early in the Vietnam conflict he'd again left stateside duty and flourished in the field, once again as an intelligence officer. There, in 1970, he had been the victim of devasting injuries. His withered and useless left arm proved immune to surgical rehabilitation, and he'd been retired with full honors. Thomas Vernon Burgess, "Colonel" in his own home, wore his scar with pride and loathing.

In the intervening years he conquered Winchester.

His politics were extremely conservative, hawkish, Republican, and he supported candidates of similar inclinations with substantial cash donations. He hired a team of researchers and compiled two large research volumes on the Vietnam conflict. They had been detailed, incredibly researched and documented, and were generally accepted as the most objective assessment of that conflict by military historians.

The report on the Colonel's desk detailed the particulars of the Colombian departure, the weight and cost of the goods shipped, the fees and bribes incurred en route, the officials to whom the bribes were delivered, the amount of funds paid to the members of *The Atlantic Maiden*'s crew, an account of the pirate attack, and the measures used to neutralize that threat. The report went on to tell of the success at off-loading the contraband, the projected gross profit from the operation, and proclaimed a healthy net profit.

Burgess tugged off his polished gold-framed glasses and squinted at the spotless lenses as if expecting to find the source of his irritation in the glass. He replaced them upon the bridge of his nose and again read the material.

"Additions, Weems?" the Colonel asked.

"Well, no, sir."

From behind the lenses magnified, soulless eyes peered at Weems. The crinkled lids blinked slowly, like the cold appraisal of a reptilian predator.

Colonel Burgess cleared his throat with a spine-straightening cough. He raised his knotted right hand and lowered it beneath the desk. He pressed the concealed button, ringing for coffee, then moved to the central drawer. He opened it and removed a thick envelope. "You disappoint me, Weems." He spoke in controlled, bored tones, inviting no reply.

Weems glanced about the room, once more seeking the chair or resting place a thousand visits to the room had failed to reveal. There was no seat but the one filled by the gnarled form of the Colonel.

"Your ineptitude," the Colonel said, "coupled with the haphazard actions of that narcotized fool, Maltessa, have placed this organization in severe peril. The cost, Weems, the ultimate cost of your stupidity, is yet to be determined."

"Yes, sir," replied Weems.

Burgess hadn't simply walked out of a respectable military career to become a major drug source. The man had always been a CIA liaison officer, but his military intelligence assignments in Asia had put him too frequently under CIA command. The influence was always evident. Burgess had been a very dirty participant in the dirtiest of wars.

The Colonel had specific operational rules and punished their violation. Weems, in his dealings with Maltessa, had broken one of the rules. He had authorized a new hire without first getting clearance from Burgess. At the time Weems had seen himself as using initiative to solve a tricky problem. If the shipment made it through, success would speak for itself. Burgess couldn't object to the slight extra cost. And if the frightened captain and his shotgun rider had been lost to the pirates, then the new man's clearance would have been irrelevant.

Weems said, "But, sir—"

"You hired a federal narc!" spat Burgess.

A knock preceded the entry of the daytime housekeeper, Mrs. Davidson, with her gleaming tray and implements. She placed them within easy reach of the Colonel's functional hand and left with a whisper of abrading support hose.

The Colonel astounded Weems by taking a gold-banded Turkish cigarette from an inlaid box and lighting it with a gold desktop lighter. Exhaling with a hiss, he threw the lighter across the polished wood surface, leaving a jagged scar in the wax. Weems had never before seen the Colonel smoke.

The Colonel ripped the contents from the packet and cradled them in his right hand. He held aloft a photograph, one taken of Party John and Dan Fields together on the Hilton Head dock at dawn. He pointed and said, "Is this your shotgun rider?"

Weems looked, nodded.

The Colonel ducked his chin down to the awkwardly held cigarette, pursed his purpled lips, and inhaled sharply. He flipped through a thick packet of printed material. "I do hope you enjoy reading this first document. You might find it fascinating. It's a summary of your shotgun rider's employment with the Bureau of Narcotics and Dangerous Drugs, lately known as the Drug Enforcement Agency."

With blinking eyes Weems read. He turned page after page. Dan Fields, his very own shotgun rider, in addition to having a list of drug-enforcement commendations two pages long, had actually written the agency's combat-shooting manual.

Weems noted the initials at the far left-hand corner of the last page. F.A.M. At least he now knew who'd done the research. Fanny. She was at it again, and because of it, he was standing in the eye of the hurricane. Weems laid the pages facedown upon the desk. He averted his eyes and retreated a half step.

The Colonel lurched aggressively forward in his chair, shifted the short stub of the burning cigarette to his withered hand, and thrust a second, shorter document across the ash-littered expanse of polished wood.

Weems took the paper, holding it as one would a poisonous insect, and scanned it rapidly.

TO: Center
FROM: T-4
URGENT, repeat, URGENT. The following craft have been reported as missing or overdue. CARAVELLE and three crew. MISS QUINCY and four crew, BARBARA JEAN and four crew, and VIRGINIA LADY and five crew. No sign of wreckage, crew, or cargo. Extreme activity noted among Savannah subjects of your latest inquiries. Request instructions.

Weems knew the Colonel employed a variety of personnel and communication methods to keep abreast of developments in the field. He had never questioned the man's methods in the past and was not about to express his curiosity now. He trembled. Each of the ships named were carrying valuable cargo, literally scores of tons each of presold marijuana. The losses, not including the cost of replacing the vessels, were unimaginable.

"Weems?" the voice rumbled out of the wattled throat. "Do you know what you've done? You stupid son of a bitch!" The Colonel ranted, not interested in Weems's acceptance of guilt. He said, "A simple clearance, Weems, a simple phone call to me, and those four shipments would be in port by now. You not only hired a federal narc, Weems, but by using him you indirectly targeted all of my other shipments for revenge. Not only is this whole goddamned organization in peril of federal infiltration, but," he roared, "because of you, you dumb fuck, I've lost the complete cargoes of four ships. And that does not include the cost of the vessels involved." He paused, shuffled the documents back into the envelope, lowered puffy lids, and peered at Weems. Dismissing other options, the Colonel proceeded in softer tones. "However, despite your influence, all is not lost. In reality"—he paused to draw on the cigarette and exhale—"in reality, Weems, the vessels will undoubtedly be covered by maritime insurance."

Weems, ever sensitive to changes in barometric pressure, sensed a glimmer of faint hope. His position might well be redeemed. His eyes brightened with new interest.

"And, of course, we can replace the crew from the ranks of commercial shrimpers and fishers who no longer find it profitable to ply their trade. But, as to the actual cargo losses, they represent a more difficult matter. Our cash investment in those goods is being calculated at this very moment. The loss will undoubtedly approach a figure that more than triples the amount of funds I hold for you in your trust fund."

Weems felt the weight of the blade above his neck. At the earliest point of his entry into criminal duplicity with the Colonel, the powerful man had made an irresistible offer. In each successful transaction where Weems made a direct contribution, the Colonel set aside a percentage of the net profit for Weems. That amount had been reinvested in subsequent ventures, with each investment cycle providing Weems with an ever larger "trust" fund. The "fund" had started modestly but had grown in geometric progression, with each of the Colonel's ventures multiplying its value instead of merely adding to the total.

The Colonel straightened the uncommon disarray upon the desk. He frowned at the evidence of his tantrum, the disorderly remnants of ash, the butts of custom-made cigarettes. He adjusted his posture to his characteristic military rigidity. "Weems," he continued, "as I stated, all is not lost. Much, including your own trust fund, is in jeopardy but not lost. We may well be able to recoup or, at the very least, minimize our losses, while at the same time shore up the breach of security. A breach, I do not hesitate to remind you, that rests upon your shoulders alone." He glowered. Tempt with the carrot, threaten with the whip.

"While you've been congratulating yourself for bringing one overdue shipment in, I have been forming a practical solution to this debacle. First, I dispatched Miss Marcel to Hilton Head Island for information regarding Fields. Her report should be forthcoming. Second, I've begun serious inquiries to identify all the members of the pirate organization. That is a necessary step to take before staging a firefight with our competitors. Everyone in the business has been hurt by these animals. Now that they've gotten a taste of big money from a full shipment, they'll be twice as aggressive. It's obvious they're being tipped in advance, probably by the same men loading our ships. And it's been happening to all the major suppliers who run that part of the coast. I'm agreeing to hold the 'kitty' and pay anyone who can eliminate the *whole* problem. I intend to claim that bounty, Weems, claim it and apply it to our losses.'' He paused and fixed Weems with a menacing glower. ''But only if you perform your assigned duties with a measure of competence that has escaped your grasp to date.'' He cleared his throat.

''Should you do so,'' he continued, ''should you decide to become a man and follow my instructions properly, your share of the profit fund will be protected, your position with this organization will be enhanced, and we shall all return to the uncomplicated routine I worked so hard to design.''

He pressed the button below the desk, summoning the housekeeper to remove the debris. ''However''—the Colonel spoke just above a whisper—''if you fail me again, ever dare to disregard one of my rules again, you will die.''

Weems's eyes filmed over with a wet sheen. He blinked rapidly, attempting to dispel the moisture.

The Colonel noted the effect. ''You are being monitored. Make one error, display the slightest lack of enthusiasm for the tasks I assign you, make the slightest attempt to flee, and you will die within minutes. I am fully prepared to kill you now, before you leave this room. And I am totally capable of doing so. The choice is yours. Long life and wealth, or instant death. Do I have your attention and cooperation?'' he asked.

''Yes, sir. Certainly, sir.'' Weems forced his words.

''Very well, Weems,'' the Colonel responded with resignation. ''Return to your office and await further instructions. When you return home this evening, I strongly suggest you pack a bag. I will require your services in the field, and you should be ready to depart on very brief notice.''

Weems bobbed his head in agreement, paused three beats to

determine if the castigation was over, and, certain of his dismissal, walked stiffly from the room.

As the door clicked shut, the Colonel indulged in a malicious death's-head grin. The trust fund, accurately detailed and updated monthly, had never existed. And never would. It could only be collected upon retirement, and retirement from his organization was not permitted.

CHAPTER 8

THE sculptor, standing alone in the bright morning sunlight, attacked the stone with precise, swift strokes. Again and again his chisel darted and hammer fell as Fields raced after the image in his mind. Particulate dust softened the hard edge of his movements, blurring them while the *chink, chink, grack* of his blows kept up a manic tempo. Beyond the pit, blending with the shadowed green of subtropical plant life, the overlarge Airedale sat sphinxlike with his thick-boned forelegs pinning down a wooden baseball bat. The terrier's neck arched and corded as he worked powerful jaws to crunch and chew and splinter the hardwood. Above him, a woodpecker with an improbably long tail drilled the bark of a tall live oak.

Fields rounded the rock and dropped to his knees. Again the chisel flew, following his internal guidelines, *chink, chink, grack*; *chink, chink, graaack*! Sweat flowed down the hollows of his muscled back and soaked the waistband of his shorts. His chisel stabbed. His hammer rang. Once, then twice, he blew and dusted a crevice, then wedged the razored and tempered edge of his tool onto his mark. He tapped once and scored the surface of the stone. He angled the chisel into the body of the rock, cutting dangerously across the grain. He drove the heavy hammer down, hard, with a full-shouldered, violent follow-through. The stone surrendered

49

with a vacuum-sucking sound like a shell peeled from a hard-boiled egg. A wall of sheeted fragments crumbled from the rock, and the sculptor danced back out of the way of the fall. He turned his back and stepped out of the pit.

"Hello."

Fields was nose to nose with a beautiful woman. He blotted the damp spray of dust and perspiration from his lips with the back of a hand. "Hello."

The Outlaw trotted to them, his legs barely touching the sandy soil, his head outstretched, his nose working. He halted, lifted a paw not quite from the ground.

"Oh! Excuse me!" she said. "I didn't mean to intrude, it's just that they told me if you were working, it would be okay to watch."

Fields dropped his tools, snared a towel, worked it over his face, arms, and chest. He dropped the towel and said, "They?"

"The people at the art shop in the Hilton," she told him. "I saw the sculpture in their display case and, well, I tried to—"

"It's not for sale." He wagged his head with a polite show of regret, shooting a quick glance to the Outlaw. The animal was frozen, head forward, drinking the air.

She smiled, full force, capturing daylight and night-dreams with her eyes. "That's not exactly what I was told," she countered, her voice a dusky contralto. She touched a blood-red nail to his chest. "They told me it was for sale, only you wouldn't sell anything to a tourist." She dropped her hand, looked at him with accusation. "Is that true?"

Fields confessed with a subtle drop of his shoulders. He said, "It's not for sale. To anyone."

She crossed her arms, cocked her head. "They told me you had other pieces for sale."

He touched a hand to his temple. "I apologize," he said. "There's been a mistake. Nothing is for sale. I made that decision some time ago but neglected to call my friends at the Hilton." He grinned with counterfeit shame.

"Um-humm." She nodded. Then she turned to the sand-filled arena. She looked past his shoulder and said, "You didn't forget to call the gallery in Savannah, though, did you?"

Fields, who had not forgotten the seven works he'd had out on consignment at the art gallery, who had in fact ordered them withdrawn from the display floor and shipped at his cost back to the island, looked at her with new appraisal. "You were in Savannah?"

"Yesterday," she answered. She dropped her eyes from the incomplete sculpture, caught the Outlaw as he circled her beyond arm's reach. She said, "Your dog doesn't like tourists, either?"

Dan didn't blink but stared straight into the compelling strangeness of her eyes. They were wide and promising with pale green irises flecked by gold and black. He explained. "The Outlaw thinks with his nose. You smell wrong. He's found something troubling in your scent and doesn't know what it is."

The woman laughed deeply and richly in her throat. She held up a hand, pushed the intimate hollow of her wrist to his face. "Smell," she told him. "See if my perfume has the same effect on you. If it does, I'm going to ask for my money back."

Her scent was an erotic invitation, a penetrating scalpel of fire. His eyes flared.

Again she laughed, depriving him of her hand. "Two hundred and twelve dollars an ounce to give an Airedale a case of the heebie-jeebies!" She bent at the waist, slapped her palms to her thighs, and pursed her lips. She made kissing noises in the Outlaw's face.

"Do you have a name?" Fields asked.

She straightened and offered her hand, this time at a level intended for shaking instead of sniffing. "Marcel, Fionnula Marcel. My friends call me Fanny."

"The piece in the hotel?" she prompted him. "The asking price was—"

"It is not for sale, Fanny." Fields put emphasis on the consonants, made the words sharp and final. They faced each other across a small table inside his home and sipped from cold glasses of mint-sprigged tea. She'd had a personal tour of his home, and its own gallery of his recaptured and withdrawn works. "You don't understand. Yes, I've sold pieces before but only because I had to. If I hadn't been squeezed financially, I'd never have done it."

"And now, just when I appear on your doorstep, drooling, checkbook in hand, you are suddenly no longer squeezed?"

Fields made her wait for an answer while he sipped from the tall glass. He said, "Nothing as dramatic as that."

"No?"

Something had changed. He heard it in the edge of her tone. His pulse quickened, but his face showed nothing. He said, "I'm not—"

"Twenty thousand dollars strikes me as pretty damn dramatic."

After a long beat Fields said, "I beg your pardon?"

She repeated it for him. "Twenty thousand dollars. I have twenty thousand dollars with me today, over there in my purse." Fanny drifted out of the chair and bisected the room with sensual strides. The filmy wrap of her sundress first snugged, then silhouetted, her dancer's legs. She wheeled with the purse in hand, held it aloft. "C'mon!" she taunted, advancing. "Twenty thousand dollars. That's how much I'm authorized to spend on a Dan Fields sculpture today."

Fields followed her with his eyes. She stopped at his side, close enough for him to feel the warmth from her body. Again the intimate finger of her perfume and body pheromones touched him.

"You don't seem very excited," Fanny accused from above. Then her exuberance and allure seemed to deflate. She withdrew from his side and dropped to her seat to face him. "Tell me," said Fanny, showing a mocking, inviting smile. "Tell me you're going to turn down twenty thousand dollars?"

He said, "Fanny, this is Hilton Head. Every third tourist the Outlaw knocks on their ass gets up yelling about how much money they have in their pocket. Or purse." He returned her stare, matched arctic ice to her tropical green.

"Sell me one piece. Any piece. I don't care which one it is, I'll take it and hand you twenty thousand in cash." Fanny didn't gush, didn't bubble, but made her offer and touched a hand to her bag.

"This is absurd," said Fields. He flattened both palms to the tabletop and leaned forward. "No one in their right mind would make that kind of offer."

She noted the strength in his braced hands, the stonecutter's thick wrists. She put her palms on the table, licked her lips, and said, "I'm making a mess out of this. Let me start over. I represent a man who has a proposition for you. Before I make his offer, though, I'm supposed to put this in your hands." She opened the purse, slid out a fat envelope. "If you won't accept it as payment for a sale, I'm to give it to you, anyway, and tell you it's a bonus."

"A bonus?"

"Yes. For services rendered." She performed a pantomime for him in total silence. Fanny held an imaginary rifle, loaded a shell, sighted down the barrel, and squeezed. Then she no longer had the weapon, and her arms were blooming up and out in graphic imitation of an explosion. "As in pest extermination," she said, hinting. "Pest extermination at sea."

Fields was as still as death. Beyond the window-wall of plate glass, eight hundred pounds of granite gave incontrovertible testimony to the destiny of all women. A woman-child-hag figure, at once young and innocent, from another perspective blooming and fertile, and then, from the last, shrunken and withered, fought for freedom in the stone. His time-stretched creature revealed the ripe contours of feminine youth, the swell of her womb, and the chewed and sagging breasts of age. He said, "I don't know what you're talking about."

She took his reply without surprise or offense but tucked her hand into the purse once more. She flipped a stiff-backed photograph on the table. Dan Fields and Party John Maltessa stood together against a brightening sky.

He blinked, drew a breath, then began his search. He started with her purse, dumping its contents to the table and examining each item to the most minute detail. Next he went straight to the woman herself and searched Fionnula Marcel thoroughly, right down to her skin. When he'd run his fingers through the blond silk of her hair and explored the textural contours of every seam of her clothing, he left her, barefoot and naked, in his house and stalked out to the drive. He searched her car, working methodically, bringing to his task the eye of a trained professional. When he returned, the Outlaw was trailing behind him.

Fanny, her head level, eyes unwavering, said, "Satisfied?"

"You're not carrying a wire," he admitted.

"Then I can get dressed?" She faced him directly, wearing her nudity without shame.

"Yes," said Fields. "And as soon as you do, you can get the hell out of here. I'm not interested in your proposition, your bonus, or anything else you might have to say." He was ice and control.

"Oh, yes, you are," she answered. She stepped into her wisp of a dress, shrugged it into place. "You're dying of curiosity. And fear." Fanny smoothed the fabric over her thighs, flipped a manicured hand at her hem. "You were scared to death I might be wired, dying to know if I'm a narc. You're still dying."

Dan Fields, the Airedale at his side, walked to a chair and sat. He said, "Okay. Talk to me. Maybe that's the only way I'm going to get you out of here."

She sat before Fields, trying to read his closed face. "The man I represent was at first unaware of your identity. As soon as he learned who had handled his problem, he called me and instructed me to see that you received the rest of your fee, an amount more in line with your worth."

"Who is this man?" said Dan Fields.

Fanny laughed and said, "See? You are curious."

"Who is he?"

"He's very careful about that, just as he's very careful about everything he puts in motion." She touched the tip of her tongue to her upper lip. "He prefers simply to be known as the Colonel."

"The Colonel? I don't recognize the name."

"You shouldn't," she assured him. "He works at keeping out of the limelight. That's one of the things he wanted me to impress upon you. His is a very professional organization, run in a businesslike manner."

Fields let cynicism animate his sneer. "Weems is a pro?"

Fanny reflected his distaste. "Hardly," she granted.

Fields shifted, moved close to her face. "And your proposition?"

"The Colonel wishes to contract your services on a onetime-only basis."

"As in?"

"As in pest eradication," she told him. "Pirates. More of the same group."

Dan pushed himself back into the cushions.

Fanny laid an exquisite hand on his forearm. "There's a difference between running illegal drug shipments and eliminating vermin, a difference that should appeal to you. The Colonel's much too wise, much too intelligent, to insult you with an invitation to join his trade. But—and you've already demonstrated not only your willingness but your competence as well—working to stamp out murder on the high seas is another matter. How you handle them would be your business. Of course, you'd have full support, all the information, equipment, supplies you might need. And when the problem is neutralized, you'll see a payday to make your pension check look like small change."

Fields raised an eyebrow. "What kind of payday?"

"One hundred thousand," she answered without a pause. "The minute the pirates out of Savannah are eliminated, the Colonel will deliver to you, anywhere in the world, in any currency you name, one hundred thousand dollars."

"Do you know what you're asking?" Fields narrowed his eyes. "You're using words like *eliminate* and *eradicate,* but what you're talking about is murder, taking the lives of human beings."

Fanny disagreed with a shrug. She said, "That didn't seem to interfere with your performance out on the water."

He looked at her and asked, "Have you ever killed a man?"

She frowned, chased it immediately, and said, "No."

"Then don't talk to me about killing being 'eradication' or 'extermination.' Killing is killing, whether it's done for the state, God, country, or personal gain."

"But that isn't true," she insisted. "Do you think I haven't seen your service record, haven't studied your career? You've killed men before, not only killed them but then gone on to defend your actions in front of federal juries and done so successfully. What the Colonel wants is to have you do the same job you've done in the past, eliminate the vermin, but this time with full support from the very beginning. And then a payday to match what you're worth."

Dan Fields put himself in motion. He stood up and walked over the green-dappled spaces of his cathedral of light to where she sat. "Thanks but no thanks," he told her. "I have no desire to kill anyone, vermin or not."

"But the money—"

"Fuck your money," said Fields.

"Yes, ma'am," he said over small, rectangular spectacles. "How can I help you?" His face was warm and sincere.

"I have a reservation," she answered smoothly, bathing him with pale green, luminescent eyes. "Marcel," she added, "the last name is Marcel."

The desk clerk tapped the keys of his desk console with confident rapidity and glanced at her again as he waited for the terminal's response. She was worth a second appraisal. He estimated her age to be in the early twenties. She stood five and a half feet tall, and her slender build was delightfully feminine.

Despite his wish to study her breasts, he focused instead upon her eyes. The green irises were uncharacteristically light, and the large black pupils conveyed surprise, pleasure, innocence, and invitation simultaneously.

"Here it is," he said, addressing her as the data appeared on the screen. "Could you satisfy my curiosity?" the clerk inquired conspiratorially. Her smile and her posture said that she could. "How do you pronounce your first name, Miss Marcel? I've never seen it before."

"Of course," she answered. "Fa-nu-la," she said slowly, articulating each syllable. "Fionnula Marcel. Is my room ready?" she inquired, reflected light dancing in the silvered transparency of her blond hair.

"Oh," he replied involuntarily. The audience had ended. "Yes, Miss Marcel. It's ready. I'll have your bags taken up with you." He peered over the counter at the formidable stack of baggage. Pliant, rust-colored leather. Seven full-size bags. And a matching overnight case. And a portable typewriter. "Front," he called in a clearly enunciated, but subdued, voice. A tall, liveried black appeared immediately. "Mickey," he said to the black but kept his eyes on the girl. "This is Miss Marcel. She's in 606."

He handed the room key to the black, busy eyeing both the woman and the mountain of weighted leather.

At the age of twenty-three, Fionnula was an accomplished world traveler but had never quite been a "tourist." The only child of her parents, she had developed a cosmopolitan perspective that was augmented by a disposition that welcomed the unknown without fear or apprehension. She was remarkably unlike both mother and father in appearance. He was short and dark, while the wife was a plump, freckled redhead. Fanny's complexion was creamy and uniform. While her parents' facial features had been blunt and coarse, hers were not. Her arched eyebrows framed wide-set eyes of the palest green. Her nose was sharply drawn, the bridge an unbroken, uncurving line. The nostrils were curved but not flared. Fanny's cheekbones were high and protruded beyond the more regular plane of her unlined forehead. Her jawline was rounded, curving gently from small, buttonlike, lobeless ears to a rounded chin. Her mouth was a touch large, the upper lip slightly bowed and thin; the lower one full, moist, and shaped in a pout.

"Can I arrange a hired car while I'm here?" Fanny asked the

desk clerk.

"Yes, Miss Marcel," he replied eagerly. "I can take care of everything for you right here. We have several rental companies on the island, and you can have just about anything from an economy sedan to much more expensive models." He beamed at her.

"I'd like something very nice," she said simply, turning to locate the elevator bank.

"What about the cost?" he asked, halting her.

"The cost?" she inquired.

"Yes," he answered. "What price limit would suit you?"

"Just make it very nice," she said, and drowned him in an overwhelming smile. Her teeth were perfect squares of whitest ivory.

The bellhop pushed the wheeled cart that was piled high, wide, and deep with her luggage. He monitored her passage discreetly, aware of each sensual motion, memorizing the fluid melody of her body. It was a catchy tune, one he would not easily forget.

Fanny settled quickly into her commodious quarters and tipped the grinning bellhop. After his light-paced departure she ordered a bottle of Asti Spumanti, chilled, from room service and examined the view. Beneath her lay an Olympic-size pool with service cabanas, an informal, grassy lawn interspersed with rough-barked palmetto trees, and a spread of white beach. Beyond the broad white beach the Atlantic stretched darkly out to the horizon.

Fanny dined that evening in the hotel restaurant from a buffet that combined opulent quantity with surprisingly excellent quality. The service was eager and attentive but always unobtrusive. Her estimation of the hotel and its staff was not uninformed, for Fanny had traveled extensively and had learned the difference between good, mediocre, and poor service.

Her father, Robert Marcel, a tenured professor of literature at Northwestern University, had emigrated to the United States from Paris in 1948. Her mother, Kathleen O'Brien Marcel, emigrated with her parents from Dublin in the same year. Robert and Kathleen met at their naturalization ceremony and had remained inseparable since that date. Fanny was the product of that union.

At her parents' insistence Fanny toured Europe upon completion of her education and visited the divergent representatives of her far-flung family. While in Europe she encountered a moderately well known author of romance novels. Similar to one of his often repeated plots, the middle-aged writer and the refreshingly naïve young girl formed an intensely romantic liaison. While the writer steadily cranked out no less than three new works each year, they traveled the continent together as lovers.

She politely read one of his novels and then avoided the remaining bulk of his work. He was totally unperturbed and secretly complimented her literary taste. Fanny was his consort without strings or possessive conditions, and she infrequently but openly loved other men without the ugly impediment of her own guilt or the author's distress. After more than two years Fanny returned to the States during her father's prolonged illness. She did not return to the author's side. They wrote infrequently thereafter; long, informal chats between good friends.

Fanny then modeled professionally in Chicago, capitalizing upon her cosmopolitan poise and frank beauty. Her efforts in that profession led to an encounter with the indolent son of a well-known cosmetics manufacturer. Shortly thereafter she and the son toured South America with a group of jet-setters.

At one of the popular South American resort cities Fanny was introduced to a displaced French importer who was ruggedly handsome and thoroughly charming. He lived well, deriving his income from the illicit distribution of cocaine. While he operated from Bogota, they traveled frequently to both Europe and the States. Fanny was intimately aware of his illicit activities, accepted his rationalizations, and experienced neither guilt nor fear. For eighteen months their affair flourished against a background of luxury and travel. As their romantic fervor began to cool (he was rapidly deteriorating both mentally and physically), she was introduced to Colonel Thomas Vernon Burgess.

Burgess was authoritative, informed, and intellectually compelling. They enjoyed a far-reaching and pleasantly stimulating conversation. At the evening's end Burgess quite unexpectedly offered Fanny an employment opportunity in his organization as an investigator and coordinator. In effect she would travel extensively, functioning as the eyes, ears, and occasionally the voice of Colonel Burgess. His description of her duties did not include physical obligations. She accepted his offer immediately.

In practice the Colonel called upon Fanny to give him her personal evaluations of targeted individuals, to provide background data on certain others, and occasionally to make direct business proposals. She found that she could develop a "feel" for someone through casual observation, and, when necessary, could be convincingly persuasive. She acquired easy access to a variety of classified or guarded information and was soon a viable asset to the Colonel's organization.

She flicked on the lights and opened the sliding glass panels to the night breezes. She removed all of her clothing except a small pair of briefs and a lacy wisp of a bra and settled herself before a portable electric typewriter. Without hesitation she inserted paper, no carbon, and began her report. She worked steadily for more than an hour, reread her report, packed away the typewriter in its case, folded the report into thirds, and secreted it in a drawer. She then climbed into the awaiting coolness of the soft, night-chilled sheets. She slept the untroubled sleep of an oft-hugged child, snuggling deep within the folds of cover and spread.

Fanny Marcel smiled in her sleep. As often as that smile had flashed or lingered during the day, it had at all times been genuine. She was not able to flash it on call, was not able to feign enjoyment when it was not truly present. Everyone she had met had been warmed by both her smile and her obvious pleasure. She had the capacity to find something essentially good and pleasing in each person she encountered. Because of her attitude, appearance, and pleasure in all sorts of people, the world had been kind to Fanny, leaving her unhurt, unchallenged, and incredibly naïve.

Fanny declared she had never met a violent, troubled, or evil person. In truth she met them every day of her life. But her grace and beauty, her sincere approval, and her sexuality made men behave like pussycats when in her presence. Fanny was not blind or unintelligent. Rather she was the rare product of a charmed life. She truly failed to understand the worries and pain of others because she never had received a hard knock or a low blow. But while she was essentially ignorant of the dark side of the human condition, her own intrinsic qualities brought comfort and ease to those other pained inhabitants of the planet Earth. She smiled in her sleep.

CHAPTER 9

A few blocks from Drayton in old Savannah, Thirty-seventh Street was lined with derelict houses too large for most single families to maintain. In the midst of this decay stood the three-storied dinosaur that for the evening welcomed the brutal majesty of Savannah Pink. The house had been painted six times. At any one of the myriad paint fractures one could count the coats of different-colored paint. In the littered rear drive a metallic bronze Eldorado convertible sat in misplaced splendor. The license tag read only PINK.

Savannah was at his leisure on the second floor. Clad in dark briefs, Savannah Pink's flesh gleamed wetly in the lamplight. He was on a king-size bed, monstrously hunched over a large, oval mirror pulled from the wall. Pink's complete attention was on the straight razor in his right hand, fingers curled away from the edge. He had separated a small clump of crystalline powder from the larger central mound on the mirror and was systematically chopping the crystals into finer particles. He worked the razor through the substance, first horizontally, then vertically, then diagonally. With practiced sureness he swept the powder with the angled edge of the blade, first into a rectangular pile and then into three long, sweeping lines. Each line stretched for the length of the mirror. He tapped the razor, causing the residue of powder to fall from the blade. Pink licked the remaining particles from the gray stainless steel, moved them with an agile tongue about his cavernous mouth and over his lips. "Okay, ladies," he rumbled. "Anybody want another line?"

The dark-rooted blond was the first to move. She had been lying facedown on the right side of the wide bed. Her skin was fishbelly-white and dimpled with fat, her sagging bulk striated with stretch marks both wide and long. Her hamlike haunch jiggled when she moved. She wore fist-size bruises on her pendulous breasts, and an old scar crossed both her swollen thighs. With grease-caked hair and greedy, dark eyes she was a rare beauty.

Another white woman sat at the velvet-green headboard, her knees up and her thin arms drawn protectively around her legs. She weighed well under a hundred pounds and was dressed in loose-fitting dark slacks and a pale blue tube top that revealed the modest outline of her small, budlike breasts. Her dark hair was combed in boyish fashion, falling over her narrow forehead. Her eyes were unfocused. In slower response to Savannah's invitation she crawled to the oval mirror and its temporary promise of a jolt and the illusion of confidence.

Taking a shortened plastic drinking straw in hand, Savannah Pink lowered his massive and closely cropped head to the mirror. He held his left nostril closed with a splayed finger and aligned the bottom of the straw with the far end of powdered cocaine. With a steady, forceful inhalation he snorted the substance into his nasal cavities, drawing in bushels of air, following the line to its end. He pinched his entire nose between spatulate thumb and curled forefinger and blew forcefully against his stoppered membranes. For good measure he bent forward and quick-snorted two inches from the other two lines. He passed the straw to the dark-haired, birdlike girl. She, and then her bloated companion, duplicated his actions but employed varying techniques. One divided her line into halves, using right and left nostrils in short bursts. The other took hers in one long, liquid snort.

Scarce seconds after the lines were inhaled, the trio lit menthol cigarettes and smoked in sniffling euphoria. When Pink stubbed out the remainder of his smoke, he smacked the sagging thigh of the bruised blonde. "Roll us a couple of joints," he ordered, and punctuated his command with a forceful snort. The blonde rolled off the bed and moved to a small table at its side. She spread cleaned marijuana on cigarette paper and rolled the substance into a remarkably uniform white cylinder.

"And you, you skinny bitch," Pink said in his basso rumble, "you come here and let me teach you some of the joys and pleasures of cocaine." He reached out a bear-size paw and grabbed the girl, stripping the clothing from her thin frame, tearing the fabric as if it were wet paper. His maroon eyes mixed hate and lust as he kneaded her upper and lower torso. In other circumstances the thin girl would have cried out at his first touch, but the coke coursing threw her system numbed her to his initial assault. But his sadistic handling quickly reached the point at which even the influence of the drug failed to mask her discomfort. "Oh, God, no!" she screamed, and twisted. Her tiny breast was reddened, and her face wore the memory of startling pain.

Pink stared at her in cool appraisal. He touched his nose, rubbed at his lips. "This is gonna be more fun than I expected." The gold crown on his tooth reflected the light. "I like it when you scream." Pink's father had been an animal of a man, filled with hate and violence. He was a Georgia dirt farmer, and a bad one. His black bride bore him child after child every other year, but still he beat her, in and out of pregnancy. When the children were at last old enough for him to notice, he beat them until his wife would protest, then turned his anger at her for interfering. He didn't smile, didn't wash, and he taught the child who would later call himself Savannah Pink to detest white skin and blue eyes. On the day the young teenager with the body of a man killed his father, the blue-eyed demon had been swinging a thick branch down on Pink's mother's shoulders. He'd laid open her ear with a glancing blow beside her head, and Pink had walked in the door to see her sprawled on the floor, the cartilage of her ear bare and white, the club still in Pa's hand. Pink had looked from his mother to the club to the man's cold blue eyes. And then he'd killed him, broken every bone the man had, pounded his skull to cracked pulp. He reached out, his arm slow, hypnotic. The girl whimpered. Pink whipped his broad head to the door, eyes squinting, and moved on silent feet. He jerked the frail door open.

"Hey, Pink?" a voice called from below. "Pink? Hey, Pink. It's just me, man. Birdman."

"Okay," Pink grumbled down the darkened stairway. "Come on up."

A tall, muscled black with a deceptive smile entered the room. Pink stared at Birdman, then waved an arm at the mound of cocaine. Birdman took the razor, sliced out a very modest line of crystals, and snorted the line loud and quick. "We got business," Birdman said. A flicker of his dark eyes indicated the women.

"Fuck it," growled Pink. "They ain't gonna repeat nothin'."

Birdman said, "The brother in Bogota just called. That Colonel dude has stopped everything comin' up by water. Said the man was going nuts trying to figure out how we know every shipment he tries."

Pink was rocking in the rhythmic cadence of a cocaine body-high. He grinned and fondled the bony bottom of the dark-haired girl.

Birdman laughed. "But, of course, since he loads the boat, he got the plan from the man, anyhow. They got to send it soon, and we gonna know when and where just the same."

Pink grinned again, his close-set maroon eyes gleaming. He cut a huge mound from the cocaine and began to celebrate in earnest. With luck the girls might survive his triumphant glee. Pink took perverse pride in being able to tear and rip white vaginas with his donkeylike penis, but his joy would push them to the limit this night. Birdman, as the bearer of good tidings, was made honored guest, and the cycle of snort, smoke, toke, screw, and snort was renewed with animal abandon.

CHAPTER 10

"*WEEMS!*" A harsh electronic voice lasered him from the desk intercom. He stood up and trotted for the door. Three days had passed without a word from his employer. The Colonel had failed to summon him, failed to speak to him over the one-way communicator. Weems had spent agonizing hours waiting for the call, fearful of initiating interaction himself, more fearful of leaving the room for any reason. His nerves were stretched to the thinnest, and the unpleasant snarl that the Colonel made of his name was welcome.

Engrossed in correspondence, the Colonel ignored his aide, exceeding the normal inattention by a full two minutes. Finally he tilted his aggressive jaw upward and stared at Weems with his two lifeless eyes.

"Weems, I've decided to give you a chance to redeem yourself. I find it difficult to say why, though. Yes, you push the papers well enough, dot your *i*'s, and cross all the *t*'s. And yes, I know I can trust you not to be fool enough to steal from me, but goddamn it! I can get the same damn thing from a classified want ad. So look sharp, boy. Do what I tell you to do, exactly the way I tell you to do it. One more improvisation from you and you've had it." Burgess stabbed Weems with his eyes. "Benny's here today and not for the hell of it. Do you read me, Weems?"

"Yes, sir."

Burgess stood. A suit of finest wool, cut to display the older man's crisp physique, stood dark against the perfect white of his shirt. The scar of his hand and fingers hovered at the knot of a blue silk tie. He dared Weems with his eyes to cast one brief glance at his disfigurement. He circled around Weems. From behind him he said, "But you have been loyal. And not many men could have taken the money I've paid you over the years and kept it as quiet as you have. I think that's why I'm not going with my first inclination." He stopped square in front of Weems, showed him the bottom of the wells of his eyes. "I was going to give you to Benny. You know that, don't you?"

Weems, knowing all too well what being "given" to Benny meant, would have been in another country if he'd thought such a fate awaited him, but he saw the demand for agreement in the Colonel's glare and nodded his head.

Burgess sliced the air with his chin. "You bet your ass I was! Goddamn, Weems! I tell you one thousand times not to use a single sonofabitching man until I clear him through *my* sources, and your second time out you go and play Mr. Big-shot Drug Dealer and okay a shooter on the spot. And you hire a narc." Burgess went up on his toes, rocked back on his heels, and wagged his head. "You hired, you *paid—hand to hand! You dumb motherfucker*—not only a narc but a federal narc with one of the longest, hottest enforcement streaks ever."

Weems endured a silence, then, desperate to fill the void, nodded his further agreement.

Burgess pivoted and stalked back to his desk. He sat. After a pause he said, "Don't let me down today, Weems. You play heads-up ball, follow my lead. Miss Marcel is waiting for us in the study. I've seen her report and I've mapped out a solution to the fucking mess you've made, but implementing the operation will require her cooperation. So what I'm saying is, don't fuck things up."

"Yes, sir."

"What?"

"No, sir. I won't."

CHAPTER 11

HE was a military man from a family of military men. He insisted upon being addressed as Colonel, even now that he no longer wore the uniform of the U.S. Marine Corps. He stood like a ramrod at attention, jutting a chiseled jaw. He was sixty-one years old, trim, groomed, and had the eyes of a dead snake. He said, "Miss Marcel, you disappoint me."

"But, no, Colonel," she objected, flashing her eyes in pardon. "Dan Fields disappointed you. I presented your proposition with full use of all of my skills, and he declined."

The Colonel, wearing the claw of his hand with obscene pride, marched up and down the length of the room. "Then we must see that Mr. Fields finds some other motivation."

"You're going to need some luck." Fanny smiled. "Dan Fields doesn't seem the kind of man one can push."

The Colonel halted in front of her. "I push who I choose, when I choose, and where I choose. You should remember that."

Fanny, shocked by the sudden change in tone and demeanor in her employer, covered her moment of disquiet with a sip from her glass. The wine had a unique clarity, a flavor pure and bright. She lowered her glass and said, "I didn't mean to suggest—"

"I know exactly what you meant," said Burgess, flapping his good hand at her and his own outburst. He took a seat beside her. "Have no doubt, Fanny. I have my plans for Mr. Fields firmly in mind. I am not searching for anything other than the best means by which to implement them.'' He was on his feet again, moving to the wall, passing Weems in his chair. He said, ''What about his financial situation? Isn't there more to what we learned?''

Fanny crossed one knee over the other. ''I'm afraid not. He lives modestly, doesn't show anything in his checking account other than pension deposits and money from a few sales of his sculpture. By the time he pays his bills and child support, he has enough left to buy stone.'' She tracked Burgess as he rounded the room. ''The first payment, twenty thousand dollars, represents great wealth to him.'' She smiled a very appreciative grin.

Burgess let the tension out of his torso. He said, ''Some men have such limited horizons, they can find wealth in pocket cash. I expected more from Fields.''

''There are his sculptures,'' offered Fanny. ''He is not a man without passion.''

Burgess arched a brow. He blinked, then cleared his throat. ''Benny!''

The study door opened and in walked Benny. A man of normal height, he bulged with the massive physique of a professional bodybuilder and wore a longish mane of blond hair. He slid into a chair, keeping his eyes on Burgess, looking neither left nor right.

Weems shifted, sat more erect.

Fanny lifted sculpted brows in question.

''Benny''—Burgess smiled—''is another member of my little unit. You haven't met him before. Although I must say he has certainly spent many hours watching you. I thought it was time you and he met.''

She felt her chest tighten but turned to the enormously muscled man and said, ''How do you do?''

Benny did not respond.

His name was Benny Montrose and he had the face of an angel. He had been an orphan since the third week of his life, and unlike contemporary myth would have it, he had lived hard and lean in state institutions. At the age of five he had been segregated from the general orphan population and packaged into an extended and cruel isolation. The notations from his own little folder in the administrator's office of the state orphanage listed several justifications for the unorthodox treatment. The child Benny, at three months short of his sixth birthday, was an accomplished liar and thief. This label was in no way remarkable, for many of his peers in the same institution were similarly disposed. However, Benny did differ in certain significant aspects of his behavior. When others of the homeless and forgotten children were caught in a theft or untruth by the staff, they could be expected in most cases to confess, apologize, accept punishment, and then move on to the next day. But not Benny Montrose. He, at an age presumably too young to know criminal desire, responded differently. He attacked his accuser.

Twice Benjamin Montrose handled tattletales by smashing in the faces of his sleeping accusers. The first child, a girl, was eight years old when Benny bashed in her face with a door weight as she slept in the adjacent girl's dorm. His second retaliation, leveled at a younger boy, left the sleeping tot with a permanently disfigured eye and a manic fear of sleeping in the dark. His third victim, one who accused young Benny of stealing a pouch of shredded bubble gum from a dorm-mate, was no child. She was a fifty-eight-year-old resident supervisor, and Benny sneaked into her room and doused her and her bedclothes in kerosene. It was only because of the prompt response of an on-duty floor proctor that she did not become cindered testimony to Benny's violence. Two months later she experienced a bad fall, tumbling down two flights of uncarpeted stairs. Her account, incredible but made more real by her resultant permanent paralysis from the waist down, described Benny Montrose, the boy with the face of an angel, as a demon. At five years of age he had smiled at his victim, chatted pleasantly about several of his chores, then offered to help her down the stairs. She had declined and passed him to descend to the main dining room for dinner. He had rushed at her and pushed her until she lost her grip on the worn banister. Then Benny had followed the woman as she rolled down the concreted stairway and kicked her down two flights of stairs.

"Benny," explained Burgess, taking pleasure in Weems's pained expression, "doesn't speak to anyone but me, I'm afraid. Not to anyone. He's peculiar in that way." He turned his eyes to the bodybuilder. "Aren't you, Benny?"

"Yes, sir." His voice was hoarse, wavering in pitch.

Fanny Marcel sipped the excellent wine again. She had totaled her accounts and charges. If she were to walk away from Burgess, she would leave with more than enough funds to sustain several years of travel. She said, "I don't understand why any man would speak to only one other person.''

"Then I will explain it to you." The Colonel grinned. His scarred hand spasmed. He said, "Besides, I had planned to tell you this little story. And Benny won't mind. Will you, Benny?"

"No, sir."

"I found Benny in Vietnam in 1970. He was being held under arrest by his unit commander, something about an assault on a Vietnamese woman. I was running intelligence for my unit and doing liaison with the CIA then and recognized his potential.'' Burgess beamed at the younger man. "Saved your ass, didn't I, Benny?"

Benny gulped. "Saved my ass just in time." His eyes did not leave Burgess.

"You bet I did." He pointed his chin at a far wall. "The world was insane in 1970. We were in a war where we could've beat the piss out of Charlie anytime we wanted to, but the goddamn pansies in the government wouldn't let us. Instead Congress wanted to tell us how to fight a war. It was insane." Burgess nailed Fanny with a dead gaze. "They tried to rewrite the rules of war. But there are no rules. Not in the field. In the bush, soldiers do what they have to.''

She nodded.

"Benny was about to face a rape charge brought by some goddamned gook bitch, and his command didn't understand the realities of the country. They were acting like he'd committed a crime."

"But, Colonel—"

"You had to be there, Fanny," he said, overriding her protest. "I yanked Benny out, just like I'd yanked most of my command from different jams. I gave him a chance, a chance to use his talents for his country." Burgess tilted his head back and inhaled through his nose. "Those were glorious days, Fanny. I had one tough bunch of men in my intelligence command, one tough bunch. Weren't they something, Benny?"

"Head-knockers!" said Benny. He smiled in remembrance. He wore the face of an adolescent, the eyes of a forty-year-old man.

"Damn right. Damn right." Burgess straightened, remembering his audience. "Congress was trying to direct the war from Washington. You've never seen such a mess. If an enemy unit attacked our troops, they'd flee at the very first sign of our reinforcements. But—and I still find this hard to believe—the very second the enemy troops put their little yellow feet across an international border, we had to halt our pursuit. That was law. But, Fanny, when you're on the ground, in the bush, there is no law. And for the professional soldiers there was no such thing as a goddamned international border. We crossed when we had to, did our business, got the hell home, and then denied everything. That's what I mean when I say that the world was insane. Brave men went out to battle and then had to lie, had to deny the glory of their bravery. It was a civil war in a country of villages, thousands of independent villages. Within the context of the civil war the CIA and the military command supported counterinsurgent factions all over the country with guns and food. And it was working, Fanny. So when our own goddamned Congress stabbed us in the back, sliced off our funds, we improvised. We used confiscated drugs as substitute currency, that's what we did. Opium, heroin, morphine base, hash—we used it all as currency to keep our insurgents motivated. Used it to keep our own people like Benny motivated too. You get a lot more out of a soldier if he knows he's going to make a couple thousand dollars each time he goes out behind the lines.''

"I see," said Fanny. She was uncomfortable and moved to another chair, one farther away from Benny.

"I don't think you do," replied Burgess. "Intelligence operates in a much different fashion than normal military operations. It is a dirty field, one which quickly kills off the incompetents. Good intelligence officers learn that there is no morality, no such thing as right and wrong. Only what works. For us, me, Benny, and the others, raiding heroin from one village and delivering it to another village worked. The heroin was diverted from its target, the enemy was punished, while the insurgents, my men, and yours truly were all compensated. Hell, for what we were doing, we deserved to be paid. In intelligence, if you locate a particular individual working for the opposition, one who is doing damage to your troops, you excise that individual. Excise. As in surgery. You pick up a scalpel and you slice him off." A light was burning in the Colonel's eyes. "I took Benny with me and my tough bunch of head-knockers on a mission to excise a man. A man who sold information to both sides of the conflict, a man who prostituted every member of his family to deliver heroin and other contraband. And, yes, goddammit, we crossed the border, you better believe we crossed it. We had to. Because that old fucker, Hsing Pao, he was too smart to set up camp where we could reach him. Legally."

Benny Montrose squirmed, rubbing massive deltoids against the back of his chair. Donald Weems watched in silence.

"The guys from the CIA told me something before we left, which made the target that much sweeter. They let me know that this Hsing Pao not only was selling information about troop movements to both sides, but also he was sitting on top of half the heroin in Asia right in his village. And they let me know where I could drop it off for them too. You understand, Fanny? The CIA was in the trade before I was."

She shrugged, but Burgess was up and moving again. "My objective, my intelligence assignment, was to enter the village of Hsing Pao, excise him, and seize the contraband. We were to go all the way in and make it back out without radio communications, and every member of the squad was sworn to secrecy. We were also to split some of the reward money from the company. Didn't I promise to split with the boys, Benny?"

"Yes, sir. All of us was in for a piece."

"Damn right," said Burgess. "But they didn't ever collect. None of us did." He moved in short, abrupt steps, stopped in front of the woman. "What we didn't know," he spat, "was that the goddamned president of the United States had put his finger into the same damn village. And at the same damn time! It was incredible. Some backwater mortician—a funeral parlor director for chrissake!—who happened to be second cousin to the sonofa-bitching commander in chief did the preparation for a GI who'd been shipped back for burial. Seems this second cousin found a kilo of heroin sewn into a chest wound in the dead soldier, and he went straight to the private quarters in the White House. The president hears about this just when he doesn't need to and goes through the roof, pulling strings, yanking anything that came to mind. What he did was call the director of the BNDD, passed the information, and ordered him to put agents onto the case. The federal drug agents were working with agents of the Laotian government to put a case together against, that's right, Hsing Pao. I didn't have this particular little piece of information until months later, but the Laotians had marked Hsing Pao for goddamned utter and total destruction the moment the case was made. That was their idea of justice, swift and sure. Can you picture it, Fanny? Me and my men are moving in to take out Hsing Pao and his heroin, a United States BNDD enforcement agent is somewhere in the brush making heroin deals with the son of a bitch, and all the while standing by with their binoculars are the Laotians waiting to call in an air strike."

Burgess saw her comprehension. He said, "You should feel privileged. Weems has been with me a good deal longer than you, and he never has heard this little anecdote. Have you, Weems?"

"Um, no. No, sir."

"We were caught in the middle of holy hell," Burgess whispered. His eyes glossed and lost focus. "We didn't have any way of knowing it at the time, but the BNDD agent had completed his transaction, made his case against this old bastard Hsing Pao, and the Laotian contact had moved off to radio his troops. But, and God only knows why, for some reason this agent stayed behind and tipped off the old gook. And instead of making a run for it, this Hsing Pao sat around long enough to warn his family, then killed himself. That's when we arrived, Benny and me and my men. We thought we were laying an ambush, and instead we walked into the wildest crossfire anyone's ever seen. Good men, brave men, died all around us. We couldn't move. We didn't know why, but we took air strikes all afternoon, while at the same time Hsing Pao's filthy family members slipped through the brush and smoke and slit my boys' throats. When it was over, when the strikes finally stopped, me and Benny were the only ones left. Weren't we, Benny?"

The man's face was flushed. He said, "We were the only ones."

"By the time it was over, we had the bodies of Hsing Pao's relatives and our own men stacked around us like logs. After a while we had enough to use them to stop the shrapnel. When the rockets finally let up, it took me and Benny another half day to track down the last villagers in the brush. Then, just when we think it's all over, just when me and Benny were standing in what was left of the old man's hut looking at all the rice sacks filled with heroin, talking about splitting up the CIA bounty and how we would spend it, planning to make the deaths of our comrades have some meaning, we were interrupted." Burgess snapped his chin down, conscious of her stare. "A man, a living, breathing man was crouched on the matting, holding the body of Hsing Pao. And, Fanny, he was a white man. Do you want to know what he said? I bet Benny remembers.'' Burgess whipped around. ''Benny? I know it's been a long time, and I know we don't talk about this, but do you remember? Do you remember what the man said to us?''

Benny blinked three times and nodded.

''Say the words, Benny.''

''Get the fuck out.'' Benny bobbed his head. ''He told us to get the fuck out.''

''Excellent, Benny!'' said the Colonel. ''You remembered them exactly. 'Get the fuck out.' That's what he said. After we'd crossed forty clicks of brush and jungle, staying off the trails to arrive unseen, after we'd watched our boys die all around us, after we'd survived one hell of a rocket and artillery attack, he tells us to get the fuck out.'' Burgess gazed at his claw. ''Since the man spoke in English, I didn't try to kill him. I picked up one of the sacks our brothers from the CIA were willing to pay so handsomely for and told this man that Benny and I were simply taking the packages and that we meant him no harm. Again he ordered us out.''

Benny worked his thigh muscles and rolled his shoulders.

''He used the same words. I remember too.'' Burgess grinned a shark's grin. ''Benny jumped at him first. Didn't get far, though.'' He turned. ''Did you?''

''He shot me,'' said Benny. A bicep twitched.

''Damn right, he shot him. I saw it. This white man came up with a small pistol and nailed my Benny right in the abdomen with a shot that took care of the boy's right kidney forever. Dropped him cold before Benny had a chance to squeeze his trigger. And I, Fanny,'' he said, and smiled an evil, diseased smile, ''I, like a fool, also tried to shoot that man. And he, well before I could kill him, shot me too. His bullet struck me here.'' He touched a good hand to his chest. ''Here, where I had an incendiary grenade ready for any more villagers.'' He fixed her with dead, black eyes. ''They say you panic when exposed to flame, but I had the presence of mind to use my left hand.'' He grinned again, his head a skull without flesh. ''Now you know how I acquired my mark of honor.'' He stopped grinning and waved his claw. ''Benny and I, we made it back. Obviously. But those forty clicks back to safety took us nineteen days, and we both should have died several times over. I won't distress you with details, but we did some hard things to survive.''

Burgess moved to face the three of them. ''I've never known who that man was. I was able to determine which agency he'd belonged to but nothing else. You see, the Laotian response to the narcotics agent's case was an embarrassment to our administration. Everything on the incident was incinerated. I know. I've had people go through their files. But through the years Benny and I, we never stopped looking. Did we, Benny?''

''Never.''

''Never, Fanny. Not until I saw this picture.'' He held the shot of Fields and Maltessa. ''Now that my little personal history is over, I'm certain you can supply the concluding passage. Can you, Fanny?''

She'd expected the question to go to Benny, but she answered with her next breath. ''Dan Fields.''

''Exactly,'' growled Burgess. ''Benny saw him first, in person. He brought me the photograph and I, too, recognized the man immediately.''

A fragile quiet hung in the room. Fanny uncrossed her legs, straightened her hem. ''Colonel, I do understand. But I don't believe I want to hear any more. True, I've profited from our association and I am deeply grateful, but you are entering water I don't care to—''

''Murder?'' barked Burgess. ''Are you quibbling with murder? You, you think you're clean? You think some of the money you've delivered wasn't in payment for murder? Do you think your research hasn't gone straight from me to Benny and that he hasn't gone right out and used it to commit murder? You are not clean, Fanny. You're a talented woman, smart, and with a beautiful face and body, but you are not clean.''

She stood.

He faced her. ''Fanny, don't be impulsive. You are going to help me.''

She sighed, met his eyes. ''No, Colonel. I cannot help you with this.'' She turned toward the door. A chair scraped on her third step, garments rustled on her fifth, and on the sixth pace a crunching pain erupted below and behind her right ear. She took no seventh step.

* * *

A colorless dream enfolded her. She could not move. A gray spider on a gray web crawled upon her gray limbs. She fought the gray covers. Gray hands from gray arms roughly pulled aside her gray clothing, exposing her gray nakedness. Sharp, gray stingers penetrated the flesh above her gray pubic mound. White pain bloomed, made her arch from her heels to her neck, and she urinated. She felt warm liquid splashing between her thighs. It was not a dream.

Fanny coughed and spat to her left. She was stretched upon the floor, her panting the only sound. Her wrists and ankles were securely bound by the terry cloth of fine towels. Her naked body lay faceup upon cold tile. Her neck ached with a throb that matched her pulse. Cooling urine dampened her labia, thighs, and buttocks. Two pinpricks, wasp stings, burned insistently in her lower abdomen. Fighting nausea, she lifted her head and inspected the area of pain. Protruding from her naked abdomen, slightly above her trimmed blond pubic hair, were two metal electrodes with barbs attached to fine gray cables. Blood dotted the juncture of untanned skin and probe. The cables led from her body to a rectangular device held in the hand of the Colonel. Pistollike, the device was mounted with a red trigger. The dead-eyed man wore a frown. To his side, Weems grinned salaciously, an erection apparent in his untailored trousers. The room was uniformly lit from above. Fanny tried to speak but retched.

"Miss Marcel?" The Colonel's voice penetrated her distress. "Miss Marcel, can you hear me?"

She nodded, and her diaphragm convulsed.

"Good. Please pay strict attention to what I tell you. I won't repeat it, and the knowledge I'm about to give you is the only thing that can save your mind from absolute destruction. Fanny, you can't escape the 'conditioning' that awaits you. Abandon thoughts of escape. You will be able, however, to survive it, and with your mind intact. But"—he peered at her humiliated form with compassion—"if you aren't able to fix your thoughts upon what I tell you now, you may experience permanent psychological damage."

Fanny calmed her racing fears and listened. The nausea faded slightly, and her eyes focused. Her clothing lay draped upon an adjacent leather-covered chair. Her life force seized upon the content of the Colonel's words. She would survive.

"No one resigns," he said softly, in a monotone. "Listen to me, Fanny. No one resigns. No one resigns from my little army. You are of great use to this organization. It's all very simple: You can't walk away. And I will not waste any more time, words, or valuable energy to try to convince you." He pushed the device in his right hand out from his body. The motion caused the gray cables to sway. "This fascinating device will convince you," he murmured. "It is a Taser. It was developed for use by law-enforcement personnel as a nonlethal weapon. When activated by the trigger, it impels two electrodes into, hopefully, the flesh of the target. In your present position no great marksmanship was required to place the barbs." He smiled over empty eyes. "What I want you to remember is this, Fanny," he continued softly. "I had the device modified. With each depression of the trigger an enormous amount of electrical current is discharged from one of the electrodes. The current traverses the tissues of your body and is returned to the device through the second barb. The current, while it will involve your body in a great deal of pain and convulsion, will not in itself do lasting damage. That is what you should strive to remember. Do you understand?" His question was a lover's caress, soft and caring.

She nodded and tried to speak.

He interrupted her. "No, Fanny," he warned. "Don't speak. Not until your conditioning is completed. Then, if your mind has survived, we will talk."

His gnarled finger leapt to the red trigger.

A thousand angry wasps materialized upon her flesh and stung her in unison. Her head struck the floor with an audible crack. Bowlike, her body arched from head to heels. The wasps attacked, again and again and again, and Fanny's teeth clacked in horrific rhythm. At last the arch of her contorted spine relaxed, but she trembled uncontrollably, her brain a scramble of electro-chemical messages. Her limbs danced in crazed vibration, her heels sounding a flesh-muffled tattoo upon the hard floor. Thought did not, could not, exist.

The wasps vanished, and she lay fighting for breath. Her heart beat with terror, and her mind fitfully clung to the slippery edge of reason. Consciousness asserted itself, and she forced her lungs to draw a breath. She dragged her shocked mind to focus on Burgess's last words. She would survive. She exhaled in a strangled sob.

Her second cry was wrenched from her lungs by a giant fist that lifted her bodily, stretched tight the limits of her bonds, then dashed her mercilessly to the unyielding tile. Angry wasps with a thousand busy stingers tore her mind from its moorings. She twisted, jerked, writhed, and clacked aloud. In alternating cadence, Burgess first jolted and then paused, jolted then paused, until his attack ceased and she babbled incoherently, spitting foam from rubbery lips.

In Fanny's mind, consciousness and will disintegrated. The gray dream of mindlessness returned. She fled in slowed, syrupy motion from her gray demons, always pursued, always captured, always wrenched in mid-flight to an onslaught of convulsion and fear. Her mind, her "self," her rationality banged in terror like a captured creature. She sought death, but it escaped her disrupted will. She sought mind death, the confused peace of insanity, but that was barred from her by the Colonel's last words. She could survive. She would survive. Time lost relevance, for her world consisted only of the red trigger and an eternal gray dream of fear and flight.

Her hearing and vision returned before she possessed the comprehension to unite their meanings. Fanny was in a barren and white exercise room, a place of cold tile and heavy metal. A high ceiling with molded corners told her she was still inside the Colonel's Winchester mansion. Weight benches and other training apparatus had been dragged into place around her, and she was tied to their immovable cast-iron legs. Burgess was working his lips again and sounds were escaping them, but the meaning eluded her.

He spoke again. "Listen to me, Fanny. Fanny? Can you hear me? If you can, nod your head."

Her head and shoulders convulsed with a confused spasm.

"Good. Try not to worry. Your body will return to your own control soon enough—soon enough, *if* you survive." He pushed the Taser out from his waist, dragged the wires against the inside of her thigh. "You want to please me, Fanny. More than anything else in the world you want to please me. Anything I want, you want. And you know why. Pleasing me, Fanny, is the only way you can be safe. The only way Fanny can be safe is to please

Colonel Burgess." He moved his arm, let the wires caress her pudendum. He touched a whitened tongue to purpled lips. "You will do anything I say because that is the only way to be safe. You want to please me, no matter what I ask, no matter what the task. Always remember, Fanny. If you forget, then this"—he caressed her labia with thin gray wires—"is what will follow immediately after."

Fanny's pelvis shuddered.

"No, Fanny!" cautioned Burgess, his tone at once intimidating and filled with threat. "Please me."

She met his eyes. Fanny commanded her legs, lifted her hips, and met his gray obscenity with her pubic mound. Her eyes were locked to his.

"Good, Fanny," he cooed. "A very good beginning." Burgess turned to the two men behind him. "Isn't she doing well?" he asked. He turned without expecting an answer. Weems was transfixed by the spectacle of Fanny, and Benny was sitting with clasped hands and knees pressed together. "I think you're going to make it, Fanny. Of course, there's a way for you to go yet, a little post-shock orientation, but I think you're going to make it."

Fanny's physical perceptions were returning. She felt the tiles beneath her, the stickiness of her urine, the nap of the towels that were her bindings. She saw only the opaque black of Burgess's eyes.

"Pleasing men is your strength," said the Colonel. "Remember your talent, Fanny. Pleasing men. That's why I first hired you. Because you were so adept at pleasing men. You have been an effective tool when you've used your strength too. Very effective."

She saw approval animate his face and clung to hope. The fingers in both her hands were numb.

"So, I want you to please men, the men I select, and I want you to please them for my purposes only. Without the slightest question. Do you understand me, Fanny?"

She was quick to nod, and her neck muscles did not rebel at the command.

"That is your basic usefulness, Fanny, your native currency. To help you remember your place, your role, I'm going to have one of the other members of our little army help you practice. Any objections?"

Her pulse spiked. She fought the surge of fear and wagged her head. She objected to nothing.

Burgess jutted his jaw, nodded with satisfaction. He turned, jerking the barbs where they pierced her flesh. He faced Benny Montrose. "Benny?"

"Yes, sir." He stood up and let his hands fall to his sides.

"You let me down, boy," Burgess growled.

Benny's face showed a minute widening of his eyes. "I'm sorry, sir."

"You didn't kill that son of a bitch when you saw him standing in the marina, did you?"

"No, sir." The bulk of his chest rose and fell with short, shallow breaths.

"You recognized him, didn't you?" It was a sharp demand, an accusation.

"Yes, sir, Colonel. I recognized him." Benny's lids blinked with more speed.

"But you didn't kill him."

"N-n-no, sir."

"You took his picture, though, didn't you? You held a goddamned camera steady enough to take his picture—a good picture too!—but you couldn't pick up a rifle and aim it, could you, Benny?"

The big man closed his eyes. He said, "I tried, Colonel."

"You tried shit!" screamed Burgess. "You took his fucking picture and then tucked your fucking yellow tail between your ball-less legs and ran to me like a scalded dog!"

Benny opened his eyes, then lowered them. "I did try. I couldn't hold the rifle. I was shaking."

Burgess scowled. "You were shaking." He pivoted to Fanny. "He was shaking. He was shaking because the last time he tried to shoot the same son of a bitch, Benny had to crawl through the jungle with an intestinal infection, living on slugs and mice. Because the last time Benny tried to shoot Mr. Dan Fields, Benny had one of his kidneys and most of his stuffing shot out of him instead." Over his shoulder he said, "Right, Benny?"

Montrose let his gaze fall on Fanny. He said, "I tried to shoot him, Colonel. I tried."

Burgess didn't reply. He advanced a pace, tugged out first one barb, then the other, using abrupt jerks of his wrist with no concern for her pain. But Fanny did not cry out. Burgess waggled the blood-clotted barbs in Fanny's face. He said, "I should give you to Benny. I should but I won't. I never reward cowardice. Instead, Fanny, because I need you soon, I think I'll let Weems be the one to help you remember your place. How do you feel about that, Fanny?" He loomed above her, bloodied electrodes dangling from his grip, his scarred claw curled in close to his chin.

Fanny swallowed and breathed out. She said, "I want to do anything to please you." Behind Burgess she caught the blur of Weems as he moved closer.

"Good, Fanny," Burgess said. "You're going to make it. I know you are."

Burgess stood in the hallway addressing his troops. "Weems, listen to me. You need to understand something. Yes, the shocks I administered to Fanny were devastating, taking away something as basic as the control of her own body, but we still need to do more. To insure her complete cooperation."

Weems nodded, hard and sharp.

"Fanny has to give up, Weems. She must surrender her will in everything to me. It is not enough to touch her mind. We must deprive her of ownership of her own body. To cement the nature of our bond she must now be abused. Sexual assault is peculiar in this way. Nothing quite seems to get a woman's attention like rape. Rape, Weems. Violent, abusive, humiliating. That is what you will give to Fanny Marcel. Repeated assaults. No quarter, no regard for her person or wishes at all. We will drive her mind, her will, into inaction. Then she must come to see me," Burgess said, "as her savior, as the only one she can turn to for release. And you must be the one to drive her into my forgiving arms. Do you read me, Weems?"

"Yes, sir. I do understand. Of course, I've kept current on all the readings—"

"Benny," Burgess said, cutting Weems off.

"Yes, sir."

"As punishment for your cowardice in the field, you will watch."

The man with the immense slabs of muscle blinked.

"Then, Benny," Burgess said warmly, "we'll put the past behind us, behind all of us. I want you to take that fool Maltessa and put him on hold. Then, but only if Maltessa is in live and functional condition, then will I let you have something truly wonderful.''

Benny's shoulders lifted. ''Something wonderful?''

Burgess nodded, paused, made him wait. ''Dan Fields has a family, Benny. An ex-wife and a daughter.''

''Two women?''

''Yes, Benny. Two women.''

CHAPTER 12

"*MAY* I come in, please?"

Fields pulled the door open and admitted her. He guided her to the main room with its loft and skylights and greenery. The Outlaw rounded a corner and romped a few paces toward her, then skidded on all fours. He wagged his stump of a tail and sat, his head held at an expectant angle. Fields took her elbow and ushered Fanny to a wide, comfortable chair covered in earth-toned cloth. She sat. The Outlaw crept three steps closer, then resumed his wagging sit. When the girl spoke, his wagging increased, his hindquarters rose, and he looked to Fields. Then he sat again, as if by command.

Fields, yet to speak a word, left the room, turning into the compact kitchen. Fanny could hear the opening and closing of a refrigerator door and the clink of ice cubes against glass. When he returned, he handed her a large goblet and sat before her in a large natural leather chair.

She tried to smile her gratitude but failed. She sipped strong tea, lightly flavored with mint, pleasant and stimulating. "Mr. Fields," she said quietly. "I have a message for you."

Fields's expression did not change, nor did he invite her to continue.

"Mr. Fields," she stated with more volume, "you must accept the contract I proposed, and you must begin immediately."

Fields showed amusement at the corners of his mouth and eyes. The Outlaw wagged and wriggled, inching forward a pace.

"No!" Fanny responded with force. "Don't take what I say lightly. There's no humor in this at all! The lives of your daughter and her mother both depend on your cooperation!"

The mirth vanished from Fields's face. He fixed his cold blue eyes on her. The Outlaw sniffed the air tentatively.

"Mr. Fields!" Fanny urged, "you have to take this contract! It's the only way you can save their lives!" Her eyes darted. She gulped air, fought for composure. She said, "Both your ex-wife and child are under our control at this very moment. Unless I call my superiors with your acceptance within the next fifteen minutes, they—they will not live another day."

Fields pressed his lips into a thin line, and his eyelids drew down to hooded slits. The Outlaw retreated three paces and sat. A full minute passed in which Fields's clouded eyes studied her in detail, seeming to creep over her skin, through her flesh, and into her very bones. "Can you substantiate your claim?" he asked in a flat, atonal voice.

"Yes!" Fanny answered, frantic, digging into the small clutch at her side. She pulled out an envelope, fumbled through several photographs, and passed them to Fields. Their fingers barely touched, and she recoiled immediately. His flesh was hot to her touch.

He examined the photos. A blond little girl and a darkly beautiful woman were posed artlessly before a brick wall. They were not smiling. Fields tucked the photographs into his shirt pocket.

"I don't believe you," he said, again atonally.

"Please, Mr. Fields!" she nearly screamed, rising from her chair. The Outlaw retreated two more paces. "Don't doubt for a second that these men are anything less than monsters!" The girl's body twisted, torn by her own private terrors and her fear for the pleasant, innocent faces of the man's wife and child. "They have no respect for life or love or anything normal human beings hold dear! I swear to you, they would happily destroy those two lovely people. Please!" she urged. "I can live with the hate I see in your eyes, but don't, please don't tempt these men to demonstrate their cruelty!" Her face was anguished and gray. "Don't you understand? They would be just as happy to destroy you and your loved ones as to have your cooperation. Please!" she begged. "Believe me. I must make that call. Please believe me!"

The Outlaw retreated from the volume of sound. He peeked at her from behind a pale sofa. Fields observed her delivery without expression, but his eyes were dark and cold. Either, he thought, you are very, very good, or they—whoever they are—have deliberately exposed you to their cruelty to convey just such an impression. But it remained possible that she was duping him, manipulating him with three easily obtained photographs. As he weighed the probabilities his thinking was interrupted by the unbidden image of his daughter.

The swirling waters of the Atlantic tugged at their feet and ankles. The broad white beach of Hilton Head stretched interminably toward the darkening horizon. Dark clouds bunched against the too blue sky, and the reddening evening sun broke through to bathe them in an orange glow. The little girl and her daddy, hand in hand, marched through the push and pull of the rising tide. She sang with an innocent soprano a song made popular by a green frog of a puppet. It was a song about rainbows, and she had offered it to him to cheer his sadness at the broken marriage that hung around his neck so heavily. She sang. They walked. The recollection had neither beginning nor end, but what remained in his mind was the song, and the voice, of his child.

Fanny eyed him, her panic undisguised. She had been purposely brutalized to make the message real.

"Make your call."

Fields allowed the words to pass his lips. She passed him in a rush to the phone. The Outlaw nuzzled his cold hand and wagged his tail feebly but could not distract his master from his thoughts. The animal had tried to do so many times before. Sensing the unnamed distress in his friend, the Outlaw tried again.

Weems arrived at Fields's home in twelve minutes flat. Fanny opened the door to admit him, and he entered wearing ludicrous print shorts and an open shirt. The Outlaw met him, too, jumping up on his forelegs first and punching him in the balls.

Fields watched with apparent disinterest as Weems recovered from the assault and walked stiff-legged into the room. He was followed by the excited animal sniffing at his heels.

Weems positioned himself in front of Fields. "I'm glad you decided to be reasonable, Fields," he said, and readjusted his shorts. His tone was superior. "We're going to have a little planning session," he announced, "and then we're going to—"

Fields leapt out of the chair, grabbed Weems by the shirt lapel with his left hand, and sharply smacked Weems with his open palm, resteadying the man and repositioning him for the next resounding blow. Weems's reddened cheeks flapped loosely against his facial bones with each blow, and tears brimmed wet and full in his eyes.

"First," whispered Fields, his lips millimeters from Weems's face, the left hand still tightly grasping the bunched shirtfront. "First we're going to establish that Donna and Marianne are alive and well." Fields jerked Weems off-balance again, struck him with the hard flatness of his palm, creating a sharp, cracking sound. The Outlaw retreated to the stairway and peeped at the conflict. The girl stood several feet away, well within Fields's peripheral vision. She gnawed a knuckle. Fields's soft whisper issued forth again, like a rattler giving fair warning. "Then," he continued, "after you've proved they're alive, you're going to prove to me you're capable of carrying out your threat. And if you fail to satisfy me in either case, then, you son of a bitch, you're going to be the first man I've ever slapped to death." Fields dragged Weems a few paces forward. "Do you understand me, worm?" he whispered.

Weems nodded.

Fields frisked him with his other hand while holding him up on his toes, not in the least gentle with his groin area. Weems paled but voiced no complaint. Finding no weapon, Fields released his hold with a jerk to the left that brought Weems to his knees. The Outlaw pulled his head back behind the stairwell.

Unsteadily regaining his feet, Weems glowered at Fanny. Terror was written upon her whitened face. Weems turned back to Fields, straightened his crumpled clothing, adjusted his support hose, and spoke. "Now listen here, Fields," he began. "Of course, I'm prepared to demonstrate the validity of the situation, but you're not making any points this way."

Fields grabbed Weems again, jerked him forward and to the side, and administered three more ear-ringing slaps to Weems's chalky face. "You still don't understand me, worm," he hissed up Weems's nose. "If you have them, prove that they're safe right this minute. If you do, then we'll discuss my cooperation. But if they're not perfectly healthy," he said softly, "then you die today." He jerked Weems to the side, administered another lightning blow, and released his grip. Weems tumbled to the carpet.

He struggled to his feet, his face deep crimson, small droplets of blood dotting his cheekbone. He staggered to the telephone. Fields pointed at a chair, ordering Fanny to sit. She did. The Outlaw climbed to the second floor and was still.

Weems lifted the receiver and dialed under Fields's silent glare. "This is Weems," he said into the device. "Code B, as in boy." Weems replaced the receiver on the cradle but kept his hand on the phone. Within thirty seconds it rang, and he lifted it to his ear. Weems massaged his inflamed cheek. "Yeah, this is Weems. Put the woman on the phone, then the little girl." He held out the phone to Fields, who whipped it from his grasp. He placed the receiver to his ear. The line was silent a moment, then he could hear muffled voices, cloth or other material brushing against the phone, then the strained voice of his estranged wife.

"Hello? Dan?" she asked. The wires sang with her tension.

"Yes," he replied. "Are you and Marianne okay?"

"So far," she replied after some hesitation. Then, "Dan?"

"Yes," he answered.

"Dan, I don't think they're kidding around."

"Have you been hurt?" he asked.

"No. Not really," she answered. The space between the words filled him with dread. "Dan?" Her voice quavered, then he heard the phone brushing against fabric and more muffled voices.

"Daddy?" His daughter's voice floated across the connection.

"Yes, Princess."

"Daddy, I'm scared and Mom is too!" She began to cry.

Fields started to reassure her, but the line went dead. He walked on unfeeling legs to the main room and sat deep in the padding of one of the chairs. His chiseled face had gone hollow.

Weems strode very tentatively to a position some eight feet in front of Fields. The left side of Weems's face couldn't decide whether to be red or blue. As he spoke, a slow march of tears left the eye above and fell upon his inflamed flesh. He ignored them. "Now, Fields," he began, the words coming from his numbed jaw. "That's the last you'll hear from them until the contract is filled." He touched his cheek. "And from now on," he said, "any rough stuff you dish out, multiply it by ten and that's what they're going to get. Do you understand me?" Pleasure glinted from his reddened eyes.

Fields eyed him coldly and nodded.

Weems twitched his shoulders in an involuntary shudder. He maintained his distance from the stationary man. "Fanny," Weems directed, "go out to my car and bring in the folder on Pink. It's lying on the front seat." The girl rose obediently and exited. A car door slammed and she returned. Weems indicated that she take the folder to Fields. She placed it beside the brooding man and returned to her seat. Weems kept his distance.

"Listen, Fields," he began. "If you'd acted reasonably with us in the first place, you wouldn't have created the need for this unpleasantness." He paused and gathered his thoughts. "There's no reason why we can't do business together. The money is still good, your family hasn't been harmed. They've just been inconvenienced and frightened a little bit. You can still play on our team," Weems said, "all of us can make a nice piece of change, and nobody has to get hurt."

Fields's mind raced as he searched for the weaknesses that had to exist in an organization relying upon so many marginal talents: Party John with his unorthodox chemical requirements, the girl who flickered between perfect execution of her duties and terrified panic, and the fruit who called himself Weems. The unknowns were still too many to determine a proper course of action. Who was behind the clown corps? How many more individuals were involved and in what capacity? Of prime importance was the location of Donna and Marianne. Could they be rescued?

He fought his guilt, forcing his thoughts to focus on what had to be done. His prior experience shouted that similarly held hostages were rarely recovered unharmed and that his own life expectancy would shorten drastically when he himself was no longer needed. He turned his back on the pleading faces of the dark woman and the fair child. They needed his mind, not his guilt.

Weems pointed to the folder and continued his role as conciliator. "Fields," he said. "That folder contains the full data on this Pink and his operation. You better get to work pretty quick absorbing it, because we'll be joining Maltessa on *The Atlantic Maiden* as quickly as possible."

Fields raised an eyebrow.

"That's right," Weems continued. "The jungle drums will be delivering the message to Mr. Pink that a fat one is coming down the pike with a full load." Weems smiled an oily smile. "You don't have much time to get ready," he said, "even if you are such a smart-assed hotshot.''

Fields winced. He said, ''Do you want these people removed?''

''Naturally we want them removed,'' Weems replied.

''Then why go out of your way to diminish the probability?'' Fields asked, his eyes narrowing. ''Why take the battle to their territory and warn them in advance?''

''Because that's the plan. You worry about how to deal with this group of animals,'' Weems countered, ''and let us worry about the staging. There are some very good minds planning this exercise—in fact, some of the best,'' he boasted. ''You just review the dossier, prepare a list of supplies you'll need to put them down, and we'll take care of the rest. When Pink and his bastards reach for the bait, that's when you do your stuff, Mr. Hotshot.'' Weems smiled slickly. ''And then, when it's all over, we all go home.''

Fields eyed him. ''You sound as if you're going along for the ride.''

''Naturally,'' Weems replied but with a faint tremor in his baritone. ''Fanny and I, we'll both be accompanying you on *The Atlantic Maiden*. You didn't expect to be on the honor system, did you?''

Dan Fields said, ''If I don't kill these men, what's going to save your ass when they come climbing on board?''

''That's all been provided for in the overall plan.'' Weems was smug. ''We have backup and cover. If you fail, the plan will compensate quite adequately.'' Weems added, ''And that cover will be watching you, Fields. If you try any kind of rescue, a message will go out immediately. Before you can spit, they'll both be dead.'' Weems smirked. ''You've been ringed, Mr. Hotshot, and you better buckle down to your homework right now. By the way, the girl and her mother have been moved by now. That was part of the overall plan. We anticipated you'd demand to speak to them and so we planned for it. But the minute my call ended, they were both being moved. There's nothing left for you to do,'' he intoned, ''but bite the bullet.''

Fields rose and walked to the phone, ignoring Weems's instruction to return. He dialed the house in Charleston. The phone went unanswered. He returned to his seat. ''I've got a question,'' said Fields as he touched the folder.

Weems peered at him, waiting.

''What did you and your whore do?''

"What do you mean?" Weems sneered.

"I just wanted to know what the two of you did, specifically," Fields continued. "I can understand why your boss would want to get rid of you both. I was just curious about the specifics. What exactly did you do that would make him want to have you killed along with me?" His words had been mild, his tone even.

Weems paled and pointed a manicured finger at the folder. Fanny stared at Fields, her eyes wide and blank.

He dismissed them both from his mind and opened the folder.

Fields, intent upon his assimilation of the material in the dossier, was disturbed by the Outlaw. The animal crept down the stairway and placed its huge, broad head directly in his lap. The large brown eyes showed their whites as the dog looked inquisitively upward. Fields caressed the wiry hair on the strong neck and tossed the material to the side. "What have you got on board the trawler?" Fields asked, interrupting a hushed conversation between Weems and the complacent beauty.

"What do you mean, Fields?" Weems replied, maintaining his distance.

"What will you have on board in the way of arms, explosives, timing devices, and weaponry?"

"Oh, that," said Weems. "Well, since we're leaving a lot of the operational details of the exercise to you, just let me know what you need, and it'll be on board before you are." Then, quickly, "What do you need? I'll get started on it now." The Outlaw ambled toward the man in the touristy garb, stood on his rear legs, and affectionately poked him in the balls. Weems anticipated the thrust too late and turned slightly green. He pushed the animal roughly from him. The Outlaw ducked his clumsy swipe and backed two paces. He sat facing him, his tail stump wagging sheepishly. He looked to Fields for direction and received none.

Fields requested a power launch, specifying one with maximum speed and range. He added to that demand a quantity of plastic explosives, automatic timers, blasting caps, and reserve fuel for the speedboat.

"Okay," Weems said. "They shouldn't be a problem. What else?"

Fields, knowing there were no witnesses to his last encounter with the pirates, requested bait bales to be loaded with explosive centers. At Weems's direction the girl retrieved the folder and made note of his needs on the inner side. Fields then added that he would need the shirt that Weems was wearing and a broad-brimmed straw hat.

"What about arms?" Weems inquired.

"I'd rather use my own," Fields answered evenly.

"Where are they? I want to know exactly what you'll be taking along." Weems took two strides forward.

Fields raised his glance to the approaching Weems. The silence stretched tautly; the girl fidgeted and recrossed her legs. Only after Weems had retreated back a step did Fields rise. He walked to the far bookcase, a thick-shelved affair, removed three concealed bolts, and tilted the case forward from below. Moving on a concealed swivel, the dark wood shelves and cloth-bound volumes remained secure at their upper juncture with the wall. From a hollow behind the shelving Fields removed a battered green wooden case nearly five feet in length and roughly eight inches in both height and width. He replaced the shelving, secured the bolts, and placed the box with pitted brass fittings upon the unoccupied sofa.

"That's all I'll need."

"Open it," Weems commanded imperiously.

Fields turned his back on him and walked to the stairway. The Outlaw followed him with a bounce, with only a brief glance backward. Fields mounted the stairs and climbed, ignoring Weems's protests.

Donald Weems strode to the sofa, snapped open the tarnished fittings, and tossed back the fitted lid. A gleaming blond stock and cold, blued gunmetal caressed the velvet interior of the box. Weems could not identify the make or caliber of the weapon, as it was free from visible markings. During his inexpert examination of the piece he discovered a hollow beneath the molded velvet surface. Lifting the box from the near edge, he located the two Giles Colt automatic pistols, each equipped with sculpted combat grips. Beside them he found boxed ammunition for each weapon. He returned the heavy weapons to their molded compartments and reclosed the box. He turned to Fanny.

"Listen, cupcake," he started. "I'm going up and telling him to stay here with you. You keep an eye on him. Keep him diverted if you can. You know what I mean." He winked salaciously at her upturned face. "I'm going to report in and get to work on rounding up this list. I should be back"—he turned to look for a wall clock, found none visible, and checked his wrist—"let's say in ten hours, by midnight or a little after. We can all leave from here. You keep an eye on him. Someone will be checking in by phone periodically. They'll ask to speak to you. Just answer their questions."

He gathered the folder together, placed it under his arm, and marched up the stairs. Fanny could hear the voices of the two men from the loft where Fields had been packing a small bag. While she couldn't make out the exact exchange she had no difficulty in separating Weems's controlled whine from Fields's bland replies. Weems marched back down the stairs and bent over the wooden arms container. "No sense in leaving this here. I'll just load it in the car now." He bent to lift the heavy mass of wood and metal.

"Do you believe him?" she asked in an urgent whisper.

"About what?"

"About, you know. About the Colonel wanting us to die?" Her fingers were twisting her left thumb.

"Oh, that," he answered with a sarcastic turn of mouth and eyes. "Of course not. He's trying to sow doubt in our minds. It's one of the oldest techniques in the world. Divide and conquer. Don't give it another thought." Weems marched out of the room, hunched forward over his burden, baby-stepping to keep his balance.

Fanny mounted the dark carpeting of the stairs. Once upstairs, she turned to her right into the spacious loft. The far wall was comprised of a large expanse of vaulted plate glass, affording a view directly into the upper boughs of a huge live oak. Its limbs were alive with animal and bird life, the branches draped with dry hangings of Spanish moss. Sunlight filtered through the leafy arbors and danced fairylike within the room. Fields was seated upon the far edge of a low-framed bed, packing clothing in a small duffel. The Outlaw was at the window, his head matching the movements of Mr. and Mrs. Cardinal, his nose imprinting the glass with damp reminders of its passage.

The girl moved to sit beside him, facing the darting light and feeding cardinals. "Do you mind if I get comfortable?" she asked, touching him lightly upon the shoulder.

"I don't seem to have much choice, do I?"

"It's so beautiful here." She stood and moved to join the Outlaw at the window. The dog took faint notice of her presence, his huge head following with intensity the actions of the creatures outside. As she stood framed against the uncurtained view, Fanny obeyed the instructions Weems had given her. She unfastened the clasp of her belt, letting it drop noiselessly to the carpeted floor. She then opened the two hooks that held the wisp of blue and green fabric in place, shrugged her shoulders, and allowed the dress to drop to the floor. Standing with her back to Fields, pale flesh interrupted only by the small island of lace bikinis, she seemed innocent and childlike. Fields stuffed a thick wool sweater into the top of the duffel and tossed the bag onto the floor. Fanny stood absorbed by the nearby antics of the unfearing birds.

Stirred against his will, Fields watched the bizarre tableau. Fanny hooked thumbs into each side of the insubstantial panties and slid them over her buttocks, past her thighs, and onto the floor. Retaining her heeled sandals, she stepped out of the garment right foot first, then left. Maintaining her poise, she dropped the feather-light fabric where it joined her dress.

Angered by the pulse roaring in his ears, Fields strode from the room and descended the stairway. The girl, hearing his movements, did not turn away from the view, nor did she leave the green place of peace for several moments thereafter. When she did join Dan Fields in the compact kitchen of his home, Fanny was redressed, her hair newly combed, her makeup perfected.

"I'm sorry that things have become so ugly," she volunteered.

Fields eyed her and gave no reply.

"It wasn't my idea to expose your daughter to danger," she added, wiping imaginary crumbs from the counter's surface. "Actually," she continued, "I had no idea any of this was going to happen."

Fields's skepticism and contempt were expressed in thickening silence.

"Please believe me," said Fanny. "I really had no choice in this. I see the way you're looking at me, but it's not my fault. I really had no choice."

He raised impenetrable blue-darkened eyes to hers. "We all have a choice, Fanny," he responded evenly. "There is always choice. You may have been threatened, but you've chosen, for whatever reason, to align your fortunes with those of some very evil men. You've chosen to threaten my life and the lives of two innocent people to further your own goals. You are party to kidnap, extortion, and will soon be up to your ears in murder. Those are the choices you've made, and you can't escape them with an 'I'm sorry' or some bullshit about no choice. No one's watching you right now, but you still choose to play the dramatic whore when you could be changing things.''

Fields wore a mask of control, as though he were a competent surgeon faced with massive but manageable trauma. For the briefest of moments the artist within the man canceled his disguise and showed the face of a desperate man. "Fanny, if you are sorry, this is the time to prove it. You can help me, you can help Donna and Marianne. All you have to do is tell me where—''

"But I can't!" She screamed it out and stood rigid, electrified.

He stood beside her, touched a hand to her arm. "Fanny, you don't have to do this. You don't . . .''

But Fanny, withdrawing deep within something soft and gray and vaguely comforting, wasn't listening. She stood rigidly, her face suddenly blank. In her secret, silent mind she watched herself being zapped into contorted, jangled spasms. She heard no words from Dan Fields.

The afternoon progressed. Twice the telephone rang; twice Fanny stirred herself as in a dream, answered; and twice she said to the caller that there were "No problems." Fields perceived no pattern to the calls.

They passed the evening in silence.

CHAPTER 13

THE meteorologists called it a tropical depression posing no hazard, a sea storm of no consequence. Fanny was too ill to give name to anything. For three nights and two days she lay immobilized by recurrent nausea, weakened by alternating fever and chill. Her rebellious stomach refused all solid nourishment, accepting, and then only conditionally, clear fluids. The youthful flesh surrounding her eyes had hollowed as if the gravitational pull on the sea were stronger than on land. Her perfect grooming had gone over the pitching side of *The Atlantic Maiden* with the storm. She was a nauseated hag, sour of breath and ugly. The sea was a coconspirator, reinforcing Burgess's conditioning. Mal de mer robbed her of poise, beat her to a mindless ganglion of abused nerve endings, and denuded her of the benefits of feminine art.

Chemically suspended between up and down, dull and acute, Captain Party John Maltessa fussed with his instrumentation. He ignored the real hazards they revealed and agonized over imagined catastrophe. He turned toward the coast in a looping circle, snugged *The Maiden* up against the protection of the coastal landmass, and began his charade of commercial shrimper. He slogged up the coast at fishing pace, drawing nearer to the waters controlled by Savannah Pink.

Party John was in pain, true pain. He jumped at each question from Weems, quick and eager to answer. But in growing measure, as the image of Benny Montrose faded, he answered Weems more and more with anger. Benny had stimulated the captain's cooperation with a pocket lighter, had pinned Maltessa to a bulkhead, and had held the butane flame to the captain's exposed nostrils. John had been a shrieking, wailing wreck until his mate, Ritchie Weaver, found him and tended to the burns. He'd smeared the man's charred nasal membranes with a jellied paste of his own herbs, all the while clucking and talking to the captain, cooing to him in the calypsoed rhythm of Gullah. Weaver, an intelligent man fenced into a narrow, racist world by the accident of his birth and language, had for the moment put aside his hatred for the white man. He'd held the captain and chirped in the melody of his tongue, soothing him until Maltessa had calmed and the herbs had worked their magic. Then, when Party John started making sounds like a rational human being again, Ritchie had pulled to his full height and said, "Where 'e put 'e toot now?" and laughed.

But Party John, a man who always numbered his options, was resourceful. Yes, Montrose had burned the membranes in his nose, but John could still create a vacuum with his lips, and so he coked up using a short straw. He plugged the end of the straw with coke, placed it into his mouth, held his lips around the cylinder, held his finger over the open end, drew a vacuum against the stoppered straw, then pulled off his blocking finger. The result, a "shotgun," blasted cocaine crystals onto the back of his throat. He pumped his shotgun through enough repetitions for the freeze to reach his lips and nose. Then, in further defiance, John added coke to his Jamaican marijuana, rolled a killer joint, and smoked it to an ember.

While Weaver returned to his nets Party John battered his senses with his pharmaceutical storehouse in a vain attempt to remove the fire-fingered pain from his nose. Weems, with his questions and commands, spurred Maltessa to increase the dosage and frequency.

Weems, keyed up and alert, also maintained a close watch on Fanny, ever vigilant for her recovery. His sexual interests had been obstructed, not by her will but by her odor and appearance. He had risen to Colonel Burgess's demand for brutality, had taken Fanny as often as he desired. While at the mansion Weems had amazed himself with his sexual performance. Never before a virile man, Weems discovered the aphrodisiac of power. With each subsequent taking, with each new rape of the girl, Donald Weems found himself enlarged and emboldened. He'd reached the point where he could command her to smile, to shout out cries of pleasure while he bruised her tissues. He'd shown a strength and tension in his stride and voice since receiving license to rape. To Maltessa he was forceful and demanding. Weaver he treated with disdain. And Fanny, until the storm attacked and she found safety in illness, sat in her cabin and waited for Weems to want more.

Weems had watched Fields at work in the hold as he placed explosive charges and blasting caps into watertight plastic envelopes, each of which he then inserted into the center of roughly rectangular bales of marijuana. When pressed by Weems for information about the devices and their ultimate use, Fields agreed to explain, but only if Weems volunteered to participate in the attack. With an oily grin Weems climbed the metal-runged ladder out of the iced hold and left Fields to his preparations.

Fields then began an inspection of each device and substance he had requested. His greatest concern was for the compact power launch that had been hoisted aboard and lashed to the decking. Once out to sea, Fields checked and double-checked the powerful twin Johnsons, deafening the ship's occupants with the unmuffled roar of the exposed outboards. When John's idea of good running weather set in, Fields assumed an exposed observation post at the rear of the winching gear. Clothed in yellow oilskins, he peered with unseeing eyes into the foreshortened grayness that was both day and night.

But the Outlaw found excitement and adventure in each separate area of the wallowing vessel. In his boundless enthusiasm the animal had punched Maltessa in the balls on two occasions, Weems three times, and had similarly destroyed Fields's silent composure. Fanny he did not so reward but trailed her shufflings with a concerned and wrinkled brow. Then, locating the perfect scent, the Outlaw crept in and deposited his substantial leavings at the foot of Weems's cramped bunk. In a remarkable display of canine craftiness he feigned total ignorance when confronted by a befouled and irate Weems. The dog made it a ritual. He struck at irregular periods but made sure to gift Weems at least once during each watch.

On the third evening the rocking ship entered the northward leg of the circuit that would guide them parallel to the coast. The grizzled captain anchored upon the offshore flats. The weather information escaping from the hiss and crackle of the airwaves told them the storm would pass in the early-morning darkness.

The cramped galley of the trawler combined an economical cooking area with a high-backed wooden booth. The small quarters gave access to stove, oven, refrigerator, and freezer. The evening meal of Maltessa–fried chicken and greasy potatoes went untouched by both Fanny and Fields. With the dropping wind she was recovered to the point of sitting at table and sipping weak tea. In truth Fanny's seasickness had run its course. In the absence of better weather she still would have shown the signs of recovery. The green pallor and waxy sheen had faded from her skin, her hair was pulled neatly back, and she had changed into a high-necked sweater. But her eyes, former objects of beauty, looked out through windows of fear.

Fields sat beside her in the stained and scarred booth. Facing them were Weems, bright points of light dancing on the irises of his eyes, and Maltessa, overfed and inhaling audibly from a rolled joint.

"All right, Mr. Hotshot," Weems began. "Tomorrow's the day, isn't it?"

Fields shifted his eyes to his left, focused upon Weems, but failed to reply.

"Look, hotshot," Weems intoned, his baritone booming in the confined quarters. "Nothing's changed. I've put up with your bullshit as long as I intend to. You're going to lay out an operational plan, and you're going to do it here and now—or else."

Fields took in the party at the table. Maltessa studied the imperfectly burning paper of his smoke while Fanny searched the contents of her empty cup. The Outlaw had obligations elsewhere.

"Or else?" Fields baited.

"Or else some very innocent people are going to lose their innocence tonight." Weems dug inside his shirt pocket. He flipped a poorly lit Polaroid photograph onto the Formica table-top. It was Donna Fields. She was sitting on the floor, in a corner. Her legs were tucked neatly beneath her and to the side. Her skirt was slightly askew, her blouse disheveled. Blood trickled down the left side of her face, beginning its course at her swollen and purpled mouth. Her face was a barely controlled mask of fear.

Fanny and Maltessa regarded the shot in silence.

Fields touched the horror with an index finger, then flipped it facedown upon the table.

"That," said Weems, jabbing a squat, white finger at the photograph, "is your fault, hotshot. You slapped me around, she got slapped around."

Fields was rock-still, his eyes hooded and smoky blue.

"Don't you get it yet?" demanded Weems. "Every time you throw your weight around, every time you drag your feet, every time you play the smart-ass, she and the girl get banged around, or worse." Weems's sallow skin looked yellow in the lamplight, and moisture covered his face.

"You've had that in your pocket how long?" Fields whispered, his lips barely moving.

"Since we left Hilton Head," Weems replied. "I've just been waiting for you to get out of line again." The illusion of power brought a glitter to his dark eyes, made his flesh the color of candlelight on tarnished brass. He checked his wrist timepiece and tugged at the top of his socks. "So, Mr. Hotshot," he continued, brushing hair from his damp forehead, "you shape up and shape up quick. Or else." Weems let the threat hang.

"Weems," Fields said, his voice cold in the warm, muggy air. "I'll make you an offer. You tell me where they are, give me enough information to get them safely out of this, and I'll let you live."

Party John stubbed out his smoke, keeping his eyes on the table. The girl stared, unhearing. Weems blinked and forced his constricted chest to draw in breath. His eyes met those of Fields and locked briefly. Fear twisted his bowels, and his pale hand trembled. "And if I don't?" he asked with mock bravado.

"Then you'll never touch land again."

Weems hesitated indecisively, then the moment passed. "I don't think so," he said, puffing confidence back into his lufting sails. "You know damn well that would mean death, a very unkind death, to both of them. Cut the party games, Fields," he ordered. "Let's hear your plans, with no more bullshit. Now. Or else."

Fields nodded with his jaw clamped, the mandibular muscles flexing. "In the morning," said Dan Fields, "we'll hoist the launch over the side." Weems started to protest, but Fields cut him short and continued. "Unless you're determined to commit suicide on this ship, I need to take the launch and bring the odds down. Doing that, you ass, requires speed and mobility.

But''—he fixed Weems with a glance—''if you want to accompany me, you can.'' Weems's silence answered him.

Fields turned to the red-rimmed eyes of the captain. ''John, you take *The Atlantic Maiden* up the coast, shrimping as you go. You're far enough south that while you'll probably be observed, you won't be boarded until you're closer to Savannah. The boats Pink and his friends use don't have the fuel range to come this far and be able to return. I'll scout them, stir them up a little and even the odds if I can, and probably meet you about midway between our present position and Savannah.

''Weems,'' Fields said, ''you and Fanny will play the part of shrimping deckhands. Before I set out in the morning, we'll show you what that entails. It's not difficult, especially with Ritchie to operate the winch and set the nets. We don't want to attract the attention of the Coast Guard, so our camouflage is important.''

''They've been taken care of.'' Weems was breezy in his confidence.

Fields nodded. ''You'll do it, anyhow—''

''Wait a minute,'' Weems interrupted. ''I told you the Coast Guard's been taken care of. I don't see why we have to masquerade with the shrimping routing.''

Fields exchanged a worried glance with the captain. ''At sea,'' Fields began patiently, ''you attract attention if you don't look normal. It's like that above and below the water. Any creature deviating from its normal pattern stands out from the rest and is quickly eaten. The same holds true for ships. Trawlers in this area are here to shrimp. If you aren't shrimping, you attract attention. It might be attention from a Coast Guard captain that you somehow missed, or it might be someone else.'' He fixed Weems with a thin-lipped stare. ''There are other pirates out here. Pink isn't the only opportunist on the water, or had you forgotten that?'' Weems's objection collapsed and Fields continued. ''The weather is clearing now,'' Fields said, ''and there'll be excellent visibility by morning. You'll be visible. Your efforts to duplicate shrimpers may prolong your lives.''

Fanny jerked her head up sharply. Prolong?

Fields continued speaking. ''By late afternoon, things should be resolved one way or another. If I don't return''—Fields was barely audible—''then Weems, here, can call in his backup forces.'' A thin smile played on his lips, but his eyes were lifeless. ''But if I do return, if it's possible to fill this contract, then, worm," Fields hissed, turned hard on Weems, "you're going to produce Donna and Marianne alive and well, and quickly. If you don't, then you belong to me. And you know damn well what that means, don't you?"

Weems stirred in the cramped booth, jostling Party John's shoulder. He put a plastic smile on his face. "That kind of talk," said Weems slickly, "just isn't necessary. This thing will go or it won't. If it does, Fields, then you'll have everything that was promised, we'll all be richer, and everyone can go their separate ways."

The rain stopped. The wind howled in protest at its abandonment and fled. *The Atlantic Maiden*, lit only by her red running lights, rocked in the dark night. Weems approached Fanny at the exposed stern of the ship. He stood close to her, placed his left arm over her shoulder, and slid his right hand under her shirtfront. His pulse quickened.

Not protesting, not responding, Fanny gazed out over the rail at the emerging pinpricks of light.

Annoyed at her lack of response, Weems grasped the nipple of her breast and twisted it viciously. She yelped and attempted to back away from him. His left arm slid from her shoulders, locking tightly against her head and crushing her to his chest. With his right hand Weems worked brutally on her breast. He muffled her cries with a hand clamped over her mouth. Suddenly her body relaxed, and Weems could elicit no further response. It was as if she had voluntarily shut off the impulses of pain and was no longer aware of his abuse.

"Why do you have to hurt me?" she inquired placidly.

"You bitches!" Weems burst forth. "You think that with your clothes and your education you exist somewhere above it all, don't you? Well, listen, cupcake"—he punctuated his words with a violent twist that brought tears to her eyes—"this is the real world. And the real world is like this!" Another twist. "I have the power, the real power, not some illusion from the pages of a magazine. Power is reality. And in this reality you do exactly what I want, you say what I tell you to say, and you enjoy what I want you to enjoy. You cry if I want you to cry, and you lay on your back and spread your legs if I want it. You, and your poise and charm, have nothing to say about it. Why do I have to hurt you?" he asked, and gave her reddened flesh another savage twist.

Because I want to, and you have nothing to say about it. That's why." Weems pulled aside her slicker and sweater and worked brusquely with both hands upon her exposed breasts. Fanny whimpered in the grip of his harsh fingers and the empty night air.

"Go to bed, Weems," said the voice of Dan Fields.

"Get out of here, hotshot!" came Weems's startled reply.

"Go to bed, Weems." The voice was soft in the night.

Weems dropped his hands from the girl's breasts and turned to face the sound. "Look, this is none of your business, Fields," Weems replied. "Fanny knows what she's into, and I didn't hear her ask for you or your help. Let it go. You have enough problems of your own to be thinking about."

Fanny stood mute and bare-breasted.

"Go to bed, Weems," Fields's voice said soothingly, with no hint of menace.

"Fuck you!" whipped Weems. He grabbed the docile girl and thrust his hand into the space between her corduroy trousers and flesh. "Tell him you like it, cupcake!" Weems urged with venom in her ear. "Tell him you really, really want it!" Again he used the brutality of his hands and fingers for emphatic punctuation.

"Please!" Fanny cried. "Leave him alone. I don't really mind."

Weems grabbed a fistful of pubic hair and pulled sharply.

She rose onto her tiptoes to ease the pain and cried out. "I like it! Please, stop! I like it!" And she began to cry the tears that so far had eluded her. Her body twisted in the direction of Weems's unrelenting pull, and sobs racked inside her breast. Weems searched the darkened deck behind them with frenzied, white-rimmed eyes. He could not see Fields anywhere, nor did he hear the man move.

"Fields? Are you still there? Fields?" He released the girl after a last probe of her parted labia and turned to face the open deck.

Released, Fanny sank to the concrete roughness of the trawler's deck, clutching her bruised breasts, pressing her trembling thighs together.

Weems sneered. "Hotshot got the message. Now, let's you and me go on into the bunks and get into some serious catching-up. You haven't been any fun at all for the last couple of days. It's my turn again," he said, "and tomorrow's a big day. I've got things in mind for you tonight you just won't believe." He grabbed Fanny above the elbow and pulled her to her feet. They neared the bulkhead behind the darkened winch.

Fields appeared before them, his lips pulled back, his teeth clenched. Cobralike, the stonecutter's hand darted forward and clamped with speed and force upon Weems's larynx. Fields flexed, pushed steeled fingers past the interference of Weems's tissues until his fingertips met.

Weems could not speak. Weems could not breathe. The fingers were cold metal bands bringing dark blue pain, bringing paralytic fear, bringing the promise of death.

Fields's grimace relaxed. The grip did not. "Go to bed, Weems," came the skittled sand of his voice.

Bug-eyed, Weems nodded. His vision was exploding with red light.

Fields dropped his arm. Weems bent in half and gagged. He woofed for breath, staggered down the walkway and into the ship's tiny sleeping quarters. His strangled gasps receded in the chill.

Her eyes were those of a rabid bat. She stared out like a terrified animal. Her body began to tremble, and then her knees refused to support her further. Fanny dropped, but Fields grabbed her and lifted her. He looked into the face of insanity.

He carried her to where the launch was lashed to the deck. Holding her upright, he pulled back the protective tarp, then lifted her limp form into the upholstered cockpit. He touched her and said, "I'll be right back," then turned and vanished. Then he was back, wrapping her in a stiff, woolen blanket. But the warmth of the blankets failed to soothe her. Rather, the kindness he had shown released some unguarded inner sanctum. Hot tears flowed down the contours of her face, and deep sobs shook her compact frame.

Fields joined her in the cockpit. He folded her body close to his own, folded her within his arms, wrapped the woolen blanket around them. Fanny, mindless, sightless, tunneled into his warmth. She raged. She poured out her fear against his warm shoulders, soaked through his shirt with tears of shame and violation.

He enfolded her with a gentle pressure, opened himself to her fear. Her shame gave way to anger. In sob-choked words she railed against the cruelty of men but took comfort from his embrace. She cursed a world where force gave brutal license to twisted men but found shelter in his strength. She spewed it out in mucus-clogged rush of hate and beat upon his unresisting chest with futile blows.

The *chop-slosh-chop* of the quickening tide rocked them in their embrace. Emptied, she slept. Fields sat wide-eyed and sleepless. He drifted through the dark tangle of his thoughts, seeking the clearheaded resolution his survival would demand in the morning sun. He tried to think but couldn't. He even tried to be angry, but anger, too, eluded him. He accepted instead the simple comfort of the passing Outlaw, inviting the stiff-haired animal into the cockpit with a pat. The big dog bounced in, turned, and burrowed into Fields's opposite side. The Outlaw sighed and slept.

Fields watched the constellations in their slowed-time swirl across the black sky. At the unwelcome pinking of dawn he slid out, leaving the tousled girl and the dog to each other.

The rising sun showed the sky to be hard blue, the sea a green murk. Gulls flapped in crisp strokes, and the ship's crew moved in stark efficiency. Party John and Dan Fields released the launch from its lashings, secured couplings to the hoist, and brought the racket of the gasoline winch to angry life. They raised the small boat from the deck, lowered it to the sea, then tethered it from the trawler's stern. Weems observed these actions, expectancy bright in his sun-squinted face while the Outlaw patrolled the perimeter with rapid, light-footed paces. A dark tonneau covered the bow of the launch, extended over the passenger's compartment, and left a small bit of room at the controls.

Using a language of grunts and waves, Ritchie and Party John rigged *The Atlantic Maiden* for fishing. Her diesels throbbed deep and rich. The captain, juggling joint, beer, and coke bottle and shotgun straw, guided the ship onto the flats. He revved the engines to fishing speed on the twin tachometers, set the autopilot, and scanned his instrumentation. He scurried crablike to the rear deck. He and the Gullah mate released the broad, funnel-shaped nets from their ties and swung the massive booms outward to either side of the ship. The winch barked to life. Ritchie dropped the nets into the murk of the sea. The rusted and scoured old lady began her stiff-legged deep-water walk.

Following the contour of the muddy flat, Party John nosed the trawler northward in a narcotized haze. After less than an hour the nets were creating sufficient drag to warrant examination. Leaving the vessel on autopilot, he joined the others on the rear deck. The teeming life within the nets was winched on board. The working birds screamed in frustrated greed.

Party John reached up, tugged a slipknot on the port-side net. The mass divided, fell to the deck, and separated into recogniz able forms. Shrimp were present in flicking abundance. Blu crabs scuttled defensively, claws upraised and clicking. Flounde arched their contorted spines. Shark, small hammerheads an larger gray nurse, lay tangled in the netting. Globs of brightl colored jellyfish quivered in the increasing heat. From the othe side Ritchie dumped the second net, which rose eighteen inche above the deck and measured more than twelve feet across Ritchie winched the nets back to fishing position, and Party Joh executed a brief correction of course and engine speed.

Weems balked at manual labor. He refused to join in an charade that required him to handle the haul from the nets. H eyed the mass of shark and shellfish, shrimp and man o' war, an would not go near. Instead, mindful of instructions to keep the gir off-balance, he volunteered Fanny's services. Once on deck an blinking in the sun, she showed a certain enthusiasm for cullin the shrimp from the tangle of bottom life. She hid her form in pair of baggy slacks and a shirt borrowed from Party John, took cap from Weaver, and reported to the Gullah mate for duty. Sh and the mate were able to communicate without assistance, a fea due to Ritchie Weaver's cooperation. If he didn't want *Buckra* t understand, *Buckra* did not understand. But if he felt like i Weaver could make himself perfectly understood. Fields and th captain, after watching Weaver demonstrate to Fanny the way o grabbing a spine-tailed ray and tossing it overboard without bein badly stung, climbed to the iced hold.

They sat on a straw-covered bench, deep in the chill o ice-covered shrimp. The two men had not been alone since Field had boarded the trawler.

"I—I didn't want to do this," said Party John, looking straigh ahead and not at Fields. "I wasn't ever going to bother yo again."

Fields, aware of John's nose injury, nodded. "Who was it? No Weems?"

"No, not Weems. I'm afraid of everything else in the god damned world but not him. It was some muscle freak." He flippe a hand at the deck above. "They know him. He's a jerk, a menta case."

"Where is he?"

"Fuck if I know." The dark man sighed. "He's got a hot speedboat, one of those cigarette jobs. He left me and hopped into that thing and took off just before you and the rest of them came on board." John worked his pockets. He dipped a straw, pulled a vacuum against the coke, then shotgunned the back of his throat with chopped cocaine. "He didn't say a goddamned word, Dan. He got me from behind, didn't make a sound coming on board, but the whole time he had me, he never said a word. He watched me, watched my face, watched me scream, but he never said a single word. Not that he had to, goddammit! You hold a fucking cigarette lighter to a man's nose while you pin his arms and you don't have to say anything. I got the message loud and clear."

Dan Fields fixed his gaze to a frozen avalanche of chopped ice. He said, "Did you know you were a legend, John?"

Maltessa cocked his head to the side. "What?"

"With the agency, with most of the Coast Guard too."

John drew a chest-inflating breath. "I never did anything big enough to be a legend."

"Sure you did," countered Fields. "You were never caught. Not by us, at least. Everywhere our men went, they heard about Party John. The case agents had the Atlanta office walls papered with sketches they'd had informants and artists patch together of your face. Some of them even looked like you. But not much."

The captain grinned, shotgunned his throat. "They never asked you to—"

"You were too small a fish."

"But the others, you could have—"

"I never spoke your name, John. I wasn't asked to and had no reason to target you. Besides, I was busy."

"Shit, tell me about it!" Party John laughed. "Now you're talking about the kind of stuff for making legends."

Fields grinned but wagged his head. "That's why I want to talk to you, John."

"About legends?"

"No. About reality, our reality."

Maltessa peeked at Fields from the corner of his eye. "Look. Whatever you're going to say, I don't need to be scared more than I already am."

Fields turned, arched a brow. "You do want to live, don't you?"

"Yes. What the fuck kind of question is that?"

Fields turned away. After a long, chilled pause he spoke. "I don't think you should be counting on me. You can't."

The captain was very still. "I can't?"

Again Fields wagged his head. "This is a bitch, John, from the start. Whoever is heading up this craziness is very smart: He shoves Weems at us, Fanny, and now this muscle man, but he stays out of range. He hands us throwaway talent like them, as if to say they're expendable. I can break Weems like a dry twig, but what does it get us? Nothing. This Savannah Pink. You should have seen the dossier they've put together on him. He's a sharp man, brutal and intelligent, with enough ships and men to have his own shallow-water navy." He dusted at his thighs. "When I take the launch, I'm going to talk to Pink."

"No! Goddamn, he—"

"Lower your voice."

John rubbed his hand over his hairline, down over his eye, brushed his nose, and jumped. He squinted his eyes and said in a whisper, "What the fuck for? He'll eat you for lunch!"

Fields agreed with a nod. "He might. But I read the file they put together on him. Between the lines I see an intelligent man, a leader. And no one holds onto leadership long without the ability to reason—not on a ship, not in the street. Pink won't be any different. All I have to do is show him how cooperating with me today can save his skin."

Party John was stunned. "That's all?"

Fields ignored him. "If I can get his cooperation, I'll rig some fireworks on the water for Weems and this backup man of theirs to gawk at."

"Fireworks?" Party John whispered the question but filled it with skepticism.

Fields shrugged. "A few of Pink's boats. He's damn near commanding his own squadron."

"You expect Pink to help you blow up his own boats?"

Fields caught the stiffened posture, turned, and grinned. Above the grin he wore the eyes of a very sad man. "A few boats are a small price for staying alive."

"He's gonna eat you for lunch." It was a pronouncement, and Maltessa delivered it with conviction.

"If I enlist Pink's help—"

"Jesus Christ!"

"—then when I get within range of *The Maiden*, I want you to keep Weems from getting too close a look at what's going on. I want him to be impressed with the bright lights and the big bangs but not close enough to look for bodies. As soon as I'm back, I'll press him for Donna and Marianne. He'll use some code if they're alive. If they're not, he'll try to kill me when the pretty explosions are over. Either way, when he moves, you'll know what to do.''

John waved a loose-fingered hand back and forth. "No problem. It's against my religion to get close to violence, anyhow." He leaned forward, poked Fields on the knee with a pointed finger. "What I want to know is what to do if you don't get Pink to blow up his own ships? What do you expect me to do if I look out there"—he waved a hairy arm at the sea beyond the hull—"and see you with a bunch of sonofabitching pirates on your ass? Because if you're expecting me to stop to pick up a passenger while they're loading up the motherfucking rocket launchers, I ain't saying I promise to do it.''

Dan Fields turned and faced him. "If you so much as smell one pirate ship, you're going to run like hell."

John thought, bobbed his head. "Yeah."

Fields turned away, slouched back into the cold straw. "Good idea."

"Huh? You think I should run?"

Fields inhaled, let the breath out. "They're going to let me use the launch. After enforced isolation, no freedom of movement, they're going to let me cast off in a fast boat with extra fuel tanks and let me go wherever the hell I want. Does that tell you anything, John?''

"Uh, they think you can do better if you're fast and mobile?"

"Hmmm, in part. But it tells me, John, that they don't care if I bolt and run to the police. They don't care if Weems and Fanny are arrested. Or killed. Up until I saw that Weems was going to give permission to use the fast boat, I was holding on to hope. But now I don't have much. Not for Donna and Marianne, and next to none for us.''

"But—but wait a minute. You've got that hot little boat, more explosives than I feel safe carrying, all those guns. . . .''

"John, you don't understand. What I did for you before, rigging a bale and placing a shot to detonate it, that was something I could do, something I knew would work. But Pink and his people are not sitting ducks. They shoot back and they're carrying automatic weapons, Uzies, Ingrams, and military rocket launchers. Whoever backs Weems and company knows this, John. He's sending me out to get killed and hoping I'll eliminate some of his other problems before I die."

"But in the agency you were a combat shooter, I heard—"

"John. I haven't fired a pistol since I retired. I'm forty-three years old. I practice with stone now, not firearms."

Party John listened. He shotgunned his throat with a double-loaded straw. "Why are you telling me this?" he asked.

"Because I have to leave," said Dan. "If I'm going to hit Pink's territory early, before his people start to sweep the channel, I have to leave now."

"So?"

"So this bodybuilder will be somewhere on my tail. If he's smart, he'll be camped out watching Pink's people or their boats. He won't be watching you."

"I still don't understand. What are you saying?"

Fields stood, stretched. "It means don't wait for me, John. If I don't catch up to you by the last inlet to the Savannah River, keep going."

Fields was climbing to the deck, Party John following. The captain said, "You give one hell of a pep talk."

On the slimy deck the primeval shape of a second ray twitched in the glistening mounds of shell, scale, and flesh. The animal was fourteen inches long, more than two feet from wingtip to wingtip, and whipped a barbed tail eight inches in length. Under Weaver's eye Fanny pinioned the creature with a rake and grasped the ray with thumb and forefinger, placing each in the eye sockets. She threw the fish into the sea and smiled.

In short minutes Fanny's deftness at the task of culling became apparent. She intuitively came to understand the unspoken kinship that exists between all persons who can and do function well upon the sea. The sun rose higher, grew hotter.

Satisfied with the performance of the "crew," Fields prepared for his departure. The power launch was checked and rechecked. The course that Party John would follow was reaffirmed.

As Fields descended the rope ladder to the launch, Fanny touched his hand briefly, hesitatingly. Their eyes met, locked, and mated. Then he was over the side, and the powerful twin outboards rumbled to angry life. Fanny stood square-shouldered and erect, watching as the small boat breasted the swells and grew smaller in the distance. She waved at the diminishing speck that was Fields. The Outlaw yelped in angry frustration at her side. She reassured the animal with a pat on its rib cage and returned to her duties. Weems eyed her with glowering hatred.

When the retreating speck was no longer visible, Weems rose from his low perch and walked purposefully toward the girl. Sensing his approach, she stood abruptly and faced him. The short-handled culling rake was clutched tightly in her small, white-knuckled hand.

He stopped, beyond reach. "That's okay for now, cupcake, but this job is coming to an end, and you're going to pay for last night. And I don't think it's a payment you can afford to make."

She gave no reply.

Dan Fields, alone with his thoughts upon the glare of the sea, pushed the craft to its optimum speed. The returning tide made the powerful boat broad-jump from crest to crest.

The deaths of the first pirate crew members had affected Fields badly. Like an addict reverting to his drug after a long abstinence, he had loathed himself and his lapse. He had pulled his consignment pieces of sculpture from public display, hid them in his own rooms while he questioned the worth, the right to exist, of each. His art had been at fundamental odds with his actions, and seeing the size of his error, the artist in the man had to have the pieces back, had to see if they were as deeply flawed.

Clamping his jaw muscles against the slamming jar of the speeding boat, he acknowledged animal fear. Fields understood that paralyzing fear existed deep within the soul of all men and women. He knew that it was a powerful emotion, that it could consume its host at any moment. It could lie dormant for a lifetime, or it could emerge and make each torturous second feel like eternity. The path a man chose, the importance he gave to the emotion of fear, was a personal choice. Fields chose. In the choosing, he did not deny what he was feeling but found a way to brake its velocity. Strengthened and resolved, Fields directed the craft toward Savannah.

At the common docks of Savannah, Fields refueled the launch. He nosed the small boat into a slip in a crowded marina. Fields secured his craft, pocketed the key, and hesitated. His weapons were aboard, but he'd be moving through several blocks of public streets and then into Pink's territory. He tried to imagine himself in Pink's shoes and realized that the presence of weapons would lead to hostility and suspicion. Unarmed, a tanned and ambling tourist, Dan Fields left the dock.

He'd memorized the material in the file. If the intelligence was correct and current, Pink frequented a tavern in the very worst section of Savannah, near the docks but several streets toward the old town center. He strolled in that direction, hands in his pockets, and reviewed his arguments, searching for the one correct phrase to assure Pink of his safety while yet gaining the man's cooperation. He was at the heavily armed and alarmed door, and no great phrase had been found.

The bartender, a graying stick of a man, eyed the slender white man standing in the shadowed coolness of the bar. The white man, dressed in clothes that failed to place him in any definite category, was not one of the white addicts who periodically entered the tavern. Nor did he stand with the footsore posture of a police officer. And he did not have the look or feel of a misdirected tourist. The white man returned his stare. After diligently wiping a nonexistent spot of liquid from the scarred wooden surface, the old man approached. "You lost, whitey?" He continued to rub phantom drops.

"No. I'm not lost," came the soft reply. "I'm here to see Pink."

"Oh, yeah?" the stick man laughed, showing gold. "Does he know you're comin'?" he asked, and laughed again.

"No," Fields replied, and again his voice was mild and pleasant. They were close friends enjoying an intimate joke. "But," said Fields through the laughter they shared, "he'll break your balls if you don't fetch him, and pretty soon too." Fields's eyes twinkled.

The bartender stopped laughing. The other patrons, three men and a huge woman, turned their faces away and were silent. The old man hesitated a few beats, then lifted the bar phone from its cradle and dialed. He spoke into the mouthpiece and hung up. He said, "Now we gonna see who gets their balls broke." He grinned goldly.

"I guess we will," Fields said, laughing back. "Give me a beer while I wait." He flipped a bill on the bar. The bartender moved with practiced grace, placed a long-necked bottle on the bar, and pocketed the bill. He offered no change.

Fields walked down the bar, passed a row of too small tables, reached for a discarded sports page, then sat with his back to the wall. He sipped and read.

"This better be good, white meat!" A voice growled from above him.

Fields lowered the crinkled paper, and his pulse escalated as adrenaline spurted into his veins. Before him, hands balled into ham-sized fists, stood a sleek and burnished Savannah Pink. Dressed in tight double-knit slacks, an open tropical shirt, rose-tinted shades, and a broad-brimmed white hat, the man towered above him. His legs were shortened telephone poles, his arms python-thick.

"What? Oh, yes. It is good," replied Fields, blinking rapidly, his hands toying with the bottle. "Mr. Pink? Should I call you that?" Fields asked, a jittery trace of laughter betraying his instant fear of the man.

"Don't matter what you call me, white meat," the monster uttered, pulling an obviously too small chair into position. "What the fuck you want with me?" Pink asked suddenly, hatred flaring in his maroon eyes. Pink looked deep into the hard blue eyes, eyes exactly the same color and intensity of his own father's.

Dan Fields sat before him, alone and unarmed. He said, "I've brought you a proposition."

Pink stared and waited.

Fields continued. "You may find this difficult to believe, but—"

"I find you sittin' here hard to believe," Pink said, and smiled. It was the most malevolent smile Fields had ever seen.

Fields nodded his head in wonder, breath escaping from his nose. "I'm sure you do." He nodded again. "But what I have to say is important to both of us, and time is critical." Then the words tumbled out of him. "One of the drug rings you and your men have been plundering has contracted for every last one of you, ships included, to be eliminated."

Pink's eyebrows moved a quarter acre up his forehead in surprise.

Fields went on. "They've had the profit cut out of their operation," he said, "and they decided you and your men have got to go. Just the start of their contract cost you a boat and crew not too long ago."

Pink leaned forward, his elbows taking up the entire table surface.

"What I propose," Fields jabbered, "is that you save yourself and your men. I can arrange that, if you act quickly and position your boats in a certain way so that I can destroy them without witnesses and without danger to you or your men."

Pink frowned. Two acres of facial flesh moved downward.

"Otherwise," Fields continued, his eyes blinking and his hands turning the tall bottle, "otherwise you and all of your men and all of your boats will be destroyed." A new element added a stripe to Dan Fields's growing band of fear. There was something new going on, something the combat veteran had not experienced. Face-to-face, close enough to smell each other's bodies, personal combat always differed from a firefight. But even still, this confrontation sizzled with a new flavor. At once it struck him. Race! He was reacting to the racial difference in his opponent, fearing the unknown, equating the foreign appearance of the man with evil. Recognizing the irrational pattern of his thoughts, Fields imposed his will, narrowed the focus of his control. He'd lectured to young agents about this very phenomenon, that of being mentally intimidated by an opponent, and he recalled his own words to look at the man's hands, always at the man's hands.

Savannah Pink squinted his maroon eyes to tiny red slits. Then he tilted back his basketball head, threw open his mouth, and laughed. He wiped the smile and laughter from his broad face with a meaty hand. "Tell me somethin', white meat. Why should I do this for you? Who the fuck are you that I should let you blow up my boats?" He spread his two fanlike hands in an inquisitive shrug.

"Well," Fields replied, the weak smile twitching at its far ends, "since I'm the one who took out the last crew, I thought you might understand." He clamped his jaw tightly to stifle a growing facial tremor and rotated the dark bottle in jittery fingers.

Savannah Pink's massive face shifted slowly, melting to a smoking, malevolent glower. Pink shot his catcher's-mitt hands forward across the table, aiming for Fields's neck and shoulders.

Fields had focused on Pink's hands. He dodged them and, with staccato jabs, struck him with the narrow end of the bottle, successive thrusts that drove deep into the flesh behind Pink's left ear, into the left carotid artery, into his larynx. He completed the series by trying to drive the neck of the bottle into and past the man's cavernous nostrils.

Pink, stunned and falling to his right, locked his sausagelike fingers around Fields's shirt.

Sensing the oncoming grasp, Fields jumped up, pushed off with the balls of his feet, and moved to the man's left. In a scream-filled blur he streaked out of the bar at sprinting speed, tearing away from the stunned monster and leaving his shirt in the angry beast's grasp. Pausing in his pumping strides only long enough to topple over every chair and stool that he passed, the bare-chested Fields stretched out into the driving pace of a very scared man. He was out of the bar, completed an angular one-hundred-eighty-degree turn, and was racing flat out down the littered alley on the tavern's left. Running in panicked, zigzagged haste, Fields ignored the shouts and clamor behind him, pushing his knees up high, driving his legs and lungs to maximum performance.

The adrenaline-charged fear, speed, and endurance created by the confrontation were genuine. Shouts, car doors slamming, wheels squealing, and slapping feet pursued him in earnest. The four blocks from the tavern to the common dock area passed him in a surrealistic nightmare of motion and noise. Reaching the tied launch, Fields gasped, tried to slow his breathing while he released the line. The key turned in the ignition, and the powerful outboards coughed to life. With no regard for his wake, Dan shot out into the channel, then idled down. Within heart-thudding seconds Pink, accompanied by three wide-eyed blacks, was exiting from a lurching Eldorado. Fields waited until Pink's hooded, maroon eyes focused upon him, then he waved to the angry giant and pushed the throttles full forward. Fields cleared the dock area before Pink and his companions could board their docked boats.

Leaning into the rhythmic, bone-jarring crunch of the launch, Fields flipped through the marine CB channels and was soon rewarded with the excited voices of at least two separate boat captains—blacks by the sound of their dialect and obviously under extreme pressure to find him. He pointed the compass southward and relaxed. Large, deep breaths left his open lips, the muscles in his tanned face relaxed, and a full-lipped grin appeared. He had accomplished his first goal. Pink and his men would be on the alert and on the sea. And they would be actively searching for Dan Fields and the small launch with the distinctive dark tonneau cover.

Fields stripped away the dark tonneau he'd used to cover his unusual cargo. He pulled on Weems's brightly colored print shirt, a flimsy straw hat, and wraparound dark glasses.

Dan Fields opened the throttles to their maximum and leaned into the arrhythmic impact of the veed hull on the gray swells. The afternoon sun spread a shadowless glare upon the sea, obscuring the distant shoreline. The streamlined craft fell into stride with the crests of blue-gray foam; lunging, crashing down upon the hard surface, spitting spray and fumes in its wake. He adjusted his course slightly, aiming for the Savannah shipping lanes. He monitored the crackle of the marine CB, alert for the cryptic, guttural mouthings of his quarry. Gauging himself short of their range by some minutes, he softened the focus of his eyes, slowed his respiration rate, and shrugged the tension from his tightened shoulders. The crash and jar of the small boat's banging thrust grew faint.

Fields lashed the wheel with nylon tethers and moved to the items concealed beneath a dark, thick-grained tarpaulin. He withdrew the battered green weapons box. Flipping back the pitted hinges with a deliberately slow hand, he opened the scarred lid. He removed the gleaming Weatherby, checked its action, and stowed the rifle beneath the boat's dash. Next Fields lifted the well-worn velvet shelf and extracted the two large Giles Colts. He examined the magazine of each, assuring himself that each was fully loaded with seven rounds of .45-caliber projectiles. They were tipped with soft lead, the nose of each filed into tiny crosses. The combination of caliber, powder load, and filing created a projectile that left the muzzle of the automatic at a little less than eight hundred feet per second, mushrooming within several yards to an irregularly shaped, flattened disc that quickly reached the size of a large coin. The shells were simple and devastating. Upon impact with human tissue they did not merely penetrate; they removed a jagged swath of flesh and bone that was followed by a mind-numbing shock wave. Pinpoint accuracy with the pistols was not a requirement. All that was needed to disable an opponent totally was to strike him at any point on his body. The projectile would do the rest.

Fields placed each pistol upon the seat cushions and laid a flotation vest upon them. He then placed two extra magazines, each containing seven shells similarly prepared, into his large shirt pocket. The activity left him in a state of unfocused relaxation. Continuing to monitor his course and the crackle-laden radio, he grew introspective. He avoided concentrating on the

specifics of the forthcoming conflict, for his combat plan was
solidly formulated where possible. The rest would be improvised
in the field. Fields knew too well that his martial skills had
atrophied in the last years as his physical edge had blurred and
then softened. The cumulative effects of inactivity and too many
violent injuries were something he could not change. He avoided
too frank an examination of his waning abilities.

In strange parallel to his physical limitations, he was plagued
with emotional weaknesses as well. Negative emotions flooded
him momentarily. The possibility—no the probability—of the
deaths of his child and former wife stood out starkly in his mind.
Fields had known this from the first indication of their status as
hostages but had forced himself to act out of the forlorn hope that
they would emerge in some way unharmed. He toyed with the
leverage that those two lives exerted over his own actions. He
questioned himself, inquiring as to what leverage his ex-wife
possessed, independent of the child. Would he have permitted his
involvement in this bizarre counter-criminal extermination on her
behalf alone? Without the child's involvement, would he have
simply informed the authorities and allowed them to use their
unwieldy methods to either extricate her or confirm her death? He
was unable to answer.

His was a life of debt and obligation to friends. For him,
friendship required loyalty proportionate to the strength of the
bond. Where did she rank in the ordering of his priorities? Again
he was unable to respond. With the passage of time the wounds of
their separation and divorce had healed over with emotional scar
tissue that both protected against additional injury and simultaneously prevented full repair. His trips to the remembered shrine of
their marriage had grown more and more infrequent, his thoughts
of her less and less kind. Absence had failed to make the heart
grow fonder, had, in fact, made him view her with less emotion of
any sort. He could imagine the justifiable rage with which she
would view this violent intrusion of his life into her insulated
world.

Fields looked at his own death. It was a less stressful fantasy. In
truth, he had faced that probability on far too many occasions in
the past. On this day, when it was most likely finally to occur, he
was not overly concerned. He knew that in the throes of combat,
fear would grip him and then would pass and leave him essentially
unchanged. Similarly, if death should take him this time, he was

also prepared. He was ready for nonexistence, a mindless, dreamless sleep that possessed neither fear nor pain. And he was prepared for an afterlife, if he found one. He smiled at the prospect of confronting "God." Fields wondered if he would falter at that moment and meekly ask for forgiveness or if he would retain his sense of outrage and present the deity with his current list of grievances. God might be as inept and venal a manager as the DEA administrators had been. Or perhaps, he mused, God would be a kind and understanding old fellow who really had little control over the passage of human events.

Fields laughed out loud at himself and his fanciful thoughts. Death would come. Or it would not. Donna and Marianne would be unharmed. Or they would not. He accepted the turn of the greasy playing card, the roll of the weighted dice. It was not his game, not his table. But there would come a time when it would be his game and his table. When that time arrived, there would be hell to pay.

Fields began a slow crisscross of the Savannah shipping lanes. He passed quickly by the larger trawlers fishing the channels, waved to a quartet of bikini-clad teenagers as they awkwardly maneuvered Daddy's refurbished ketch. He slid into dangerous waters with decreased throttles. The radio squawked a multitude of conversations both commercial and conversational but gave no sign of Pink or his men. On his third sweep of the primary lane Fields spied a solid cabin cruiser with two blacks on the flying bridge, and silhouettes of two others on the deck. He throttled down to stalling speed and scanned the distant craft through his binoculars.

It was a large craft, better than thirty-four feet, with a wide beam. Dark wisps of oil-laden smoke rose from the boat's wake, attesting to its lack of maintenance. The men below were stripped to shorts or bathing suits; the men on the flying bridge wore dark caps. Fields saw no fishing gear and no sign of women. He was startled to find that one of the men on the lower deck had him in reciprocal focus through a pair of wide-angled binoculars. Fields waved at the man slowly, his arm describing a lazy arc, and throttled the launch forward toward the cruiser. He read the lettering on the stern through his lenses: *The Piranha*. It was one of several boats described in the Colonel's dossier on Savannah Pink.

His launch was a different color, since he'd peeled off the salt

arp, and his own appearance not at all consistent with the one
he'd shown in Pink's domain, Fields dropped his glasses and
wheeled the launch toward the bobbing cruiser. As the distance
shortened, he was able to distinguish more clearly the men on
board. The black at the controls of the flying bridge was in dark
shorts and a yellow shirt, his hair flecked with patches of dingy
gray and his mustache drooped downward to his chin. He wore a
pair of tinted glasses, and a neglected cigarette dangled from his
full lips. His stomach extended over the waistband of his shorts.
He issued instructions to the others, and the cigarette jiggled ash
onto his waiting abdomen. Tucked into the waistband of the man's
shorts was a large automatic pistol.

Fields pegged him as the crew leader and marked him for a
strategically early dispatch. Beside the pilot on the flying bridge
stood a tall, slender black man in his late twenties sporting a
charter captain's hat, a gold wristwatch, and a chunky gold neck
chain. He wore a faded green pair of swimming trunks and
displayed no weapon.

On the deck below them, two alert and athletic blacks stood in
the stern, the sun glistening from their faces. The taller of the two
casually cradled an ugly automatic rifle in his knotted arms. Fields
thought it to be the Colt AR-15 but was not certain. The tall man
became his first target. The shorter man beside him was stocky
and thick-limbed, wearing denim cutoffs and a sweat-stained
shoulder holster snugging a small revolver. Fields guided the
launch toward the cruiser, positioning the twin Colts within inches
of his grasp.

Two uncovered bales were now openly displayed in the rear of
his launch. Dressed in the garish printed shirt, wide-brimmed
tourist's hat, and wraparound glasses, Dan Fields eased the small
boat to within a few rocking yards of *The Piranha*'s rear deck.
Fields smiled and hailed the craft. "Hey, there! Can I ask you
fellows to call the Coast Guard for me? My CB is on the fritz, and
I found a couple of bales of pot floating out there in the channel."

The mustached pilot on the flying bridge stared down at Fields
with startled incredulity. The dumb-ass tourist had not noticed the
open display of arms and was actually asking them to summon the
authorities. He smiled a flash of gold at the tall, slender man
beside him and rumbled down to Fields, "That won't be necessary, Cap'n. We'll take them bales from you right now and save
you the trouble. Police reports and all will take up the rest of your

vacation, for sure." He called down to the taller of the two men
on the deck of *The Piranha*. "Hey! Snake! Help that cap'n tie up
to us and get those bales on board."

Snake shifted the AR-15 to the crook of his muscled left arm
and beckoned with his right hand for a tossed line.

Fields nursed the throttle controls, keeping his craft astern and
roughly perpendicular to *The Piranha*. "Hey!" he shouted in
irritation. "You didn't understand me. This is pot! I mean, it
looks like marijuana! You know? Drugs! They were just floating
out in the channel in broad daylight. I need to turn them over to
the Coast Guard!" Fields the tourist waved at the bales with his
left arm and yelled, "Don't you understand? These things were
probably dropped off by smugglers." His voice vibrated with a
tone of wonder and excitement.

The captain of *The Piranha* looked down at Fields again, all
pretense of civility gone from his barking voice. "Listen, turkey.
Throw a line over to Snake, there, and be smart about it. *Now!*"

Fields stared up at the captain, his expression bleak, shading his
face with a flattened palm. He tugged the broad-brimmed hat
down farther onto his brow. He spoke quietly, abandoning the
touristy, nasal honk and using his own softly modulated voice.
"Captain, I don't think so. I think I'll take the bales into port
myself and contact the Coast Guard when I get there." Fields sat
motionless at the control panel, dropping his arms loosely to his
sides.

The captain hissed, "Take him, Snake." The tall, muscular
black rotated the short snout of the AR-15 a few degrees toward
Fields. Snake's right hand reached for the trigger guard, an evil
curl transforming his face into a savage snarl.

Dan Fields stood fully erect in the cockpit of the launch, each
hand holding one of the huge Colt automatics. He fully extended
both arms in front of him, hands curled around the molded grips,
thumbs locked securely down, forearms parallel and directed
toward Snake, and pulled each trigger. The impact, accompanied
by a deeply resonant roar, drove the man and his weapon brutally
backward and over the cruiser's rail in a red profusion of plasma
and tissue. Squinting into the sudden recoil, Fields brought them
both down again, forearms locked rigid, veins bulging, and
turned his aim into the flying bridge.

The mustached captain recovered quickly, drawing across his
pendulous abdomen with his right hand to pull the large-caliber

automatic pistol from his waistband. Simultaneously the man in the hat beside him reached down and raised a pump shotgun.

Fields shifted his aim, separated the muzzles of the heavy Colts, and fired again. The shotgun-wielding black was struck in the right shoulder, the flattened lead projectile obliterating the full shoulder joint and a substantial portion of his upper arm. The second projectile, milliseconds behind the first and striking with the mushrooming surface area of a tumbling silver dollar, impacted squarely upon his left elbow. The limb below vanished.

The rapid series of explosions literally deafened Fields, but he could see the open mouth of the captain shouting in rage and the automatic pistol leveled in his direction. He fired both pistols again, snapping the shots off as he forced the recoiling automatics down upon the captain. The drooped mustache was suddenly gone. The small Plexiglas windscreen of Fields's launch shattered. A series of zipping shells cut jagged patterns in the planking before him. The last pirate, a fist-sized snub-nosed revolver extended dueling fashion, was firing rapidly.

Throwing himself to the left, Fields fired once more with the Colt in his right hand. The dumdum struck the pirate in the thigh. His leg shattered, and the man tottered briefly. He shut his eyes tightly, as if to deny the next round and the vision of his own death. Fields sighted and fired. The man died.

Fields exhaled for the first time since the combat began and blinked several times. He dropped the Colts to the cushions and pressed his palms against his ringing ears. The two boats rocked in rhythm to the gentle chop, and the afternoon sun shone brightly. He turned in the cockpit and surveyed his surroundings. No other craft was in sight, and while he was certain that the gunshots would carry for miles across the warm waters, he knew from experience that it was impossible to determine the direction and origin of such sounds while at sea.

Suppressing a mounting tremor that threatened to consume him if unleashed, Fields forced himself to test the operation of the launch's controls. Finding no functional damage, he implemented the second phase of the attack. As he worked, the ringing in his bruised ears diminished and again he could hear the throb of the powerful Johnson engines, the thunk and slosh of water, and, in the distance, the scream of a hungry gull.

He picked up the tourist's wide-brimmed hat and moved to the rear of the launch. Selecting one of the electronically timed explosive packets, he set the dial for fifteen minutes and flipped the device onto the rear deck of *The Piranha*. Staring into the sun, he throttled the small launch forward while locking the wheel hard over. Clearing the bow of *The Piranha*, he opened the throttles and motored out one hundred yards from the boat. Throttling back to neutral, Fields moved gingerly to the rear of the small boat and quickly tipped the two explosive-rigged bales over the side. Fields opened the throttles of the Johnsons and skittered across the mild chop.

When the flying bridge of *The Piranha* was a barely visible speck upon his horizon, Fields killed the engines, placed the well-maintained gray binoculars on the cushions beside him, and reloaded the clips in the Colt automatics. While doing so, he flicked through the CB channels, searching for other members of Pink's organization. Noting a garbled, yet distinctly hostile, black voice, Fields paused in his manipulation of the dial. They were angrily trying to raise the captain of *The Piranha*.

From the stern of *The Piranha* a bright orange flash obscured the horizon, followed by a roiling black cloud that swallowed the original fireball. The sound, traveling at lesser speed, arrived in a booming roar and echoed on the water. Fields turned the binoculars to the mushrooming darkness and saw the bow of *The Piranha* jutting at a crazed angle from the blue-gray chop. The rising plume of blackest smoke rose high into the cloudless sky. An exchange of inquiries upon the CB informed Fields that the second pirate craft was powering up to investigate, with Pink responding from a more distant point.

In minutes, Fields spied a quick-moving vessel, sleeker and more powerful than the sinking *Piranha*, churning directly to the flames. The course of the vessel brought the first of the bales into its path, and the pilot slowed his craft. Combining the use of binoculars and the CB, Fields was able to both witness and comprehend as the craft slowed, pulled the closest of the bales on board, and proceeded toward *The Piranha*'s debris. From the CB, Pink's voice urged them to verify *The Piranha*'s wreckage.

Presenting the smallest possible height above the horizon Fields peered over the low sides of the launch and observed as a second vessel, *The Black Widow*, also circled the wreckage. Fields counted five blacks on board and had no difficulty in spotting their weaponry, a variety of rifles, and shortened automatic weapons. A member of *The Black Widow*'s crew then used the CB. Pink responded in a harsh growl above the static that he would arrive in three minutes. Fields gunned the launch into an angry burble, spun the wheel hard over, and opened the throttle controls. The craft leapt over the low chop and sped toward the blackened debris and the circling *Black Widow* and the second smaller boat.

Barely audible above the roar of the straining outboards, Fields heard the pilot of *The Black Widow* over the CB as he informed Pink of the launch's approach. Pink's prompt response, "Burn the honkie and burn him now!" left Fields with clammy flesh and a racing pulse. The sharp crack of rifle detonations from *The Black Widow* followed close behind the command, and he whipped the launch into an irregular zigzag.

Projectiles from the concentrated fire of *The Black Widow* were whipping like angry hornets into the gray waters, their trajectories bracketing Fields and the launch in an ever-tightening space. Fields pulled back the twin throttles, dropping the launch into the rough of its own wake. He flinched as one of the men from *The Black Widow* found his range. Splinters of flying wood erupted around Dan's clenched shoulders. A hail of staccato rounds tore through his small craft, chewing chunks of wood from the decking. Fields wasted no time, regretting the lost moments and the approach of Savannah Pink. He snapped the Weatherby to his shoulder, wound his left arm through the webbed strap, sighted through the scope, aligned the cross hairs on the center of the bale in the stern of *The Black Widow*, inhaled slowly, exhaled half of the breath, and evenly squeezed the striated trigger.

First he saw a white flash, then heard a sharp crack, followed by a muted, water-softened explosion below the waterline. The craft paused indecisively. Then the boat bucked violently as her fuel tanks erupted in an ear-ringing explosion, hurling shredded debris hundreds of feet skyward. The force of the explosion was transmitted through the seawater and was instantly followed by a blinding yellow-orange fireball. It hovered directly over the nearby second craft and savagely consumed the boat and all aboard in a fire storm that formed a vacuum as oxygen was pulled quickly inward to feed the growing, greedy flame. The heat from the fire burned Fields's lungs and stung his eyes, and then was no longer there. Every stick of wood, every ounce of fuel had been consumed in that urgent, brief moment. A dark, dense cloud of acrid smoke billowed lazily, and the scent of charred flesh pervaded the afternoon air. *The Black Widow,* her sister craft, and all aboard were gone.

Fighting back a desire to retch, Fields pushed the throttle forward, felt a chill rise along his spine as the engines responded sluggishly, and directed a course for the coast. He turned up the volume on the set, switched through several channels, but was unable to raise any sound from the CB. The pockmarked and splintered deck of the launch gave silent testimony to the cause of the malfunction. He pushed the throttles to a position where the engines ran with the least amount of hesitation. The high-pitched drone of tuned exhausts drew his attention rearward. He was relieved to spot a small, sleek craft occupied by a solitary young white man. The youthful pilot had a bodybuilder's physique and flowing blond hair.

The sleek craft pulled abreast of Fields, and the man flipped Fields the finger from an upraised, muscled arm, then roared off, leaving a frothy wake.

Burning the man's face into his memory, Fields steered the crippled boat toward land to the shelter of the Inland Waterway, part of a well-traveled body of navigable water that wanders between the shelter of marshy islands and coastal landmasses. It is an alternative to travel on the open sea, affording protection from severe storms and other deep-water hazards. Fields sought its shelter for other reasons. His craft was no longer performing properly, and he intended to locate a similar boat and borrow it. Among the numerous private docks and small marinas lining the Waterway he would find a suitable replacement. He sighted the channel marker to the Inland Waterway. At the same moment he felt the presence of his pursuers.

Fields turned to scan the unbroken horizon behind him and saw no other craft. He lifted the worn binoculars and scanned from left to right. His first complete arc revealed no cause for fear, but the sensation was irrationally persistent. He repeated the arc. A flock of distant seabirds attracted his attention. He fixed them with the glasses. The speck was a thin needle of a boat moving with such speed that a plume of agitated water followed its passage like a bantam rooster's tail. Fields whipped the throttles full forward and slammed the reluctant launch into the Waterway. The small boat labored, the engines thrusting unequally, forcing Fields to fight the small wheel. As Fields's launch thundered through the narrow, twisting passages of fertile marshlands, aquatic fowl took to the air in alarm, pinpointing his progress for those who pursued.

Pink, accompanied by his three personal guards, crashed onto the Waterway. Their boat was built for speed alone and was filled to capacity with the four men aboard. Their weight kept the hull of the craft down upon the water despite the full thrust of the engines as they strained above the red-lined limits of the tachometer. Behind the wheel was the monstrous Pink in a sleeveless green tank top and overstretched dark slacks. He hunched his hamlike shoulders over the tiny wheel and oversteered his turns.

Seated beside him was Birdman, a tall, sinewy black who cradled the ugly snout of an Israeli Uzi automatic rifle in his long-fingered hands. A light smile played upon his lips. He disdained the use of his arms to maintain his balance but rode the careening boat with the skill of a practiced cyclist. Behind Pink sat Yorkie, a man of medium height but considerable stockiness, who refused to carry firearms; he preferred the more personal use of a short blade honed to a razor-sharp edge. A thin fringe of beard marked his chin, barely visible against ebony skin.

Behind Birdman rode a middle-aged man with mottled skin that blended dark patches of umber with strawberry swaths of violent birthmarks. The contrast was most marked upon his broad face where one side was dark brown, the other pale red. He had briefly played pro football, later wrestled to no distinction, and finally located his niche in life as an arm-breaker for Pink. He was tall, heavy, brutal, and went by the name of Lester.

Fields's faltering launch popped into Pink's view as they rounded a sharp turn. Birdman reacted, raised the shortened barrel of the Uzi to his chest and squeezed off a burst of cartridges. The water behind Fields erupted in a tight line of minor fountains, and then the shells cut across the stern of the boat. Fields clamped down on his jaw and spun the wheel right-left-right while trying desperately to become a smaller person. But Pink oversteered the turn, and the automatic weapon's fire was pulled away, off the launch. Birdman continued to smile, lowered the weapon to his lap, and waited patiently for his target to reappear.

Fields, in contrast, screamed frantic curses at the stuttering engines. He held the wheel in a white-knuckled grasp and steered a tight, erratic course, praying for any kind of a break. At no point had he seen an opportunity in the landscape to facilitate his escape. He cut close to the mud banks of the channel and throttled back to hold tight to the turn as he rounded one of the last fingerlike peninsulas between him and the Savannah quay. Rounding the sliver of reedy land, he throttled back sharply, cut the wheel over, and narrowly avoided ramming a small sailboat. Its sail lufting in mid-tack, its captain stared wide-eyed and open-mouthed at the onrushing craft. Fields pushed off against the polished hull of the day sailer and rammed the throttles full forward. The launch responded with a surprising lurch, the miss in her engines smoothed, and the boat jetted forward.

The vacationer at the helm of the sailboat yelled over his shoulder and tried to bring his boom over. As the sail filled, Savannah Pink and his men roared around the small peninsula and bore down upon him. Sighting the hurtling speedboat and its complement of armed, grim-faced blacks, the vacationing sailor, an accountant from New Jersey, whispered, "Mother of God!" and jumped over the side.

Pink saw the oncoming sailboat and watched in contempt as the honkie captain leapt spread-eagle over the stern. He cut the wheel of the speeder sharply to the left. His boat careened past the bow of the sailboat, shot across the width of the narrow channel, and grounded itself with a crunch on the mud of the opposite bank. With gruff commands and one hard slap, Pink had the two rear passengers out of the craft in water up to their thighs. They pulled and tugged the speeder back to the shallow channel. In brief moments the sloped hull was free of the mud and suction, and Pink had once again rammed his throttle home.

Fields clamped down tighter on his jaw and threaded into a channel that would lead him into the Savannah common docks and the public marina. The straightaway was nearly three quarters of a mile long and afforded no shelter. Miraculously the battered launch sped even faster, the bow lifting out of the gray-brown channel waters. At full speed he shot past the channel marker that ordered *No Wake* and aimed his boat at the marina. The dopplered howl of a powerful speedboat stung his ears, and the frantic zip of bullets cut across his path. Crouching low within the bullet-ripped launch, Fields waited until the last moment, then wheeled acutely to the left and fishtailed the small boat up against a low-railed pleasure boat moored at the foremost berth.

He grabbed the twinned pistols and scrambled onto the low deck of the empty cabin cruiser, pushing his abandoned launch out to bob in its own wake. His passage across the empty boat was greeted by a short burst from the auto rifle in Birdman's confident grasp. Again, the zip and zing of the hornetlike projectiles squeezed a jolt of adrenaline into his racing bloodstream, and Fields dashed down the floating pier, varying his course, avoiding a rhythm.

Scant seconds behind Fields, Savannah Pink whipped his custom craft against the dock a few yards in front of the drifting, pockmarked launch. Birdman and Yorkie scrambled off and pursued Fields down the pier while Pink and the blotch-faced Lester on board lurched into a tight circle and began a slow, questing loop around the marina.

Running on legs trembling with a surplus of adrenaline-charged energy, Fields reached the main dock. He placed a battered working boat between himself and the steady advance of his two assailants. Birdman, the smile grown wide upon his face, stalked purposely down the weathered gray planking, his Uzi held at the ready. Yorkie, a respectful five yards behind, walked catlike, his bunched thighs absorbing the rise and fall of the floating dock.

As Birdman and Yorkie reached the juncture of the main pier and its first floating appendage, they widened the distance between them. Observing their silent hand signals, Fields immediately understood. Yorkie would spot and flush the quarry, followed by Birdman's swift response with the automatic rifle. As if to confirm his correct analysis of the situation, Birdman halted his progress and assumed a point from which he could clearly view Yorkie's progress and a major portion of the intersecting floating piers.

Fields moved in a tight crouch, keeping his profile below the intervening vessels. Creeping around a wide-beamed sportfishing boat, Fields noted an eight-foot gaff with a barbed point resting within the craft. He laid his Giles Colts on the grayed oak planking and silently lifted the gaff out of its hooks and onto the dock before him.

Birdman stood some fifty yards distant, obscured by several large pleasure crafts rocking in their moorings. Yorkie, his knife blade held in the grip of the professional cutter, thumb and forefinger curled around and concealing three quarters of the blade, hand held close against his hip, advanced toward the fishing boat.

Twice in the preceding moments Fields could have taken Yorkie with the Colts but would have drawn return fire from the man with the Israeli auto rifle. While nearly vacant, the marina's quiet was occasionally broken by the activity of scattered boatmen. Fields watched in increased anxiety as a family of tourists ambled down the pier, approaching Birdman. They failed to notice the weaponry in his relaxed grasp, their unsuspecting eyes devoted to admiring the gently rocking civilian navy. There had been no sign of Pink or the fourth black, but Fields knew they were engaged in the same deadly game of hide and seek.

Yorkie rounded the fishing craft's bow. Beads of perspiration framed his forehead, and the veins in his temples bulged and pulsed visibly. He saw Fields crouching and facing away from his approach, the Colts lying at his feet. Yorkie advanced eagerly, his right arm and the gleaming tip of the blade weaving snakelike in advance.

Fields felt the floating pier rise and fall with the man's approach. He wheeled one hundred and eighty degrees, simultaneously thrusting with the barbed gaff.

Yorkie's teeth were clenched in anticipation of the easy kill, his eyes fevered with predatory excitement and confidence when his forward progress was abruptly halted and then reversed as the barbed shaft penetrated his left breast and emerged below his left shoulder blade.

With the same follow-through he put behind his sculptor's hammer, Fields lifted the spitted man from the dock and drove the emerging barb deep into the wooden bulkhead of the adjacent fishing boat.

Plunged into the depths of trauma shock, Yorkie fluttered feebly against the shaft of the gaff. His glazing eyes met those of Dan Fields, felt their North Atlantic chill, and wept. The blade in the man's grasp flipped convulsively to the dock as he filled his frothy lungs with humid air to call for help.

Fields stepped in close and delivered a backhanded, knife-edged blow to his larynx.

Voicebox and windpipe crushed, Yorkie sagged down against the eight-foot shaft. He mouthed "Mama" on soundless lips and died.

Fields bent down and snared the bulky pistols. Peering over the stern of the fishing boat as it listed a full ten degrees under the dead man's weight, Fields was unable to locate the other armed man. He fought the onset of panic and began his search for an escape vehicle. On an adjacent finger of floating pier he spied a large inboard sportfisher that appeared to be very fleet but failed to provide him with cover in the cockpit. Under the circumstances Fields accepted the vehicle despite its inadequacies. Keeping low and duck-walking, Fields began to move. Birdman was no longer in view, and the family of tourists was now approaching Fields's own position.

The family consisted of a husband and wife in their early thirties and three children ranging from a chunky toddler to a boy seven or eight years old. Daddy was leading his brood, describing the functions of the various craft, speaking aloud his fantasy of boat ownership. The children were enthralled. Daddy's sour-faced wife was working on a severe case of sunburn and was painfully bored.

Fields stood erect and held the large automatics at his sides. He turned and walked. Daddy nodded as they passed, oblivious to the weapons gripped tightly in Fields's hands. He smiled thinly. People saw only what they expected to see. He was making steady progress toward his escape when the oldest of the children behind him called out in a clarion soprano, "Daddy, why is that man carrying cowboy guns?"

Dan Fields neither turned nor paused. He walked at a normal pace, willing his step to remain casual, but his eyes darted, searching for Birdman.

"Don't be silly, Mark," a baritone voice responded. "You have such a strong imagination. Here, look at this boat. It's a working boat, the kind that—"

"George!" the wife screamed. "Guns! That man's carrying guns!"

With the perfect balance of a fencing master Birdman landed on the dock, his feet shoulder-width apart. His leap from the obstructed stern of a small, neglected yacht thirty feet to the rear of Fields placed the tourists directly between him and Fields.

Eyes bright above a carnivorous leer, Birdman timed his leap for maximum advantage. From his elevated position on board the yacht he'd seen Lester's approach and had used hand signals to notify him of Fields's position. Then he had covered himself with the approaching tourists. Fields was now between Birdman and the still concealed Lester, with the tourists obstructing Fields's major line of fire.

Fields heard the thud and felt the impact of the man's landing on the dock and correctly interpreted the abrupt silence of the tourist family. He wheeled.

Sandwiched between the two armed combatants, the tourist father gaped in frozen paralysis. His wife, powered by the strongest of instincts, hurtled her stock body down upon the nearest two children, taking her husband in a rolling crackback block. The toddler watched in gleeful fascination.

Fields turned, whipped the huge Colts in parallel movements, halted their progress just above the tumbling mass of flailing bodies, and fired the pistols in unison. Birdman, the sight of his auto rifle just brought to bear on Fields, was struck in mid-chest and slammed several paces backward. The jolt of fist-sized, flattened lead projectiles not only tore gaping wounds in his thorax but also caused his trigger finger to squeeze in reflex. A spray of small-caliber cartridges ripped through the dock, reaching to within inches of the standing child.

Fields fought down the recoil of the .45s, but a second barrage was not needed. Birdman's burst ended, the auto rifle's recoil ripping the weapon from his dead hand. A smiling death mask grinned from above his gory chest. Dan exhaled noisily through his nose, eyes narrowed to blue-gray slits, and checked the tourists for injuries. Finding none, he took a half turn toward the open boat he'd selected for his escape moments earlier. Crunching hammerlike blows stunned his forearms as the ghoul-faced Lester struck downward with a massively muscled arm.

The Colts clattered to the dock, and Fields's numbed hands and arms hung useless and stunned. The black-and-strawberry-faced man leapt forward, turned, then locked an iron-hard bicep and forearm around Fields's head and twisted him into a low stoop. Fields's vision blurred and doubled in the wrestler's headlock. He heard the crunch and grinding of cartilage in his rushing ears. Fields's face was trapped against his rocklike torso. The man's stench was overpowering.

Sensing his consciousness fading with each tortured second, Fields fought the temptation to yield to the soft, comforting world of nonexistence. He screamed against the smell and taste, forced his jaws open, and sank his teeth deep into the rancid flesh of the man's side. Simultaneously he stepped behind the wrestler's legs. With an oxygen-starved effort he threw both arms straight up against the full weight of his assailant. Caught off-balance, Lester was tripped by Fields's legs from behind, forced backward from above by the thrust of Fields's arms. Struggling instinctively against the loss of balance, Lester released his viselike grip around Fields's head and neck.

Fields pushed as he would against a stubborn quarry stone, continuing to drive Lester up and back while grabbing each of the man's thighs and spreading them out in a wishbone formation. Gulping air, Fields raced headlong at a pier piling, carrying the spread-eagle Lester before him, and rammed the vee of the man's crotch into the thick piling. The black's breath whistled out at the impact. Fields dropped the retching man to the dock, pulled him four feet forward away from the piling, and rolled him to his stomach. With winter lighting in his gray-blue eyes Fields pounced, wedged his right knee in the middle of Lester's spine, reached under his thick neck with a right forearm, inhaled sharply, and jerked up and back. A moist pop emanated from Lester's neck, and the man's body went slack. Resting his knee on the corpse's back, Fields stole two short breaths; suddenly, he was assailed by an odious smell. The man's sphincter had relaxed with his death, adding one more horrific aspect to his passage.

The tourist wife clustered her children into a manageable mass and herded them from the carnage while her husband, a competent man in normal circumstances, stood slack-jawed and uncomprehending. Fields averted his face. Bunching his trembling legs beneath him, he turned to search for his pistols and spied them ten feet distant. He also spied the huge form of Savannah Pink stalking him softly on small feet. Fields gauged the distance to the pistols in that instant, locked eyes with Pink, and darted down the main pier, abandoning his weaponry.

Pink snapped off two rounds from a double-action automatic pistol. The first round struck the body upon which Fields had knelt; the second pulled high and right.

Fields streaked down the dock with every ounce of adrenaline-charged strength he possessed, weaving like a Sunday afternoon halfback, varying his stride, and avoiding any pattern. The retorts from Pink's handgun echoed sharply across the water, the slugs spitting uneven splinters behind Fields's pumping feet. He stretched out and found his stride, praying for his injured knees to hold, breathing noisily, arms swinging forcefully. A pause in the shooting tempted him to chance a rearward glance, but his curiosity was promptly answered as a lower, louder boom exploded behind him. A Chris-Craft several feet in front and to his left imploded, and Fields knew that Pink had retrieved the Colts and was using them. His forty-three-year-old body ran even faster.

At the end of the central pier stood two marine fuel pumps. Pulled into the fueling dock was a brightly painted, air-conditioned pleasure cruiser of solid proportions. She was named *The Banker's Holiday* in bold blue lettering and was occupied by a paunchy gray-haired man in middle age and a bony, hawk-faced woman of equal years with hair the color of cheap red wine. The couple had been awkwardly attempting to moor the boat for refueling when the first shots had broken the humid laziness of the late afternoon. With engines at the idle and the hawk-faced woman holding the forward line, they had unthinkingly assumed spectator status, craning to observe while maintaining their safety and lack of involvement. To their horror they were treated to an unexpected front-row view as Dan Fields sprinted toward them, pursued by Savannah Pink.

"Cast off!" commanded Fields to the bony woman as he neared her at full speed. She remained immobile. He passed her and broke stride to leap on board. "I said cast off!" he bellowed again from the carpeted rear deck.

Pink paused in his rushing shuffle, raised one of the Colts, and fired. The too close boom lifted the woman inches from the planking as a fist-sized hole was torn away from the gas pump's metal casing. She threw the heavy line onto the boat deck and clutched her thin arms around her middle, scowling over a sharply beaked nose. The woman's husband, fat jiggling around his pale belly and on his hairless thighs, danced indecisively from the wheel to the rear deck, abortively attempting to form words of protest.

With a glance at the lumbering approach of Pink, Fields took two steps, interrupted the banker in his dance, and opened the inboard diesel throttle. The heavy-bottomed craft responded slowly and lagged. Fields brought the custom-crafted wheel hard over, away from the dock.

The Banker's Holiday paused in indecisive imitation of her owner, then edged slowly away from the fueling dock. Savannah Pink growled in animal frustration and galloped down the weathered boards, firing from alternating hands with the unfamiliar Colts. Explosions ripped the clear blue quiet of the afternoon. Irregular portions of *The Banker's Holiday*'s bulkhead shattered and were torn away leaving jagged holes and showering the interior of the wheelhouse with flying pieces of custom-tinted glass. Fields lay upon the carpeted deck, again trying to be a very small person.

The cruiser's diesels wailed to a full-throttled roar, and the broad-beamed motor yacht gained momentum. She labored through the tight turn, exposing her stern to Savannah Pink not more than fifteen yards distant. The enraged black stood full square upon the grayed oak planking and alternated rounds from each ham-sized fist, spacing and placing his shots with purposeful concentration. The instrumentation in the gleaming teak dash panel was torn, broken, and reduced to an unrecognizable mass of ruptured components and sparking wires of red, black, and green. The flabby banker lay curled against the stern gunwale, his eyes clenched tightly against noise and danger.

Pink raised the Colt in his right hand and fired. The magazine was empty. He quickly raised the weapon in his left and discharged a final round that impacted within inches of the ship's wheel, gouging an elliptical hole into the electric maw of the wounded vessel. Fields dared a glance from behind his teakwood shelter, straightened the wheel, and steered the wallowing yacht out of the harbor.

Pink dropped the Colts in disgust and pulled his double-action automatic, sighted down the short barrel, but declined the shot. He turned and sped back down the complaining dockway, intent on retrieving his swift craft.

Fields rose shakily in the debris-strewn wheelhouse, noted Pink's heavy-footed retreat, and silently thanked the fates. The ringing in his ears diminished to an angry buzz, and he could hear the impassioned screeching of the hawk-faced woman on the dock.

"Stanley!" she screamed, "Get back here, *now*!" Her pitch rose another octave. "Stanley! Do you hear me? You get that boat back here right now! Stanley!" Her harsh vocal chords, aided by years of practice and an unaccustomed charge of fear, stretched her husband's name to an improbable three syllables.

Stanley, suddenly vulnerable in his scant gray trunks and rolls of flab, stared at the destruction of his favorite toy. With sad brown eyes he faced Dan Fields. The banker looked at the once beautiful wheelhouse and shrugged his shoulders in wordless desolation.

"She was beautiful," said Fields, sharing the man's loss.

"Yes, she was," he replied, his voice hushed by the devastation of such craftmanship and artistry. The yacht, her rudder straightened, gained speed steadily. Fields spoke again. "He'll be coming after me."

"I understand," the banker replied. With a saddened smile he surveyed the profane destruction of his prize. He grabbed a flotation vest from a belted fishing chair and strapped it to his round-shouldered torso. Fields cut the throttles, and the banker, a man who lived by his ability to cut his losses and run, slipped over the side. Without complaint or a rearward glance he began a steady breaststroke toward the dock. The woman's shrill voice floated over the marina waters. "Stanley! He's taking our boat! Stanley! Stanley!"

Her screeching receded as Fields opened the throttles, a kind smile below his cold blue eyes. He felt open admiration for the wisdom of the slowly swimming man. Fields scanned the marina docks but failed to locate Pink or his sleek powerboat. He viewed the remnants of the motor yacht's instrumentation. The weather was clear according to the barometer, and the temperature was a solid eighty-six degrees, but all other information regarding the yacht and its mechanical condition had been obliterated by Fields's own abandoned pistols.

With frequent rearward glances he began a systematic search of the wheelhouse cabinetry and then extended his rapid examination to the rear-deck bench compartments. While he was able to locate one serviceable fishing knife, he failed to secure any type of firearm. Fields lashed the wheel to a course east by northeast, again scanned his wake and the receding marina, and carried his search below decks.

He used the activity of the search to fight the threatening surge and pull of fear. He knew the frenzied questings of his mind wouldn't aid his struggle but instead would lengthen his response time. Furthermore, unspent adrenaline coursing through his system would create additional fatigue in his nerve-tightened muscles. Counting the possible reasons for Pink's failure to appear in his wake wouldn't assist him. Fields knew he was in the strategically limited position of the hunted. He could run and could improvise in response to the actions of the hunter. He could do no more. He searched futilely among the domestic possessions of the banker and his wife, hunting for what he would not find, chasing the phantoms of his fears with the meaningless actions of his hands.

Savannah Pink rumbled down the worn oak planking and rounded the turn to the floating pier where his low-riding powerboat was moored. Sighting his boat and cursing Fields's luck, Pink slowed to a casual walk and tucked the automatic pistol in his waistband.

A tall, gangly police officer in a perspiration-stained blue uniform stood in animated conversation with a grizzled boatman. The officer, a blond wearing reflective sunglasses, placed a calming hand on the shoulder of the gesturing man and stepped off in the direction of Pink. The officer's hand darted immediately down to the polished black holster at his side, releasing the catch with the edge of his palm and withdrawing his revolver in a well-practiced, fluid movement. Pink, his reaction ingrained by years of survival on ghetto streets, walked casually toward the officer, hands held open, palms forward at shoulder height. He smiled. "Hey, Officer," he began, his tone subservient, his smile ingratiating. "There was all kind of shootin' goin' on up there," he said, pointing toward the main pier while his steady gait brought him closer to the poised officer.

"Just halt right where you are," the officer ordered, leveling his pistol at the huge black man's middle.

"Yessir, yessir, Officer," Pink replied, palms showing, "but you better git up t'other end of the dock. There's two men up there been shootin' up the place."

"I'm going to check you out first, son," the officer replied curtly. He was at least ten years Pink's junior. "Assume the position," he ordered. "I'm sure you know it." His voice of authority cracked at the edges. The man facing him was a human mountain whose smile and easy, shuckin' manner did little to dispel the intimidation caused by his immense physical size.

Savannah Pink shrugged two or three acres of shoulders in amused resignation, shuffled to the bulkhead of a moored cabin cruiser, and leaned forward with his arms outstretched.

"Feet farther back. Let's go, Buck, you know the drill," the voice behind the mirrored eyes ordered.

Pink, who as a boy had been "Buck" to his rawboned, malevolent father, complied, sliding his narrow feet back and out, taking his weight on widespread palms. He said, "Officer, you know I ain't done nothin'. I'm just a workingman. I work every day. I don't make no trouble.''

''You just keep 'em spread and keep your mouth shut, Buck,'' the officer commanded, his voice gaining in confidence now that the giant was off-balance. The officer held his revolver leveled at Pink but tucked it back against his right hip. Assuming a fencing position, the young officer glided in toward the man, his left hand extended. As he touched Pink at the rear of his neck the giant pushed effortlessly off with his fingertips and pivoted, his long arms rotating. His right hand spun the officer's outstretched, empty hand and smacked it aside. His left hand completed its arc and grabbed the officer's right hand and revolver, clamping down painfully.

The officer tried to pull the trigger, but Pink's grip had locked the revolver's chambers and prevented rotation and discharge. With a resounding crack Pink struck the officer with his open right palm, knocking his cap and glasses to the dock. The outsize left hand then effortlessly twisted the service revolver from the officer's grip, and Pink flipped it contemptuously into the marina waters. Pink lifted the horrified and helpless man from the dock by his bunched collar and held the pale face inches from his own. ''White-meat motherfucker!'' he growled. ''My name ain't Buck, and you're one dead piece of white meat. Give my regards to the white man's God, piglet!'' His voice had been a deep rumble in the officer's consciousness, the warning prior to a major earthquake. Then, much as a hunting dog will shake vermin, Pink shook the officer, then drove his plate-sized fist into the officer's horrified face. The young man was driven forcefully to the dock where he lay motionless. Pink administered a vicious kick to the officer's temple, then turned from the unconscious officer and walked with studied nonchalance down the dock. A gaping old boatman fled.

The discordant wail of ululating sirens alerted Pink to the advent of assisting officers. He gunned his speedboat and throttled off parallel to the docks, skirting in and around moored vessels. Fields might gain a few minutes from his evasive action, but Pink would not waste time seeking unnecessary confrontation with an angered police force. Individually they were harmless flies, but they could overwhelm an adversary with their combined numbers and technology. Mindful of that swarming advantage, Pink wove a random pattern among the docks and piers, working ever gradually toward the open channel.

The arriving officers, weapons drawn and voices tightened with emotion, scurried in defensive crouches from body to body and from witness to witness, attempting to administer emergency aid, preserve the numerous crime scenes for forensic analysis, and discover an intelligible chronology of events.

Pink left the marina at a sedate pace, attracting nothing more than an errant glance. Once clear of the dock area, he opened the throttles to the powerful engines, his streamlined craft lifting her bow well out of the water and shooting a plume of spray into the trough of her wake. Fields and the motor yacht were not in view. Pink began a wide, sweeping pattern, moving farther out to sea with each successive sweep.

Dan Fields had completed his exhaustive search of the yacht's finely appointed compartments without locating a rifle or other firearm. Grim-faced, eyes narrowed to slits, he returned to the shattered wheelhouse and tried to coerce more speed from the deep, booming diesels. His ministrations failed, however, and the wide-bottomed craft maintained its stately rate of progress.

He had dissipated the surplus adrenaline from his limbs with his futile exertions. The absence of pursuit heartened him, and he began to entertain the hope that he could safely elude the raw, physical terror that was Savannah Pink. Given the opportunity, Fields would avoid that one man for life. But faced with the current realities, he vowed to waste no more of his energies in face-to-face combat with the man. Next time—if there was a next time—he would kill him at long distance, very long distance.

Scanning his wake and the horizon behind, Fields found no sign of his adversary. The minutes passed with creeping slowness. His breathing patterns mimicked the drone of the diesels and the steady rise and fall of the boat as she broke over the stronger chop of the outer channel. Fields adjusted his course a few more points to the north and allowed himself the forced luxury of sitting in the padded leather contours of the pilot's chair.

The afternoon sky was a brittle bright blue, and the silhouettes of working shrimp trawlers were grayly visible. Selecting the one silhouette most closely resembling the size and configuration of *The Atlantic Maiden*, Fields focused his glasses. Running at a course oblique to his own, it was *The Atlantic Maiden*. Her nets were fishing the flats, and he could see tiny figures on the rear deck. He adjusted his course, calculating a point of intersection, and turned the glasses to his wake. A sprayed plume of foam rising from the sea followed close behind a glint of light upon the water. The boat was at the far range of visibility of his glasses, but her course and speed left little room for doubt. It was Pink, and he was coming at full throttle.

Fields closed his eyes. He focused internally upon the pattern of his breathing and the sound of air flowing in and out of his nasal passages. He envisioned the three vessels, their courses, and their speeds. He plotted their vectors and permitted himself one small hope. It would be very close. If the three craft maintained current speed and direction, he might possibly reach *The Atlantic Maiden* prior to Pink's arrival. He shuddered at the ease with which he was able to delude himself. Any mental device was preferable to the thought of death at the hands of Savannah Pink. It was no marvel that Pink was such an absolute success in his trade. The man was a primal terror, a merciless, soulless killer who brought death after prolonged indignity and pain. With some reluctance Fields opened his eyes and again played the glasses first upon *The Atlantic Maiden* and then upon the steadily gaining light boat with its trailing plume of gray.

The slamming rock and splash of the flattened hull upon the white-crested waves beat a steady, rapid rhythm into Pink's mind. Each beat reinforced his hatred for the white man who had devastated his organization and murdered his men. The jarring physical impact was a driving drum of war that raised his pulse to an animal fury. He screamed above the roar of the engines, his hatred overflowing his capacity for words. This man, with his father's hated eyes, would die slowly, begging for his death long before it came. *The Banker's Holiday* grew larger in his sight, and the drumbeat grew louder, more maniacal. Savannah Pink bellowed into the salty water that sprayed across the slashing bow.

Fields calculated again and saw that the speedboat would overtake him prior to his rendezvous with *The Atlantic Maiden*. Fields was able to distinguish Party John at the rail adjacent to the pilothouse. Aft of him, along the rail, he saw Weems and Fanny. Party John was hopping up and down, waving frantically, pointing to the rooster's tail of water plume that trailed Pink's knifelike craft. Fields responded with a one-handed wave and turned to gauge the time remaining before Pink's intersection. As he rotated in the chair the diesels coughed, hesitated, and then resumed their throb. Fields silently cursed the obliterated instrumentation and the destroyed fuel gauge. To the rear, Pink slowed his approach.

Fields rotated the custom wheel a few points off his course. A sharp crack echoed across the water, and a projectile smacked into the bulkhead above him. Fields dropped from the leather seat and hugged the carpeted deck. A second round ripped through the rear of the chair back as Pink closed to within thirty yards. Fields snaked an arm up from the deck and pulled the spoked wheel sharply. The craft hesitated for long seconds and then responded. Two rounds struck the dash beyond the wheel and a high-pitched whine filled the shattered compartment. The diesels rose in rpms, coughed, hesitated, coughed again, and died.

"Shit!" whispered Fields between tightly clenched teeth. He reached for the starter switch, exposing an arm and a shoulder to Pink. Two more rounds imploded into the teakwood bulkhead. The engines responded with clicking noises. Another shot spat sharp, flying splinters of teak into Fields's right forearm. He jerked the arm back spasmodically and hugged the carpet again. Fields rolled onto his back and, with tremulous fingers, extracted a polished shard from the belly of his forearm muscle. The wound bled freely, and the muscle quivered with an erratic rhythm of its own.

Fields rolled to his stomach, gathered his legs beneath him, and sprinted through the passageway to below decks amid a splattering of impacting bullets. Once below, he slammed the sliding teak door and secured it with an ornamental brass latch. He drew the heavily lined drapes for the small advantage of darkness.

His wound continued to flow with blood, and he grimaced as he flexed the injured tissue. It was painful, but his hand and arm were still functional. Fields removed the fishing knife from the rear of his waistband and hefted it in the weakened right hand. Dissatisfied with the feel, he switched the blade to his left hand and flattened himself against the bulkhead beside the cabin door. He waited there, listening for Pink's approach.

Party John had eased the throttles at first identification of Fields in the plushly appointed motor yacht. His narcotized mind easily accepted Fields's appearance in the riddled craft, noting only that something had gone wrong. His bible of fear had clearly prophesied disaster, and he was more than quick to recognize it. After observing the speedboat's pursuit, Party John shotgunned his throat with cocaine. A spontaneous rush flowed through his capillaries and into his jaded system. As the stimulating alkaloids traveled into his bloodstream his pulse mounted and his pupils constricted. Party John stood a little taller, a little straighter. He witnessed the battered yacht lose its weighty momentum and coast to a rocking drift. As the pursuing vessel closed the distance Party John had a virginal experience. He tasted courage. Party John devout coward with Bolivian bravery in his veins, stepped resolutely into the trawler's wheelhouse, yanked the throttles all the way down to idling speed, and pulled an ancient 30-06 scopeless rifle from the rack behind his map cabinet. A black-stocked weapon of dubious vintage for use against an occasional live shark brought on board by the shrimping nets, the rifle was pitted with neglect.

He rested his pendulous abdomen against the top rail, chambered a tarnished brass round, and sighted down the rusted barrel. He aligned the light pursuit boat and its black occupant in the sights and jerked the trigger. The round went high and to the right and the huge black flinched. The rifle kicked back viciously against Party John's fleshy shoulder, turning him half a turn to the right. He chambered a second round. The drag of the nets combined with the absence of forward thrust, had brought *The Atlantic Maiden* to a semi-stable position one hundred yards abreast of the yacht and the trailing speeder.

Party John again shouldered the cumbersome rifle, took measured aim at the small boat, and fired again. Amazingly the slug smashed into the fiberglass prow of the boat and spit fine splinters of ruby-tinted plastic into the air. Pink growled with irritation wheeled his craft to the sheltered far side of *The Banker's Holiday* and clambered over the chrome railing. He tethered the speedboat to the railing and moved on cat's feet to the wheelhouse. Party John, astonished at the accuracy of his last effort, chambered another cartridge and waited for his next clear shot.

Pink's huge right hand held his freshly reloaded automatic pistol tight against his hip as he moved silently into the wheelhouse. He had seen Fields dart below decks and was confident the man would have opened fire by now if he had weapons. Pink eyed the closed passage door and the debris littering the compartment. Bright red blood was pooled on the carpet and was streaked upon the grain of the polished teak door to the lower compartments. Pink grinned. His prey was wounded. The annoying fir from the trawler was of no consequence, the distance far too great for accuracy. He dismissed the men on the trawler. Pink was engaged in the pursuit and punishment of one who had hurt him and hurt him badly. It would take months to locate and recruit trustworthy men, but years would pass before he regained something of far greater value. Savannah Pink was a man who relied heavily upon his "rep," his essential reputation in the criminal community. In his violent world a man's rep was his foremost possession. It was his defense against theft, encroachment, and prosecution. His rep stood guard against the savagery of his own brutal environment and the effectiveness of law enforcement. Without it Pink would be constantly tested by those who coveted his power, informed on by those who envied his wealth, and harassed by local law-enforcement agencies.

Animal rage coursed like fragmented razor blades through his veins as he considered the damage inflicted by the white man below decks. The scrawny honkie had not only left his men broken and dying in a path for all of Savannah to see, but also had dared to challenge Pink empty-handed on his own territory. The man had to be destroyed. Fueled by the fires of personal shame and personal loss, Pink disdained a more cautious approach and faced the passageway.

He grasped the burnished brass handle and yanked mightily with his left arm, muscles bunching like writhing snakes beneath his skin. The inner latch strained in its ornate fittings and popped free. He threw the door back into its fitted sleeve. Pink paused in the passageway as he adjusted to the lack of light. Fields held his breath as the huge man's body engulfed the doorway. The black man stooped his basketball of a head to enter the compartment and led with his right arm and the pistol as he turned sideways to squeeze through the opening. With lightning speed Fields desperately swung down with the fishing knife in a straight-armed overhead smash that drove the sharpened blade deep into the massive black wrist.

A primordial bellow burst from Pink's titanic mouth, the automatic thudded to the carpeted deck, and his convulsive response flipped the fishing knife from Fields's grip and into the vibrating air of the cabin. Savannah Pink screamed a wordless challenge that both deafened and disoriented his opponent. He hopped forward, pivoted, and sought to embrace Fields with his deadly arms. White-flecked spittle formed in the corners of his lips. Bellowing, he lowered his broad head and shoulders and charged. His enraged rush crushed the breath from Fields's chest, lifted him off his feet, and smashed the smaller man against the curtained expanse of heavily tinted glass. The window shattered.

Fields clawed at the toughened skin of Pink's rubbery neck and drove his knuckled thumb into Pink's exposed mastoid. Breathless and fearing that the next few seconds would bring his own death, Fields struck at the small hollow with a looping inward stroke and felt the crunch of fractured bone. Pink sagged, loosened his grip, and dropped to one knee.

Fields gasped for breath, and a stabbing pain shot white lights behind his eyes as the expansion of his chest caused broken ribs beneath his left arm to puncture adjacent tissues. The pain angered him beyond his terror, and he smashed his knee into the stunned face of the kneeling monster. Pink's nose flattened, cartilage ground audibly, and he rocked back. Fields drew a second, searing breath and drove the knee forward a second time, using both hands to steady the bloody mass of Pink's pumpkin-sized head. Instinctively Pink leaned into the thrust, grabbed the swinging leg with both arms, and rolled to the side. His massive weight pulled Fields to the carpet, wrenching the knee out of its socket and forcing the knobby end of the bone to roll painfully over supporting tissue and nerves.

A high-pitched scream whistled from Fields's grimaced lips as the brutal strength of Savannah Pink flung him across the cabin. With a horror born of pain Fields crabbed backward on his elbows, dragging the mangled leg. Pink, snuffling, filled his lungs with a bushel of frothy air and crawled forward, a bloody grin fixed on his pulped face.

Fields's intellect reeled. He had delivered three killing blows in rapid order, and yet the man crawled steadily forward, his demented smile flashing gold. Fear pervaded Fields's mind and body. He scrabbled farther backward and reached with both hands to his dislocated right knee. He snapped the joint flat, forcing the bone to roll again over the swollen and screaming tissues. Behind his slitted eyes, bright lights flashed in kaleidoscopic fury, and his body jerked with the excruciating pain. Fingers of agony traveled bone-deep and upward, moving up his skeleton and exploding in his skull. His head was thrown back, and a frozen rictus transformed his face into a savage mask. His hands stood rigid before his face, his fingers clawed the chilled air, and a primal scream escaped his lips.

Mindless of the pain, mindless of everything except the death of his adversary, Dan Fields flung himself forward, driving stiffened fingers into Pink's maroon eyes. Ocular fluid splashed wetly to his wrist, and he turned his rigid digits in the gory sockets.

Pink twisted and roared with a bellow that shook the cabin as he stood fully upright and sightlessly clawed the air.

Fields stepped in, ducked the windmilling arms, and drove a stiffened and arched hand deep into Pink's solar plexus, the follow-through reaching up and in to crush the man's aorta. Pink retched and gasped, but still he remained erect. Windmilling blindly, his meaty left hand closed upon Fields's right wrist and held tight.

In amazement and desperation Fields hacked at the locked hand with repeated knife-edged blows, backing constantly to evade the other groping arm. He ignored the protests of his anguished knee and tortured lungs, literally dragging the sightless man in his wake.

He slashed repeatedly at the iron claw that paralyzed his right hand, ducking the sightless efforts of Pink's other arm as it cut the air in violent thrusts. Reaching the passageway to the rear deck, Fields was trapped. Knowing the man would surely kill him if both arms were again allowed to seize him, Fields aimed a kick with his injured leg at the crotch of the gory-headed leviathan. Lacking balance and follow-through, the blow glanced from the giant's groin but achieved a limited effect. His grip relaxed momentarily, and Fields fell backward. He scrambled crablike through the passageway.

Undaunted, Savannah Pink, yellow fluid dripping from his destroyed eyes, blood flowing from his mangled nose, pursued the sound of Fields's exertions and followed the smaller man onto the open rear deck.

Fields danced from the groping paws and circled. His efforts demanded oxygen, and he drew a rattled breath. Pink turned and sought him. Sighting a rigged fishing pole in its clamp, Fields grabbed the device and whipped it through the charged air. The line extended with the centrifugal force; weights and hooks whistled noisily and wrapped tightly around Pink's gruesome face and head, and Fields jerked backward, with all of his torso and shoulder behind him, as if setting the hook in a surfacing marlin.

The barbed hooks bit into the bloody flesh of Pink's neck and face, and he roared in anguish, pawing the air for his unseen tormentor. Fields jerked again, setting the hooks deeper. The thick line snapped.

Fields cast aside the stiff rod, took two long strides into Pink's range, and leapt into the air. He brought both open palms powerfully together upon Pink's ears and burst the giant's eardrums. Fields landed square before the agonized hulk, drew back as if to cleave a mighty rock, and launched a rigid line of bony right hand into the gory face. The strike was known as the collapsing fist in martial circles and was a killing blow that broke the bridge of the nose with the first impact of curled knuckles, then followed through as the fist collapsed and the heel of the palm drove the fractured bones deep into the skull and brain tissue. Fields, seized by the blood-passion of his own body, envisioned the hand emerging at the rear of Pink's skull as he delivered the strike.

Pink staggered back two steps but retained his stance.

Incredulous at the man's ability to withstand such an attack, Fields stepped forward again and sliced at Pink's larynx. Pink reeled, his source of oxygen occluded. He windmilled his arms, fighting for balance, looking for any hold that would deliver Fields to him.

Fear banished, his rationality swept aside, hatred burning in his reddened eyes, Fields ducked the massive arms. He grasped Pink's front waistband and a fold of skin below the gargantuan neck, and incredibly, as he'd done so often when loading his own stones, he lifted the full weight of Savannah Pink from the deck. Screaming against the strain of the impossible lift, Fields dropped to one knee, letting the huge man's own improbable weight smash the exposed small of his spine against Fields's braced knee. The fall impacted the monster's spine at its weakest point and snapped the thick structure. The dead weight of the body flattened Fields, and he lay gasping for shallow breaths, his vision shot with red hues from his pained knee and splintered ribs. When at last he rolled the slippery carcass off him and onto the deck, Fields crawled to his knees and hands and retched.

Avoiding any further sight of the dead Pink, Fields clambered over the side and fell into the tethered speedboat. He turned the starter with quaking fingers, edged the throttle forward, and guided the craft away from *The Banker's Holiday*. Fields was thrown back against the cockpit cushions as the small boat leapt forward. Intense pain seized his rib cage and blurred his vision. He raised a hand to wipe the offending cloud from his eyes, remembered the blood from the defeated monster, and rinsed his hand in the rushing sea. Two parallel *Atlantic Maiden*'s danced crazily before him, and double suns lit the harsh blue sky. He eased the throttle back, the craft slowed, and Dan Fields steered a course midway between the rocking double images of the trawler.

From *The Atlantic Maiden* Party John had viewed the awesome combat through battered binoculars. Twice he had sighted down the barrel of the ancient rifle, and twice he had lowered the old gun, fearful of striking Fields. When Pink was lifted and then fell heavily to the deck of *The Banker's Holiday*, Party John uttered a swallowed prayer of thanks, then held his breath until he saw Fields rise. "Thank you, sweet Jesus!" he screamed when he saw Fields crawl over the side. John winced empathically for the younger man's obvious pain. Again he cursed the lack of a second launch in which he could have gone to his aid. And inwardly he remembered his own religion of cowardice and knew any help he would have rendered would have been from a remote distance or not at all. He snared the vial of cocaine crystals from his pocket, unscrewed the cap, and paused. He watched across the choppy waters as Fields, clutching his side, stumbled over the rail of the motor yacht. Party John tapped the crystals back into the bottle and screwed tight the cap. He placed the bottle back in his pocket. Not a man to spend too much time in self-recrimination, Party John scanned the far horizon and took comfort that no other vessels were in range to connect the gory scene on the drifting yacht with *The Atlantic Maiden*. He turned to face the other spectators at the rail.

The girl beamed broadly at the approaching small boat, but the lines beneath her pale eyes and the lines framing her smile suggested an undercurrent of something else. Farther down the rail, Weems stood grim and damp with perspiration. His exposed skin was pinked from the sun. The man was deep in his own thoughts and unaware of Party John's scrutiny.

On the rear deck the Outlaw caught his master's scent on the freshening breeze and barked and yelped, tossing his firm body in tight, concentric circles.

"Get the nets up, Maltessa," Weems ordered, his narrowed eyes focused on Fields's approach.

"What?" asked the captain, returning from his musings.

"Get the nets up," Weems barked. "The nets are stretched out behind us, and we better be ready to get the hell out of here as soon as Fields is on board. Get the nets up, man!" Weems spit the last word out, and the captain hurried to the task. Weems frowned deeply, his elbows resting in dejection upon the rail. He cocked his head to the left and eyed the steady progress of the boat as it circled the yacht and neared the trawler. Then he drew in a breath through his nostrils, pulled in his relaxed stomach, and bent to tug his support hose into place. He straightened quickly and strode to the stern. He evaded the yelping Outlaw, leaned far out over the low gunwale, and extended a hand to catch the line from Fields.

Dan Fields sat motionless in the cockpit of the speedboat. His face was bloodless and vacant, his clothing spattered with drying fluids of red and milky yellow.

"Well done, hotshot," Weems shouted from above.

Fields looked up in vague surprise. Above him were the faces of Weems, Party John, and Fanny. He was below the stern of *The Atlantic Maiden* and could hear the frantic, happy yelp of the Airedale. Fields stared in amused wonder at his own disarrayed clothing and giggled slightly at the seeping wound in his forearm. Something terribly funny must have happened for him to look as he did. He knew he'd recall what it was at any minute. Weems had his hand out for some reason. Fields knew that he couldn't reach him and giggled again. Silly Weems. Then Party John's face was above him, smiling kindly. Good old Party John. He always enjoyed a good joke. Perhaps he would remind Fields of the funny thing that had happened.

"Dan," he called. "Dan, throw us the line, Dan."

Fields looked in puzzlement at the line coiled in the bow of the speeder, then knew what Party John and the others wanted. They wanted the line. He giggled and stretched forward to hand it to them. A bright arrow of pain shot through his thorax. With the pain came arrested movement and the return of clarity. The crippling jolt of sharp-ended bone on raw tissue cleared away the foggy euphoria of shock. He remembered.

Fields clutched his right hand to the fractured ribs and stretched forward with his left. He snared the coil of line and tossed it in a looping, unfurling arc to Party John. The captain secured the line, then quickly dropped a stained rope ladder with wooden slats for rungs and scurried down to him. He enfolded Fields in his hairy arms, supported his weight, and gingerly helped the ashen-faced Fields on board.

Party John propped Fields against the gunwale and tossed the line to the speedboat over the side. He then performed a cursory examination of Fields, noting the broken ribs and the punctured forearm. With gentle yet insistent hands he felt the man from head to toe as he searched for concealed wounds.

When Party John completed his brief examination, he stepped aside, and the irrepressible Outlaw sprang forward in a series of whirling yelps. He licked Fields wetly on the face. The stump of his tail worked in triple time, and his front paws vibrated on the deck. Fields moved to push the dog gently away, and the excited animal stepped squarely on his groin. Fields groaned audibly, pushed the Outlaw more firmly, and smiled a thin smile. "Not now, Outlaw," he whispered hoarsely. The Outlaw retreated two paces and sat, his stump of a tail wagging, his head cocked to the side.

"Fanny," Party John called. "Get some blankets and some brandy and bring them out here. And bring me the first-aid kit too."

The girl took off at a lope. The Outlaw turned his head but did not follow. He crept a half pace closer. Fields smiled at the beast, patted his uninjured knee lightly, and the Outlaw crept the remaining distance to Fields. The dog rested his massive head lightly upon Fields's leg and whined. The tail stump halted its wag as the animal sniffed Fields's spattered garments, then resumed its steady thump. Fields ruffled the black-and-gold coat and sighed, catching his breath as the movement caused the bone tip to jar against the offended tissues.

Ritchie was below decks in the iced hold and would not answer the captain's call. Party John nervously secured the half-filled nets above the deck, released the slipknots below the mass of fish and shrimp, and dropped the slithery catch onto the deck. He rapidly stowed the nets, shut down the gasoline-powered winch, and returned to Fields. "Dan," he began, "Dan, I've cast the speeder adrift and rigged the nets like we're returning from a normal run. I'm going to get *The Maiden* under way, and then I'll wrap those ribs for you. Can you hold out that long?"

Fields nodded.

Party John continued to speak while his eyes scanned the sea. "My bones are telling me we better put some distance between us and this area pretty quick, Dan, so I'm going to get us under way. Are you sure you can hold out for a few minutes?''

"I'll be fine."

John placed an open palm on Fields's clammy forehead, frowned, and shouted over his shoulder, "Fanny! Get those blankets out here. He's in shock!" The girl emerged from the passageway in a loping trot, carrying stiff, gray woolen blankets and a small flat flask. John rose to meet her.

"Fanny," he said, "my boy's in shock, probably from the broken ribs. I can feel at least two that are pretty jagged. I checked him out, and except for the ribs and a pretty nasty puncture in the arm, he looks okay. Just cover him up, keep him quiet, and give him a few sips of brandy. I'm heading for port on Hilton Head. I know a doctor there who'll give him a look and not ask questions." John turned, then scurried down the deck and ducked into the wheelhouse.

Fanny moved swiftly to Fields and tucked the stiff blankets around him. He winced as the girl tucked the blanket's edge beneath his right knee but said nothing. Fanny then uncorked the small flask and poured a limited amount of amber liquid into a dented tin cup. She offered the cup to Fields, who extended a hand and missed the cup by several inches. She guided the cup to his hands, and he sipped carefully. The brandy burned on the way down, then spread warmth and life through his stomach. He returned the cup and looked into her wide green eyes. The pupils were constricted in the glare and darted rapidly, constantly shifting in fevered tempo from one of his eyes to the other. Watching them flit blurred Field's vision, and he looked away. The Outlaw nuzzled his tanned hand, lifting it with his large black nose.

"It's okay, Outlaw," said Fields. "Just a little tired and a little sore. It's okay, Outlaw." Hearing its name, the dog perked up, took reassurance from Fields's voice, and laid his massive head again upon Fields's outstretched knee. The thick stump of tail wagged tentatively. He wasn't convinced.

The diesels thrummed, their revolutions increasing. The trawler shuddered with the effort and slowly began forward movement. Fields braced his back and extended his left hand for the cup. Fanny poured another small dollop of brandy, and Fields downed the warming amber fluid.

Weems moved a few steps forward and assumed a square stance

some six feet from the recumbent Fields. The deck behind him was littered with the spilled contents of the nets. Flicking brown shrimp performed their death dance; blue crabs scuttled, claws upraised and defiant; flounder arched in suffocating agonies; and a small ray whipped its poisonous, spiny tail in futile threat.

"Well, hotshot," Weems projected, extending to his full height. "How did it go? You've had a few minutes to pull yourself together. I need some idea of how the job went." He stood there, puffed up in the humid afternoon sun.

"The job is done, worm," Fields replied. "Now it's your turn. Fill your half of the bargain." He stared into Weems's pink face and squinting eyes.

Weems scowled down at the injured man. "You're right, hotshot," he answered, his voice dropping from the projected baritone and becoming a menacing hiss. "It is my turn." He backed two short steps and whipped out a chromed automatic pistol with an effeminate pearl grip. He trained the small-caliber weapon upon Fields's chest.

Fanny had jerked around at the change in his voice, her attractive face transfigured with loathing and fear. During Fields's absence Weems had limited his abuse to verbal harassment, his remarks pointedly sexual and demeaning, but he had not placed hands on her. She had declined to respond to his comments, had met his gaze steadily, and had not tried to disguise the hatred in her eyes. She had resolved to take her own life rather than endure another assault at his hands. Her eyes flickered to the gun in his hand, and she froze as hate and fear fought for dominance in her contorted face.

"That's right, Mr. Fucking Hotshot," Weems said, continuing his hiss. "This is your payment!" He gestured with the pistol.

Fields tossed the blanket aside and drew his left leg in several inches.

"Stay where you are! You son of a bitch!" Weems shouted in response. "You move one more muscle and I'll blow your fucking brains all over this deck!"

Fields was very still, eyes steady, mind racing. The Outlaw, on his feet, whipped his broad head between Fields and Weems.

The girl twitched her shoulders and clenched her white-knuckled hands into small fists. "No!" she shouted, refusing to be responsible for this man's death. "No, you can't!" she shouted, her voice strangely deep and threatening. Her tightened body twitched again, and she hurled herself at Weems. He took a short step forward, met her rush, and brought the barrel of the small pistol savagely across her sculpted cheekbone. The force of the blow carried her around to Weems's side where she thudded heavily to the deck, face and arms lying very unprettily upon the mass of netted life. No sound escaped her lips as a bloodless gash appeared upon her cheek. She raised on one elbow and glared at the man, the hatred of repeated injury and humiliation obscuring her beauty. She touched her face but remained still. Weems had knocked her aside effortlessly and brought the short-barreled weapon quickly back to bear upon Fields's chest. The Outlaw whined in distress. Fields had not moved. The Outlaw wagged his thick stump of a tail uncertainly, turning to glance at Fields.

Weems nodded his head, certain of himself and his mastery of the moment. He had succeeded. The Colonel's plan had been executed satisfactorily, the pirates were no longer a matter for concern, and Fields was injured and waiting docilely for his death. The man had obviously lost his sharpness in the ghastly conflict on the yacht and was reduced to his proper level. Weems laughed a barking laugh, keeping Fields transfixed with his eyes. Weems was wealthy, his position with the Colonel more firmly established than ever before. He was an unqualified success, triumphant in a world barred to him in the past.

"How does it feel, hotshot?" he taunted, his thin lips sneering. "Come on!" he said derisively. "Can't you answer me, you smart-mouthed shit?"

Fields gazed steadily at the excited man. The diesels shifted to a higher level of revolutions, and *The Atlantic Maiden* moved several points to the east. Party John was making way for Hilton Head.

"I have an answer for you, Weems," Fields replied in even tones, stalling, praying for Party John's return. He needed a diversion more potent than that created by the girl's futile attack. Fields struggled to keep the malice from his face. Weems was right at the edge, intoxicated with his power. It would take very little to detonate the explosive package within his twisted brain. But he was enjoying the moment, prolonging the gloating. A pro would have shot Fields without announcement.

"Weems, listen to me for a second," Fields urged, his voice soft sand. "I've fulfilled my part of the arrangement. You can go home now with a success for your boss. Why spoil it with unnecessary risks now?'' he inquired.

"What risks?" Weems inquired, his tone disbelieving, taunting.

"Party John, for one," Fields replied, moving his left hand imperceptibly closer to the deck. "If you shoot me now, he's certain to hear the shot. He's not about to let you kill me and go unpunished."

Weems chuckled and wagged his head in disagreement. "No way, hotshot," he countered. "The man is a sniveling coward and you know it. He'll do exactly what I tell him to do and will be glad for the chance. You'll get no help from that fucking hophead, and you know it. You'll have to try harder than that." Weems drew a deep breath through curling, flared nostrils. He stood taller on the concrete deck.

"That may be true," Fields agreed evenly. "But in all good conscience," he continued, inching his left hand minutely closer to the deck, sliding his leg a millimeter more beneath him, "in all good conscience I had to give you this warning. I don't want to see you hurt," he said.

Weems snorted in derision, but Fields continued.

"Sure, we've had our disagreements, but that's behind us now. Face it, Weems, I need you. We can all go home peacefully and you can release my family, all without the need for taking this any further."

Weems chuckled again. "I sure got to hand it to you, hotshot"—he laughed—"you sure got a lot of shit in you for a man who knows he's had it." The pistol remained focused on Fields's chest.

Fields allowed his eyes to flash for a brief millisecond from the pistol to the scene behind Weems. The girl lay open-eyed but immobile, the blood seeping from her shattered cheek. Party John had not emerged from the wheelhouse and, in all probability, would be of little or no help. He returned his stare to Weems and the ludicrous, but no less deadly, pistol.

"Weems," he pressed on, "I'm trying to save your life, believe me."

The puffed man curled his lips in disbelief.

"Weems, this is your last chance to settle this reasonably." Fields spoke with concern in his even tones. He could see that Weems was tiring of the verbal game of cat and mouse, could read the man's body as he steeled himself for the kill. "Weems!"

Fields spat sharply, his tone grown menacing, "you either put that toy away now or you're a dead man, as dead as Savannah Pink." His eyes shed their subterfuge, grew cold and murderous. He bunched the muscles in thighs and calves and placed the edge of his palm upon the deck. "If you hurt me in any way, if you fire that gun, the Outlaw will tear you to pieces."

Weems laughed his barking laugh, relieved at the emptiness of the threat. "No good, hotshot," he replied. "That dumb son of a bitch is the least of my worries. I'm tired of your shit. I've wasted enough time on your ass." The pistol centered on Fields's chest, and Weems's finger tightened its pressure on the chromed trigger.

"Outlaw!" Fields snapped, his voice the unmistakable tone of command. "Take him!"

At the command of "Attention," the animal had frozen rigid, his body squared and facing Weems. With the command to attack, the thick-shouldered Airedale sprang across the short distance to Weems with a snarl of unleashed fury and sank its large back-curled fangs deeply into the man's crotch. The Airedale originally bred in the British Isles for use in hunting the otter and other fierce prey, had been used with stunning success to hunt bear, mountain lion, and wild boar. The Outlaw, true to his heritage, stood as an excellent standard to his breed. He was even-tempered, irrepressibly happy, and loved in his daily life. But responding to the urgent tone of Fields's command, he obeyed instantly. His formidable neck muscles bunched powerfully as the merciless jaws clamped violently through Weems's trousers and penetrated the man's flaccid flesh. An ugly, vicious snarl emanated from the dog's locked jaws, rising with savage fury as the Outlaw bit deeper. He tasted blood, shook his broad neck and shoulders, and tore the wounds deeper. The snarl rose and fell in pitch, obliterating Weems's high-pitched shriek of startled terror.

As the fearless dog hurtled through the air to attack, Dan Fields pushed off with his left hand. The effort of rising filled him with nausea and vertigo, blurring his vision. He lurched unsteadily to his feet, yielded to the searing pain in his chest with an animal scream, and stumbled to his knees. He steadied himself with a palm upon the deck and lurched again toward the snarling Airedale and the shrieking man.

Weems backed ineffectually against the gut-wrenching onslaught of the Outlaw. The beast tore through the flesh of his penis, ripped thigh tissues, and grazed the surface of adjacent bones. Weems was terrified. The dog was hurting him incredibly, stripping his manhood, panicking his mind. With a clarity that exceeded his capabilities Weems lowered the pistol to the Airedale's head and jerked the trigger. The snarls stopped abruptly and the dog sagged. Despite the pain and the shock, Weems saw Fields as he lurched to his feet for the second time, and Weems fired again, turning to aim point-blank into Fields's headlong rush.

Fields was shot, thrown backward onto the deck. His angular face was contorted, drawn back in a clenched, soundless scream, and the blue eyes burned bright with hatred. Fields writhed under the impact, jagged ribs stabbing deep into his flesh. He rolled with the pain, but his eyes remained locked in fury with those of Weems. The great dog lay motionless at Weems's feet.

Weems howled in hysterical pain, holding his bloodied crotch with his empty left hand, stooping with the effort to retain his feet. The pistol wavered, then focused upon the twisted form of Dan Fields. "God! Oh, God!" Weems howled. "Oh, God! It hurts! Look what you've done to me!" he screeched. "Oh, God! I'm gonna kill you now, motherfucker! Oh, God! Oh, God! Oh, God!" Tears streamed down his flushed cheeks, and his face was tortured with the pain and shame of his injuries. Blood spread downward and soaked into the thighs of his trousers. The muzzle of the pistol waved crazily in his grasp but remained leveled at the prone body of Fields. Weems howled in agony, clutching his mutilated groin. He sobbed, gasping for air, and hobbled a step closer to Fields.

Fanny's eyes widened in horror at the grisly scene. Ritchie Weaver, the Gullah mate, his head inches below the hatch to the hold, was calling to her. "Frail 'im!" he whispered. "Frail 'im, frail dat larging man!" While they'd worked, he'd spoken to her as he had never spoken to any white. And he had talked in his tongue, Gullah, to her without shame for the language based on baby talk to African slaves.

Fanny heard him and understood. "Frail 'im" meant "flail him," "whip him." Her face hardened. She recovered from the initial shock and drew her knees beneath her. Weems was oblivious to her presence, injured and obsessed with his wounds and Dan Fields. Fanny stood slowly, tentatively, then outstretched her hand to the small ray that lay grayly upon the deck. She placed her thumb and middle finger in the sunken sockets of its sightless eyes, exerted inward pressure, and lifted the primitive creature. She crept forward on soundless feet, her face a mask of contempt and concentration.

Weems lurched forward, stooped in the pain, and lowered the pistol's snout to Fields. His moans subsided and he sobbed. "Fields! You bastard! I'm gonna kill you now!"

Fields stared defiantly into the barrel of the automatic, his eyes glittering with hatred. The girl stepped obliquely out beside Weems and whirled the ray at Weems's tear-streaked face. The spiny, poisonous tail of the creature whipped out with centrifugal force and struck Weems squarely across the eyes.

His scream pierced the harsh blue afternoon. It rose continuously as he dropped the pistol and reflexively covered his blinded, agonized eyes. The poisons from the ray's spine penetrated his eyelids, attacked the vulnerable membranes of the eyes, and shot their venom deep within his system. Weems hopped with the unbearable, blinding sting, hooting and howling with earsplitting intensity. Fanny dropped the ray and ran at the helpless and blinded man. She struck him with her shoulder and knocked him screaming to the gunwale. Weems wobbled, blinded and bellowing, his arms rotating for balance. Fanny struck him with her shoulder across the shoulder blades. Weems windmilled, fighting for balance, then tumbled over the low gunwale, disappearing into the white-crested foam of the wake. Fanny shook herself in a cleansing motion. She knelt quickly beside Fields and peered at his gunshot wound.

The small-caliber bullet had entered his body just below the right side of his rib cage, its passage marked by a small, rounded hole that bled slowly. Fanny eased Fields gently onto his side and gasped. Located high on his back, the exit wound lay between his spine and the edge of the shoulder blade. It was the size of a nickel and was bleeding strongly. Fields's shirt was soaked in red, the deck beneath slicked with blood.

Fanny gently lowered Fields back to the reddened deck and soothed his face with her fingertips. She was surprised to see the soft smile upon his face. The lips moved wordlessly, and she bent close to catch his sound.

A very agitated Party John pushed her aside. "Get out of the way, girl!" he commanded. "The man's got a hole in his chest and you can't think of anything better to do than pass the time in idle conversation!''

Party John's hands shook with rapid tremors as he squinted into the glare. "Jesus Christ!" he roared. "Get me the sheets from my bunk, and this time don't forget the goddamn first-aid kit!" The girl was off and running, sobbing as she fled.

John examined Fields's wounds, clucking aloud and cursing. Gauging from the trajectory and the size of the exit, the slug might have struck bone. "Cough for me, Dan," he ordered. "Come on. I've got to know if he hit the lung. Cough, damn you!" he shouted.

Fields raised his head slightly and coughed weakly. The action triggered a spasm of deeper, racking coughs. Fields arched with the effort, then spat upon the deck. Both he and the captain turned to look at the moisture on the concrete surface. It was clear, with no sign of blood.

"Well, at least we don't have to worry about that," said Party John with some relief. His hands still trembled. "At least I don't think we do." He lowered his head and placed his ear close to the wound and listened. "Sounds clear, Dan," he said. "I don't hear air sucking." Then he gingerly turned Fields to the side and listened at the rear wound. He smiled at the younger man as he lowered him. Fields was moving his lips again, the sound inaudible against the throb and thrum of the diesels. Party John drew closer.

"Outlaw?"

"Dan," he replied sadly. "Dan, he's gone."

He had to know about his wife and child. Weems was dead, and Fanny was his last link. He worked a hand to her, pulled her close. "Fanny, I have to know. Where are they?"

She looked into his eyes, saw the blood from his wound where it leaked to the deck. "I don't know," she said. "They were with Benny somewhere."

"Benny?" Fields's voice was far away.

"The Colonel's goon," offered John. "The one with the lighter."

Hope died on Dan Fields's face. Benny would not have left them. Not if they were still alive. His lips worked, formed a soundless "Why?"

Fanny sagged, torn between guilt and fear, between the pain worn by Fields and the threat of Colonel Burgess. Her mind seized on the man's wound, bound her eyes to his blood. She started in a small, detatched voice but carried through, telling Dan Fields the story of Colonel Burgess, Benny Montrose, and Hsing Pao.

Before she was finished, Fields's eyes filled, his jaw locked, and he closed his eyes and drifted in the sweet gift of unconsciousness.

CHAPTER 14

FIELDS felt the gentled swirl of sun-warmed waters above and around him. The tropical sea bathed him sensually. He opened his eyes. Drifting green strands rose, bent and twisted in the deep-water eddies of the current. The white sand beneath his feet was fine, his buoyed weight not denting the dimpled surface. The sea floor was unmarked, freshly vacuumed by the currents, vacant to the limits of his sight.

A constricting pressure tightened his chest, forcing crystal bubbles from his lips. They floated obliquely up from him, trailing markers on the currents. He looked at his chest and saw a large, flat, white snake slithering against his skin, drawing itself ever tighter against his lungs. His hand rose in submerged slowness to arrest the actions of the snake but was gently pushed aside by unseen fingers. *Oh, well,* he thought, *I really don't mind.* The snake continued its winding constrictions, biting him sharply in the side. Fields started at the pain, but the waters soothed him and he lowered his hands and did not interfere.

The stark sandscape in front of him blossomed, greened to abundance, and became land above the sea. The plant life was dense, lush, and overcrowded with twisting and spreading greenery. The sky was obliterated by an intertwined ceiling of living green, and the sounds of the rain forest penetrated to his ears. Brightly striped lizards flitted in stop-and-go fits of motion and

repose. A small clearing in the bush materialized, the bare ground
blackened by fire. Party John walked toward him and Fields tried
to hail him, but burbled sounds and oblong bubbles escaped
uselessly from his lips. He remembered his watery environment
and clamped his lips tightly.

It was strange. Party John was not under the water as he was.
Fields promised himself he would ask about the inconsistency at
the first opportunity. Before that, he would keep his mouth shut
and not drown.

Party John approached him, feet crunching in cindered ash, his
back framed by lush greenery. He halted, either unaware or
unconcerned about the waters that flowed about his friend, and
held out his arms. Fields did not understand the gesture and was
about to make some physical sign to convey his unspoken
questions when the limp and bloodied form of the Outlaw
materialized upon the captain's outstretched arms. The great
canine lay motionless and slack in John's caring embrace. John
spoke. "Dan, he's gone, boy. Dan, I'm sorry. He's gone."

Fields choked against a sob, tasting his own swallowed tears
and the salty waters that imprisoned him. He nodded in understanding to Party John, lifting his glance from the once gay animal
to his friend's face. He saw the lines of guilt and remorse. Party
John had known of Dan's life-and-death struggle, but he had
withheld his help. The man's darting, constricted pupils confessed
as much. Party John had waited in the wheelhouse, imprisoned by
his fears.

Fields wanted to embrace him with forgiveness, to speak to
him, but the waters impeded his efforts. He tried to think of some
bodily gesture he could offer, some movement or posture that
would tell John that he, too, understood the power of fear. But
while he sought vainly for the means to ease his friend's
discomfort, Party John's face blurred in the shifting currents.

The Outlaw shimmered in the watery eddies, then blurred. John
held a larger, human form. It was a young man with an angelic
face and blond hair, his face pale. Fields stared in wonder at the
youth. It was Cadet, code name for the best of his handpicked and
personally trained covert agents in the Baltimore campaign. The
youth had been quick, successful, and fearless. He was the perfect
all-American boy, actually believed he'd been fighting for good
against evil, and he had died alone in a trash-littered Baltimore
alley, castrated by unidentified drug traffickers and left to spill his

blood on empty hamburger wrappers and the debris of the ghetto. Fields wept until his tears blended with the warm currents. He wept for the dead boy, and he wept for John, and he wept for all who betrayed and were betrayed.

The flow of tears subsided, and a different figure stood in the cindered clearing. It was a larger man with silvered hair and sad brown eyes. His words penetrated the sea in muffled distortion. Fields heard him repeating, "I'm sorry, boy. I'm sorry." The form he held in his arms was shrouded in a blanket, but he could see a feminine leg and ankle. Fields struggled to penetrate through the clouding waters with his eyes but failed.

The clearing faded, and Fields looked into the face of God as He sat peacefully upon a short stump of oak. Then God turned to face him directly and Fields saw that it wasn't God at all but the kind face of his grandfather. The man looked at him with twinkled amusement in his all-knowing face, arched his bushy eyebrows, and laughed and slapped his knee. "Danny, that's one fine dog you got there," he rumbled, mirth escaping from a thousand seams in his lived-in face. "Yessir, that's one fine dog. Fine, fine, fine." One large tear escaped from the corner of his crystal-blue eyes, and he returned to his contemplations as he sat motionless on the stump, a crumpled Stetson in his gnarled hand.

Fields winced at the pain in his side and told himself that he was in a dream and could rouse himself with an effort of will.

A large, furred spider in the center of a three-dimensional web robbed him of the power to concentrate, fascinating him with its movements. The spider tramped on ciliated legs up and down the fine threads of the web, repairing a tear here, spinning a new design there. The web extended in all directions, touched all people, and threatened all lives.

The spider crept down a trembling thread, approaching Fields, its mandibles working as if the creature were tasting Fields prior to actually biting him. Fields attempted to flee but found his legs mired in the fine undersea sand. As the beast drew closer and placed its furred leg on Fields's arm, the spider grew human eyes in its rounded head; they ballooned outward, filling the warm waters with a new shape. It was Savannah Pink, his empty eye sockets staring and huge jaws snapping. Fields struck out with an arm and severed the monstrous head from the bloated body, only to find a new head with larger jaws snapping goldly in the dimmed aquatic light. The sharp teeth sank into the flesh of his shoulder and twisted violently, tearing muscles from his shoulder and sending reddened clouds billowing into the currents. Fields opened his mouth to scream and choked as the warm, salty taste blocked all sound. The destroyed eyes of the monster smiled in evil satisfaction and shook him again.

Fields opened his eyes with a start. Party John loomed above him. He was lying in the tiny cabin of *The Atlantic Maiden*, ribs bound tightly in a twice-wound sheet, the gunshot wound tightly bandaged front and rear with makeshift pressure bandages of folded gauze. Fields was drenched in cold sweat, fire lived inside his rib cage, and his shoulder ached as though it had been struck repeatedly with a heavy maul.

"Dan? Dan?" Party John kept saying, his face screwed with concern. "Dan, come on, boy. Snap out of it. Dan?"

"What?" Fields croaked through dried and cracked lips.

"You were shouting and kept turning," Party John replied. "I didn't want you to reopen the gunshot wound, that's all." Party John smiled with relief. "Look, while you're awake, we need to talk. Can you talk for a few minutes?"

Fields shifted his weight, easing the pain in his side slightly. "Yeah, John. What is it?" He chased the dream from his mind.

"I've got most of it worked out, but I wanted to check with you first, if I could." He smiled again. "I really didn't know if you'd be available for interviews for a while."

Fields smiled back painfully into the captain's deeply tanned face. "Go ahead."

"First off, Dan," the captain began, "I need to know. Are you hot, personally? Can anyone tie you to what's been going on in the channel today? You know, police types?"

Fields shifted position again. Nothing was comfortable. "No, John," Fields stated with certainty. "The best thing anyone has is a description of my face. If they don't see me or my picture for a few days, they'll never know me." He winced at the effort required to speak. The throb in his shoulder was increasing, and the sound of his own echoed pulse threatened to cover all other noise. The room began to swim.

"Dan, wait a minute, boy!" John implored. "Dan, don't leave me just yet."

Fields opened his eyes. The room was brighter and larger. He managed an "Okay."

How about Pink's men? Will they be coming after us?" The

fear was strong in the captain's voice, and he covered the tremor with a dry cough.

"No," Fields answered. "They won't be after us or anyone. They're all gone, John."

Maltessa frowned in puzzlement, then grasped Fields's meaning. He could not suppress a broad, relieved smile. "Okay, then, Dan," he rushed on, "you just leave the rest to me. I've got a doctor on Hilton Head who'll patch you up with no questions. It'll all be fixed as a shrimping accident. You know, the winch cable snapped and the wire cable came back and busted you up. We'll do it away from the hospital so there won't be any nosy witnesses." Party John noted the alarm in Fields's eyes. "Don't worry about the doc," he continued. "He's a client of mine. In fact, he's supplying coke to the whole hospital, and probably half of the damned island. You just take another catnap, and before you know it, I'll have you back home." Party John allowed his excitement to light up his face. He could barely sit still. "Listen, Dan," he said, his voice climbing higher, his hands gripping the side of the bunk. "Listen. Since old Weemsy boy decided to cancel our contract the hard way, I'm certainly not going to make delivery of this coke and pot to his people. That'd be plain foolish. No, I'm going to make a quick deal at a discount, probably to the doc and a few of his friends, and take the full amount for us. No split to Weems's boss, no split for anybody but you and me. I got ten keys of ninety-six percent coke and a hold full of pot. At fifty thousand per pound on the coke, that comes to more than a million bucks at the full market price. I'm going to discount it to seventy percent for a quick sale. That's three quarters of a million bucks for you and me, Dan. And that don't include the pot."

Fields was eyeing him coldly.

"Dan," he urged, "we earned it. Those bastards were gonna blow all of us away. You can be sure of that." He lowered his voice conspiratorially. "Dan, I'm gonna dock this old scow, get you patched up, then I'm gonna drop clean out of sight. These boys play too rough for this old smuggler. They'll be coming after me for the drugs, no doubt about it." His face grew thin and worried at the thought. "And they'll be coming after you, too, boy. Think about it," he urged. "I'll split even with you, and then I'm gonna disappear. I'd be more than proud to have you come with me. We can do a lot of oceans on that kind of money. What do you say, Dan?'' he asked, his eyes bright and burning. ''Do I make accommodations for two?''

Fields narrowed his eyes. ''Have you written off Donna and Marianne that easily?'' he asked, his voice iced.

''No, Dan,'' Party John answered apologetically. ''I just figured that if the plan was to drop you in the ocean, well, they have no reason to, you know . . .''

''I know, John,'' Fields replied. ''No reason to keep them alive.'' He closed his eyes. ''Get the doctor to put me on my feet and be quick about it. I've got unfinished business. You do what you want with the money.''

Party John sat on the edge of the bunk, struggling within himself. He wanted to say to the injured man that he would come with him, help him locate the girl and her mother, and, if necessary, avenge them. He truly wanted to be able to say such things. But he could not, for fear paralyzed his will and controlled his choices. He owed much to Dan Fields but was not able to repay the debt with courage. He looked at the man and was ashamed of the minutes he had spent cringing in the wheelhouse while Weems played tyrant on the rear deck. He longed for the chemical relief of his tensions.

''Dan,'' he said, rising, ''I'm gonna get *The Maiden* well up into Skull Creek and get the doc out here. From what I can tell, you've got at least two broken ribs. That and the pistol wound. The bleeding's stopped pretty much, and it looks pretty clean. You try to rest for a while. I'll be in the wheelhouse if you need me.'' He started to leave the small cabin.

''John,'' Fields said, stopping him.

Party John halted, fearing Fields would now ask why he hadn't come to his aid.

''What about the Outlaw?''

John looked at the deck, averting his eyes from Fields. ''I put him over the side, Dan,'' he mumbled. ''You were out cold, and I didn't know if we should be expecting marine police or not. I did it to protect us, Dan.''

Fields clamped down on his jaw and the pain, looking past the captain into space. ''Okay, John,'' he said very quietly. The paunchy captain slid through the passageway and was halted again. ''Hey,'' Fields called.

John poked his apprehensive face back into the cabin.

''You did what you could,'' Fields said. ''You did okay, John. Thanks.''

Maltessa acknowledged the remark, looking into the pained eyes of his friend, seeing the forgiveness. "I could have done a lot more, Dan," he replied, his heart thumping.

"Maybe," Fields replied, "but what you did was fine. You did okay, John."

The fear left Maltessa. "Thanks, Dan," he mumbled. "Can I get you anything?"

"Yes," Fields answered. "Send the girl in, would you? There're a few questions I need to have cleared up, and this looks like the time to take care of them."

"Sure, Dan," Party John agreed. He waddled down the passageway.

Fanny stood upon the freshly scrubbed stern deck of *The Atlantic Maiden*. She wore loose-fitting tan slacks and a large man's shirt. Her fine blond hair was combed severely back from her face, tied with a patterned blue scarf. She wore no makeup, and the gash on her high cheekbone was scabbed with crusted flecks of dried blood. The widely spaced, pale eyes were unfocused, directed at *The Maiden*'s swirling wake. Her lightly tanned arms were folded protectively across her chest. She had stood upon the deck for unbroken minutes, her mind blanked to the recent past.

Fanny had helped Party John to carry Dan Fields into the small cabin and had then been ordered to leave. She had busied herself with the condition of the culling deck. She had quickly shoved the catch that littered the deck through the ports of the gunwales. Using a large push broom, she had indiscriminately discarded shrimp, fish, crabs, and shark into the passing sea. Her mind raced with incredulity as she dumped the dead ray over the side. *She* had not used the ray to kill a man; that had been the action of someone else. Certainly *she* was not capable of killing; that was the exclusive province of animalistic men. Her self-protective mind rebelled stubbornly at the unresolved clash between reality and what she wished to believe. Once again she sought the safety and innocence of the unpeopled green place. Her thoughts insulated from the truth, she then completed the tasks on the deck. Bringing buckets of seawater aboard with the use of a galvanized bucket secured to a line, she doused the painted concrete deck, scrubbed the clotted blood from the rough surface with stiff-bristled brushes, and then rinsed the dislodged stains with fresh bucketfuls of seawater.

Still engaged in the contemplation of her fantastical green place, she then bathed the corpse of the Outlaw, sponging the gore from his dense coat. She covered his limp form with a faded green tarpaulin. Then she faced the empty sea and drifted in the purposeless void of her mind.

Her vacant stare had been interrupted by the captain as he uncovered the fallen Outlaw and unceremoniously tossed the corpse over the side. Watching the lifeless animal tumble into the receding foam, Fanny had burst into spasmodic, choking sobs. It was so much easier to cry for an animal, but her tears were shed equally for herself and the other lives she had touched. She longed for the security and supervision of her parents' home and for the safety of their simple, ordered lives. The catharisis of the sobs eroded the protective bastions of her mind. Now she felt guilt and reproach.

The murders, the rapes—they all became partly her own responsibility, she now saw. Each incident had been in some way directly traceable to her own shortcomings, to her own greedy desire for material goods or status. And each had been tied to her sexual ease and promiscuity. She believed her licentious attitudes had prompted others to act as they did; to involve her in crimes against civilization; to use her to further the spread of addiction; and to lust after her body and gain its access, either through the lure of money or by the use of animal force. She no longer felt she was the victim but rather the catalyst, the enticement for the destruction of others.

With each breath, with each acceptance of diminished self-esteem, her natural femininity faded, to be replaced by the feelings of a sexless, fearing, self-hating child. As these thoughts of self-accusation flitted unopposed into her conscious mind, she believed them. And because she believed them she was certain that others would also perceive her shame and unworthiness.

The summons from Fields filled her with dread. Fanny walked slowly, her shoulders slumped, her arms folded, to the small cabin. If *this* exchange was the one in which her ugly, true self was announced to the world, she would escape into the peace and solace of suicide. If not, if by some miracle Fields wished to discuss some other topic, she would hang on to her life. But only until that terrible moment of discovery. Then she would escape to the one safe place where no one could detect and announce her sins.

She entered the cramped cabin. Fields lay propped up against a small pillow and a rolled blanket. His eyes were closed tightly, and he was obviously fighting the discomfort from the injuries, unaware of her presence. She maintained her silence and leaned patiently against the bulkhead, content to allow any number of minutes to pass. She had but two duties left in life—to be wary and then to commit suicide at the proper moment. A distorted sense of self-preservation was her only deterrent to a premature death. She would seek death only if her secret were revealed.

Fields opened his eyes and looked at her. At first his eyes were clouded with his efforts against the pain, but their expression quickly softened. She did not go to him but remained upright against the bulkhead. Her green eyes searched for the sign that would tell of her denouncement. But his face was composed, and he smiled sympathetically. "Fanny," he began, "I want to thank you. You acted very bravely. I owe you my life."

The void grew unbearable. She filled it. "Weems was going to kill me too. You can hardly owe me a life. I acted for myself, not for you." She pointed out her worthlessness, hoping he would not accept it.

"That's probably true," Fields said, shifting slightly and wincing. "But your bravery saved me, and I owe you a life. Nothing can alter that." He smiled. "But I have to ask you about the other members of this organization before we get into Hilton Head."

"Okay," she responded, searching his face, searching his eyes.

"Tell me everything you know about them and what your involvement was. We'll go from there. I'm sure you understand the reason for my questions. I only want to see that my daughter and her mother are released." Fields stopped and watched the girl. Damn those eyes, he thought. She's still scared to death.

"There's really not much for me to tell," Fanny offered. "Most of their people I've dealt with have been outside consultants, like you. The only true members of the organization I knew were Weems and the Colonel."

"Tell me about this Colonel. Who is he? Where can I find him?"

Fanny began slowly, haltingly. She told Fields of her first encounters with Colonel Burgess and how she had prospered in his employ. She withheld nothing, explaining her sporadic services, his rates of remuneration, and the means she'd used for maintaining contact with the Colonel. She supplied Fields with the Winchester address, a description of the house, its contents, and physical layout. After some prodding by Fields, she described the Colonel and his relationship with Weems.

"And what of Marianne and her mother?" he inquired, his voice strained either with pain and fatigue or emotionality; she couldn't determine which.

"Knowing what I do about the cruelty the Colonel's capable of, I fear greatly for them," she said softly. "I'm sorry, but I do. He's a monster. He doesn't—I mean, he simply isn't human. I can't begin to describe how *much* of a monster he really is. I'm truly sorry about your wife and daughter. I never knew, or I wouldn't have become involved—never." She eyed him, searching his face, hunting for any sign that his feelings toward her were turning negative.

He listened calmly, as if expecting her words. "Do you have any idea where they were being held?" He might have been asking if the weather report included rain.

"No," she replied truthfully. "No. At that point in the planning I was as much a prisoner as they were. They weren't telling me anything but where to go and what to say."

Fields nodded in understanding, eyed her again, forcing his face to remain calm, friendly, understanding. The girl was such a wreck, it was nearly impossible to tell the difference between self-serving lies and the results of her abuse. He must not allow the slightest sign of rage or disbelief to show through, or he could lose her cooperation totally.

She said, "I know Weems was very, very frightened of Benny. I think Weems was afraid that the Colonel was going to have Benny eliminate him after he had killed you. Oh, and there was some discussion that Benny would finish the job if Weems couldn't do it." The girl was searching her memory. He saw her struggle with something else. "Oh, one more thing," she added hurriedly. "If you were killed by the pirates, Benny was to take care of their elimination." She stood braced against the bulkhead, fearing that Fields would realize she had known of his planned murder and had failed to tell him.

"At the time it was said," Fields asked, "did you believe the Colonel? I mean, did you get the impression that this Benny was capable of eliminating the pirates?"

"Yes," she replied. "Definitely. And that he was capable of

killing you also.''

Fields allowed his gaze to drop from her face. It was maddening. "Fanny?" he asked. "Do you have the slightest idea where Donna and Marianne were taken?" His voice remained steady.

"No, I don't," she replied, an edge in her voice. "They were still at their home in Charleston when you spoke to them on the phone. After that I have no idea."

Then that, Fields thought, *is where I'll begin, and God help them all if they've been harmed. God help them all.* He thanked her again for her assistance and patience. He reminded her of his obligation. A life. He smiled again, thinly. She left the cabin.

Below decks the worn diesels shifted pitch. Fields could feel the sea-scoured trawler enter the crosscurrents of the sound. They were beginning the last leg of the return to Hilton Head. Another twenty minutes and they would be at anchor in Skull Creek. Dan Fields lowered his head and closed his eyes. The electric-blue throb of the gunshot wound filled the corners of his thoughts, obliterated his will and ability to think, and he again sank into the gentle waiting arms of unconsciousness. God help them all. God help them all. God . . .

Unconsciousness took him. Again he dreamed. A shortened gnome of a man with tobacco-colored skin and a wisp of grayed beard smiled benevolently through rheumy eyes. It was the Cambodian, Hsing Pao—pirate, smuggler, and father of nineteen sons. He was the creator of the strategy wherein packets of heroin were sewn into the deceased bodies of American soldiers and returned without fear of inspection by customs. He was fat, shrewd, and saw all white men as barbarians. He recognized the authority of no government, feared no man, and was a doting parent. Fields had infiltrated the man's organization, won the old man's confidence through bluff and bravado.

The plump figure sat squatting in the ashes, smiling broadly at Fields. He chuckled and the triple chins jiggled. Fields blushed with remembered shame. He had undertaken the arrest of the tough patriarch himself, informing Hsing Pao personally of his true role. Hsing Pao had sat expressionless through the account, then had asked Fields one favor. He had quietly, unemotionally requested that Fields permit him to commit suicide. Fields understood the savagery that passed for justice in the bush culture and was genuinely fond of the old man. He declined with regrets and excused himself momentarily. Upon his return Hsing Pao lay

dead upon the earthen floor of the hut, a bitter-scented liquid on
his lips.

Fields had loved the old smuggler and envied the man's sense
of history and family. In the perverted morality of a spy who
should not have been, Fields had betrayed a friend and his family
into the hands of a government dominated by cruel, savage men.
And yet Hsing Pao sits gleefully in the mud and ashes now and
smiles broadly without a trace of anger or resentment.

"Greetings, Yankee policeman." The gnome beams. "Your
face is greatly missed at the rice bowl. Your name remains upon
the lips of the family Hsing," he said, and smiled broadly,
peacefully. "You give great face to this unworthy smuggler. In a
civilized land where each life is but the turn of a waterwheel, you
perform a great honor to this one." The voice is neither English
nor any foreign dialect spoken by Fields. The words appear in his
thoughts without benefit of language. "Remember, Yankee Dan
policeman," he continues, the toothless grin wide upon the portly
face, "in our land, the Land of Civilized People, deceit is an art
form and not a matter for disgrace. It is only when you judge your
civilized soul by their barbarian standards that unhappiness comes
to you. You did as they asked and allowed me great face at the
same time. Next turn of the wheel, I shall show you new tricks
and we will eat rice and laugh together."

The fat form bounced on inner springs of glee, and Hsing Pao
was rushed by a multitude of giggling sons, daughters, grandsons,
granddaughters, cousins, nieces, and nephews. They bore the
gnome away among them, chattering loudly.

The great white snake seized Dan Fields and wrapped its coarse
coils tighter, ever tighter. He opened his eyes. He was tied to
crossed saplings in a small grassy plateau. The trees were
deciduous and North American. Below his knees, tongues of
yellowed flame licked upward lovingly, but each caress brought
searing, burning pain. Surrounding the fire and saplings, a
weaving line of nude figures danced, shuffling to the rhythm of
unheard drummers. The figures crouched as they hopped and
shuffled from right foot to left. Before each was a mask. The glow
from the flames painted the masks and the smudged and dirtied
nakedness of the bodies in shadows of red and bright planes of
orange.

The masks were caricatured faces of the men Fields had
infiltrated as an undercover agent during his career with the

bureau. Each had accepted him as friend, partner, or fellow traveler; each had been imprisoned for his misplaced confidence.

The tempo of the dance increased; the dancers whirled demonically. With a great shout they halted, faced the center of the clearing, and lowered the cartoonlike faces. Behind the masks were the faces of his daughter, Marianne; her mother, Donna; and John Lennon. The faces were much older and hardened than Fields knew them to be. In silence each dancer raised a pointed finger at Fields. The flames grew higher and burned without relief at his knees. The silent accusations filled him with dread. He began to shiver uncontrollably with some unknown fear, then the surrounding circle dispersed, and the obscenely naked body of Hsing Pao appeared in their midst. He was clapping his hands, hopping from one foot to the other, singing, "Same, same, nevermind. Same, same, nevermind."

Fields's eyes popped open, and he stared into a closely shaved, bespectacled face. "I sure hope you're the doctor," he croaked hoarsely, his body deep in fever. The face frowned in puzzlement at him and nodded affirmatively. "Thank God," whispered Fields, and lapsed into a dreamless sleep.

CHAPTER 15

DAN Fields awakened and leaned back into the feminine luxury of the bed. The linens were printed pastels, the mattress only slightly more dense than a cloud, the large pillows fluffy and lightly scented. The bed was king-size, high-posted, French Provincial. Diffused light from a wide stretch of gauzily curtained floor-to-ceiling windows filled the corners of the room. Carefully he drew an ever-deepening breath, expanding his lungs. Pain from the injured ribs surged through his chest but to a lesser degree than before, and starting much deeper into the inhalation. He explored the firm resistance of a tightly wound bandage holding the ribs in place, restricting the expansion of his chest. Then he focused his awakening consciousness upon his abdomen. The wound ached dully, throbbing in cadence with his slowed pulse.

An unfocused headache made his eyes squint. His mouth was dry. Very carefully he flexed the knee joint of his right leg. The joint responded but with limitations. It had been wrapped, and the tightness of the bandage restricted his movements within the limits of tolerable discomfort. Fighting against the fogginess of his narcotized mind, Fields began a thorough examination of his body, fingertips lightly exploring. He discovered a broad chest binder extending from his lower abdomen to just below his arms; wide adhesive bandages with thick gauze beneath the front and rear of his left shoulder; a tightly placed elastic bandage that extended eight inches above and below his right knee; and a small bandage on his right forearm. The exploration further revealed muscle tenderness in the right hip and that he was naked beneath the soft linens.

Fields tossed back the sheet and light comforter and sat. His vision swam and his stomach twisted. He closed his eyes and fought the nausea. It passed. He slid his legs over the side of the soft bed, resting his feet upon the thick carpeted floor. He blinked rapidly, then opened his eyes. He tried to breathe deeply but halted well short of his goal. He tried again. The combination of tight bandages and pain would not permit him a full breath.

Steadying himself against a nearby bureau, Fields rose and teetered precariously as his vision fuzzed and another wave of nausea washed over him. He thought of resting, returning to the bed, but dismissed the thought and again dominated the queasiness. His leg was solidly locked in a brace. He gradually placed his full weight on the injured knee. It would hold his weight, but it would not perform any turning motions. Adjusting for the dysfunction, he took a tentative short first step, taking care to avoid any rotation of the joint. Balancing himself against the furnishings, Fields made his way to the end of the bed. His goal was the door, and it lay more than ten feet beyond the aiding support of furniture. He decided to skirt the perimeter of the room, using the walls to support his unsteady progress.

Nearing the door, a third onslaught of vertigo assaulted him, and he groped blindly for support. He knocked a small figurine to the carpeted floor and winced at the careless noise. The sound of approaching footsteps raised his pulse and respiration, but he was unable to move quickly.

The door opened, and a tall, tanned girl with neat, shoulder-length auburn hair faced him. "You shouldn't be out of bed," she admonished, her face concerned and her voice throaty. Fields immediately liked the guileless, broad planes of her friendly smile.

"It seemed like a good idea at the time," he said, using both hands on the near wall for support. He looked at her, forced his eyes to focus on her face, and said, "Where am I, how long have I been here, and where are my clothes?"

The girl laughed, her head tossed back on a fine, strong neck, her smile showing bright, square teeth. "I was told you'd be something else when you came around"—she chuckled—"but I wasn't quite prepared for this." She gestured with an arm at Fields, who was bandaged, clinging to the wall, and completely naked. She smiled again and reached forward to take his arm, the good one. She was very tall, looking him full square in the eye. She wore a faded green T-shirt and tan shorts. No shoes. "Why don't you slip back into bed and rest for a minute?" she asked. "I'll get the doctor and he can answer your questions." With gentle pressure she tried to guide Fields back to bed. He resisted.

"No," he said, the sand of his voice packed and hard. "It took too much effort to make it this far. Before I move an inch, I want to know where I am, how long I've been here, and where the hell my clothes are."

The girl again smiled her broad-toothed smile. Eyes of brown flecked with gold took in his nakedness, then looked at his face again. Amusement twinkled across her face.

"Come on." Fields softened his approach slightly, liking her more with each exchange. "How about my clothes, at least? We haven't even been introduced." He smiled, she smiled back; they both meant it.

"About your clothes," she said, again increasing the gentle pressure on his arm. "I'm afraid I had to cut them off you last night when you came in. They're quite useless to you now."

He began to yield to the firm grip and let her guide him to the edge of the bed.

"If you'll rest here a minute," she said, positioning him, "I'll lend you something to put on. Please? You shouldn't be standing until the doctor looks you over." Her concern was genuine, and he sat. The tall girl moved fluidly to the chest beside the bed, opened the second drawer, and pulled out a shirt similar to the one she wore and placed it beside her, out of his reach. Then she opened the third drawer and pulled out a light tan pair of well-worn slacks. She talked as she moved. "Before you put these on, let me get the doctor down here. He'll only make you take them off again to examine you. I know you're sore. Any unnecessary movement is going to hurt." She moved to a small table, lifting the pastel blue princess phone. "I'll get the doctor. He's right upstairs." Without waiting for a reply, she tapped at the keys, her fingers moving with speedy familiarity. Fields leaned toward the clothing on the bed, but she fixed him with her clear eyes. "Wait," she said firmly, and he did.

"Hello, Mark," she said into the mouthpiece, her weight on one leg glancing at her wristwatch automatically. She was tall, broad-shouldered, and long-legged; easily six feet but retaining her full femininity. "He's awake, full of questions, and mobile, very mobile. Can you come right down? Fine. I'll tell him. Maybe that'll slow him down a little. Bye." She hung up. "He'll be right down," she offered. "He was still sleeping. You had us all up a little late last night, and he was grabbing a quick nap. He's only two floors above us. You can wait until he gets down, can't you?" She saw the hesitation in his eyes. "Good. We wouldn't want you to undo all of our hard work from last night, would we?"

It really wasn't a question. Fields ignored it and said, "Where am I?"

She smiled again. She could see the strength and purpose within the man, remembering Party John's description of his personality. She abandoned the standard instructions to keep the patient immobilized and unanswered until the doctor's return. "You're in Sea Pines Plantation, in one of the Turtle Lane condominiums on South Forest Beach. Do you know it?" she asked.

Fields gave her a nod. It was one of the more expensive developments on the island. Most of the dwellings were single-family affairs; the only condominiums were oceanfront and very, very expensive. Fields relaxed a notch. He withheld the questions springing to mind about the likable girl and her identity. He had no idea what arrangements had been made by Party John, didn't know how much, if anything, his hosts knew of him. "And I've been here since last night?" He made the question bland, unimportant.

"Yes," she told him but did not go further. The doctor's first examination of the conscious patient would include an exchange of questions and answers probing the patient's orientation and awareness. She had already overstepped the proper boundaries of nursing care by responding as she had, but the man sitting naked upon the foot of her bed was intense and driven and looked the type to bolt. She knew her business. She was very good.

"Before we go any further"—she diverted his next questions, feeling them forming in his mind—"let me get some vital signs. The doctor will want to know what they are." Without waiting for Fields's agreement she walked out of the room and returned with a thermometer, blood-pressure cuff, and a stethoscope dangling from her neck. She did not comment on the shirt and trousers being moved to a spot closer to the naked man but promptly placed the thermometer under his tongue. She then took his right wrist, the firm pressure from her middle finger seeking and finding his pulse. It was strong and elevated. She timed it with the sweep hand of her plain-banded wristwatch. She ignored tactfully the inquiring arch of the man's eyebrows and placed the pressure cuff upon his left bicep. She inflated the cuff, placed the stethoscope's diaphragm upon the blood vessels of his inner elbow, and observed the gauge as the systolic and diastolic pressures registered. The pressures were consistent with those she'd logged throughout the night.

"Do you jog?" she asked.

The thermometer still under his tongue, he wagged his head.

"Some other form of regular exercise?" she inquired, knowing the answer. His body was hard and lean, the muscle tissues firm and resilient. She had been there when Dan Fields had been carried into her apartment the night before, and she had spent the early-morning hours assisting in the treatment of his wounds. She knew full well the man was in excellent shape, a condition that did not occur accidentally. Fields nodded noncommittally. She extracted the thermometer from his mouth and quickly turned away to read it beyond his view. It registered 99.4 degrees.

"Well," Fields inquired, "how am I doing?"

She shook the thermometer down with three smart snaps of her wrist and dropped it into a plastic case. "The doctor should be here any minute," she said, evading his question again. "I need some information before he arrives. Do you have any pain?"

Fields laughed but stifled the laugh as soon as his ribs expanded. "Yes," he answered. "Everywhere."

She smiled down at him. "I'm not surprised," she responded warmly. The man had arrived in rough shape the night before. Two compound fractures of his right floating ribs, a small-caliber gunshot wound through the upper abdomen which had exited through the meaty tissues of his right shoulder, a severely dislocated right knee they had nearly failed to discover in his unconscious state, a deep puncture in the long extensor muscle of the right forearm, and a concussion. You *should* have pain, she thought, and plenty of it. But you'll survive. Judging from the numerous scars decorating your body, you've been there before.

"How's your vision?" she asked, bending and looking from one pupil to the other. As she raised his upper eyelids with a warm touch she asked, "Any blurriness or double vision?"

"At first, when I woke up, but not now."

She stood erect. His pupils were even, both the same diameter. The concussion had passed. "Nausea?" she asked, hands on hips, arms akimbo.

"No," he lied, and reached for the slacks.

She was faster, scooping up slacks and shirt and whisking them behind her onto a tall chest of drawers. "Why don't you get back under the covers now?" she urged. "The doctor will be here very shortly." She glanced pointedly at his nakedness. "We wouldn't want you to take a chill." They grinned together, and he felt himself stirring.

"I really am fine," Fields said, pushing off from the bed, needing the movement to halt any further developments. As he stood, a clean-shaven silver-haired man entered the room.

The doctor was very young, and the incongruity of the silver hair and dark black eyebrows gave his face a comic aspect. "Ah," the doctor said, his voice a strong baritone. "Good to see you feeling so well this morning." He took Fields firmly by the arm and guided him to the bed. "Give me a minute with my assistant, Mr. Jones, and I'll be right back in."

Fields caught the intelligent eyes, looking for signs of understanding. He allowed himself to be positioned on the bed, but he remained sitting. "I'm in a real hurry."

The doctor with the young face arched an imperious eyebrow. "I'll only be a minute," he replied, smiling with his mouth. The eyes were hard and alert, appraising him.

Must be a surgeon, thought Fields, bristling at the unspoken arrogance.

The young face with the white hair and the tall girl swept out of the room, snatching the clothing she'd offered him from the top of the chest of drawers. The door clicked behind them.

Fields could hear their muted voices. His was crisp, impatient, demanding; hers was smooth and unruffled. Definitely a surgeon, he concluded. His thoughts were interrupted as they reentered the room.

"Mr. Jones," the doctor began brusquely, courtesy an unknown attitude in his hurried world of life and death and profit. "First I'm going to examine you. Kindly hold your questions until I'm done." He did not wait for assent.

Fields gave no sign of agreement or understanding, disliking the man instantly. A surgeon for certain, he thought.

The doctor began a thorough examination of Fields. Eyes, ears, nose, throat, head, chest, neck, arms, shoulders, hands, legs, knees, and feet. He was brusque, fast, and communicated in short commands and grunts. His questions were direct, and he barely listened to the answers, secure that he knew the response in advance. His manipulations hurt Fields, shot flames of fire into his shoulder and knee, but Fields would not protest or cry out, hating the man and tolerating his examination but only barely.

"Fine," the doctor concluded, and stood. "Mr. Jones, your friend arranged for your care here as long as necessary." The doctor jiggled change in the pocket of preppy green slacks. "You'll be here for at least two more days, possibly three or four. It depends on your progress and on what kind of arrangements can be made for supplementary care. You can expect some pain, but I've left medications with your nurse. I would caution you not to use them indiscriminately, but do ask for them if you need them. You are to rest in bed and let my work have a chance. I'll look in on you from time to time, but for now you'll be attended by the nurse." He pointed his chin at the tall girl. "You can call her Mary. Do you have any questions?" he asked, clearly not wanting any.

"No," came Fields's short reply.

The doctor smiled again with just his mouth, beckoned authoritatively to the girl, and they both left the room.

Fields waited short moments, then rose from the bed. The pain during the examination had cleared his head of the last remnants of the mind-dulling narcotics. He favored his knee but walked more firmly than before, reaching the chest of drawers on the far side of the bed without support. He quietly slid open the third drawer and removed a faded pair of jeans. He closed the drawer and opened the one directly above it, removing a short-sleeved sweatshirt of faded gray.

Fields slid the slacks over his left foot first, then more slowly over his right. The jeans were the right length but fit snugly in the waist and crotch. He zippered them partially, far enough to hold them securely, but abandoned any hope of closing the catch at the waist. He then lifted the sweatshirt over his head. It was large and bulky and made the passage over his head and left arm uneventful. But, pushing his right arm through the armhole, he drew in his breath sharply as pain sliced through the bullet's exit wound in his shoulder. He cursed and fought the pain.

Fields rested, letting the rush of his pulse diminish and his vision clear. He steadied himself and looked into the mirror above the low chest. His face stared grimly back at him. He tried to smooth some of the ruffled hairs back into place, then abandoned the efforts. It was Hilton Head, and a tousled, windblown appearance would raise no eyebrows. He moved on bare feet to the door and listened. The room beyond was silent.

Slowly and silently Fields turned the knob and opened the door. He peered out. A wide, colorful splash of Oriental carpet framed an enormous room. Floor-to-ceiling plate-glass windows opened onto the Atlantic. Fields eased out of the doorway and began his search for the exit.

Knowing that the apartment would have an entrance away from the view, he moved to the opposite side of the apartment. Nearing the end of the room, Fields peered into the hallway and saw the entrance doors. They were custom-carved double doors, bedecked with rich brass hardware. He moved toward them.

"Aren't you the perfect patient." Her voice speared him from behind.

Fields turned to face her. She was alone, smirking, her hands on her fine hips again. "No," he replied good-naturedly, "I'm not. No reflection on you or your abilities, but I have to leave." She eyed his clothing. "I'm sorry about your clothes," Fields apologized. "I'll see that you get them back." He turned to leave.

"You're quite safe here," she volunteered, and wedged herself between Fields and the door. "We haven't told anyone about you, and I don't think Party John would tell anyone. Please come back to bed. You shouldn't be up yet. You are seriously injured."

Fields saw the concern on her friendly face. Everything within his efficent, professional being shouted that he should leave and disassociate himself from the girl, the surgeon, and his current vulnerability. His continued presence violated the rules of survival. Too many unknowns were floating, too many people were involved, and he did not have control. He knew nothing about the girl or the doctor, had no idea how much security had been in force when he was brought in, nor what they had been told. He needed to leave immediately and sever all connections with these strangers. Any information they already possessed could be a threat to him and his ability to work effectively for the release of his daughter and ex-wife. If they were alive. But her face was open and trusting and still amused. "Do you have any idea what you're involved with?" he asked, ignoring his own philosophy.

She cocked her head to the side. Her full lips pursed pensively, and she eyed him thoughtfully. "Yes, I think I do," she answered. "Party John speaks very highly of you. And he assured me you weren't hiding from the police. I believed him." She shrugged. "Yes, I know what I'm doing."

"You don't strike me as one of Party John's chippies," Fields offered.

Her molded eyebrows went up a quarter of an inch. "You don't exactly strike me as one of his normal associates, either," she countered.

Fields smiled, properly rebuked. "I'm sorry," he said, and turned to go. "You've been very nice, but I have business that won't keep. Thank you very much." He smiled a near smile, opened the dead bolt, turned the lower latch, and left. Fields walked down the corridor and punched the button for the elevator. She joined him, standing by his side. He could see her repressed grin from the corner of his eye.

"You don't know what you're getting into," Fields reasoned, turning to see if they had been observed in the hallway. "Listen," he continued in a whisper, "I'm involved with some very bad men, and just being seen with me can be very, very dangerous to you. Please go back to your apartment. I like you. I don't want to see you hurt."

She stared at the illuminated orange circles above the elevator door. The elevator slid noisily open. "Where are you going?" she asked, voice innocent, eyes amused. The elevator doors began to hiss closed, and he stopped them with his arm and stepped in, his eyes darting to check the hallway. She stepped in, and he noticed she clutched a small purse. He frowned at her and stabbed the lobby button.

"First," he snapped, "I'm getting the hell out of here. Second, I'm getting some clothes that fit." He looked at his bare feet. "And some shoes! Then I've got business out of town. Now, please," he said more pleasantly, "you've done your job, I'm certain you'll be more than well paid, so why don't you just let me alone?"

"You shouldn't walk too far on that knee," she said. "Too much strain and it will start to swell again, and then no matter how big and brave you are, you won't be able to go anywhere."

Fields looked at her, exasperated, but knowing she was right. The knee was throbbing already, and the bandages were biting into his flesh. "I was going to flag a ride," he said halfheartedly.

Translation: "I'm going to steal a car." And she knew it.

"Why go to the trouble?" she asked. Again she was innocence and mild amusement. "My car's downstairs. If you insist on leaving, the least I can do is give you a lift." She paused as the doors opened. The lobby was vacant. "Party John made me promise to look after you. Let me keep that promise."

Fields wagged his head. "Listen, Mary, or whoever you are," he began, anger stirring in his voice. "I must not be getting through to you. I don't want you to know who I am or where I go." His eyes narrowed as he focused on her. "Even if you don't have the good sense to recognize danger, I still do. It's best for both of us, believe me, that you know as little about me as possible. But if you want to be so damned helpful, give me the keys to your car and I'll see that it's returned." Fields held out a hand.

A middle-aged couple entered the lobby, arguing harshly. They stopped when they saw Fields and the girl in the elevator. "Oh, Hello, Tracey," muttered the man. He was short, bald, and plump, dressed in bathing trunks and a flowered shirt. His companion was tall and thin, and she wore a matching flowered shirt over a dark swimsuit. She glowered, radiating hostility to him in particular and the world in general.

"Hello, Mr. Weinglass," the girl replied cheerily. "How's the beach today?" She guided Fields out of the elevator.

"It's too windy for us." The man was eager for conversation with anyone, but his mate dragged him into the elevator. "Why don't you come down for a drink later on," he continued. "Oh, and bring your friend, too. . . ." The elevator doors closed, and his companion resumed her litany. Her shouts floated higher and faded as the elevator rose. Fields and the girl were left alone in the air-conditioned greenery of the lobby.

"As for secrecy," she whispered from the side of her mouth, "I know who you are and where you live, and have for more than a year. Why don't you let me drive you?"

Fields was stunned and stood motionless. Her fine, long fingers wrapped themselves around his elbow, and she steered him through the lobby.

"Did Party John . . . ?"

"No, of course not." She laughed deep in her throat. They passed through two sets of heavy outer doors. "One of the girls I work with lives down on North Forest Beach," she explained.

"She's pointed you out to me a couple of times on the beach, and well, I've seen you around the island."

Fields was reappraising her, the dawn of suspicion lighting his cold eyes.

"Come on, now," she said with a slight tug. "Don't go paranoid on me. My interest in you was strictly physical." The frank admission was followed by a smile that showed all of her teeth. He believed her. They stopped beside a maroon Pontiac Trans-Am with a golden eagle emblazoned boldly upon the hood. "Go on, get in, Mr. Dan Fields Jones. I'm a safe driver, you won't have to worry." Again he believed her. He sat in the car. She trotted to the driver's side, slid into the deep bucket of the seat, and roared the car to life.

"Do you want to go to your place?"

"Yes," he replied, "I need some clothes and a few other things. And a car."

She steered the racy car out of the parking area and onto Forest Beach Drive.

"It's down from the circle, just off of—"

"Oh, I know the house," she said without turning to face him. She drove with smooth competence. "I've walked past on several occasions with Gail. She's my girlfriend. She lives just up the street from your place." Fields shrugged, his gesture an apology for not noticing. "Yeah," she continued. "We've passed your house a lot of times, back and forth on the way to the beach. A couple of times you were outside with your dog and waved to Gail. Don't you remember me at all?"

Fields lied. "Oh, that's where I've seen you."

"By the way, where is your dog? He's such a cute thing. I don't think I've ever seen a happier animal in my life. Is someone looking after him for you?"

Fields turned from her to look at the occupants of a car they passed. When he turned back, his face was set and the blue eyes were very cold. Looking at the road before them, he said, "He's dead, Tracey."

She darted a quick glance at the man beside her and felt the change in his mood. "I'm sorry," she offered. She motored the width of the island, filling his silence with idle chatter about herself.

Her name was Tracey Barkley, she was twenty-five years old, the only daughter of a moderately well-off industrialist. Her father had encouraged her to complete her nursing education and had rewarded her accomplishment with clear title to a Turtle Lane condominium on Hilton Head. That revelation almost elicited a response from Fields but not quite. A property that sold on the market for a minimum of a quarter of a million dollars was some graduation gift. Fields redefined the term *moderately well off* for future reference.

Tracey began work at the Hilton Head Hospital shortly after graduation from nursing school. She was assigned to the emergency room and liked the work. She had never been married, was under no pressure from her parents to do so, and thoroughly enjoyed the life on Hilton Head. She divided her time between the pleasures of island life and her work, reading widely and perfecting her golf and tennis, the mandatory sports of the island. And she totally enjoyed the favorite pastime of the native islanders—gossip. She delivered this short, personal history without prompting, all the while assuring Fields she would never discuss him with others.

Tracey despised the doctor. She supplied Fields with the man's true identity, said yes, he was a surgeon, and then answered Fields's unspoken questions. She had agreed to help Party John not for money but as a personal favor. Treating any gunshot wound without reporting it to the police was a crime and cause for loss of her nursing license, but sometimes special favors were rendered in the medical community. She was aware the doctor had agreed to treat Fields to facilitate a large transaction of cocaine, but she was quick to add that she was in no way involved with drug traffic. Tracey gabbed about cocaine abuse, common among hospital personnel, admitted to having tried it one wild night, but had never used it again. She said that it burned her nasal membranes and was more bother than it was worth.

"Then why are you involved in this mess?"

"Because," she answered, pulling onto his street, "Party John asked me to. He did a very big favor some time ago for a friend of mine."

"And on the strength of that alone," Fields asked, "you agreed to risk your license and God knows what else?" His doubt was clear, unmistakable.

"Yes," she answered evenly, ignoring his tone. "It was a very big favor, and the friend was very close." She volunteered nothing further, and Fields accepted her justification. He noted her closemouthedness regarding a private matter. She would treat his privacy with the same respect.

She pulled the car to rest in front of his sandy drive and killed the motor. Fields eased himself out and hobbled to the rear of the garage. He located a large stone in the brush and sand and turned it over with his left foot. Tracey bent to the ground, sparing him the effort, and retrieved the key. She handed it to Fields, and they walked together to the front door. Fields focused on reading the air and the signs around the house. He looked for anything out of place or out of the ordinary but found nothing.

"Tracey," he said, turning to her, "you've been great. I think you'd better go now. Some people have no respect for innocence." He paused and smiled at her. "I like you. I don't want to see you get hurt."

"That's wonderful!" she exclaimed, flashing that devastating smile again. "But it's broad daylight, and I doubt anything terrible is going to happen." She saw the firmness of his rejection coming. "Why don't you go in and check the house if you want. I'll wait out here if it makes you feel any better."

Fields prepared to dismiss the lovely girl in such a manner as to leave no room for further maneuvering on her part. He forced his eyes to harden and turned to face her. "Look, Tracey," he snapped, his voice lashing out, "I don't give a good—" The ringing of the telephone stopped him. "Wait here," he ordered, and turned the key in the lock. He went in, reaching the phone on the third ring.

"Hello?"

"Hello," the voice answered. "Is this Mr. Fields? Mr. Dan Fields?"

"Yes, it is," he replied, not recognizing the caller.

"Mr. Fields"—the voice was thin and frail with age—"this is Henry Thorpe from Charleston. Do you remember me? You gave me your number some time ago, when you were visiting."

"Yes, Mr. Thorpe." Fields placed the name and voice. Thorpe was an elderly neighbor of his ex-wife and daughter in Charleston. Fields felt a trickle of sweat sliding between his shoulder blades.

"Mr. Fields," the old voice continued, "I thought I'd better give you a call. There's all kinds of police cars out front and back of the house."

"How about Donna and Marianne?" Fields demanded. "Are they okay?"

"I don't know, Mr. Fields," the old man replied. "I haven't seen them the last few days."

"What happened?" The control was slipping from his voice. "What's going on?"

"I don't know. All I know is that there are more police cars outside than I've ever seen together in one spot. A neighbor told me they're going to break down the door to your wife's house. That's all I know."

"Can't you tell me if they're okay?" Fields asked, his voice pleading.

"No, son."

"I'm on my way," said Fields, and he hung up the phone. Tracey had padded into the room and stood before him.

"Has something happened?"

Fields stared at her in confusion, then remembered. He stepped closer to her. "Yes," he answered in a small voice, his eyes distant and clouded. "Something's very wrong. I'm going to Charleston right away."

"Oh, no! Has something happened to Party John?"

"What?" Fields asked, confusion still clouding his eyes. "Oh, no, not Party John. It's my daughter and ex-wife. They live in Charleston."

She sped past his answer. "Dan, don't worry too much. It's probably not as serious as it sounds. Don't think the worst. Get your things and I'll drive you," she offered. "I'm off today and I don't mind. Besides," she said, "I'm your nurse for today, whether you like it or not."

Fields stood in the dappled sunlight falling from the windows above. He dialed the number of the home in Charleston. In monotonic precision a recorded voice informed him that the number was temporarily out of order. He lowered the receiver to its cradle.

"Tracey," he asked, "would you mind going upstairs for me? The large dresser at the foot of the bed. Top drawer is underwear and socks; slacks are in the closet. Oh, and a shirt too. That's in the same place. And I'll need some identification; there's a wallet lying on top of the dresser. If you don't mind?"

She started up the carpeted stairway before he had finished speaking. "Of course I don't mind," she said. "You shouldn't be running up steps for a few days, anyhow."

"Right," Fields replied, moving to a heavy wooden bookshelf.

He bent to the side of the shelf and removed the hidden screws that secured the unit to the wall and lifted the bottom of the shelf away from the wall. The top remained in place, fastened by a concealed hinge. From the cavity within, Fields withdrew the one remaining weapon. It was a .45-caliber automatic pistol, 1921 model, also customized by the Florida gunsmith, Giles. Totally remachined to perfect tolerance, the weapon would fire reliably, accurately, and with an action so smooth that an adolescent could fire the pistol one-handed without severe recoil. Fields repositioned the shelf, replaced the hidden screws, and secreted the weapon beneath the sofa cushions. He stood waiting for Tracey, the sounds of her movements spilling over the loft.

"Hey!" she called from above, "how about some shoes?"

"Right," Fields answered. "The tan loafers."

"Okay," she called, "I see them."

The tall, warm woman brought the clothes down the stairs and laid them on the edge of the sofa.

Fields took them and limped into a small room off the entrance and dressed. After long minutes he stepped out, pale, and laid the clothing he'd taken from her room in her arms. "Thank you, Tracey," he said, "but this is where we part company." Fields moved to an Oriental bowl on the countertop that divided the small, airy kitchen from the open space of the first floor. He fished inside and palmed a spare set of keys. Dan Fields then marched to the sofa, retrieved the pistol from beneath the cushion, and tucked it in his waistband.

Tracey watched him, wide-eyed and openmouthed. "Dan! Whatever is going on, I don't think you're going to solve it like that. Please, put that thing away and let me drive you."

Fields strode past her, out the front door. She followed him outside. His face was set, his jaws tightly locked; his eyes were dark and cold, the blue barely visible. He entered the garage.

Tracey pursued him, pressing her argument. "Dan, your knee is one thing, but your wound needs rest. Please!" she shouted. "Let me drive you! You're likely to hemorrhage if you drive that distance!"

Fields ignored her. He moved to the front doors of the tiny structure, released the catches, and opened them wide. Sitting inside was a gleaming yellow sportster. It was a 1954 TF by MG, its boxed and louvered hood secured by a broad leather belt. The fenders were sensually rolled, and the leatherwork was a soft, supple black. The interior was a combination of rolled and tufted leather pleating, the dash a highly polished walnut. The top was down, and the chromework danced and sparkled with reflected sunlight.

Fields walked to the driver's side and opened the small, low-cut door. He lowered himself, his eyes closed against the white starbursts of fire, into the perfectly restored cockpit and worked the key.

"I'll be damned if you're getting away that easily!" she shouted, and plopped down in the deep-cushioned passenger's seat.

"Tracey," he snarled, "this is none of your business. Get out of my car and go back to the safety of your own world. You don't belong in this one." Fields used his thumb and depressed the remote starter button located in the exact center of the walnut dash. The engine leapt to life with a deep-throated growl. He revved it twice.

"The only way I get out of this car is if you let me drive you!" she shouted over the loping snarl of the engine. "That, or put me out physically. And I don't think you can do that right now, at least not without hurting yourself very badly."

Fields glared at her and jammed the car into first gear. He popped the clutch, and the sportster leapt forward. At the end of the drive he changed into second, and the tires bit into the sand and gravel of the street. The acceleration pressed him against the seat back, but he clenched his teeth and leaned into the pain. His mind zeroed in on the task of driving, and he blanked all other thoughts from his mind. The motorcar was going like hell before he turned onto the paved road in a showering spray of dark sand and fine gravel. Nearing the first traffic circle, he touched the walnut wheel, jumped over two lanes, and passed a line of gawking tourists. He downshifted again, the tiny engine howling, and cut the tourists off as he pulled onto the only highway leading off the island.

He accelerated in perfect harmony with the peaking rpms of the tuned engine, then reached over and flipped a wooden toggle switch. Immediately a howling whine screamed from beneath the hood. He had engaged the Borg-Warner supercharger, and the horsepower of the four-cylinder engine doubled. The car shot forward in a surging thrust that pained his ribs and pressed Tracey deep into the cushions.

The low-slung car jetted through the slower traffic, careening wildly and closing the distance to the next clump of traffic. The speed markers whisked by, and Tracey leaned forward to check their speed. She looked away when the speedometer touched ninety miles per hour but felt the car continue to accelerate. She gripped the dash handle with one hand and used the other to keep her hair from blinding her as it whipped at her face in the rushing wind.

Fields flew down the island highway with no regard for restrictions or traffic. Twice he braked suddenly to avoid a rear-end collision with more moderate drivers. The small car nosed down each time but skidded in a tight, straight course, avoiding the crash. In scant minutes he piloted the howling vehicle over the bridge and streaked for the mainland.

Wheeling sharply to the right, Fields cut north onto the highway, changed rapidly up through the gears, and the car settled into the road. Throughout Fields had blanked his mind to all thoughts except the problems of the road. Easing the straining engine into a steady cruise at ninety-five miles per hour, he checked the rearview and side mirrors, found them empty, and sighed shallowly. Tracey sat beside him, her knuckles white as she hung on to the dash handle.

With an effort at mental discipline Fields kept his thoughts on the traffic. He sighted the congested vehicles ahead and either slowed or accelerated to shoot the responsive car through their midst. Frequently his startling presence and then abrupt disappearance into the distance ahead was saluted with horn and epithet. Grim-faced, he ignored them.

He drove hard against the upper limits of his ability. The miles to Charleston passed by in a kaleidoscopic rush of sound and color, and soon he wheeled the sleek car into a screaming turn at Old Town Charleston.

Mid-morning Charleston traffic brought his mad rush to a crawl. Making what progress the press of vehicles would allow, Fields flipped the toggle and killed the supercharger. Its howl dropped immediately, drawing a curious glance from an old man in a weathered Cadillac. Excess energy overfilled Dan Fields, and he banged on the walnut wheel with the flat of his hand.

Tracey relaxed her death grip and pushed her tangled hair back from her face. "Where on earth did you learn to drive like that?" she asked with fear and grudging admiration in her voice. He did not respond. "How do you feel?" she asked in a more controlled and professional tone. Silence. He accelerated the car into a closing space between two cars, shot forward forty yards, and slowed again. "I'm concerned about your wounds," she continued, trying to distract him from his fears. "How is the shoulder? Is the pain much worse?"

Fields spun the wheel, shifted down into second gear, and took a hard left across the flow of oncoming traffic. Horns blatted angrily in his wake. He shot down the near empty side street and jumped the stop sign at thirty miles an hour. He accelerated quickly through the gears, the engine growling. He jumped three stop signs at a roll, screeched into a right, and again cut in front of traffic as he turned left onto a tree-lined boulevard of restored town houses.

Sixty yards beyond, the street was blocked off by two marked police units, three double-parked unmarked detective cruisers, and a van that housed the mobile crime lab of the Charleston Police Department.

Tracey felt the hair on her arms and neck raise. A lump of sidewalk spectators stood whispering. Fields slid the pistol from his waist. Her eyes widened in horror, but words would not come to her lips. Fields tucked the weapon under the low seat as he braked the car at the blockade. A uniformed officer authoritatively waved him on, signaling him to turn left into a narrow alley, a makeshift detour around the bottleneck of departmental vehicles and onlookers.

Fields killed the engine, the mirrored chrome bumper inches from the officer's legs.

"Hey!" the uniform shouted from behind dark glasses. "You can't stop here. Get that car out of here! This ain't no circus!" Fields had levered himself awkwardly out of the low seat. He slammed the door shut and stepped forward, his eyes seeing only the crowd and the empty police cars.

"Wait just a damn minute!" the officer ordered. He moved to block Fields's path and grabbed him by the arm. Fields met the officer's gaze. His eyes were chunks of North Atlantic ice, his face a frozen sculpture of hate and fatigue. The officer released his grip.

"Listen," said the officer more politely, "you can't just leave your car in the middle of the street. Why don't you . . . ?" Fields passed him, limping toward the middle of the block.

"I'll move it, Officer," Tracey volunteered, catching the policeman in mid-turn. "His family lives here." She pried her long legs out of the well of the seat and moved swiftly around the bright yellow car. "I'll park it down there," she said, gesturing to the alley.

"All right," the officer stated, "but don't put it in the alley. Go over to the next block."

Tracey turned the key, but the starter did not engage. The officer was frowning. He advanced toward her when she remembered the separate starter switch in the center of the walnut dash. She stabbed at it nervously, suddenly terrified that any incident would lead to the discovery of the pistol beneath her seat. The engine coughed and took; she fought the gearshift lever into reverse and backed away from the stern-faced officer. Turning to enter the alley, she could see Fields as he parted the outer limits of the spectators.

A very tall, lean police officer in a wilted uniform stood sad-faced at the door to the town house. Since the start of his shift that morning he had been in the same position, except for a brief look at the first floor of the home. That short glance had dislodged his breakfast and coffee. Since then he had sadly maintained his post, admitting teams of investigators, mobile lab technicians, and a continuous flow of ranking police administrators. He had denied entrance to representatives of two newspapers, three radio stations, and the live minicam crew from the television station. His bladder was painfully overstretched, and he was praying for the arrival of his patrol sergeant and a few moments of relief.

He saw Dan Fields as he knifed through the crowd. The man did not have the expensive clothing and grooming of the old Charleston neighborhood. Rather he was dressed casually, his face was deeply tanned, and his hair was roughly windblown. The second the sentry saw him, he knew the man was coming straight for the door. The officer hitched his blue uniform trousers farther up his hips and shifted the position of his holster.

"You can't go in, sir," he ordered as Fields placed his foot on the first of the three steps.

Fields stopped. His face was immobile, frozen with his effort at control. "My name is Dan Fields," he said softly. "My family lives in this house."

The officer's eyes winced, and he sighed. "I'll have Lieutenant Gordon come right out and talk to you, sir," he said sympathetically. Fields noted each innuendo of sadness and steeled himself. The officer reached in and opened the door a crack; keeping his eyes on Fields he murmured to a figure within. In response to an inquiry he nodded his head. He pulled the door closed.

"I told him, Mr. Fields. He'll be out in just a few minutes." He let his eyes find relief in a quick scan of the strangely quiet crowd. The television crew was setting up for a take on the sidewalk. Fields was buying none of it.

"Move aside, Officer!" Fields snapped. "I told you who I am, and I'm going in *now!*" The officer was stung. He'd heard the same tone only once before in his career when a night-shift police captain had caught him in a darkened alley with a prostitute in his car. The memory was seventeen years old. He was torn with conflicting impulses. His trained ear jumped at the tone of command, his paternal emotions went out to the man in an empathic flow of sorrow, and his instinct for covering his own ass demanded that he bar the door.

The conflict was satisfactorily resolved when a solid man in a crumpled dark blue jacket stepped onto the small porch. He was of medium height, but his shoulders were very broad and rounded. They sloped from his thick neck and curved on down into his bulging upper arms. He was thick-bodied, his stomach spreading the buttons on the front of his wrinkled white shirt. His trousers were gray, too short by several inches, and they revealed two inches of scaling white skin at his thick ankles. His dark socks were being slowly eaten by his well-worn shoes.

"Thank you, Officer," he said in a gravelly voice that matched his beefy, reddened face and squared jaw. His hair was white and trimmed closely in a recent crew cut. Watery blue eyes were enlarged by thick, bifocal spectacles in simple black frames. "Mr. Fields?" the lieutenant growled as he came down the steps in an arthritic waddle. He took Fields's right hand in an outstretched paw and put his left arm around Fields's shoulder, encircling him and guiding him away from the door. He smelled strongly of cheap cigars and Lavoris. "I'm Billy Gordon," he said affably. "I'm a lieutenant detective with the Charleston Police Department. Let's talk over here for a minute, can we?" Subtle pressure took Fields four steps from the door. A rising murmur from the crowd accompanied their movements.

"What's happened?" Fields inquired, his voice hoarse with fear. He knew the answer by looking at the collection of official cars and personnel, the crowd, the blockade, the news team.

"Mr. Fields," the chunky lieutenant replied, "you came up from Hilton Head Island?"

"Yes," said Fields, blinking too often in the sunlight. "What's happened?"

"Let me get a few things clear first." The white-haired man was kindly. "You're the child's father?"

"Yes," Fields said testily. "I'm Marianne's father. What the hell's going on here, Lieutenant?" he barked. "Where are they? Are they all right?" His voice was growing louder, more urgent.

"They're both dead, son." The older man said it with a shrug of his bunched shoulders. Kinder to get it over quickly. He stood still and watched as Fields shrank into himself, the eyes blinking rapidly as they fought the pressure of hot tears. His jaw muscles twitched in rhythmic spasms. Fields turned right and left blindly. His body demanded that he move.

"Look, son"—the white-haired man tugged at Fields's elbow compassionately—"I'm sorry. I'm sorry you had to hear it out here like this." The older man tugged a little more firmly, turning Fields toward the impromptu municipal parking lot. "Let's go over and sit in my car for a few minutes." He was leaning in that direction, towing Fields behind him. Fields slipped his arm out of the man's grasp and stepped toward the door.

"Mr. Fields!" the lieutenant ordered. "Don't go in there. Not now."

Fields hesitated and said over his shoulder, "I'm not sitting in any car, and I'm not standing out here while you—"

A perfectly coiffed platinum blonde in a lightweight tailored suit and heels strode forward, microphone in hand and camera crew filming from behind her. She waved the microphone in the lieutenant's face. "This is Martha Parker with your Action-Cam News Crew. Lieutenant Billy Gordon of the Charleston Police Department's Homicide Squad has just stepped outside the Baker Street residence. Lieutenant?" she called, her voice strident, "is it true, as earlier reports indicated, that the occupants of the house were dismembered into pieces with an electric carving knife?" She expressed the perfect amount of unspoken horror and shock that would attract the attention of her viewers.

Fields turned, his face white, his jaw slack.

The camera crew filmed him as he bolted for the front door of the town house, took two of the three steps, and tossed the uniformed sentry to the side. In the same motion he turned the knob and ran into the main room.

"Where are they?" he bellowed. A portly technician in protective overalls dropped his expensive Nikon and emitted a responsive "Arrrghhh!" as the camera lens shattered on the hardwood floor. A thinner, older man in identical overalls, collecting specimens on his hands and knees, leapt to his feet and turned his rodentlike head in tight sweeps. A uniformed police major descending the stained carpet of the stairs froze in mid-step, and a thin-lipped investigator in a smart summer-weight vested suit ran in from the adjoining kitchen with his revolver drawn. He slipped in a pool of dark liquid on the polished wood floor and fell heavily. Lieutenant Billy Gordon, despite his arthritic joints, was two steps behind Fields.

"Where are they?" came the bellow again, Fields's terror, hatred, and primitive rage vibrating against the red-smeared walls. The house was overfilled with the compressed emotion of the sound.

"Mr. Fields!" Lieutenant Gordon pleaded, wrapping him in a huge arm, "come on back outside," he urged gently. "There's nothing you can do for them in here. You know that. Come on back outside." Again he was steering Fields, turning him away from the horror. Fields's eyes took in the numerous signs of butchery that were manifest in the room. Each new visual image intensified his panic and magnified his feeling of impotence and frustration.

"No!" he shouted, tearing free from the big-boned man's grasp. "Where are they?" he roared again as he whirled around the befouled room, then dashed for the kitchen and dining area to the rear of the house. Gordon was a half step behind, wincing at the effort but maintaining his pace.

"Mr. Fields!" he urged. "Don't go out there. Please!"

Dan Fields stood paralyzed at the rear door leading from the kitchen to the small brick areaway that connected with the garage on the alley. Below him, the coroner and two forensic specialists were framed in hot, white light emitted by powerful portable lamps. Upon the garage floor were dark green garbage bags, their contents wetly exposed. Each bag had been sliced open and the plastic pulled back to reveal the contents. There were seven bags. A gristled thigh jutted upward from the maw, its end darkly clotted. Sightless eyes locked in eternal agony and terror stared from a bloody grimace above a severed neck. Small arms, larger arms, a leg and foot that began improbably from a flat, sticky surface and went brutally into another unidentifiable lump of gore. Flies hummed noisily.

Fields stared, numb, his eyes gone wide with horror and disbelief. Then a sound that traveled from the depths of his ancestry up through time and into his throat began and would not end. It was a cry of wounded guilt and outrage, a cry that rose the hackles on the necks of all those present. It increased in volume, peaked, and sustained a keening wail. His arms flapped helplessly at his sides, and his eyes rolled up until all sign of pupil and iris was gone, white alone remaining.

The lieutenant grabbed Fields in a protective bear hug and held him. Fields struggled weakly against the restraint, but the primitive keen born four thousand years earlier continued to rise and fall.

The men who heard the sound were pierced by it. They were hardened professionals, men who lived with the brutal realities of death and tragedy who long ago had become callous and immune to the repeated assaults upon their natural sensitivities. They heard the wild, inarticulate wail of an uncultured savage, and it swept away the years of protective scarring. The howl was independent of language. It expressed, as words could not, the inescapable guilt of all parents who survive the death of their offspring. It was mindless and crossed centuries to explode clearly in the present. It mourned, raged, hated, begged, and blamed; most of all, it blamed.

Lieutenant Gordon held tightly to the anguished man, endured his feeble blows, and hugged him deeper into himself. He absorbed the man's agony, taking from him the uncontrollable overflow of guilt and outrage. He repeated continuously, "It's all right, son. It's all right. It's all right." The words were meaningless mouthings, but the repetitive sound and soothing tone were Fields's only defense against insanity. In his thirty-seven years with the Charleston Police Department Lieutenant Billy Gordon had seen this kind of grief before and knew how easily it could kill or disable the strongest of men and women. He held Fields, ignored his cries and curses, and crooned softly to him, caring for him and soothing him slowly back to rationality. Fields's howls faded to dry, racking sobs that expanded the bindings of his chest, but the pain brought no response from the man. He rocked, numb and mindless, in the protective embrace. When the sobs receded, Fields stood red-eyed and empty. Billy Gordon guided him back into the house.

TO: Police Commissioner Howard Bingerly
FROM: Lieutenant Detective William Gordon
SUBJECT: Homicide; Fields, Donna and Marianne
 Sir:
 At 0848 hours, the undersigned received notification from Communications Division of a possible homicide at the location of 374 Baker St. The request for assistance from the Homicide Squad originated from Captain Leonard Wellingham, District Commander of the Old Town District.
 The undersigned, in company with Sergeant Detective Morris Webber, arrived on the crime scene at 0918 hours where control of the investigation was assumed from Captain Wellingham. Upon our arrival the residence had been properly cordoned off, and the scene and the evidence had been adequately maintained.
 Investigation revealed that one Robert Burrell, a municipal sanitation employee, at approximately 0830 hours this date, was loading trash onto municipal trash collection truck #84, traveling eastbound in the alley behind the above address. Mr. Burrell reports that he discovered a large number of trash bags at the rear of 376 and 374 Baker St. and was in the process of loading the bags into the trash truck when one of the bags ripped under the strain of the weight. He states that as the bag ripped, a human arm and hand fell to his feet. Mr. Burrell immediately notified the driver of the vehicle, one Vernon Johnson. Mr. Burrell then remained with the discovery while Mr. Johnson used the telephone at 371 Green St. to call for police assistance. Statements of Burrell and Johnson are appended to this report.
 At 0836 hours this date, Communications Division received Mr. Johnson's request and dispatched Unit #218 from the Old Town District to investigate. The first call was dispatched as "Investigate the trouble," as Mr. Johnson was in a very excited condition when he spoke to Communications personnel and the exact nature of the trouble could not be ascertained by the police clerk. Officers Good and Branton responded to the call, arriving at 0838 hours. At 0840 hours they requested

*supervisory assistance and a unit from the Mobile Crime Lab.
Officers Good and Branton acted to protect the evidence from
further disturbance and detained Mr. Burrell and Mr. Johnson
for questioning.*

*Our investigation, supplemented by the findings of the
coroner and the Mobile Crime Lab, revealed the following:
Retrieved from the trash cans located behind 376 Baker St.
were two large green plastic garbage bags containing portions
of a dismembered human corpse. From the trash cans at the
rear of 374 Baker St. were five more identical bags containing
parts of a dismembered human corpse. The entire contents of
the trash truck were examined but revealed no other evidence.
The contents of all other trash receptacles in a two-block
radius were searched and revealed no other evidence.*

*Officers were immediately dispatched to question the
occupants of 374 and 376 Baker St. Mrs. Helen Barlow of 376
Baker St. responded immediately. Mrs. Barlow, who lives alone
at that address, stated that she had no knowledge of the bags
or their contents and stated that she had not placed same in the
trash containers. No response was received from 374 Baker St.*

*Mrs. Gail Penrose of 371 Green St., a residence that shares
the alley in common with 374 Baker St., then volunteered to
Officer Good the following data: Mrs. Penrose states that two
or three days earlier, she was not certain, she observed a white
male, twenty-five to thirty years of age, with long,
shoulder-length, very light blond hair, as the subject exited the
garage at 374 Baker St. and placed large and apparently heavy
dark green trash bags in the cans at the rear of the residence.
She further describes the subject as tall, very muscular, like a
bodybuilder, and having a deep tan. She recalls no facial hair
or other characteristics and describes the subject's clothing as
shorts and a tank top. She was unable to recall any jewelry or
other distinguishing marks but was able to assist investigators
in assembling a likeness of the subject with the Identi-Kit. That
likeness is attached to this report and has been circulated to all
districts and divisions.*

*Mrs. Penrose states she was at home with her husband and
two small children in the early evening when she heard her dog
barking at the rear door. She states she went to the rear door
of her home and released the dog into her fenced rear yard.
She states she looked out the door to see what was disturbing*

the dog and observed the above described subject carrying one of the described bags from the garage at the rear of 374 Baker St. She states she did not recognize the subject, nor had she seen him in the neighborhood previously. Mrs. Penrose added she didn't pay any further attention to the subject, as she knew the occupant of the residence at 374 Baker St. to be an attractive woman who occasionally entertained visitors. She then returned to the living room of her home and resumed watching television with her family. She recalls the program they were watching as the national news, placing the time at approximately 1900 to 1930 hours.

Mrs. Penrose further states that her dog continued to bark, and she again went to her rear door. She again saw the subject carrying an apparently heavy bag from the garage at 374 Baker St. and that he again placed it in the containers at the rear of that address. She adds that the subject secured the lid to the trash can, then reentered the garage. Mrs. Penrose called her dog indoors and did not observe any further incidents. The witness was transported to the Bureau of Identification where she viewed photographs of previously arrested subjects but was unable to locate the above-described subject. Her statement is appended to this report.

Upon arrival, the undersigned, in company with Sergeant Detective Webber, initiated interviews of potential witnesses residing in the area with negative results. Then, acting under the authority of the undersigned, uniformed officers forced open the door to the garage and the residence at 374 Baker St. That action was undertaken without a warrant to locate and assist persons in need of assistance. None were located, but examination of the interior of the garage and residence verified that the homicide and subsequent dismembering took place at that location.

Mrs. Helen Barlow of 376 Baker St. supplied the following information: 374 Baker St. is owned and occupied by one Donna Fields, white female approximately thirty-five years of age. The only other occupant of the dwelling is the daughter, Marianne Fields, white female. Mrs. Barlow states that Mrs. Fields and the child had lived at 374 Baker St. for approximately two years. She added that the mother and daughter were polite and friendly while somewhat distant and removed. She reports that she learned from conversation with *the daughter that the mother was divorced, self-employed in a local interior decorating enterprise, and without other living family.*

Sergeant Detective Webber then interviewed Mr. Henry Thorpe of 372 Baker St. Mr. Thorpe, age sixty-seven, stated that he had not seen the Fields woman or child in several days and had no knowledge of their personal life and did not concern himself with their activities. Mr. Thorpe then added that he had met the father of the child, Marianne, on one occasion late the year before and, as an outgrowth of a pleasant conversation at that time, had been asked by the father, a Mr. Dan Fields of Hilton Head Island, to accept his telephone number and advise him if the family ever needed anything. Mr. Thorpe stated that was the only occasion in which he spoke to Mr. Fields prior to this date. Thorpe added that early this date, when he observed the patrol cars converging on 374 Baker St., he did telephone Mr. Fields in Hilton Head and advised him of the unusual activities. He related that Fields had told him he would be immediately en route.

Reconstruction of the crime scene suggests the following: Entry to the home was gained without visible means of force by person or persons unknown. The deceased, Donna Fields, and the deceased minor child, Marianne Fields, were taken to the second-floor bedroom, front. There are indications that both victims were bound and secured in the bedroom. The evidence then suggests that the mother either gained her release or was released intentionally from her restraints and that her assailant(s) then pursued her through the home, inflicting numerous knife wounds on her face, hands, arms, legs, and torso. An abundance of blood found throughout the home indicates that the struggle was prolonged. In the opinion of the coroner and the forensic team the attack was deliberately carried out to inflict maximum horror.

Investigation further strongly supports the conclusion that the victim, Donna Fields, was then killed in the kitchen of the residence with a fatal wound to the throat. Our reconstruction suggests that the assailant(s) then returned to the second floor where the child was killed by knife wound and dragged to the kitchen.

The reconstruction suggests that the attacker(s) then systemat-

ically dismembered each corpse with the use of an electric carving knife, the dismembered bodies were then placed in seven plastic garbage bags, and placed in the aforementioned trash receptacles. Evidence in the form of collected blood and hair taken from the second-floor bath strongly supports the conclusion that the suspect(s) then showered in the second-floor bath.

In addition to the abundant physical signs of the attack and dismemberment (see photos attached), all telephones in the dwelling were ripped from the wall, and the entire premises was ransacked. The vehicle registered to the deceased was not located in a search of the area. Details of the registration were obtained and have been distributed to the patrol force. Numerous prints and partial prints were recovered at the scene and are currently under analysis.

At 1022 hour this date, Mr. Daniel Fields, father of the deceased minor child and former husband of the victim, Donna Fields, arrived on the crime scene, responding to the telephone notification described above. Mr. Fields was unable to supply any details of value to this investigation and was escorted back to his home in Hilton Head by one Tracey Barkley of Hilton Head Island. Ms. Barkley is a registered nurse on the island and stated that she accompanied Mr. Fields as he is recovering from injuries sustained in a recent fishing accident. There is no statement at this time from Mr. Fields, as he was overcome with grief and shock at the crime scene. A sedative was administered by the coroner, and Mr. Fields was briefly interviewed by the undersigned. Mr. Fields, a retired agent with the Drug Enforcement Agency, last spoke to his daughter and estranged wife three days ago by telephone from Hilton Head Island.

The investigation is continuing.

Respectfully,
Lieutenant Detective William Gordon

TO: Police Commissioner Howard Bingerly
FROM: Lieutenant Detective William Gordon
SUBJECT: Retirement
Sir:
Dear Howard,

Please pardon my departure from normal departmental communication and style. At the end of today's shift I am submitting my papers. As you well know, I have more than enough time in and have been thinking about retirement for the last two years since Ellen passed away. I regret any inconvenience that my sudden action causes, but I have full confidence in Sergeant Detective Webber. He has carried my unit for some time now, and I have acted mostly as a rubber stamp for his decisions. He's a good man, the best for the position, and I hope that you give the Homicide Squad to him.

Howard, this Fields case is the worst thing I've ever seen. The horrible ugliness of this killing and the crushing grief I saw today in that young man was the last straw. I'm done. I just can't take it anymore, and my report shows it. If I have to witness any more ugliness, any more sadness, I'll lose my mind. It's that simple. I've prepared the correct forms for Personnel Division and am surrendering my equipment to the sergeant when I leave today.

It has been my pleasure to work with you and for you these last years, and I'll never forget your kindness when Ellen was ill for so long. Thank you, my friend.

Sincerely,
Billy Gordon

The Charleston News Courier
Morning Edition

Bulletin: Police Department spokesmen today revealed that Lieutenant Detective William Gordon, Chief of the Department's Homicide Squad, was discovered dead in his home late last night by his son-in-law. Lieutenant Detective Gordon, fondly known to several generations of Charleston residents as "Billy," was reported to have died of self-inflicted wounds. Lieutenant Gordon was spearheading the investigation of the brutal double homicide discovered yesterday in the exclusive Old Town District. The departmental spokesman denied any connection between the investigation and the lieutenant's death but stated that the popular detective had experienced recurrent bouts of depression since his wife's death two years ago. See page C-7 for funeral arrangements.

CHAPTER 16

THE island lay slightly south and east of Hilton Head. It was numbered on most navigation charts and named on very few. Those charts that did name the tiny speck of land were very detailed. The island consisted of fourteen acres at high tide, boasted of a good wharf and its own power source, and was known to a limited number of persons as Dandma's Island. Dandma, a shriveled black woman of unknown years, was the sole owner of the island and the sponsor of its reputation.

She had three teeth, and they were all tucked safely out of sight, far to the rear of her mouth. She laughed and cackled without restraint when amused, kept her guests' business private, and was well paid for her trouble. Her table was consistently laden with tasty, healthful meals. Her rambling house, or the Lodge as it was called, was scoured regularly. And her linen was always ironed before it went on a bed. She'd been called Dandma—one child's long-ago attempt at "Grandma"—for more than four decades, sang the fear of God and the love of Jesus in hymn and song throughout the day, and hadn't filed an income tax return in her whole life. She was innkeeper to an unpredictable flow of guests: smugglers, adulterers, fugitives, and many others who sought privacy and service in king-size portions. On Dandma's Island privacy was both abundant and expensive.

The island itself was one long, flat, low-lying marshland but also claimed a few twisted live oaks, forty-three palmetto trees, a well-maintained wharf, and three man-made structures. The lodge was a rambling, E-shaped, single-story dwelling with five spacious bedrooms, a large dining area, a comfortable common room, and a well-stocked kitchen and pantry. Each bedroom had its own tidy shower and bath, and screened porches ran the entire length of the *E*.

The second structure on the island was a small cottage adjacent to the lodge. It was tilted on its foundation and badly in need of paint. Dandma's personal quarters were inside, and she hadn't invited another living soul into them in thirty-six years, the exact number of years since she'd last seen her husband. She didn't hesitate to say she was in no hurry to see him again anytime soon. The third structure was a padlocked tool and supply shed where electricity was furnished for the island by a sturdy gasoline-powered generator.

Dandma received her mail and supplies by way of a Daufuskie Island boatman on each Monday, or the next clear day after. Fresh water was collected in an elevated cistern on the roof of the lodge. That supply was then augmented with bottled fresh water delivered weekly in five-gallon glass jars by the boatman. Showers were salty but heated. In all, Dandma's Island was abundantly stocked, the guest house was spotlessly cleaned by Dandma herself, and the mechanical needs of the premises were maintained by lockjawed Daufuskie craftsmen. Dandma was discreet, self-sufficient, and her integrity was unimpeachable.

Party John Maltessa and Dandma had shared a pleasant business relationship for the last of these sixteen years. She'd frequently given him sanctuary away from federal observation and other pressures stimulating his paranoia centers, but she permitted no cargo to be unloaded on her island and would not tolerate illegal drugs or their use on her territory. She extended credit to no one but, beyond those simple rules, didn't interfere in the private affairs of her clients.

Party John had arrived on the craft bringing her Daufuskie delivery, and they'd negotiated in the bright sun as her supplies were off-loaded. Yes, she had plenty of room at the moment with no current guests and no imminent arrivals. The size of the party was to be five, one of whom would be Party John. One of the guests was physically injured but would be attended by medical personnel in the party. Yes, he would pay in cash, in advance. He estimated the length of their stay at a week. Of course, her rate was fixed, and she permitted no bargaining. One hundred dollars per day, per person. He'd paid her with hundred-dollar bills, and she'd tucked them securely away into her shriveled bosom.

The "guests" arrived with Party John one day later on board a gleaming pleasure craft. The boat was emblazoned with the name *Georgia Pair,* and she was brightly new. Dandma welcomed her arrivals at the wharf, greeting each as sir or ma'am, intentionally ignorant of their names. She watched as the fifth member was carried on a light stretcher from the well-appointed cruiser. The invalid was a pale, unconscious white man who tossed and cursed in fitful dreams.

The stretcher was carried ashore and up to the lodge by Party John and a second man, who had a young face, quick eyes, and silver hair. When the injured man had been transferred to the crisp linen of the large bed, Dandma drew Party John aside in the kitchen.

"Wait a minute, Cap'n."

"Yes," Party John replied, "what is it?"

"I don't want no white mens dyin' in my house," Dandma whispered. "An' I don't want no white mens dyin' on dis island, either. Unhappy white ghosts is bad for business."

They haggled. Party John assured her the injured man wasn't going to die, that he'd be receiving the best medical care available outside of a hospital. The negotiations were concluded when Dandma folded an additional four hundred dollars into her undergarments. Placated and enriched, she cheerfully set about the business of installing her guests.

The unconscious man had been settled in the central guest room. He was bracketed on one side by the silver-haired man with the young face and on the other by the incredibly tall white woman. There had been a moment of preliminary confusion as the white-haired sir had placed the tall woman's bag in his own room. Then the tall woman had moved the bag to the large, sun-swept room on the other side of the injured man. The silver-haired man hadn't commented on the switch, but his movements became more crisp and efficient. Party John claimed the room closest to the boat and the wharf, as was his custom. The second, smaller woman with the faraway stare installed herself in the last room at the far end of the rambling structure.

Dandma evaluated her guests in those first minutes. No honeymoon this week. Not much mirth and laughter. She repositioned the extra bills and cackled quietly to herself, thanking God she was neither young nor white. She busied herself in the scoured whiteness of the kitchen, allowing her guests to familiarize themselves with the house in privacy. She began with a floating hum, but soon her voice overflowed the kitchen and stretched the walls of the lodge with an old hymn. She sang for herself and for the glory of her God, certain of her simple faith, happy with her life, and facing death with patience and calm. If she lived one more day or one more century, it would be the same to her. She was a very happy old woman.

Dan Fields slipped in and out of rationality and consciousness for thirty hours after their arrival. Waking moments, brief but startling, found him silent and brooding. His responses to questions from Tracey were monosyllabic grunts. The doctor he ignored. But in truth, the moments of his wakefulness were very few.

The hours were measured by the changing tides and the overflight of the pelicans as they fished the daylight and returned overhead with the advent of dusk. Fields lay with a fever under woolen blankets and shivered despite the subtropical temperature. The auburn-haired nurse left him rarely.

The young doctor with the silver hair checked his patient regularly but remained only for the briefest of periods. He administered antibiotics for an infection in Fields's shoulder, along with periodic injections of Demerol for pain. The doctor was made restless by his own forced inactivity and angered by the open hostility from a should-be grateful patient, but Party John had made Fields's full recovery the hinge pin of their transaction. Only upon Fields's complete recovery would Party John deliver the remainder of the cocaine.

The surgeon calculated the profit again for the twentieth time. The total investment required from him and his two associates had been a bargain price plus whatever amount of his own time was required to see the disabled man back to relative good health and lucidity. His associates had readily agreed to cover the demands of his practice on the island, and the cash had been no problem. In fact, the entire operation had been financed completely from the accumulated profits from their prior entrepreneurial efforts in the cocaine market. Party John's teaser, one small ounce of bricked crystals, had withstood heavy dilution with inositol and yielded a product that had greatly satisfied their top-ranked dealer. The man was delirious with the prospects of an unlimited supply of the substance. The potential profit exceeded their wildest hopes. If they could be patient and trickle the coke out through their own dealer network at the full price, the potential for profit soared geometrically.

As a consequence, the young face with the silver hair endured the boredom of the island and placated himself with visions of his forthcoming wealth. The infection troubling his patient was of marginal concern. Fields was in peak physical condition, his body toned and resilient. The doctor felt far greater concern for the man's mind. But after the infection ran its course, then the doctor would deal with the man's mind, if necessary. In the interim he counted his profits and improved his tan.

Fanny became a mannequin. Her eyes stared, her hands didn't move. If she spoke, she said, "Why bother?"—whether to an offer of food or an inquiry into her health. She was incapacitated by a paralytic fear of being seized and punished by the Colonel. While Party John was uncertain of her exact role in the Colonel's operation, his blossoming paranoia had demanded she be immobilized until Fields was conscious to provide guidance or instructions. Fanny walked the perimeter of the island and then crossed the marshlands. Her appearance had lost all traces of style and fashion, and she dressed in overlarge shirts and ill-fitting trousers. Her face had not the slightest sign of makeup, and her nails were bitten short and jagged. Her amblings had no purpose or direction, while her mind achieved the greater sanctuary and the greater danger of her unpeopled green place. Her expression was vacant. She sat silently through the nourishing meals provided by Dandma's strong hands, present but untouched by hunger. Fanny no longer had any notion of time. She was in a world without a past or future and with scant acknowledgment of the present.

Party John, in accordance with the inflexible rule of Dandma, abstained from the use of chemical substances while on the tiny island. He did, however, make numerous journeys to the moored cruiser where he had an ample stash of the necessities of civilized life. He maintained his precarious equilibrium in that manner, lifting his depressed fears for Fields's well-being with cocaine and soothing his tensions with Jamaican marijuana. Party John had begun his convoluted preparations for a safe harbor and secure retreat the moment after Fields was placed in the medically competent hands of his associate and new partner. The doctor had nearly wet himself at first mention of the sizable coke transaction and had given every assurance that the huge amount of cash would present no problem. Party John had then rapidly hidden the cocaine and begun implementing his plans for total disapperance. He'd rushed through the negotiations with Dandma and then paid cash for the *Georgia Pair*, taking ample precaution that the vessel's registration would not mark a trail for the Colonel to follow.

The veteran smuggler had then alerted the tightly knit island telegraph of Hilton Head, arranging to be instantly notified of any inquiries, official or otherwise, that centered upon himself, Dan Fields, or Fanny. While Hilton Head does function as a popular tourist resort for the nation's wealthy, the island is in truth a small town, and it is virtually impossible for an outsider to make inquiries without tipping his hand in some way to the central community. Consequently Party John was able to monitor his level of safety from a remote distance.

He did not underestimate the Colonel's tenacity or cruelty and would not sleep soundly until he placed half the globe's circumference between himself and the man. And Party John was resolute in his determination that Fields accompany him. The horrific deaths of Donna and Marianne Fields terrified John. It was a credit to his loyalty he hadn't dumped Fields and headed for China the minute he learned how they died. But, however monstrous the murder, his terror had not abated his lust for one more score. He deemed the Colonel's consignment legitimately forfeit. He diverted his fearful mind with dreams of enough wealth to sustain him for a lifetime, planning his leisurely meanderings in detail.

His greed in no fashion weakened his natural caution, and his dealings with the consortium of Hilton Head physicians had been guarded and meticulously planned. He'd quickly negotiated the remaining sixteen tons of prime Colombian marijuana, striking a bargain with an island building contractor, settling upon two hundred dollars per pound, delivered. The price was high for the quantity, but John had made his pitch to a mid-level dealer, previously unable to gain access to the importation fraternity. In so doing, John collected eighty dollars more per pound than from his regular drops and simultaneously avoided involvement with the Colonel's organization. The buyer had been ecstatic. He'd been able to purchase the contraband at fifty dollars less per pound than his previous supplier could arrange and did so in such quantity that his operation would operate on inventory for many months.

The laws of supply and demand were working smoothly in an uncontrolled and unregulated marketplace, and at no time did Party John face exposure to robbery or loss of his treasure. His total coup represented the grand culmination of a lifetime's experience and risk in the drug trade, and he had learned his lessons well.

Tracey Barkley, the tall, auburn-haired nurse, had few ties to the fears and hopes of the other guests on Dandma's Island. She did not stand to profit from the several transactions that were under way, nor was she in danger of retaliation. She had not been victimized, as had Dan Fields and the strangely quiet blonde. But the maelstrom of emotional currents swirling violently about Dan Fields had swept her into the vortex of the conflict, converted her into the most involved of spectators, and had drawn her into an ever-deepening involvement with the man and his fate.

In Charleston, when Fields left her on the glutted street, he had been deeply anguished over the probable deaths of his estranged family but had been in grim-faced control. When next she'd seen the man, he'd been slack-jawed and staring. And with cause. Oh, God, with cause. She had gently extricated him from the home she could only describe as an abattoir, coaxed him into the classic MG, and driven him in silence back to Hilton Head. Fields had not awakened upon their return to her condominium at Turtle Lane and had been carried back up to the apartment with the help of the doctor.

A quick examination revealed his fever to be dangerously high, his pulse rapid and reedy, and his blood pressure dropping. They responded with intravenous antibiotics, but the doctor knew the symptoms of central nervous system shock behaved in the same manner. With each hour bringing no change in Fields's condition,

Tracey feared the oddly compelling man had shut down his formidable engines and was willing himself to death.

Three hours after her return to Hilton Head, Tracey had left Fields's bedside and found Party John and the doctor in hushed conversation. After a moment of silence in which she could feel Party John measuring her, she'd been given the news. The island telegraph was buzzing with numerous inquiries regarding both Fields and Party John, and those inquiries were not originating from any official quarters. Gauging her reaction to that particular item, Party John completed his revelations. Hours before, Fields's home had been engulfed in a fiery blast that had reduced the dwelling to ashes. Investigators had wasted no time in classifying the fire as arson, and witnesses had supplied the authorities with a description of a man seen fleeing the premises.

The wire services had nailed the similarity in the victims' names linking the Charleston and Hilton Head incidents, had done some hasty checking, and were headlining the connected incidents, complete with the speculation that the atrocities were retaliation for Fields's past enforcement activities. The former agent had been reported missing, and a full-scale search of the rubble that had once been his home was under way.

Tracey received the news with controlled terror. She listened calmly and rationally as Party John encouraged her to drop any and all ties with Fields. Then she firmly declined his suggestion and insisted she would accompany Fields until he no longer required nursing care. But nonetheless she had agreed to a strategic relocation.

Tracey examined her unrealistic involvement with the unconscious form of Dan Fields. She acknowledged she had been initially attracted to the man on a physical level, and yes, the attraction had grown rapidly under the intoxicating influence of excitement and intrigue.

But now, after all that he had suffered, she refused to leave his side, arguing that his comatose condition was not typical of a raging infection. She scoffed at the conservative treatment by antibiotics and launched upon her own personal holistic approach. She spent every waking moment in a concerted attempt to reach his wounded mind. She continuously spoke to the unresponsive man, affirming and reaffirming his right to live, combating the death-seeking guilt in the ugly trenches of his delirium. She crooned to him when garish nightmares drenched him in sticky perspiration, constantly adding her own voice in opposition and counterbalance to the stricken man's subconscious will to surrender. For thirty continuous hours she did not sleep, did not leave his side for more than a few minutes. She opposed the destructive trend of his mind with her body and her will. She refused to let him die.

In the thirty-first hour Dan Fields propped himself up on an elbow and asked for food and drink.

"How long have you been awake?" she asked hoarsely, her broad, toothy smile bathing him in comfort.

"Not very long," he replied. "How long have I been out?"

"Two days," she said over a stifled yawn. She stirred herself to action. "I'll tell the doctor you're up." She stood and rubbed her red-rimmed eyes.

"Tracey," said Dan Fields, his voice kind and even. "Thank you. I know what you did for me."

She smiled again and left the room in long strides.

He tested the air, smelled the salt-scrubbed wind, and knew he was far from the mainland. Then he caught a whiff of spice and pine oil. He didn't know where he was, but his animal senses told him it was a good, safe place.

Dan Fields wobbled to the adjacent bathroom, stepped inside, and locked the door. He propped his back against the closed door and lowered himself to the cool white octagonal tiles. With an Atlantic-freshened breeze in his lungs and the afternoon sun full upon his face, he accepted the reality of his own continued existence and wept. He allowed himself the small but necessary luxury of grief expressed, blew his nose on stiff tissue, then levered himself to unsteady feet. He faced himself in the silvered mirror, shuddered through a last tremulous sigh, then unlocked the door and stepped out.

His first meal was weak tea and thick pea soup. The taste of the fluids was so intense, so acutely delicious, he raved over them and demanded to meet their creator. With good humor and great ceremony Party John presented Dandma to Dan Fields. They were immediate and fast friends. He supplied outrageous compliments to her talent, style, and beauty. She cackled toothlessly, said "Law', Law'," and called him a scamp and a lazy scoundrel. Fields continued to ignore the doctor with the silver hair and young face but began to do so with humor and a sense of devilment. Dandma scoffed and scorned his bad manners, but she brought him a continuous feast, then stood careful watch while he napped. Tracey collapsed in satisfied exhaustion and retired to her own quarters.

Fields awoke refreshed and hungry again. He feasted on fresh shrimp and vegetables and quaffed gallons of spiced tea. Then he leered at Dandma and asked if she would care to soap his back in the shower. She tilted back her grayed head and cackled at the roof beams.

"Why are you laughing at me like that?" he inquired with feigned innocence. "You're going to hurt my feelings."

"Honey," she said, and worked her gums, "I wuz laughin' at what would happen if I said yes. I think you'd need that doctor again pretty quick." She fled the room in a rustle of crinoline and raised her voice in an old Baptist hymn. It was a joyful noise unto her Lord.

Fields bathed as best he could, making detours around wounds and bandages. He dried, then dressed in loose, comfortable clothing. Over weak protests he joined Party John outside the lodge. They walked.

The two men trudged slowly upon the narrow, dry path through the marsh. Party John huffed and blew noisily, jaded years taking a heavy toll on his lungs. Dan Fields moved silently, placing his feet upon each new footfall with caution. He was deeply fatigued but pushed past his limitations.

"Okay, John," Fields said, encouraging him, the Lodge lost from view. "It's time to catch up on current events. What's going on out there?"

Party John was in front of him on the narrow pathway and did not turn to face him but spoke as he walked. The marsh was alive with a thousand lives: insects, marsh birds, frogs, microscopic shrimp, and soft-shelled crabs. The sounds of their dance of life and death filled the humid dusk. A small white sun with a yellow nimbus hung suspended in a reddened sky.

"How much do you remember of Charleston?" John began with a question. Discreetly he did not turn to face his friend.

"Everything," came Fields's measured reply, but he missed a beat before answering.

"By the time you and Tracey were back on the island," said John, "your house was burning like a son of a bitch, so—"

"What?" Fields said, interrupting. "My house? What do you—"

"Dan," John said, overriding his friend, "relax, son. It's all over now. Do you want to hear about it, or do you want to scare all the little fishies out of the marsh?"

They walked. Finally Fields asked the man to continue.

"Like I said"—Party John picked up his story—"it was burning like a son of a bitch. The whole thing went up and was leveled flat before the first fire company was on the scene."

"Shit!" whispered Fields, dragging out the curse. "Was anyone hurt?"

"No," Party John answered, "I don't think so. Some of the trees behind the house went up, too, but your neighbor, you know, the guy from South Africa, he was out there with a hose and wet everything down and kept it from spreading to the other homes. Lucky there was no wind or the whole block would have gone."

Fields marched behind him. "Did you go by there?" Fields asked.

"Yeah, Dan," he replied. "There's nothing left. I mean, well, the chimney and the fireplace are the only things standing. The rest is ash."

"Arson?" Fields asked, certain of the answer.

"Yeah," responded John, fording a shallow spread of the marsh where it flooded the path. "The fire chief called it arson right off the bat. Said no fire would burn that fast and that hot unless it was set." He took three more steps. "Then everybody was getting in on it, and those two dykes that live in the green house up from you, they came out and said that they had seen this guy leaving your place just seconds before the fire."

"Did they know him?" Fields asked, his voice under strict control.

"No. But they said he was a beach type. You know, blond hair to his shoulders, muscles on top of muscles."

Fields said nothing.

"Well," Party John continued, "everybody was trying to find out if you were burned up in the fire. They were going through the ashes before the place was cold, and I figured it wouldn't hurt any to keep everybody guessing for a while." He had reached the end of the narrow path. They stood together at land's end, facing the white hole in the red sky.

"In fact, Dan," he said, "I think you ought to leave it like that. We've got all the bucks coming that we should ever need, and I can have us eight thousand miles away from here in a heartbeat. If you leave it so this Colonel bastard doesn't even know you're alive, it might be the best thing we could hope for."

Fields scrutinized the weathered face. He said, "What else?"

Party John was digging in the loamy marsh soil with a begrimed toe. "Okay, first thing that happens is the TV guys, after they made the connection to the fire at your place, they took this artist's sketch of the bad guy from Charleston down and show it to the two dykes who live up the street from you. They did it in front of a camera, right? Well, the two dykes say something like, 'Shit, that's the guy!' They blooped out the 'shit,' but there it was on the TV, the two of them holding hands like they're scared and saying, 'That's him.' So the TV guy goes on to say something about this whole mess being some kind of retaliation for when you were a narc. Next thing you know, the papers and the cops are saying the same thing."

Fields was resting, one leg shot forward, a bandage visible through the fabric of his trousers. He wagged his head slowly, incredulously. "Lieutenant Gordon?"

"No," John replied. "That guy was an old guy who started out on the case, right?"

Fields nodded.

"Well, he died or killed himself or something the same night that you were up there."

Fields stared at him in puzzlement. "He died?" he whispered, not believing.

"Yeah," John said, "but they don't think it had anything to do with the case. He was an old guy, and his wife died some time back, and they said he put in for his retirement, then changed his mind and blew himself away."

"He was a nice old man, John," said Fields, his voice flat and toneless.

Party John gave him a minute, digging more trenches in the sandy soil.

"Go ahead," Fields urged, turning back along the path.

John followed. "Okay," he said. "Anyhow, this sergeant who's got the case makes a statement to the papers and to the TV stations the next day. It's turning into a zoo, you know. The mayor is calling for more money to fight crime; people who live in the rich-bitch part of the city are frying his ass but good. So this sergeant comes on with a statement to the press. The sergeant says the case is still under investigation. Then he comes on with this sketch of the beach-type guy and asks if anyone has seen him that they should call the cops and let 'em know.''

Fields picked up the pace to fight the chill brought by a wind from the Atlantic. "Have you heard if they've found him?" he asked.

"Well," John answered with a chuckle, "it seems that half the guys in Georgia and all of 'em in South Carolina fit the description. The cops have jacked up every beach bum between here and Miami, but they don't have him yet." He paused. "It's the same one who toasted my nose, isn't it?"

Fields stopped and faced him in the dying sun. "I saw him on the water, I think," he said. "It has to be the same guy. He's the hitter for this Colonel of yours." Fields resumed his trek.

"I'm sorry you got messed up with these animals," Party John said to Fields's back. "I thought I was bringing you into a quick score. I didn't know it would turn out like this." He took a few more paces. "I'm sorry about the kid and your old lady, Dan."

Fields stopped and turned to face him. The reddened twilight lit the planes and angles of his face. "John," he said, fixing him with cold blue eyes, "if I thought you were directly responsible, I'd kill you where you stand." The silence stretched awkwardly. Sweat trickled uncomfortably down Party John's nose despite the cooling breeze. Fields sighed, and the tension fled with the breeze to the sea. "We all live with the consequences of our actions," Fields said, resuming his march. His leg was throbbing again. "You face yours, I face mine, and this Colonel and his friend will face theirs." They marched in silence, nearing the lodge.

"Hey!" said Party John enthusiastically. "Look. As soon as this coke deal is done, I'll have more than enough money to pay some hitters. Pros. You can have this Colonel and his friend taken out the smart way, from a safe distance." He pressed on, speaking to Fields's retreating back. "Listen, Dan, I'm not saying you don't know what you're doing or that you don't have a right to go after them. But these guys have been winning, in case you didn't notice. Look at you! You're all fucked up, you got busted ribs, a hole in you, your house is a wet pile of ashes, and your kid and old lady are both gone. What I'm saying is, these guys haven't even got a bloody nose and you've been down for the count enough times to have the fight stopped. I don't want to see you hurt any more, boy. Let me put us about a million miles from here and these animals, and then I'll have some friends find us the best hitters around. Christ, Dan, I feel responsible, don't you understand?''

Fields maintained his pace in silence. After a very long while, a time in which he accused himself and found himself guilty, Fields answered. "Yeah, John. I do understand."

"Then you'll let me take care of things my way?"

"No," Fields answered. "The Colonel and his beach boy belong to me and me alone. Not to the police, not to contract hitters, not to anyone but me."

They boarded the boat. Party John switched on the generator, and the cabin was freshened with conditioned air. Fields sprawled in a comfortable chair and eased his throbbing knee. Party John worked smoothly behind a stocked bar and poured Fields an undiluted four fingers of Jack Daniel's.

Party John flopped ungraciously onto the cushions of a tufted beige couch, sipping noisily from an iced beer. He rolled a potent marijuana cigarette, completing the ceremony with an exaggerated flourish of his tongue. He flamed the tapered joint and inhaled deeply.

"What about the girl?" Fields asked.

"Which one?" croaked Party John, speaking bellows-fashion without loosing the acrid smoke from his lungs.

"Fanny. What's going on with Fanny?"

John exhaled slowly and slurped again from the beer. "I didn't know what to do with her. She didn't have anywhere to go, and even if she did, I wasn't exactly sure what her connection with these clowns was. So I kept an eye on her—you know, made sure she didn't drop a dime on us or anything like that." John knocked an ash from the joint. "If you ask me, she's just another spacey broad. I was hoping you'd be able to tell me what to do with her." He drew again on the glowing joint, gagged, and broke into paroxysms of violent coughing.

Fields waited for the fit to subside, sipping at the Tennessee sour mash. "They hurt her, John." He paused, working the condensation on the glass with a fingertip.

"But what the hell should I do with her?"

"I don't know," Fields replied. "You can keep her on ice for now. I don't think she has any desire to help this Colonel, but I'll shake her cage a little and find out for certain." Fields fidgeted with the knee bandage. "How about this doctor friend of yours?" he asked. "What's going on there?"

"First," said Party John, "this dude is not a friend. This is strictly business." He sucked again at the joint and conquered the futile attempts of his lungs to expel the cloud of blue smoke. Fields waited patiently for him to exhale. "But it's good business, Dan," John continued. "I won't argue with you about his personality. He's a yuppie, preppy prick, but he's taking good care of you and can keep his mouth shut. Christ, he's as anxious to finish the deal as I am. I checked him out for somebody else a few months ago. He's slick and runs a very clean operation. No pun intended. And," he added, "he's got the cash anytime I'm ready to deal."

They discussed the practical aspects of John's remaining cocaine transactions. Fields's interest was passing, but he extended him the courtesy of listening. Party John had rigged a series of drops for greater safety, minimizing his exposure at any one time. The total transaction was to be broken into a series of six smaller exchanges. In each case Party John would receive the cash from the doctor and his associates, then direct them to a location at which the cocaine would be found. The method was a time-tested one that provided maximum safety and the least possible exposure to arrest or robbery.

After listening to the plans Fields said, "Where are you going to go?"

Party John butted the joint with his callused fingertips, twisting the burning ember into a crystal ashtray. "I've got several places in mind. I've never really spent as much time as I'd like in the Japan seas. I've got a line on a beauty of an ocean-going yacht, and I thought I might take her over there and check out that part of the world for a few years. How about you? What are you going to do?" Party John's speech was slurred.

"I'm going up to have dinner," Fields said with a thin smile.

"And then?" pressed Party John.

"Then I'm going to work out a few kinks for a day or two,"

Fields answered. "We can stay here out of sight for a little longer?"

"Yeah," John answered, "that's all taken care of. Then what?"

Fields pulled himself to his feet. He shook his trousers back down over the bandage on his knee. He faced his friend. "Then I'm going to go find them, where they are, and send Colonel Burgess and Benny Montrose to hell." Fire danced in his cold blue eyes and sent a chill running down Party John's spine.

"I thought so," worried the little smuggler, climbing to his feet. "I thought so."

CHAPTER 17

IN the following four days Dan Fields retreated deep within himself and began his physical preparations in earnest. By the very act of giving voice to his intentions, he became a total slave to the goal of rehabilitation and vengeance. He sat silently as the silver-haired physician outlined a schedule that would gradually restore his abused body to its former condition. He enumerated a long list of forbidden activities, urging Fields instead to rest frequently, abstain from all strenuous exertion, and to regain his prior form through judicious long, slow walks.

Fields did engage in long walks, but they were not slow and they were not his sole activity. He swam in the briny shallows of the island, his ribs encased in tightened bandages, then lay naked in the hot glare of the sun. He ran; he waded through the marsh. He pressed beyond the pain, beyond fatigue. The exit wound in his shoulder had developed a layer of new skin, and by the third day of his efforts he was satisfied with its improved function. On the fourth day he trotted around the circumference of the island without benefit of the knee brace. Afterward he lay down and breathed shallowly so as not to hurt his ribs. He watched a stealthy green heron as it slow-stepped ever closer to the water's edge. The long-beaked bird froze for an eternity as the sea trout fingerlings darted in the shallows. With a flash of its elongated neck, a motion too fast for the most watchful eye, the bird stabbed a fat fingerling with its rapier of a beak and rose on triumphant wings.

Fields rolled onto his flat stomach and pushed off equally with both arms, landing balanced on his bare feet. He brushed off the sand and soil and trotted easily back to the lodge. His eyes were clear, his pulse slow and steady. The injured ribs did restrict his motion and the depth of his breathing, but in four days of hard training he had measured those limits and fine-tuned his body to operate within their restrictions. He was ready.

Fields had dwelt alone for the preceding four days in the prison of his own discipline. Driven by guilt and outrage, he had devoted every waking moment to conditioning and exercise. Repeatedly he had turned away from the efforts of Party John, Tracey, and the wrinkled old woman to divert him from his narrowed focus. He had been intensely sullen and totally uncommunicative, driving himself again and again to the upper limits of his endurance.

The lodge had become a prison for each of them. The doctor argued bitterly with Party John, demanding to be returned to Hilton Head. He was incensed at Fields's stony disregard for his counsel and angrily declaimed any responsibility for the man' inevitable relapse. Party John took the irate surgeon to the moored boat and renegotiated their bargain. The doctor was assured his responsibility, for Fields's physical condition no longer determined the outcome of their negotiations. The transaction would take place within a few days, upon their return to Hilton Head. The young man helped himself to a gram of Party John's private supply of uncut cocaine and retired to his room. At meals he nodded rhythmically and hummed softly to himself and was less of an annoyance.

Fanny was lost in her half-minded exploration of the island. She fell often, soiling herself, but refused to change her clothes. On the third day of Fields's single-minded conditioning, Tracey took the girl aside and firmly encouraged her to bathe and comb her hair, but the transformation was short-lived and Fanny materialized at the midday meal the following day disheveled and soiled again from her meanderings.

Ignored by her patient, Tracey found pleasure in Dandma's company. She listened to the old woman's lore of island living, keeping a kitchen, and laughed out loud at the crone's caustic opinions about men and their outrageous emotional needs. Dandma equated Fields's obsessive intensity with a woman's menstrual cycle, claiming with a pink-gummed cackle that all men had periods but they simply didn't know it because they didn't bleed. She admonished the tall girl to enjoy the sun, assuring her the man would return to normal when his "period" had run its course.

At the evening meal of the fourth day, Fields announced they would be returning to Hilton Head on the high tide early the following morning, and each of them would go their separate ways.

Fanny's blank face was immediately animated. Her eyes widened with fear and her spine stiffened. Her fork clattered to the table. "No!" she shouted, her face twisted, her lips curled back, as she bared her teeth. "No!"

The wall clock ticked away six seconds of their lives. Fanny's shoulders twitched, hidden strings jerking the marionette within her slight frame. "This isn't a game!" she screamed. "Don't you see that yet? They just aren't going to call it even and let all of us go on about our lives. These are monsters! Monsters!" Her eyes were glazed jade, darting about in search of support or a hidden foe. "If you're just going to dump us out in the open," she shrilled, "we might just as well commit suicide here and now! I know this man," she said quietly, "and I will *not* let him get his hands on me again!"

She pleaded with each of them, alternately fixing them with the flash of glazed jade. Fields observed her dispassionately, as did Party John. They were painfully aware of her precarious mental stability, or at least the appearance of it. She had started as agent for the Colonel, and her reversed allegiance, while plausible, was not without question.

Tracey eyed the agitated girl with controlled sympathy, sensing the other currents flowing through the tense room. The doctor held Fanny in his peripheral view, observant but uninvolved. He detested this entire subclass of allegedly human creatures, but regrettably they were the only source for quality cocaine. Their fears, hopes, lives, and deaths were of no concern to him.

"Don't you understand?!" Fanny wailed. "He'll kill all of us as soon as we show our faces! Or he'll do something much worse!" Her last words were whispered, the hidden strings jerking her shoulders. "Dan Fields!" she shouted, facing him with green demons behind her eyes. "How much more do you have to lose? How the hell can you sit there and calmly say, 'We're going back now,' like it was the end of summer vacation? What the hell is wrong with you?" Her hands were balled into white fists. "Don't you care about anything but this stupid game?" she asked. "Don't you have any love or pity for the innocent people and the stack of corpses stretched out behind you? Didn't they count for anything?"

Fields chewed his last mouthful. He raised his eyes and swallowed. "You're right, Fanny," he said quietly. "But I'm sitting here remembering who brought this animal to my door. I'm remembering you and your slick presentation, I'm remembering how Donna and Marianne were alive and happy before you brought your subcontracts for mass murder into my home. And I'm remembering, as you pointed out, that I have absolutely nothing left to lose. Nothing." He let the words hang. "You were the Colonel's employee when I met you," he resumed, "and if it weren't for a change in his fortunes, you would still be his employee." Fields blinked. "Perhaps you still are. But I don't think so. I think you blow with the wind. When the Colonel has the dice, your work for him; when the dice pass to someone else, you stand behind them. Your ethics are conveniently flexible for you but dangerously unreliable for anyone else." Fields tilted his head back and viewed her through narrowed lids. "I'll feel one hell of a lot safer when there are plenty of miles between us. You said it best, Fanny. I don't have that much left to lose." A thin smile hinted at his lips, but his eyes were iced with hatred.

Fanny Marcel sat white-faced through his words. The accusation she had feared lay naked on the table, there to be seen by the unblinking eyes of the others. Her name had been called and her sins had been listed. She wavered, edging toward panic, but steeled herself with images of blissful suicide and release from the tortures of fear. She answered the greater accusations that sprang from her own self-loathings. "You owe me a life, you bastard," she said evenly, in control of her voice and her eyes. They were locked onto Fields. "You said it yourself. You owe me a life. Well, Mr. Dan Fields, who can sit there and lecture me about ethics, I claim it now." She smiled a haggard but competitive grin. "Tossing me out there as bait for the Colonel while you and the Space Ghost"—a scathing glance to Party John—"travel the seven seas is not ample repayment." She favored Party John with the same grin. If nothing else, she was a survivor. "You said you owed me a life. Pay up, Fields!" she demanded, suddenly strident. "Make me feel safe, and I mean nice and safe, or yes the Colonel will be hearing from me, and I don't care about the cost. No one can kill me more than once. Cross me and he'll know every step you make. He'll squash you flat, Fields. And we both know, he wouldn't hesitate to take Nancy Nurse over there and put her through a few nice changes to get to you. And I'm telling you," she hissed, "you goddamned ethical son of a bitch, you pay up or I'll make sure he finds out what happened to his dope, and I'll make sure he finds out what happened to you and your friends too." Fanny tucked a stray wisp of blond hair into place and looked with distaste at her unpolished nails.

Fields arched an eyebrow. "I can think of a very simple and direct solution to the problem you present." He said it in a low murmur.

"I'm sure you can," she replied, her posture growing more erect. "But you won't. You can't. Your goddamned ethics are going to prevent you. You won't kill me, Dan Fields," she said. "You'll protect me, at least until you're dead or until the Colonel is dead. You owe me a life, and your precious ethics will make you pay up."

Fields nodded to her. It was a pass-or-fail test and she had passed. Fanny would not commit suicide. Fields turned to the dark captain. "John," he said, his tone conversational and relaxed, "you keep Fanny with you, out of sight on the *Georgia Pair* for a few days. Then we'll see what needs to be done."

Party John bobbed his head up and down.

"Good," said Fields. "Of course," he added, "if she goes near a radio or phone, you know what to do, don't you?"

Party John, who had no idea what to do if she made a move, nodded his assent.

The meal concluded in awkward silence, and the company went their separate ways.

CHAPTER 18

FIELDS and Party John stood on the bridge of his fine new cruiser. An hour passed; the dawn slid by unnoticed in the gray rain. John eased the *Georgia Pair* slowly past another rusting channel marker. They were well into Skull Creek, having rounded the southern tip of Hilton Head Island thirty minutes earlier. The water lanes were deserted. The faces of the two men were faintly illuminated by the dim glow of the boat's instrumentation. Party John slurped from a cold beer; Fields sipped from a mug of black coffee.

"Are you sure you don't need anything from me?" Party John asked.

"Nothing more," Fields replied. He had sandals, slacks, a cotton shirt, and a hooded slicker. And he had fifty dollars in his pocket. "You'll take care of Fanny?" Fields asked, knowing the answer.

"You bet your ass I will," John answered emphatically. "I don't trust her at all, Dan. She's bad news from start to finish. Bet your ass she won't be out of my sight, not for a minute."

"She isn't bad news," argued Fields, his eyes searching the gray-wet rain. "Fanny is no different from us, John. Do you want to tell me you've never worked for an evil man? Or that I never followed an order I should've disobeyed? Or that both of us haven't endangered the lives of innocent people when we could have avoided it?'' Fields was cutting stone with his words, gouging them out with his hammer and his chisel. "If she's bad news," he asked, "then what does that make us? Better? Worse? I don't see a difference. So you do me a favor, John. You take care of Fanny."

"Okay. I'll take care of her. But what the hell was she talking about before, back on *The Maiden?*"

Fields arched a brow in question.

"She was saying something about Vietnam?"

"Laos," answered Fields.

"Yeah," said John, "Laos. This Colonel Burgess and his freak, Benny, they're pissed at you because of something you did in Laos?"

Fields sipped black coffee. He said, "I was sent into the bush, Laos, a few years after I met you. Military intelligence needed someone to rig a buy and bust an old smuggler. His name was Hsing Pao. They were hot on him because he'd been sewing packets of heroin into the bodies of dead American soldiers."

"I heard about that," said John.

"Hsing Pao was targeted by everybody. CIA. Intelligence. The Laotians wanted him, the Cambodians too. Of course, the Bureau of Narcotics and Dangerous Drugs wanted to do their part; that's where I came in. As an undercover agent. A big buyer from the States." Fields met the smuggler's eyes. "I stayed with him, and yes, I worked the deal for the heroin, but—maybe you'll understand—I liked him, John. He was a criminal from our point of view, but he was a hero to his people. I worked him but, well, I hated to do it."

Party John bumped the throttle, slowed the engines.

Fields said, "After I'd made the case, closed the sale, and notified the Laotians, I couldn't leave. I had to tell him myself."

John eyed him, said nothing.

"He committed suicide, John. Rather than be killed by his enemies, he took his own life. Right after he did, the Laotians tried to blast Hsing Pao's village off the face of the earth. I still don't know why. When the shelling and shooting stopped, not a single member of Hsing Pao's family survived."

"But where does the Colonel . . ."

"At the end of the firefight," said Fields, "Burgess and a young soldier crept into what was left of Hsing Pao's hut and tried to take the heroin. When I told them to leave, the soldier tried to shoot me. So did Burgess." Fields shrugged. "I shot them both and left. All these years, I'd thought they'd died."

A squall passed over the boat and the water boiled gray, black, and white. "How about that dock ahead?" Fields asked, squinting through the wall of rain. He pointed to an empty private dock that traversed a sloping incline from the land down to the river, ending in a small, floating pier. The planking above led to a large home, a massive combination of wood and glass.

"Can do," said Party John, slowing the engine and flipping a toggle to cut his running lights. He pulled the wheel over, nursing the throttle.

Fields took all of the kindness out of his face. He stared at the captain and said, "You came to me to collect a debt, John. Do you think I paid it yet?"

Party John sagged. "Christ! You know you did, ten times over!"

Fields listened to the rain and the burble of the engines. He narrowed his eyes, and when at last he spoke, he said, "You owe me, John."

Maltessa bobbed his head. "You know it! Name it. Name anything in this world." He flapped an arm. "Except, I, well—"

"Except don't ask you to come with me?" No humor, no forgiveness softened Fields's ice. "No, John. I wouldn't ask that. I wouldn't ask anyone to go with me. But I do want to collect. Now."

Maltessa looked at the gray rain and boiling water. "Yeah. Just tell me."

"You're a rich man."

"Hey, not rich! But, yeah, I'm okay for a while. I told you before to let me give you—"

"That's not what I want."

John shortened his neck by pushing his chin down to his chest. "I didn't think so."

"Fanny is the price of your debt, John."

"What! What does she have to do with—"

"Shut up, John." Fields spoke at a near whisper, but the smuggler closed his mouth and stood and waited. "You are going to take good care of her, John. Whether I come back or whether I don't, you are going to see she gets all of the medical attention she needs—*and* you're going to see she gets it someplace warm and safe where she doesn't wake up each morning scared to death."

"Hey, okay. That's easy enough. I—"

"I'm not finished."

"Go ahead."

"I'm not talking about the cut on her face, John, although I *do* expect to stand for the cost of her cosmetic surgery and *not* in some banana republic, either."

"Of course not."

"What she needs is more than surgery. They hurt her mind, John, down to its most basic and vulnerable roots. She's going to need time and patience and professional help. I expect you to find all of those things and pay for them."

Maltessa drew a breath. "I can do that."

"You *will* do it. And while she's healing, you're going to stay close enough to her to see she isn't left alone and afraid."

Party John lowered his chin further. He said, "This is starting to hurt."

"It's supposed to hurt. Something else."

"Yes?"

"Fanny will need a start when she's strong again. You be the one to give it to her, John, with no strings attached. You reach down into your pocket and you pay her exactly what you would have paid me."

"Jesus! Wait a minute! Now your talking about—"

"You owe me, you bastard. You owe me the life of my only child." Fields's eyes burned.

"Dan, I didn't ever mean for this—"

"Pay it, then."

Maltessa breathed in and out, nodded. "I'll pay it. Whether you come back or not."

Fields looked to the bottom of Party John's soul. He said, "Yes, I believe you will." Fields gulped the last of the coffee and put the mug on the dash. He raised the hood of his slicker, losing his face in the shadows. "Hey, John?" he asked.

"Yeah, Dan."

"You still betting on the bad guys?"

"What do you mean?" John asked, pushing the throttle to reverse, halting the boat's progress.

"You were telling me that I was losing this one, remember? I wanted to know if you're still betting on the bad guys." Fields's face was a black shadow.

"The odds aren't too good, Dan," he said. "You can still bail out with me, you know that?''

"I know, John," came the easy reply. The bow of the craft nosed closer to the wet-slicked wood of the dock. Fields slipped out of the protected enclosure. His shadow flitted to the side of the craft, slid over the side and onto the dock, and the dark blue slicker vanished into the swirling rain and the gray morning.

Fields slipped silently up the dock, skirted the unlit house, and gained the macadam road. He stepped out in a squishing, wet stride and made for the main road. He was a shadow in the rain, well prepared for the walk ahead. He cut off onto the empty bike trail and knifed through the plantation, passing the homes of absent owners in damp silence. After two hours of marching in the downpour he made his way to a broad expanse of beach facing the Atlantic. He removed his sandals, rolled up the soaked legs of his slacks, and headed north on the stormy beach. Water boiled in knee-high pools, and solitary vacationers were out on the sand at intervals, scouring the beach for shells or other treasures tossed ashore by the squalls. Fields gave them a wide berth and continued his progress. He reached the public beach at Coligny Circle at a little after eight o'clock. The sky had lightened to a monochromatic gray, and the tourists were stirring in small numbers as Fields approached the shopping plaza. He circled around the restaurant crowd and ducked into the hardware store. There, with his hood over his head, he purchased a hammer and brick chisel and left without comment. His drenched appearance elicited no inquiry. On the island, tourists and natives alike often walked the beach regardless of weather conditions.

Fields left the shopping area quickly and used back trails to reach the street where the ruins and rubble of his home stood. The rain continued its steady assault. An occasional car passed down the main streets, but the sandy side roads were abandoned. Fields slipped the leather sandals over his feet and picked his way carefully through the charred debris, going directly to the masonry fireplace and chimney. He pushed aside a charred upholstered remnant that might have been his favorite couch and knelt before the fireplace. Hammer and chisel in hand, he counted up four bricks, then two, and began to cut away the blackened mortar. The sounds of his efforts were muffled in the roar of rain falling noisily upon the broad fronds of the palmetto trees. A car rolled down the sandy street, tires hissing, wipers going, and headlights aglow. Fields slumped against the fireplace and was still, but the car passed by, its side windows fogged with steam.

He aimed two more solid blows with the hammer, and the brick came away in his hands. Then he attacked a second, inner row of bricks and knocked out two more. He jammed his hand through the small, rough opening and found a small metal box. He worked it through the opening and hurried it into a slicker pocket. For the first time he focused on the rubble. Rain slapped his face as he stood there trying to find something recognizable. His girl-hag-mother statue lay shattered in the pit, the sand gouged with blackened tire tracks, the creosoted ties burned down to sway-backed char. The work, all of the art that had been the man, was destroyed. Every last piece. He'd known what he would find but had to come, had to sear the visual reality into his brain, had to stand in the gutted debris of his life and confront his loss. An empty and unwilling survivor and witness to his own purgatory, Fields bent and took the shattered hand of a broken lady. The fractured granite lay rainwashed in his hand. In his pocket sixteen thousand dollars, what was left of the price he'd earned by sentencing all he loved to devastation, was dry and protected. He turned his face up to the rain, daring the razored droplets to take his eyes, inviting lightning bolts to melt him where he stood. The storm subsided. Fields moved on.

The wafting scent of cinnamon and applesauce pervaded the cool night air. Literature in the motel had called the Virginia town of Winchester the Apple Capital of the world. It smelled like it might be true as Fields breathed night air, apples, and cinnamon. He eased quietly away from the roofline and relieved himself on the graveled roof. Resuming his observation post, he gripped the concrete ledge, his heart pounding. A low-slung sportscar had pulled into the Colonel's drive, and Fields had missed its passage through the barred gate. The car pulled to rest beside a Rolls, and an obscured figure moved to a side door.

Dan craned his neck and squinted through half-lidded eyes. The door to the mansion opened, and a spreading cone of light illuminated the figure. The man entered and the door closed. At once Fields stood erect at the roof's edge, hands clenched, lips drawn into a fine, flat line. The back light had revealed the figure to be a man, a blond man with shoulder-length hair.

Pulse racing, Fields crossed the graveled rooftop and entered the stairwell. He descended using the stairs and exited through the main lobby.

"Good night," the security guard called to his back. Winchester Memorial Hospital prides itself on the courtesy of its staff.

He'd been patient because time, the very concept of acknowledging one's past and future, no longer had meaning. But on the other hand, he wasn't constrained and restricted by the restraints of his former employment. He wasn't overly concerned with probable cause, didn't give a damn about court orders or the admissibility of evidence. He was free, liberated by absolute desolation, emancipated from the flimsy prison of civilization. Yes, he'd learned enough and watched for enough days to have killed Burgess many times, but instead he'd waited, watched and waited for the bodybuilder, Benny, unaffected by the passage of time, patient in anticipation of what was to come.

Now Fields walked down the old Winchester street in darkness, willing his pace to remain casual and unhurried. One block before the walled stone barrier, he turned west. He followed a narrow alley south, continuing until he reached the corner of the stone wall. He skirted the wall's gray bulk until he reached the darkest segment, a space farthest from the street lamps. In an athlete's fluid vault, he veered from his path, grasped the jagged edge of the stone two feet above his head, pulled up with his arms while digging between the stones with his toes, and then lay flat. Shards of broken glass were imbedded in the surface of the wall. They jabbed him, but he avoided injury by distributing his weight evenly over the surface. He listened intently for two minutes, measuring the time with his own respiration and pulse, hearing only the distant passing of automobiles and the mournful calling of night birds.

Fields suspended his weight from his hands and lowered his dark-clad body over the barrier's inner side. He dropped noiselessly to the manicured lawn's soft turf and crouched. The large house lay one hundred yards beyond, its shadowed image partially obscured by meticulously trimmed shrubbery. His eyes picked out a thick-trunked tree fifteen yards ahead. Catlike, he moved forward, through the darkness, stepped inside the darker shadow of an oak, and froze. He strained the upper limits of his hearing, struggling to hear sounds muffled by the passage of street traffic. The sound from the cars retreated, fading into the distance. Fields heard a new sound, felt it transmitted through the ground. He crouched lower, his leg muscles bunched.

He heard the quickened drumming of hard pads running over turf. It was the unmistakable rhythm of a dog, and the heavy, drum-pounding thud of its paws told Fields it was a large one. The thudding approach stopped. The night was silent, and Fields knew the animal was scenting him. He looked to the wall, abandoned thoughts of retreat. The hard-padded drumming resumed with even greater speed. The dog was closing, and time for escape didn't exist.

In the time-slowed and adrenaline-charged workings of his mind, Fields noted other data. There were no sounds of human accompaniment, indicating that the animal was on routine patrol and not turned out in response to his presence. That was good. However, the animal searched for him without yelping or barking. It made no sound of challenge or warning. Either the animal had been surgically silenced or intentionally trained to seek violators of its territory without giving warning. That was bad. Very bad. The animal would be trained to attack and kill without so much as a growl.

The animal was suddenly backlit by the glow from the house. Thirty yards away, running hard with his nose to the ground, was a thick-bodied Doberman.

He'd seen it done before, once with success, once without. Fields jumped from the shelter of the shadow in a low crouch, left arm extended parallel to the turf.

The huge Doberman laid its ears flat back, bunched its muscled forelegs, and leapt.

Fields followed the animal's leap, raising his left forearm to shoulder height. The dog followed, stretching its powerful neck in mid-flight to seize his arm. Gleaming white-tipped razors slashed through thin fabric. Fields whipped his free, knife-edged hand through the cool darkness while simultaneously lifting higher with his left. The Doberman, for a brief second of initial contact, was suspended, lifted full off the ground, its neck extended while iron jaws ripped at Fields's left forearm. But the sculptor's rigid hand edge drove up and under between the dog's slavering jaws and exposed neck and snapped the animal's spinal cord. It fell to the dense grass, dead before its heavy body touched the turf.

Fields immediately grabbed the once powerful forelegs and dragged the ninety-pound animal into the darker shadow of the oak. His own pulse and rasping breath deafening him, he knelt beside the sleek corpse and examined his numb forearm. The dog had gripped him in a nauseatingly painful vice, puncturing his flesh, driving curved fangs deep into skin and tissue. Dan's killing blow had ripped out the fangs, gouging the surface of the bone. He fought the urge to cry out and stamp his feet, to yield to the mind-killing intensity of the pain. Instead he clenched and unclenched the hand, working it until it functioned properly. He wrapped it in cloth torn from his shirt. He dismissed the sanctuary of the stone wall as ghostlike visions of mutilated limbs protruding from blood-slicked plastic bags clouded his eyes. Fields worked the hand again and moved forward through the deep shadows.

He crossed the remaining yardage to the silent house. The dark blue Rolls and the sportscar, a Jenson Interceptor, rested on the macadam pad. Fields melted into the shadows cast by lights from within the house and slid soundlessly around the huge old home's perimeter. He tried each door and each ground-floor window, but the doors were locked and snugly double-bolted, and the windows were fitted with key latches and could not be opened from the exterior without breaking glass. Fields declined that course of action and began a second tracing of the perimeter.

Slipping through the dense tangle of shrubbery at the rear of the house, Fields tripped and stumbled. He caught his balance and listened. He heard no sound. He blessed his luck and began a search of the shrubs, seeking an ambush position from which to strike when the occupants emerged. Prior to moving, he looked below his feet, hunting for the limb that had caused him to stumble. He found it; a garden hose, coiled loosely in the cover of the shrubs. Fields traced the hose through the dense vegetation. It was connected to a greened copper fixture that jutted from the foundation wall. Several feet from the faucet, a rectangular window lay hidden at ground level. Fields squirmed on his stomach and elbows through the brush. He pried at the cracked wood of the window frame. Wood and blistered paint gave way. He dug at the crumbling putty, and it came away in long strips in his fingers. He exposed a corner of the pane, then worked it back and forth. More dried putty broke free, and the pane tilted forward. He laid it gently upon the cool, moist earth and reached into the opening. His blind fingers found the catch and rotated it. He pushed with the heel of his hand, and the ancient, neglected window opened inward, screeching as warped wood was forced past the frame. Again Fields froze and listened. He could hear faint, muffled music and nothing else.

Dan Fields took a slow, deep breath and lowered his feet through the opening. He eased himself through the window and slid down the foundation wall. His feet touched an earthen floor, and he released his grip, pivoting to face the cellar.

Diffused light from a horizontal crack beneath a wooden door enabled him to examine the room: earthen floor, stone-and-mortar walls, and the smell of must and age. Above him were cobwebbed joists and a crazed tangle of electrical wiring. Finding no other exits from the cellar, Fields approached the backlit door. It was secured by an ancient hook and eye. He lifted the hook and the door swung noiselessly inward. He slid flatfooted into the light and scrutinized the tiny landing. The music had faded with his passage from the earthen cellar and was no longer audible. He eased onto the far side of the first stair riser and began a painstakingly slow ascent of the stairs. Lowering his weight in small increments to each board, he discovered the lower limits of squeaks and creaks and avoided them by shifting his stance. He opened the connecting door to the first floor.

Fields stepped full into the light. The room was empty, its silence playing on his nerves. Fields searched the kitchen, turning corners in combat fashion, crouching. Successive empty rooms yawned at him, mocked his deadly intent.

Fields looked through the window. Both cars remained as before.

Thick carpet muffled his footfalls as Fields mounted the darkened stairway. He ascended, flattened against the wall. He crept down the hallway, forcing himself to breathe. Each empty room increased the odds that the next would reveal his quarry, but the vacant rooms laughed at him. He wiped the perspiration from his hands and climbed to the top floor.

Fields dominated the building charge of adrenaline and conquered the desire to move more quickly as his nerve-charged body quivered under the accumulation of unspent energy. He maintained his steady, thorough progress, searching every conceivable space in which a man could hide. He found nothing.

With feline patience, Fields retraced his steps and searched every room again. Nothing. He descended to the second floor. Nothing again. Not even the sound of music. Fields straightened and his nostrils flared. He moved to the first floor and retraced his path. He heard only the swishing passage of traffic on the distant street. A tight, thin smile flickered below the cold blue eyes. He descended the ancient stairway that led to the earthen cellar. His eyes noted the incongruent cleanliness of the steps. Dust abounded in every corner of the cellar, but the centers of the risers were dust-free. Standing on the narrow landing, the sound of the music touched his ears. The sound was faint, very faint. Fields slid on cat's feet through the doorway and stood on the earthen floor of the small room. The music was soft and muted but louder than in any other part of the house. Fields reclosed the planked door and refastened the catch. He closed his eyes and waited until they adjusted to the darkened room.

He opened his eyes and began an inch-by-inch examination of the cellar. Rough-cut and unpainted shelves, on which stood an occasional cobwebbed jar, occupied the far wall. Standing before them, Fields could hear the muffled music enough to discern both the artist and the work. It was Chris Montez performing "There Will Never Be Another You."

Fields examined the shelving, applying gentle pressure at the sides and corners. Where the dried wood of the shelves abutted the stone wall in the far corner, Fields tugged, and the shelving swung out from the wall a fraction of an inch.

He took two slow breaths, each one burning as his chest rose and fell. His pulse thundered, and the remembered sound of droning flies deafened him. He grabbed the shelving's corner and yanked. The entire assembly turned on a well-oiled hinge. Fields faced a darkened passage through a stone-and-mortar arch. It was but three paces long, ending with a metal door. Finding no indication of an upper lock or dead bolt, he tried the knob and it rotated freely in his hand. Without pause or thought Fields wrenched the knob and abruptly pushed the door open. He went through the door in a running, low crouch, turning to the side and diminishing the size of his body. Full inside, Fields halted. Hatred and disgust curled Fields's thin lips into a sneer of rage. The two men before him stood as though paralyzed. As their shock receded, neither moved.

CHAPTER 19

THE sculptor, stripped for combat, circled the looming stone, his bare feet skimming the surface of the sand. His scars showed pink and in some places were lightly scabbed, but he moved with feline intensity. His hammer struck, flashed, struck twice more, and a brick-sized shard of marble thudded to the sand. Behind him, beyond the newly creosoted perimeter of railroad ties, the incomplete structure of his house reached to the dusking Hilton Head sky.

The carpenters and plumbers and electricians had all quit for the evening, their abandoned implements and scattered debris witness to their departure. The sculptor, seizing this time for its absence of power-saw whines and cement truck rumbles, worked with speed. To the accompaniment of chattering squirrels and in the caress of a cooling ocean breeze, he whirled and the hammer followed. *Chink, chink, grack! Chink, chink, grack! Chink, chink, chink, chink, graaa-aack!*

Motes of dust and sand whoofed up and were carried away. Fields, his stonecutter's forearms bulging, his veins engorged, wiped the back of a hand over his brow.

"'Evening," said a voice.

The sculptor turned, looked, then left his arena. Spectators were part of the process of art, a much larger part than he'd ever suspected. The piece, the rock, could never be finished, could never be complete until its impact on ordinary people had been measured. No, the sculptor needed each man who took the time to stand and watch.

"'Evening," said Fields.

"Mr. Fields?"

"Yes?"

"Sergeant Detective Webber," he said, extending a hand. "We met before. In Charleston?"

Fields took the hand. "I don't remember you."

Webber, comfortable in slacks and a thin shirt, felt the iron in the grip. He said, "That's understandable. I was assisting Lieutenant Gordon."

Another wound flashed across Dan Fields's deep-frozen eyes. He said, "You were fortunate to have worked with him."

"Yes, I—I miss him." Webber shifted his notebook and recorder. The detective circled the statue and the sculptor. He raised a finger and touched, not the stone but a spot near the artist's shoulder. "Is that where you were hurt in the fishing accident?"

Fields nodded. The detective was indicating the pinkest of his scars.

"Looks like a bullet wound, doesn't it?"

The sculptor turned, pointed to a shiny, gouged starburst on his thigh. "That one is a bullet wound." He held up a forearm, pointed to two glossy dots. "These two are bullet wounds." He touched his chest front and back. "But these are from a snapped winch cable."

"Oh?"

Fields met his stare and waited.

Sergeant Webber spoke first. "Yes, I think I recall seeing something about that in the file. A report from some doctor who was attending you. Cable just snapped, huh?"

The sculptor shrugged, and a droplet of perspiration streaked down across the month-old scar. "I don't know. I was on deck, I remember that much, but as for the accident, I have no memory of what happened."

Webber put the sun behind his shoulder, made Fields look into the distant fire. He said, "I know who committed those killings." Webber was a decade younger than Fields, and his face had no guile. He was watching for a reaction.

Fields blinked and waited.

"The bodybuilder," said the Charleston investigator. "The bodybuilder. His name is Benny Montrose. He's been found. It's all over. His prints were confirmed before I left the office this afternoon."

Dan Fields looked to the bottom of Webber's eyes and said, "Good."

Webber narrowed a brow, went to his notebook. "I've got a photograph with me," he said, flipping case folders. "Here, this is him." He pushed a glossy print at Fields.

The sculptor held the morgue shot, his face a mask.

"He's dead," said Webber.

Fields handed him the photo. "Also good."

"You—you didn't recognize him?"

"Should I?" Behind the man, his newest work reached out with arms much like his own, strong and corded.

"No. They ran his ID through the DEA computers and couldn't come up with a match on anyone from your old files. Couldn't come up with a match on the other man they found with him."

Fields stood unblinking.

Webber produced another photo, also taken by a morgue camera. "This man was found with the killer. Also dead."

Fields held the print, stared at the death mask of Colonel Thomas Vernon Burgess.

"How about him?"

Fields rubbed a fading welt near his neck. He handed the photo back to the detective.

"They were discovered six hundred miles from here," pressed Webber. "The—the circumstances of their deaths were unusual in some respects. They were found locked in a hidden basement compartment of a mansion in Winchester. That's in Virginia." Webber paused.

Dan Fields drew a breath. He took the man by the elbow, guided him inside the perimeter of sand. He said, "How long have you been with your department?"

"Twelve years. Almost."

"A long time. You're married?"

"Yes."

The detective reached out and ran a finger over breathing stone. "Children?"

"Two," he answered, and couldn't stop an automatic smile. He pressed a palm against flesh made of marble, anguish made of death. He said, "They found something else too. At the homicide scene."

"Oh?"

Webber nodded, ignoring Fields, circling the statue. "Your dossier. Everything there is to know about you, including your family's address in Charleston. That and about a ton of documentation, records, reports—you wouldn't believe it—all detailing one hell of a drug operation. The bodies might never have been discovered if it weren't for a squirrel."

"A squirrel?"

"Yes. Damnedest thing. Seems a squirrel chewed some wires in the walls, shorted out the whole house. The housekeeper called an electrician, who started tracing all the wires to find the short. What he found were these two men, dead, locked in their own soundproofed vault."

"How did they die?" said Fields.

"Now that—that's what I find strange," said the detective. "These were both violent men in a very violent game. Yet, get this. Whoever killed them had them in a position where he could've hurt them bad—you know, live by the sword, die by the sword, that kind of thing. But he didn't, whoever he was. He sealed them in, cut their electricity, and covered their air vents. Then he locked up their house and went home."

A signal passed, a subvocal sign. "It was kind of strange in another way too."

With the barest of nods the sculptor encouraged the detective to heft the hammer, touch the stone.

Webber felt the warmed wood of the handle in his hand, the smoothness of its grain. Webber ran a palm over taut ribs cut into cool marble.

Fields moved aside, let the police sergeant circle the huge torso without breaking his continuous touch. Webber closed his eyes, saw with his fingers. He said, "Maybe you can explain this, seeing how your background helps you understand these people. See, Benny Montrose, he had all the bones in both of his hands broken, days before he died." Webber opened his eyes, studied the slow, gradual hollow his fingers were tracking. "The Burgess character, too. Burgess had some kind of deformity—some old war wound made one of his hands a worthless scar—but all the bones were broken in it too. That's what makes it so strange. Don't you see it? Whoever was there to kill them, if he has the edge on them enough to break all the bones in their hands, and I mean break with a capital SNAP! because the medical examiner says neither man would have been able to pick up a chicken feather afterward—how come he doesn't go all the way and kill them then? Why doesn't he do what he's there to do?'' Webber faced the sculptor. ''He seals them up, cuts off their electricity, closes their air-intake pipe, but lets them live. Only to die days later of dehydration, shock, and asphyxiation because he's smashed the bones in their hands to a pulp.''

Fields was undisturbed. ''I can see the puzzle bothers you.''

Webber nodded, but his own hand pulled him around the base of the newest stone. ''It's about the only thing left that bothers me anymore about this case. Everything else is resolved—for me and my department, at least.''

''Maybe,'' said Dan Fields, ''maybe whoever it was couldn't bring themselves to kill.''

''I don't think so for some reason,'' said Webber. He was sliding his hands over cords of abdominal ridges.

''Then again''—Fields's voice skittered like breeze-blown sand—''maybe whoever it was wanted them to have the pleasure of each other's company down to the very last gasping, choking, bug-eyed moment.''

Webber stiffened, his hands suddenly cold. He rubbed them together and said, ''Guess we'll never know. The case is closed on my books.'' Webber began to nod his head. He licked his lips as if to speak but instead fished in his pockets. When he'd found the keys to his cruiser, he said, ''That hammer you're holding. It's damn heavy.''

The sculptor returned to his mountain of marble and its arms of strength. Over his shoulder he said, ''You're wrong, Sergeant Webber. It's not heavy enough.''

Webber stopped.

Fields said, ''Can I turn things around and ask you a question, Sergeant?''

Webber nodded, his face clouding with apprehension.

''Don't worry,'' Fields told him, ''the question is hypothetical. I don't expect you to answer it.'' He stalked a pace closer. ''Sergeant, suppose when you went home to your family this evening, you discovered your wife and your children brutally and savagely murdered.'' His words were clear and measured, but the detective could hear as the man struggled for emotional control.

"And then, Sergeant, suppose you discovered certain information identifying the killers. Information you know never could be introduced into a court of law, but which nonetheless convinced you, as the investigator you are, that these men, whoever they might be, that these men had committed the *murders*"—the word hissed from Fields's lips—"in some perverted attempt to avenge themselves upon you." He eyed the man. "Sergeant Webber," he said, "my hypothetical question is this. With your experience as a police officer, with your bird's-eye view of the criminal justice system, with your inside knowledge of our system of prisons and privilege, what would you do? Would you allow the men who slaughtered the beautiful things in your life, who put a permanent bloody smear across every memory you possessed of your children, would you stand by and watch them jump the hurdles placed in their path by the courts? Or would you do something else?" Fields touched a horned and callused hand to the marble, and for one brief moment he dropped his mask. He relaxed the voluntary muscles in his face. His North Atlantic–blue eyes burned with cold animal hatred. His lips drew down into a predatory sneer. And then the moment was gone. The sergeant stared into the smooth composure of Dan Fields's tanned face.

"If you lost every reason you'd ever lived for, had it ripped away, would you stay home and write letters to the newspapers, Sergeant, civilized out of nothing but habit? Or would you do something else?" Fields took his tools from the detective. They molded to his hands, balanced and ready.

Webber exhaled. He, too, lived with an eternal nightmare, one born in the same blood-soaked house. They faced each other. Above them pelicans sliced the purpled clouds, racing home in strict formation. Far away a dog barked, happy.

The sergeant paused. "You didn't let me answer your question."

"You can thank me later," said the sculptor. He circled his marbled opponent, gliding barefoot over hot sand. The hammer rang out its life-driving rhythm. *Chink, chink, grack. Chink, chink, grack. Chink, chink, chink, gra-ack.*